The Life of Marek Zaczek

Volume I: Under the Wings of Eagles

A Novel by David Trawinski

outskirts press

The Life of Marek Zaczek Vol. 1
Under the Wings of Eagles

v4.0

Outskirts Press, Inc.
http://www.outskirtspress.com

Paperback ISBN: 978-1-9772-2776-8
Hardback ISBN: 978-1-9772-2499-6

All interior images are taken from Wikipedia Commons unless otherwise noted below:

Rear Cover Winged Hussar Photo by Elizabeth Marie Trawinski © 2020 (taken at the National Shrine of Our Lady of Częstochowa in Doylestown, PA)

Dedication Page Photo Image of Elizabeth Marie Trawinski by David Trawinski © 2020

Figure 1 - Partitions of Poland Map revised by David Trawinski

Front Cover and Interior Graphic of Winged Hussar Armor used by license from the Polish Institute and Sikorski Museum - London.

Text Edited by Elizabeth Marie Trawinski.

PRINTED IN THE UNITED STATES OF AMERICA

Dedicated to the love of my life,
Who inspires my ideas,
Sharpens my words,

And commands every breath of my soul,

"Moja Manya Manuska"
My Marie

"All contemporary social crimes have their origin in the partition of Poland. The partition of Poland is a theorem of which all present political outrages are the corollaries. There has not been a despot, nor a traitor for nearly a century back, who has not signed, approved, counter-signed, and copied, ne variatur, the partition of Poland."

"Les Misérables"
Victor Hugo
1862

AUTHOR'S NOTE

Poland and Lithuania were first joined by the marriage of the Monarch of Poland, Queen Jadwiga to the Grand Duke of Lithuania, Władysław II Jagiełło in 1386. After Queen Jadwiga's untimely death in 1399, King Jagiełło ruled over both Poland and Lithuania. In the year 1410, the King led the joint armies to a historic victory as they defeated the dreaded Teutonic Knights in the Battle of Grunwald.

The two Slavic states were formally joined as a Commonwealth in 1591, and they remained a single political entity until the Third Partition of Poland eliminated the joint state entirely in 1795. At the height of its greatness, the Commonwealth was the largest unified state in Europe.

This novel depicts the conditions of the Commonwealth during the time of the three partitions, from 1772 to 1795, under the criminal military intrusions of the Austrian, Prussian and Russian Empires. As was customary for the time, the terms "Poland", "Polish-Lithuanian Commonwealth", and "The Commonwealth" are all used interchangeably throughout this story of young Marek Zaczek's life.

POLISH TERMS (ITALICIZED IN TEXT) USED THROUGHOUT THIS NOVEL AND THEIR OVER-SIMPLIFIED PRONUNCIATIONS

Ciotka - Aunt (Pronounced CHUT-ka)

Cześć – Informal Hello, "Hi" (Pronounced "Chestz")

Dobronoc - Good Night (Pronounced "Do-BRAN-oots")

Dobrze bardzo – Very Well, Very Good (Pronounced "DUB-zha BARD-zo")

Dziadzia – Grandfather (Dz Pronounced like the J in Judge so "DZA- Dza" or more simply 'JA-ja')

Dziękuję, Dziękuję Bardzo – Thank you, Thank you very much (Pronounced "Je-KOO-ye BAHRD-zo)

Dzień dobry – Good Morning or Good Day (Pronounced "Jane DOE-brey")

Dupa - One's backside or derrière (Pronounced DOO - Pah)

Folwarks – Estates owned by the szlachta (Pronounced "FOL-Varks")

Hetman – Military Leader of All Polish Forces (Pronounced "HET-man")

Matka, or Moja Matka –Mother, or my Mother (Pronounced 'MAHT-ka', 'MOY-Yah MAHT-ka')

Na zdrowie, or Twoje zdrowie - Toast 'Cheers; To health' or 'To your health' (Pronounced NAH zdrovie, or TWOYVE Zdrovie)

Nie ma za co – "It is nothing!" Often used as "You are welcome!" or "Don't mention it!" (Pronounced 'Nee Mah ZAT So')

Pan – Mister, Sir (Pronounced "PAHN" like the word Pond without the 'd')

Pani – Miss, Mrs., Madame (Pronounced "PAHN -nee")

Pańszczyzna – System of Serfdom as enacted in Poland (Pronounced "Panz-CHEZ-na")

Proszę – Please - (Pronounced "PROSH-eh")

Rynek Główny – Kraków's Main Square (Pronounced "RIN-ek GWOV-nee")

Sejm – The Polish Legislature (Pronounced "Sem")

Siostra – Sister (Pronounced "SHO - stra")

Szlachta – Polish Nobility, Originally Landed Gentry (Pronounced "Shlahta")

Tak – Yes (Pronounced "Tahk")

Tata – Father, in the endearing form, like "Daddy" in English (Pronounced "TA-Ta")

Wisła - Vistula River (Pronounced "VEES-wa)

Witamy – Welcome (Pronounced "Vee – TAHM- Me)

Złoty - Gold. Also the name of the Polish currency (Pronounced ZWOH - Tee)

POLISH NAMES AND LOCATIONS WITHIN THIS NOVEL

The Polish language can be intimidating to the non-initiated. I have included this pronunciation guide for my non-Polish readers.

NAMES	*Pronunciation*	*Rules of Polish Language*
Marek Zaczek	MARE -ek ZAH-check	*(CZ sounds like CH in Check)*
Duke Cyprian Sdanowicz	Sip-Ree-an Zdan-AH-vich	*(SD sounds like Zd; W like V; CZ like CH)*
Władysław Kowalczyk	Vwad- ES-Waff Koh-VAL-Check.	*(W pronounced like 'ff' at end of word)*
Sister Maryja Elizabeta	Ma-REE-ya Elz-BEYT-a	*(Y sounds like a I, J sounds like Y)*
Stanisław Poniatowski	Stan-EES-waff Pon-ee-TOV-skee	*(W pronounced like 'ff' at end of word)*
Abbott Dawid	AH-bott DAH-Veed	*(W pronounced like 'v' in middle of word)*
Kazimierz Pułaski	Caz-EE-meerz Pu-WAS-kee	*(ł sounds like W)*
Tadeusz Kościuszko	TAH-Dayoosh Ko-SHOOZ-ko	(ść sounds like sh)
Grzegorz Olszewski	GRZE-Gorz Ohl-SHEV-Skee	(sounds just like its spelled)
Jacek	YAH - Ceck	*(J sounds like Y)*
Jersey	YER - Zee	*(J sounds like Y)*
Witold, or Tolo	VEE - Told, or Tolo	*(W sounds like V)*
Miłosz	MEE- wosh	(ść sounds like sh)
Ewelina	Ev-a- LEEN-ah	*(W sounds like V)*
Lech	Leh, often mis-pronounced as Lek.	*(Ch sounds like h)*
Bochnia -	BOH-nia	(ch sounds like hv)
Częstochowa	Ches -ta- HOV-Va	(Cz sounds like Ch; ch like hv; w like v)
Kraków -	KRAK - ooff	(ó sounds like oo; W pronounced like 'ff' at end of word)
Maciejowice	Mah-chaj-YO-veetz	('wice' sounds like 'veetz')
Puławy	Poo - WAHV- ee	*(ł sounds like W)*
Tyniec	TIN - yets	(c sounds like ts)
Wieliczka -	Va-LEET-Ska	(W sound like V; c sounds like ts)
Zagórz	ZAH - Goorshz	(ó sounds like oo)
Zieleńce	ZEL - Lence	(eńce sous like 'eentz')
And finally, Rzeszów	JESZ - shoff	(Don't ask, just accept it)

Figure 1: The Partitions of Poland

"We will consume Poland's provinces like an artichoke, leaf by leaf!"

Frederick The Great of Prussia

1

THE BIRTH OF MAREK ZACZEK

FEBRUARY 19, 1772

Fate is a scythe that cuts across decades, centuries, and even the intricate fabric of time itself. Its indiscriminate edge spares not the bonds of distinction so jealously guarded by the elite ranks of mankind: those of class, station, and privilege. Its sickled blade is honed on the whetstone of human suffering. Those who fatten themselves on the burdens of the unfortunate masses may stand proud for some time like the stalks of wealth that they are. Yet, ultimately, they will fall like chaff when the razor's edge of the scythe of fate is swung.

It is the winter of 1772 in southern Poland, just below Kraków, on a *folwark*, or Polish nobleman's estate, outside the nearby village of Wieliczka. An icy breath of unrelenting wind blows across the fields of the massive estate that reaches north greedily to caress the banks of the Vistula River. The howling wind drives the pelting white snow, shed like crystalized tears from an angry gray sky. As the diffused light of day slowly loses its battle with the heavy overcast clouds, the foreshadowing darkness of the storm will soon yield to the velvet blackness of the coming night.

The snows blow heavily across the great manor house, catching the warm smoke that is expelled from its hot chimneys. Its charcoal ribbons rise only slightly, before it is blown down into cooling gray spirals that rake like dancing fingers across the whitened, barren fields. At its farthest edge, these fingers of smoke, now deathly cold from their journey across the expanse of the estate, claw ominously at the thatch roof of a peasant family's simple earthen hovel.

The snow, its purity already defiled by the black char of the smoke, piles in great drifts against the humble earthen structure of the peasant hut. Amidst the storm, inside the structure, a young woman struggles to give birth to her first child.

Wrapped around her shoulders, draped like a shawl, comforting her, is a second young woman. The attending woman's hands caress the face of her pregnant friend, whose pain and fear are on the verge of overcoming her completely. The comforting woman, herself only a few years older than the birthing mother-to-be, whispers into the ear of the distressed young peasant wife.

"We know your pain is intense, young Magda, but it is this very suffering which you offer to the Lord. Your sweat, your labor, your aches will soon enough be forgotten when you hold in your tender young arms your first miracle, whose life will be breathed into its lungs from our Almighty God."

A third woman, much older, deformed by the hardship of her years, squats between the trembling, spread legs of the pregnant twenty-year-old girl. She attends to the laboring of young Magda.

The old woman is also a peasant of the estate, bearing an advanced age that attempts to imply wisdom, but instead only disdains the folly of the other two women's youth. For she knows under her wrinkled brow that youth is the only currency which these poor peasant women have, and she knows that soon enough each will squander their sole valuable possession.

The matronly woman is confident that she will deliver the child, as she has served as midwife for so many of the other peasant mothers. She has born great life, yet in doing so, she has also tasted the occasional bitterness of unexpected death.

"*Pani* Ewelina - your babbling is no more comfort to our young Magda than the howl of the winds outside this very door.

Poor Magda is suffering for her sins. God Almighty is still weighing whether she deserves His greatest gift! Wipe her face, for her greatest agony is ahead of her."

The young Ewelina cast her eyes downward upon the admonishing old woman. Ewelina held the optimism of youth in her voice. The old woman named Urszula spoke only in tones tainted with experience.

"*Pani* Urszula – you must not frighten Magda with your words, for she struggles so. I will comfort her in my own way, with my own words. For even though you have the wisdom of many more years than I, your heart has only the compassion of a Cossack's."

The wrinkled woman's head snapped up in reaction, her eyes glaring in a threat that immediately quieted Ewelina.

"I have many more years upon this earth than you, Ewelina. I have delivered many children into this world. Have I not delivered your own two boys? Never have I delivered a child born from the depths of sin such as this. Now, stop with your empty stream of disrespectful words and allow me to concentrate on the birth of this child," seethed the elderly midwife Urszula.

The comments only enlivened young Ewelina all the more.

"You will not hush me, you old woman. Magda hears you, and the words you say," objected Ewelina, in a harsh, but whispered voice. "You are putting the darkest of thoughts in her head."

Urszula ignored the young upstart Ewelina. *She is only one child comforting another,* thought the midwife, *and both have yet to begin to taste the hardships of life.*

"She has no room in her thoughts, except for those of her own fears of whether she will survive this night, for she has offended God," said *Pani* Urszula. Then she added, "And where is her husband? He is not to be found. Has he not the time to be with her?"

The young woman Ewelina at that point became pricked with anger at the cynical old woman's caustic comments.

"It is not his fault. My brother Bronisław is a good man. He has no choice but to labor in the ground beneath us," she said, "at the command of the Duke."

"Yes, of course, the Duke. He who has the honey tongue but only a heart of gall. He makes Magda's man, your brother, toil in the great salt mine, where the light of the sun never penetrates," *Pani* Urszula prattled on, "and like the father, this child is to be born in another darkness, that of a great sin."

The labors of Magda deepened as the night fell. The young woman became more vocal, uttering only a caustic stream of long, plaintiff moans. The pain rose in her as her own body's muscles seemingly betrayed her. The contractions came in waves, overtaking her, leaving her aching, breathless, drenched in the sweat of her own exhaustion and direly fearing what was to come next. As the hours passed, the cycle continued in ever-shortening intervals. She was at the height of her bearable pain, atop the crest of a wave of suffering, when she saw and heard it.

The crack of lightning seemed to illuminate every shadowed recess of the hovel. The spark searched the room like an inquisitor looking for hidden secrets. The hair of the women's necks and arms stood on end. Its instant of passing seemed to leave a metallic taste in each of their mouths.

It was immediately followed by the low penetrating rumble of thunder, which shook not only the heavens, but the very ground under the three women. The earth struggled to absorb the shuddering tremors. It did so slowly and tentatively. The quaking was ultimately subdued, however, yet not before shaking the very foundations of the convictions of all three women.

"Jezu, Maryja i Józef," moaned Magda aloud in a terrified voice. This was her first understandable words for the past several hours. Magda then screamed in agony. She had sensed that the birth had gone awry and became convinced of her suspicion upon hearing the thunderclap that had shaken the walls around them.

Ewelina caressed her friend, her own brother's wife, feeling in her a terror which shook the very bones of the laboring woman's exhausted body. Ewelina felt the thick sweat which drenched Magda's skin as it turned cold in what could only be a manifest horror.

"It is a curse! Our Lord has claimed His displeasure with

Magda's sin," cried out the old woman Urszula. It was then the midwife first realized the child's head was not properly positioned. She realized the child may be lost and took the thundersnow to be a sign of the Lord that He was displeased with this birth.

"No, *Pani* Urszula!" reacted Ewelina forcefully. "It is not Magda's sin, but a sin forced upon her by another. This child shall be born. It shall grow to be a tender young child. For *Jezu* loves all children and would never punish this child, or any other, for any of the sins of the wretched man who preyed upon its mother."

"God is angry! Our God is so upset! This birth is heresy to Him! *Jezu* protect us all," yelled Urszula in fright.

"It is unholy for you to be so superstitious, *Pani* Urszula!" says the woman Ewelina. "God will be angry at you, yes, for serving your rancid superstitions. Hear me, *Pani* Urszula! There is no innocent life which He will reject. Thus, you are to deliver this child, using all the gifts He has given you. Do you understand?"

The harshness of young Ewelina's tone seemed to steady the hands of the midwife. She refocused her thoughts and attended once more to Magda's issue.

"Hush, Ewelina, you are only a child yourself," snapped the midwife, after a long second. "This life is not innocent. It is also not yet here. Magda, you must not push unless I tell you..."

The midwife pushes the baby back into the womb, and with a gentle but dexterous movement of her hands, is able to turn the infant so stubbornly refusing to be born. Its mother screams in agony. It is a scream that sears through each woman's being. A scream which seems to climb to the apex of unbearable suffering, which then, just as it appears to have reached the crescendo, pitches even higher, revealing a new plateau of torment and anguish for the young woman to bear.

"*Jezu! Jezu!* Forgive her, *Jezu!*" Ewelina cries out through the piercing wail of Magda's excruciating suffering.

"Push, now, child!" demands the old woman Urszula.

Magda pushes, before crying out again in great pain.

"You are doing well, Magda, relax," says the young Ewelina. She speaks out of reflex to comfort her friend, but instead triggers a harsh rebuke from the midwife.

"Do not tell her to relax, I need her to push," Urszula admonishes the childlike Ewelina. "Push on my command, my girl. It is almost clear."

A howl of icy wind shakes the hut, its frozen breath sinks through the thatch and slices unnervingly through them all. Ewelina begins to pray aloud, her eyes raised upwards, her trembling hands clasped together.

"*Jezu!* My Lord, give her this life and she will dedicate it to Your Honor for as long as it walks the grounds of the earth..." pleads Ewelina on Magda's behalf.

"Now, my Magda, push," yells the midwife. "Your baby is here!"

"*Jezu, Maryja i Józef,*" Magda screams in pain again as she pushes.

"Lord, we promise the life of this child to Your Holy Church. Forgive Magda this evil forced upon her, and protect us all in Your Holy Name!" cries Ewelina aloud.

"Push again, Magda! Push, now," commands the midwife Urszula.

Magda pushes. The pain is overbearing. Ewelina wipes the sweat from her brow. It once again bears the warmth of her skin instead of that of an icy cold terror.

The horror in Magda's mind has been replaced by the rebellious pain of her body's tormented muscles.

It is then that Ewelina feels the weight of the woman collapse under her. In that second, she fears that the very breath of life has been drawn from her friend. She fears that the Lord, despite all her protestations otherwise, has indeed punished Magda, taking not only the life of her child, but the life of the would-be mother as well.

"No! No! Magda!" Ewelina exclaims in her panic. She begins to cry a mournful wail. "She is dead. She is dead. Our Lord has taken Magda from us. Why has He taken back the sweetest breath of hope that He had ever gifted to the peasants?"

Ewelina sinks into an immediate despair. Her friend is gone. She fears the Lord has taken her for her sins against God's Word. She drapes herself over the corpse of Magda, the great sinner.

Yet instead of finding the body cold with the chill of death, Ewelina finds Magda drenched in a sweat as thick as the foam covering a whipped mare. Her bosom heaves and ebbs in shallow swells. These are the respite breaths of a tormented being struggling to forget the tremendous pain to which it had just been subjected.

"No, Ewelina, your friend Magda is not dead," cries out the midwife in an unusually joyous tone, "she is very much alive and the mother of a beautiful baby boy."

At this moment, Ewelina hears the first cries of the newborn. She lifts Magda slightly, so she can see her infant son in the hands of the midwife, who then cleans him.

"You have a son, Magda!" exclaims Ewelina.

"You have a beautiful and healthy son," says the midwife, openly smiling with the responsibilities of the delivery by then safely behind her.

Magda is catching her breath. "I want to hold him. I must hold him." Tears of immense joy cascade from her exhausted eyes, their hollows of pain at that moment sparked full of the promise of hope.

The midwife passes the infant to his mother. Another clap of thunder splits the night. It is somewhat off in the distance. No one hears it.

The swell of tears becomes a cleansing wave that moves throughout the mother's being. Her muscles, weak from their hours of seemingly unending contractions, are soothed.

Magda is exhausted. She nestles the infant in the crook of her arm, upon the bosom that would soon nurture it. She feels nothing but relief. That wave of respite soon gives way to a much deeper solace. Her pains are all forgotten in the instant, although they would fight to be remembered over the coming hours and days.

"His name is Marek," says Magda, with a great smile, beaming a mother's love at the innocence of the child. "Hello, my Marek Zaczek, you will become a man of the Lord. You will grow in the Spirit, and before I die, you will forgive me of my sins, so that my soul may rest eternally."

The jingling of bells were then heard upon the howling of the wind. They are the bells of a sleigh outside the hut. The doctor, sent by the Duke, dismounts the sleigh and enters the hut with great reticence. He is uncomfortable in this peasant setting, one he has rarely encountered.

"I have come to attend to the birth of your child, *Pani* Zaczek. It is upon the insistence of the Duke, I am afraid," the doctor says apologetically.

The three women look at each other, with smiles creasing their faces as they all harbor the same thought, one that Urszula next said aloud.

"You may find that the baby was not so informed," said the midwife flatly.

Pan Grzegorz Olszewski, the doctor kept on the *folwark* for the Duke's personal care, blushed with embarrassment. He looked into Magda's arms, spotted the newborn infant, and uttered only the words, "Of course."

"I cannot remember the Duke ever having sent his personal doctor to oversee a peasant child's birth before," said Ewelina accusingly.

Once again the doctor blushed, for like the other three women, he also knew the *folwark's* great secret. And the women's comments suggested that they were aware the Duke had shared it with the doctor.

"That is because it is as my father always said, *A doctor will take care of the rich man, but the poor man is cured only by work,*" said Urszula with a sneer.

"How is the child?" asked the doctor, wishing to change the conversation.

"He is beautiful! He is perfect," said the exhausted, yet peaceful Magda, as she held onto her newborn son.

"He is the image of God Himself, perfect in every way!" said Ewelina tenderly.

"Yes, of course," exclaimed Urszula, "all children are born in

God's image. It is the shadows of man's evil that touches and disfigures them as they grow. Yet, this child has been touched with it even before his birth." Urszula looked into the eyes of the doctor with a penetrating, steely, and even accusatory gaze.

"*Pani* Urszula, quiet yourself," says Ewelina. "You caw like an old crow. No one wants a crow's cawing drowning out a newborn's coos."

Over the next few hours, after assuring the young mother and child were healthy, the doctor left the infant with the three women. The sun was rising in the east. Its red rays sliced through the parting clouds of the overnight storm. Their reflections danced with joyous mirth upon the uninterrupted blanket of fresh and deep white snow as the doctor's team of horses pulled the sleigh briskly towards the estate's palatial manor house.

The manor house belonged to the wealthy and powerful Duke Cyprian Sdanowicz, owner of massive land holdings from the town of Wieliczka to the banks of the *Wisła*, the Vistula River. Tied to these lands were the fates of thousands of peasants, including one boy who was now only a few hours old.

Upon having entered the massive house, the doctor found the Duke who had nervously awaited him in the hall. The Duke had for many years employed him as his personal physician. They knew each other well. Well enough to entrust the doctor with the most damaging of secrets.

"Well, *Pan* Grzegorz, " queried the Duke, "tell me, damn you!"

The doctor took the Duke gently by the arm, leading him to the warmth of the fireplace in the great room, away from the hungry ears of the house servants who were already stirring. He looked into the wealthy man's eyes and whispered, "Congratulations, my Duke Sdanowicz, you have a perfectly healthy son. *Pani* Magda says his name is to be Marek. He is to be called Marek Zaczek."

The Duke sighed with relief. His head dropped, as if a great weight which it had been bearing had been removed in an instant, toppling it like a child's toy.

"These peasants so love their traditions. So, my son is to bear the poverty of her young husband's family name. And what of Magda's beloved Bronisław?" asked the Duke. "Does he know yet that I have graced him with a son?"

"*Pan* Bronisław Zaczek is under our feet, working in your salt mine as you have directed. I am sure he does not yet know of the boy. Of course, Magda will not disgrace herself by telling him the truth."

"And who can be sure that the child is even of my stock?" questioned the Duke. "There is always a chance that the boy is indeed Bronisław's own, and as such, deserves to bear the shame of his name."

"I doubt that, my Duke," responded the doctor. "Magda has been wed to him for some six years. He took her for his bride at age fourteen, as the peasants will do. If she had not enflowered his seed within those intervening years, it can only be because her husband has no life in his seed. For certainly the young woman has proven herself fertile. However, even the most barren of peasant men still possess the strongest of muscles with which to do your work. So, why not let him think the boy is his? You will know the truth, and its sharpness will be a weapon like a saber's blade for you to hold over Magda."

The Duke's sinister smile creased his face. His was a smooth face, but not altogether young. It was not yet wrinkled by the parade of his advancing years.

"*Pan* Grzegorz, you have a mischievous mind. This I like, for you think almost as I do," said Duke Sdanowicz. "Yes, I will allow the peasant Bronisław Zaczek to believe the boy is his own issue. After all, it is more like I have done his work for him, is it not? In return, I am sure very little work was rendered from him this night past. I am confident he was upon bended knee, at prayer, in one of the many carved shrines in the salt walls of the mine. Yes, young Magda is fertile indeed, unlike my own wife of many years. So, perhaps I do not have an heir, but I do have a son, even if he is to be a bastard all his life!"

Doctor Grzegorz Olszewski listened as the Duke spit out the last few words like the inedible seeds of a ripened fruit.

"The boy has had no say in this," offered the doctor in the infant's defense. "He will grow in your presence, and you will have the comfort of knowing that the child is of your fine lineage. But, my dear Duke, you can never let anyone know. In your disgrace the King would take away your rights to manage the royal salt mines – the source of all your great wealth."

The Duke looked upon the doctor's face, and wondered what thoughts ran through his physician's insightful mind.

"Yes, and even more so the source of the King's even greater wealth. But you worry that the King will find another to manage these prosperous holes in the earth? You are wise to worry so, my friend. For even the leech dies when all the blood is sucked from its host."

The doctor was long accustomed to such ill-suited insults as this coming from the Duke. He ignored it, instead offering only, "You have nothing to fear, my Lord, as long as the secret of the boy is kept."

The Duke's face became flushed with a crimson pride as he recalled the event of his son's birth.

"Yes, a boy. My boy. Marek Zaczek. His secret will be kept, but I will take great joy in watching him grow," said the Duke, "may his shadow always fall upon my own."

2

SHADOWS OF A CIVIL WAR

MAY 1772

Three months later, Duke Cyprian Sdanowicz of Wieliczka hosted a gathering of the region's noblemen, or *szlachta*, in his magnificent manor house. The Duke opened the assembly by proposing a toast to their King, who was not amongst them. At the mention of the King's name, a calamitous din filled the great room immediately.

Duke Sdanowicz's voice sharpened as he continued to speak in order to pierce the near riotous tumult. "But my brothers, it is customary to toast our King who rules in Warsaw. Allow us to honor the tradition, if not the man himself."

The glasses were raised, although somewhat reluctantly by many in the hall. For the current King of Poland, having been on the throne only a handful of years, was already a divisive figure.

"To the health of King Stanisław Augustus Poniatowski!" The Duke paused for silence, then uttering the traditional toast to his health, *"Twoje Zdrowie!"*

Yet, despite their angst reserved for the monarch in the capital of Warsaw, not a single member of the *szlachta* refused to enjoy their host's finest vodka. Their glasses were drained, although the fullness of their apprehensions remained.

The crowd collectively murmured and showed great angst as they awaited direction from their host.

"Please be seated, my brothers," said Duke Sdanowicz, addressing his fellow nobles in the traditional manner. A great cacophony echoed from the long oaken table as the noblemen seated themselves. "May our gracious Lord *Jezus Chrystus* above bless this gathering! We are here to discuss the events evolving from the accord signed by our neighboring states three months ago in the city of Vienna, and the ongoing rebellion by the Bar Confederation."

They all knew the events. On the preceding nineteenth day of February, the empires of Russia, Prussia and Austria had decided amongst themselves to take territories from The Commonwealth of Poland and Lithuania's borderlands. This travesty of both sovereignty and justice was documented in formal accords signed by the three empires in Vienna, although without any representation of the Commonwealth. All the nobles assembled in the Duke's hall held their King responsible for allowing this to occur.

Poland's King, unlike the predominance of other European monarchies, was elected, not inherited. The electors were the *szlachta,* the landed gentry, or noblemen of the Polish-Lithuanian Commonwealth. Nine years earlier, in 1763, when King Augustus III had died, the Russian Tsar Catherine's agents had used their influence with the individual members of the *szlachta*, bribing many, until her former lover, Stanisław Poniatowski, could be installed as the new King of the Commonwealth.

From 1764 on, King Poniatowski ruled under a cloud of suspicion of being a Russian agent. His mother was a member of the powerful pro-Russian Czartoryski family, who along with the Russian Empress had worked feverishly to secure his election. In an act contrary to this perception, two years after being elected, the King attempted to strengthen the monarchy by reforming some of the powers of the nobility. Most grievous to the noblemen were Poniatowski's attempts to infringe upon their *Golden Rights,* which included their right to collectively elect the monarch. Also, among these, was the threat to take away their right *of liberum veto*, which allowed any member of the *szlachta* to veto any session of the *Sejm* legislature, and in doing so render any acts passed by it as invalid.

The King had known that the right of *liberum veto* had been overused by the nobles, to the point that Poland, once the dominant power through central and eastern Europe, failed to advance with the world around itself. As these *szlachta* increasingly employed the *liberum veto* as a political weapon, Poland's progress itself became the ultimate victim.

Catherine of Russia had no desire for her former lover to strengthen the Polish monarchy. It was, and had long been, nearly totally ineffective in governing the Commonwealth. In her view, the expansive rights historically afforded to the *szlachta,* which kept the country from achieving any real modernization, needed to be maintained as the status quo. The Tsar Queen's intention was to keep the Commonwealth weak. Russia thus declared that the *Golden Rights of the szlachta*, including the *liberum veto,* were to be guaranteed by the Russian Empire.

Russian troops were then sent into Poland in order to guarantee that these rights were not reformed. In Warsaw, the troops were even stationed inside the *Sejm* legislature chamber to insure that the King's articles of reformation were not enacted. Despite this invasive act protecting the *szlachta's* historic privileges, the majority of the Polish noblemen were incensed that Russia would meddle in the Commonwealth's affairs so forcefully.

Nearly all the *szlachta* laid blame upon King Poniatowski, for his acquiescence to Tsar Catherine, for allowing the Russian troops to enter Poland at all. However, a subset of fervent *szlachta* noblemen had become so distraught with Russia's influence over the Polish-Lithuanian Commonwealth, that they decided to rebel and declare war on the Russian Empire.

These noblemen formed the Confederation of Bar, with Bar being a town in the southeast of Poland at the time. The Confederation rose to fight against both the Russians and eventually their own King, when Poniatowski did not support their war declaration upon Russia.

"It is an outrage!" shouted another *szlachta* Duke, not waiting for Sdanowicz to frame the discussion. "Our 'Great' King Poniatowski allows our enemies to agree to feast upon our borders? For certain he does so, only for he is nothing but a puppet of the Tsar Queen Catherine of Russia!"

With this outburst all order was lost. A third Duke interrupted the second, who had interrupted Sdanowicz, their host.

"That is exactly why the Confederation of Bar was organized. To fight off the Russian influence that has been growing over the Polish-Lithuanian Commonwealth for many years. Tsar Catherine II has meddled in our elections, and in doing so has placed her lover upon our throne. King Poniatowski allows her to send her Russian troops onto our soil, even arresting those Poles who dare speak out against the puppet King."

The room burst into enraged jeers from almost half of the *szlachta* brothers who supported the Confederacy. The last voice then spoke even louder to continue to make known his support for the rebels, or Confederates, as they were called.

"As a result, the Confederates, all noble brothers of the *szlachta*, rose in the town of Bar to fight the Russian intruders. Instead of offering the power of the Throne of the Commonwealth to support the Confederates, our King rallies against them, siding instead with Catherine of Russia, and throwing us into Civil War. Then, he sat quietly in his Palace in Warsaw, while Russia and her allies Prussia and Austria connived in Vienna as to how best divide our stolen lands."

A great racket rose among the attending *szlachta*, with arguments being raised against the King, as well as a minority in defense of him.

Duke Sdanowicz, who hosted this congregation, was in this minority.

"My brothers, the Confederation of Bar has all but failed," Duke Sdanowicz reminded his guests, "with the fall last month of Wawel Castle in Kraków, just across the Vistula River from this, my estate, where we now meet. It was one of their main rebel strongholds, and now their remaining forces are scattered only to a handful of monasteries. They lick their wounds at *Jasna Góra* in Częstochowa, at the Benedictine Monastery in Tyniec, and the Carmelite Monastery at Zagórz. These fortresses are like separate islands, doomed to fall one-by-one. God Himself has betrayed the Bar Confederation. It is time, now, for all of us, my brothers, to throw our full support behind our leader, King Stanisław II August Poniatowski!"

The hall exploded into a frenzied commotion. Cries of "May our Lord save the Confederates, who fight from the fortresses of His Faith!" were heard, as well as, "Who will save Poland from the three Empires?"

Duke Sdanowicz, the host, called for order. "Remember, my brothers, it is only fitting, as this rebel army of Confederates was raised by Kazimierz Pułaski, along with the once powerful Krasiński magnates, over four years ago in Bar against the Russians. It is the very same scoundrel Count Pułaski who now leads the defense of Częstochowa, and imperils not only the monastery of *Jasna Góra*, but also the sacred Black Madonna."

The last reference was to the venerated icon of the Polish Catholic faith, a painted and bejeweled wooden image of The Blessed Virgin Mary holding the infant Jesus, both bearing darkened skin tones, aged by time. This icon dates back to at least the fourteenth century and is known to have endured the Hussite invasion in 1430 .

Legend held that the original image was painted by Saint Luke on a wooden tabletop in the Holy Lands. It was then brought to Constantinople by Saint Helena in 326 AD as a gift to her son, the Emperor Constantine. It is said to have arrived at the *Jasna Góra* monastery in the southern Polish town of Częstochowa in the late fourteenth century.

Death of Polish King Augustus III	5 Oct 1763
Election of King Poniatowski	7 Sep 1764
King Proposes Reforms to Szlachta's "Golden Rights"	1766
Russian Troops Occupy Polish Sejm Legislature and Forcibly Control Lawmaking Process	1767 - 1768
Szlachta Rebels Confederate at Bar	29 Feb 1768
Russian and Royal Polish Forces Attack Bar/ Bar Falls	20 Jun 1768
Att. Kidnapping of King Poniatowski	3 Nov 1771
Vienna Agreement to Partition	19 Feb 1772
Fall of Wawel Castle (Kraków)	28 Apr 1772
Austrian, Prussian, Russian Troops Occupy Partition Lands	Jun 1772
Fall of Tyniec Monastery	13 Jul 1772
Fall of Jasna Góra Monastery	13 Aug 1772
Fall of Zagórz Monastery	28 Nov 1772
Russian Troops Occupy Warsaw Forcing Polish Sejm to accept Partition Treaty	1773 - 1775

Figure 2 – The Chronology of The Confederation of Bar and the First Partition of Poland

Another eruption of discordance then rippled through the hall, its members as divided as the country of Poland itself. It was not that half the room were vocal supporters of the King, as Duke Sdanowicz was. It was more so that half of the noblemen were simply looking to put an end to the civil war that had so cruelly torn their country apart for the past four years. Another voice supporting the rebels then spoke.

"Brother Pułaski, as well as the brothers Krasiński, are not scoundrels! These brothers are rather brave Polish patriots. They fight for the *Golden Rights* of all *szlachta,* those promised to us by the ancestors of each brother in this room. One of those rights is to confederate against a King when the *szlachta* feels it necessary. So, their action is not a rebellion. It is a sanctioned right of protest! Long may the remaining Confederates hold strong in the monasteries of *Jasna Góra,* Tyniec and Zagórz. May the Lord *Jezu Chrystus* gather and protect these patriots!"

A dissonance of divided passions overtook the room, before Duke Sdanowicz wrestled order from the chaos once more.

"Yes, my brothers, some have spoken of the *szlachta's Golden Rights*. One of those rights is for the *szlachta* to elect the King of Poland and the Commonwealth. That was done as prescribed by our laws in the election of King Poniatowski some eight years ago. These rebels accused our King of being in league with the tsarists. Imagine the Confederates resorting to the point of attempting to kidnap the King last fall in the streets of Warsaw. This travesty was joined by none other than Count Kazimierz Pułaski himself. Thanks only to the protection of Our Lord they were unsuccessful, for His Hand made them as ineffective in their actions as they have always been in their planning of their radical ways. They have only given Russia, Austria and Prussia an excuse to declare to the world that Poland is in a state of anarchy, and they must take from us that which we have demonstrated we cannot effectively manage ourselves."

No sooner had Duke Cyprian Sdanowicz finished supporting the King once more before there erupted another contrarian outburst.

"The Tsar Queen in Saint Petersburg stole that election with her money and her influence over some members of the *szlachta*. Catherine craves our eastern lands, even more than King Frederick of Prussia does those of our north, or Empress Maria Theresa of Austria does those of our south. Had the Tsar Queen not interfered in our affairs, we would have had a strong and properly elected King. Instead, her lover, our puppet King, allowed the Russian troops across our borders. The Confederates of Bar were wise to rebel against the King and the evil Tsar Queen who has blinded Poniatowski to act against his own countrymen."

"Here! Here!" echoed throughout the hall. Duke Sdanowicz felt as though he was losing control of the assembly which he himself had called.

"Long may the ideals of the Confederates of Bar live, that of an independent Commonwealth of Poland and Lithuania," was shouted enthusiastically from the far end of the massive table.

Cyprian Sdanowicz once more requested order from his fellow nobles. The anger of the room resisted him, yet he was ultimately able to cajole them into an uncomfortable truce of near silence.

"*Proszę*, my lords," pleaded Sdanowicz, "please, please, let me have your attention for but a short time. After the Confederacy's disastrous plan to kidnap the King, the Russians proclaimed Poland a state unable to prevent the revolt of its own populace. Our ineffective actions have only reinforced this perception, held now, unfortunately, far and wide across Europe. As a result, yes, a conference was convened in Vienna this February past which produced an accord allowing each of the three empires of Russia, Prussia and Austria to take border lands from the Commonwealth. While there has been a great outcry against this by France and Britain, the truth is that no power is willing to going to war to prevent it."

This Vienna accord later would become known as the first partition of Poland of 1772, although the troops from Austria and Prussia had not yet moved to seize these lands. Russian troops had for some years been on Polish soil. These forces had not yet moved to secure the Partition's spoils.

The crowd erupted once more, yet Sdanowicz continued aggressively in the hope of calming their fears.

"I am happy to report to you, that I have been in contact with the Royal Court in Warsaw, and I have been assured that the King has no intention of allowing these lands to be taken from the Commonwealth."

Contrary to Duke Sdanowicz's desire, the comment only instigated further aggravation among the guests.

"With what army, exactly, will he stand up to the troops of Catherine, Frederick, and Empress Maria Theresa? They will take our lands and plunder our sovereignty as they please."

Another voice added, "You, Duke Sdanowicz, have the most to lose, for the very land, the very magnificent manor house we meet in here today, as well as both salt mines you control, are by their accord to be taken by the Austrians."

All the attending noblemen were from the southern regions just below Kraków. These lands across the Vistula from the great city were to be annexed by the Austrians, and another great clamor filled the hall.

Similar regional *szlachta* gatherings had been occurring in the eastern lands of the Commonwealth to be absorbed by the Russians, as well as those of the north of Poland to be annexed by the Prussians.

All realized what had been stated was true. Cyprian Sdanowicz, Duke of both Wieliczka and Bochnia, was the man indeed with the most land and fortune to lose. His family's *folwark* of Wieliczka stretched from the town north all the way to the Vistula River. The great salt mine beneath the town was Royal property, however, Sdanowicz was paid handsomely to manage its production, which was staffed with his own peasant laborers.

The *folwark* at Bochnia was smaller, and its mine was not as expansive. Cyprian Sdanowicz had deftly added it to his holdings in recent years. Again, the mine belonged to the King, and Sdanowicz was paid handsomely to administer it also.

In an earlier time, this combination of wealth would have made

Duke Sdanowicz a magnate, among the wealthiest and most powerful of the *szlachta* nobles. Yet this was a different and most turbulent time.

Duke Sdanowicz then continued in his efforts to calm the crowd.

"The King's Court has assured me that King Poniatowski has no intentions of allowing the royal salt mines, either here in Wieliczka, or in nearby Bochnia, to be transferred to the Austrians. They are too valuable. For what is as precious as salt? Nothing, my friends. Why, they may as well allow Kraków itself to be given to the Austrians. Of course, this they will not do."

A loud pounding upon the great oak table reverberated through the room. The nearest goblets jumped in animated response. The room quieted.

All heads turned to Duke Sroka, the second most powerful member of the *szlachta* in the room behind only Duke Sdanowicz himself.

"It is brave but empty talk!" answered Sroka's outraged voice, which was authoritative. However, despite his great strength, his words were faintly edged with the tint of his advancing age. "Who will defend us from their armies? They will take whatever they like. Our King Poniatowski is certainly in league with the Russian Court of Saint Petersburg. He has brought us to this point of misfortune. The Russians have legitimized their greed by declaring us a failed state and by inviting the Austrians and Prussians to sidle up to the trough. Any fool can see what comes next."

Duke Sdanowicz fought to be heard over the mayhem that resulted.

"I remind my fellow members of the *szlachta* that an old Polish proverb warns, *Do not separate the skins until the bear is dead*. This bear that is the Polish-Lithuanian Commonwealth is far from dead, my brothers."

From the far end of the table, Sroka's voice coldly contradicted the Duke.

"With a Russian head, this bear will not only lose its skins, but its heart as well. Prussia covets our northern lands to bridge its own two Germanic enclaves, Austria desires our minerals, and Russia demands our very souls. With their first taste, their thirst for these treasures will only become all the more unquenchable. They will return again and again until there is nothing left to steal from us. Mark my words, my fellow Poles, what these Empires crave in their greed is to expel our country and our culture forever from the map of Europe."

3

MAGDA AND THE DUKE

JULY 1772

The infant Marek grew quickly, nurtured at the breast of his young mother. Magda soon returned to her assigned chores in the keeping of the manor. She dreaded seeing the Duke again, as she feared for the safety of her infant son. Especially, should she be forced to openly defy any further advances by the Duke.

At first, Duke Sdanowicz was indifferent to Magda. He welcomed her back to his employ, politely and in full earshot of the rest of the manor staff. However, his attentions were elsewhere, with the great debates raging in Poland over the ongoing forced secession of lands to the three empires of Russia, Austria and Prussia.

Then, one day after Magda had been back at the manor for a month, the Duke had given the entire staff the evening to themselves. As they left the manor house, he called out to *Pani* Magda to clean a spill from his inkwell that he had clumsily knocked over as the staff departed. Magda cringed, as it was this sequence of events that was reminiscent of an evening nearly a year earlier.

"My dearest Magda, before you clean that stain, be so kind as to tell me of your boy, Marek. Is he healthy? How bright is the shine of his eye? Your boy is destined to be a peasant, my peasant, for all his life. Tell me, will he become a man to work the manor's stables, or another back to break under the labors of the royal salt mines below our feet?"

"My Duke, my child is indeed healthy," she responded with noticeable restraint. "Yes, he is healthy, and his eyes are truly bright, however he will neither be a man of the stables nor of the mines. For I have promised his life to the church. He will grow to one day forgive the sins of the peasant people. I pray, one day, he will absolve the very act of depravity of his own parents. He will redeem the very depths of the darkness, albeit that which brought the flame of light to his own being."

Her words were meant to threaten the Duke, but Cyprian Sdanowicz merely allowed a sickly grin to cross his tightly pursed lips. The effect was that of a beast caught in the moment before its grimace transitioned to a full snarl exposing its dangerous fangs beneath.

"I would be very careful in taking stock of your sins, my dearest Magda," responded the Duke, "and especially in sharing those iniquities with your fellow peasant women. This could prove most dangerous to you and your family."

Even though these words rolled so calmly from his tongue, Magda knew that his passive jaw contained the sharp teeth of a wolf that would next shred at her family's skin as it had already done to her personal dignity.

"In saying my family, you most certainly mean my husband," said Magda tersely. "You would not dare to take my ills up against your own child, after all. You continue to break poor Bronisław's back in those mines. Yet, I tell you now that he does not know of the sin for which I most pray forgiveness." Magda lowered her head in shame.

Her piety enflamed the Duke, who burst into a demonstrative rage.

"Sin! Sin, you say! You tempted me, you vile thing! Was that not your sin?" exclaimed the Duke. "You dare tempt me with your feminine form, steal my seed, to gestate it within your fertile womb, all because your husband is weak and vacated in his loins. He could not give you the child you so desired, so you played me in a moment of weakness. I warn you, Magda, dare you confess not your sin of larceny with any man, ever, be he husband, friend or priest!"

The Duke's voice rose sharply in pitch. His right hand swayed menacingly high over her. It was a habit, that motion, that he often employed in dealing with the house staff to show his displeasure. Magda initially cowered, before straightening herself to defiantly respond.

"I stole not from you, my Duke. It was you who stole from me everything once pure and meaningful. You stole from me the love of my parents to satisfy your unchecked greed. You stole from me the safety of the convent, where I might become learned of the world. Now, you menace me, once again. For what? To carry out the threat that you hung over my innocence like the sabers of your guards-men?"

The Duke scoffed at her outburst, turning his rigid face loose into a devious smile. The sight of which cut the girl like a dagger.

"You tempted me, vixen. You offered no resistance to my advances, because you desired only one thing: a child. A child your impotent Bronisław could not bring to seed within you."

Magda, already emboldened, exploded in turn. "You parted my resistance to your desires with your unholy menace upon my husband's head. He toils under our feet at your discretion, then and now. Are you to remind me once more how many accidents take place in the mines? It worked for you then, will it work for you again? Am I simply to recline tonight, once more, for your leisure, my Duke? Am I to merely allow you to continue to seek your pleasures under the veneer of my motherhood?"

Duke Cyprian Sdanowicz sneered at the girl's rancid outburst. He had expected as much, as she always had a sharp-edged tongue which was carried to flight by the swiftest of wits. However, he was confident of the tools of his own intellect. He knew just how to jab his words into her, then twist them with his scornful derision.

"You do so abhor yourself, my Magda," said the Duke resolutely. "You have been given an incredible gift, my child. A son, healthy and vibrant, with the blood of the *szlachta* coursing through his veins. I am sure this infant will grow to be a man of greatness, descending not into the laborious depths of the mines. Yet neither shall he ascend the dizzying heights of the church's steeples."

Magda looked upon the Duke with emblazoned contempt. "Yes, he has the blood of the *szlachta* in his veins! For Marek carries the blood of my own father, who you betrayed before forcing me into a peasant's life."

"Your father was not worthy of the title of *szlachta*. He was a traitor to the King," responded the Duke calmly. "He disgraced your family forever, as well as you, his forgotten child."

The Duke's word cut deeply indeed at Magda. Her tongue let loose in anger.

"I am indeed a Duke's daughter, yet you force me to serve as a peasant under this roof," said Magda. "Still, I prefer this than to ever sleep again under its comfort by pretending to be a ward of your pretentious care and false compassion. You may have forced me into the life of a peasant, but at least it is an honest life."

"I have not forced you into the life of a peasant," responded the Duke coldly, "for it is only a natural calling to you. As for your father, yes, he was once a member of the *szlachta*, yet no longer. His rebellious acts against the King have stripped him forever of that title. Your son Marek will forever be my peasant, as you will always be also."

The girl's eyes began to fill with tears. She fought their shedding, for to release them would only imprison her further within the Duke's cruelty.

"I will give Marek to God's church, as I have already promised to the Lord," she said, adding, "unless you wish to reveal yourself as his *tata* and take him from me. Imagine the shame which would be cast upon you."

The Duke was not moved by her threat upon him. His lips merely again widened slowly into that sickly grin, for he knew he had dominance over the girl. Complete and utter dominance.

"You forget, my Magda, that I have no need to acknowledge

the boy as my own. As a bastard, he is nothing for nothing, never to be an heir of my fortunes. Let me remind you, my girl, that any son who suckles from a peasant *matka's* breast is indeed a peasant himself. And as the peasants of my estate are my property, I am free to do with each of them as I so desire."

In having said this, her attention was drawn from the decrepit bend of his lips to the excruciating anticipation of the wanton yearning in his eyes.

"Yes, I so know your desires, my Duke. Do you desire once again the flesh of this despoiled child?" asked Magda, flowing her hands over her bodice and downward to her hips.

The Duke slowly allowed his gaze to wash fully upon her, until he noticed her blush in the shame of being measured by his eyes. He then slowly walked a small circle around her, as he might do inspecting a mare he desired for his stables.

"No, no, my lovely girl. Once again, you tempt me. Your form recovers nicely from your son's birth, it is true. For now, I shall abstain. For when one presses the fruit, he can instantly have its sweet juice, or with patience have exquisite wine. Having tasted the sweetness of its press, perhaps now I desire its intoxicating fullness. Thus, I am inclined to be patient, my child. Your time will once again come, but for now, be gone."

She walked toward the manor house door, her eyes brimming with the tears that she had successfully kept from her cheeks. She stopped under the doorframe and steeled her will. Looking over her shoulder at him, an act of defiance of its very own, she wanted more than anything to make him aware of her intentions.

"You think you have stolen me from my God, my Duke," she said before departing, "but not so my son. Despite your powers, I will commit him to the Church. He will grow to hear me confess the sin which you have so vilely pressed upon me. I promise you this much - I shall be absolved. However your soul, as unrepentant as I am sure it will always be, will bear forever that sin's infinite weight."

Duke Cyprian Sdanowicz merely ridiculed the girl. He widened the arc of his hands from his chest in mock frankness. He held his frame open, defenseless to risk of her attack.

"A woman's promise carries the weight of a full heart and the emptiness of a vacant suit of armor. It has no threat without the strength of a man behind it. You are right on one account, my Magda. The convent educated you well. You parley with me in such a delightful manner. It amuses me so."

And with having said this, the Duke's sneer opened like a sickly flower to the full bloom of his mocking indifference of her threat.

Magda's blood boiled within her. Her rage was not triggered by the Duke's having once taken her innocence under duress. As much as she detested him for it, it had indeed given her the son who was the singular joy of her life. Her blood pulsed in fury because of the way he toyed with those under his possession. These peasant people, Magda by then included, were good people who struggled under the yoke of being tied to his estate. Yet, to the Duke, they were merely belongings, to be used to his benefit, his amusement, and ultimately his pleasure.

4

THE STORY OF MAGDA

1752 – 1772

The young peasant, and, by then, mother, Magda, who had stood alone against Duke Cyprian Sdanowicz was not an ordinary peasant. In fact, she was not a peasant at all. She was born in 1752 as Magdalena Kowalczyk, the only daughter of another member of the *szlachta*. Her father, Duke Władysław Kowalczyk, was the nobleman who, at that time, controlled the other salt mine of the region, the Bochnia salt mine.

Władysław Kowalczyk was a descendant of a proud family. His ancestors had fought against the Swedes during the great invasion known as "The Deluge" in the previous century. He believed fiercely in maintaining the strength of the *szlachta* as the ruling class of the Commonwealth. His family had historically administered, on behalf of the King, the Bochnia salt mine, the oldest in Poland, and one of the oldest in the known world. His daughter, Magdalena, was denied nothing, including an expansive education, as unusual as it was for the times.

For her father, Władysław, had sent her away to the convent in Kraków, where she was to be cloistered with the intent of being tutored by a highly educated nun that was known to him. Sister Maryja Elizabeta had been tutored in her youth by a professor from

Kraków's famed Jagiełłonian University, the oldest in Poland, and the second oldest University in central Europe.

In those times, it was not permissible for women to study openly at university. Institutionalized education was forbidden to young Magda, just as it had been earlier forbidden to her tutor, the nun. Nonetheless, Sister Maryja Elizabeta, before entering the convent, had indeed devised an ambitious manner in which to gain her own education.

In fact, before she became Sister Maryja Elizabeta, this young woman, had the only option available to her of learning from a private tutor. She was not from a prosperous upbringing, and as such, had little to offer materially. Despite this, she sought to undertake her education in Kraków in the charge of a learned gentleman. This gentleman was a professor at the University in Latin, History and the Humanities.

His classes would hungrily consume his days, he had told her, yet they would allow him to tutor his potential pupil afterwards, but only as the gray and dark hours of the evening transitioned to the blackness of night.

The young woman agreed, and soon she took her instruction in his private quarters and repaid him, by cleaning, washing and occasionally cooking on his behalf. She admired the man, who was as respected as any other member of Kraków's renowned academics.

As the years progressed, this young woman of Kraków sensed a shifting of the character of her patron from dignified instructor to collegial comrade, until he was eventually exposed as the immodest and prurient predator that is subdued in so many of the hearts of even the most elevated of men.

The progression of events has recurred since time immemorial. A gentleman begins a platonic relationship with the purest of intentions, and an extravagance of restraint. That restraint is so often slowly worn away by the increasingly intensifying waves of familiarity and inseparability. This can lead a man to think of the woman under his charge as his possession. Finally, the last bastions of restraint are eroded, and his desire is set free by his misconception of intimacy. Even then, the assailing man realizes the abuse of trust which he is perpetrating, yet he invariably still gives in to the animal nature which is true to his soul.

In the closeness of their hours together, he had grown to secretly covet her. Over the course of their many shared private sessions, the coveting in him festered into a black and lustful desire for her. Under the cover of the night, and the influence of unusually heavy drink, the professor had set himself upon the fullness of this young girl's feminine form. This esteemed member of the intelligentsia ravaged his aspiring student using the crudest manifestation of his yearning, that of physical force. The girl was left bloodied and humiliated, disgraced by the coerced loss of her own chaste virginity, and at the hands of the man that she once respected most.

She could not turn to her family. While they were not prominent in Kraków, they were on the ascendency. She knew to share her dishonor with her own father would only drive him to acts of dishonor upon the professor. Thus, her shame would discredit the family. She even feared that her father would soon enough come to regret not only her shame, but eventually the loss of his own good fortune in which it resulted.

She then turned to the only institution in which she could entrust the disgrace of her having been victimized. It was shortly afterward that this woman was accepted into the convent, and very late in life. At the untenable age of twenty years of age, this deflowered child would become Sister Maryja Elizabeta.

It was Magdalena's father who was aware of the cloistered Sister's considerable education, although not of the calamity that had transpired and ended her tutelage. He then made an arrangement with Mother Angelica, the Superior of the convent. Kowalczyk would submit his daughter, Magdalena, to be cloistered for a period of five years for instruction in the Christian Faith. However, with the provision that she be allowed to be tutored by Sister Maryja Elizabeta in general education. For this indulgence, Władysław Kowalczyk agreed to provide a stipend to the convent of a generous percentage of his earnings from his administering of the Bochnia Royal Salt Mine.

The deal having been struck, Magdalena then entered the cloister at the tender age of ten years old. She immediately bonded with her new tutor, Sister Maryja Elizabeta. Even though the disparity of their ages was enormous, they shared the fact, nonetheless, of being the two youngest women within the walls of the convent. The good Sister took her tutoring responsibility seriously and instructed her pupil in all that she had learned from her own disgraced, and still unrepentant tutor. In good time, as the child matured, the tutor's instruction included the bias of her own mistrust for men. After all, all men were to be seen for what they were - predators of the pristine.

Young Magdalena at first did not comprehend all that she was being instructed in, as she was still only a child herself. She heard the good Sister's message: *trust not what you perceive to be in the thoughts of men, for they work so deviously to disguise their sordid desires. For men know the darkness within them, and fear that others may come to know it as well.*

The child came to know these words, and unfortunately would come to understand every nuanced aspect of their meaning over the years just ahead.

What poor Magdalena did not know was that she would never see her loving father or mother again. As the young girl entered her fourth year within the convent walls, her father was found guilty of conspiring against the then newly elected ruler, King Stanisław II August Poniatowski.

For when the King attempted to reform the powers of the monarchy in 1766, and thus weaken the powers of the *szlachta*, several nobles, including her father, quietly plotted a protest in rebellion against Poniatowski, and the Russian Tsar Catherine who had placed him upon the throne. This would manifest itself two years later in the establishment of the Bar Confederation, thrusting the Polish-Lithuanian Commonwealth into an effective Civil War.

It was a rebellion that Duke Kowalczyk would not see come to pass, as he was arrested before it began by the King's soldiers, already encamped around his lands.

What Władysław Kowalczyk did not realize, was that he had been surreptitiously sacrificed to the King's agents by another member of the *szlachta*. Another member who was eager to gain control of the Bochnia salt mine and combine its wealth with that of his own mine in Wieliczka. That treacherous member of the *szlachta* was none other than Duke Sdanowicz.

Magdalena's father and mother were taken in the night by Russian-aligned agents of the King. When they were interrogated, Władysław Kowalczyk did not stray from the story he and his wife had rehearsed for so long. *Their daughter had died at the age of ten*. They had even so marked a grave in a place of prominence upon their lands. Except it contained, of course, not the corpse of their daughter, but rather one of their *folwark's* peasant girls who had indeed died in childhood.

The Kowalczyks knew, at best, they would be sent to Russia to live the rest of their years in abject poverty, and possibly worked as beasts of burden for their transgressions against the Tsar Catherine's favored King of Poland.

They understood that since they had no family to care for young Magdalena, and they wished her not to be subjected to the harshness that surely lied ahead for themselves, the confines of the Catholic convent of Kraków was the safest place for her. They had entrusted her life with Mother Angelica and Sister Maryja Elizabeta.

Kowalczyk and his wife were indeed later deported to a small village some three hundred miles north of Moscow. Their every movement was watched and reported upon to Tsar Catherine. Their existence became harder than even those of the peasants who had once been tied to their lands of Bochnia.

Every day in the snowdrift village brought tears to her mother's eyes. For each day she thought of her little Magdalena, captive within the confines of the cloister.

Duke Kowalczyk's sentence in exile was made known to all of the traitorous regions of southern Poland, as a lesson to other conspirators against the King. Despite this deterrence, the Confederation of Bar would still rise in rebellion a few years later.

Magda, still cloistered in Kraków, was oblivious to all that had transpired. The Superior, Mother Angelica, of course, was well aware of her loss of a patron for the convent. Upon learning that the management of the Bochnia mines had been awarded by the King to be combined with the Wieliczka mines already under the administration of Duke Sdanowicz, the convent Mother Superior reached out to him.

The Duke's response was not exactly what she had expected. He told Mother Angelica that he would no longer pay for the education and cloistering of the young child, Magdalena. However, not knowing that the girl had been secretly cloistered there, he was furtively delighted. He then agreed to support the convent financially in the same amount as their previous benefactor, but only if the Mother Superior would release the Kowalczyk's daughter to him.

Mother Angelica protested at first, until the Duke, with the most elegant duplicity, explained that he had long ago promised the Kowalczyk family to look after the girl should any ill fate befall them. Upon hearing this explanation, and with the good Duke kneeling beside her as they prayed together to the Virgin Mother, it was agreed that Magdalena would be released to his care.

The Duke did not have to resort to his ultimate threat, which was to expose the Kowalczyk family's lie of the girl's death. This would be followed by his exposing Mother Angelica's harboring this enemy of the state within her convent. While the state would still likely have not violated the sanctity of the convent walls, even in this situation, it would have caused great hardship for the Mother Superior with the Cardinal of Kraków, and potentially with the Holy See in Rome, as well. Yet, however, the Duke did not have to resort to even threatening these events. Young Magdalena was released to him.

On the day that Magdalena was released to him, during the carriage ride from Kraków to the manor at Wieliczka, Duke

Sdanowicz explained to the then fourteen-year-old child how her parents had been betrayed by a treacherous spy for the King. He swore that thereafter she would live with him on his *folwark*, that is, on his estate, and that he would treat the young girl as his own adopted daughter.

It was a few days later that the Duke wrote a special letter to the Kowalczyk's in exile. He wanted to let them know that their daughter was safely in his care, and would remain so, as long as no renegade member of the *szlachta* attempted any acts of retaliation against him.

For the Duke feared that those aligned with Kowalczyk in plotting against the King might decide to take action against him. This assumed their having correctly inferred that he had profited from the family's betrayal. That, in turn, would mean that Duke Sdanowicz surely was the genesis of the treachery taken against the Kowalczyk family.

This, of course, was true. The Duke decided his possession of Magdalena should be known by all parties involved. She would remain with him, on his *folwark*, as his shield against the possibility of his enemies' potential retribution. He dispatched the letter to Magdalena's parents in exile by his own personal courier.

Young Magdalena slowly adapted to her life at the manor house. With a heavy heart, she mourned the loss of her family to the remote regions of Russia. Her life was, of course, physically comfortable, but her temperament was in the gravest of emotional distress.

The warnings of Sister Maryja Elizabeta echoed in her being like the murmur of malevolence itself - *Beware most those men in which you place your trust*.

Many weeks had passed, when one afternoon she was reading quietly in the manor's library, so as not to disrupt the Duke in the next room. She soon found that she could overhear the Duke having a discussion with his private rider who had just returned from Russia. The library adjoined the Duke's study, and he surely must have thought it empty, as she was out of his direct line of sight. She had always been so very quiet in her reading within its shelved walls, so as not to disturb him.

Magdalena could hear the weary rider telling the Duke that the Kowalczyk husband and wife, her own father and mother, had understood that Duke Sdanowicz had the child under his care. The parents went on to say that even were it possible, they would in no way attempt to signal any other members of the *szlachta* to take action against the Duke. In fact, the rider carried a letter, written in Władysław Kowalczyk's own hand, falsely stating that Duke Sdanowicz was raising the girl as a result of the deep and dedicated friendship that had always existed between them.

Magdalena realized for the first time that she was being used as a pawn against her own family. This malicious knowledge burned within her. It enflamed to a rage as she slowly came to realize it was the Duke who had betrayed her family to the King. Young Magdalena, a few days later, had secretly crept into the Duke's study. She found the letter from her father, tracing her fingers over his coerced signature. She could feel the utter duress, perhaps the very fear of the threat of her own annihilation, under which it had been written and signed.

It was then that the Duke walked in on her, surprised to find her rifling through his correspondence desk. She confronted Sdanowicz, who flew off into an intense rage at being questioned by the upstart child. He then responded in exactly the manner as she had been warned by the good Sister. Duke Sdanowicz grabbed the young girl of fourteen, dragged her screaming away from the manor house, until he had plowed the dirt between it and the stables with her flailing body. In anger, he then threw her forcibly against the wooden trough of water, where stunned, she slid into the indignity of the muddy slop surrounding it.

"From this point on," he screamed at her in rage, "you are not worthy to sleep under my roof. I opened my arms and my home to you, only to have you spy upon me, you treacherous young girl! You will never lay your head down in comfort under my roof again. You there!" he yelled to a passing peasant stable-hand.

"Yes, my lord?" the surprised young peasant man answered.

"What is your name, peasant?"

"Jacek, my lord," he answered.

"Peasant Jacek, take this unworthy wench to be your woman. She is to live with you on the this *folwark*. She is never to leave my lands, nor shall she ever come within my sight again. You will take her for your woman, from this point on."

The peasant looked down on Magdalena, crying, covered in filth, and with small rivulets of blood emerging from the scrapes of her resistance. His heart filled with sympathy for her.

"My lord, I beg your understanding, for I already have a wife! Yet, I know of a man who works in your mines, who is in need of a woman."

"Then stop what you are doing this instant, and take this villainous guttersnipe to him, for she is no longer of any use to me," commanded the Duke. He knew he needed to keep the girl on his estate. This did not mean he could not let her taste the discomfort of the life in which his peasants toiled.

And so, Magdalena was taken to Bronisław Zaczek, the miner. Zaczek was a good and compassionate, although poor and uneducated man. He treated her with kindness and respect, leaving her alone in his own hut, such that it would not be thought that he was taking advantage of the distressed young girl in any way. He went to stay with his sister Ewelina and her husband, Jacek. The very same Jacek to whom the Duke had abandoned Magdalena.

Bronisław neither wished to bring shame upon the girl, nor suspicion upon himself. He sent his sister, Ewelina, to care for her, to tend to her minor physical wounds, and attempt to salve the serrations of uncertainty that had ripped apart her young life.

So, Magdalena became Magda, as that was solely the name the befriending peasants would effort to call her. The months that followed exposed Magda to a new extended family. It was warm in a camaraderie borne of a communal misery, one in which she was soon to share. All those that Magda met shared with her in the intimacy that is borne of suffering under the hardship of a common yoke.

For all those peasants around her had been the subject of the Duke's contempt at some point. They had not necessarily been caught so directly in his wrath, as she herself had, yet they were forced to suffer his reckless indifference to the severe destitution of their lives.

Yet, they all felt compassion for this girl. She had been cast away in anger from under their master's roof. The peasants revered her, as she accepted and took up her burden humbly amongst them.

Magda, as she was now called, became increasingly close with Ewelina. After several months, Magda confessed to Ewelina that which the entire peasant community had long suspected; that she had been the daughter of another *szlachta* Duke. They had so assumed because of the elegance not only of her speech, but of her thought. Ewelina and the other peasants came to revere the young girl.

Magda had been viewed as a gift from God to the peasants. Yet, never in the girl, not even for the flicker of an instant, did Magda ever assume herself to be superior to any of them in even the least of ways.

The greatest comfort to Magda, that which she was most relieved to find, was that despite the vile intentions of the Duke, Ewelina's brother, the miner Bronisław Zaczek, had no intention of purloining her innocence. He was respectful to her. He looked after her, and soon she came to see him for the good soul that he was. Slowly, the respect he showed to Magda cultivated itself deep within her, where it was transformed with time into a seed of fondness for him. That seed sprouted a seedling of admiration, which within her grew to a clinging vine of deep affection.

Bronisław was a simple man, who worked in the salted darkness of the mines to provide whatever comfort he could for his family. A family that, by then, had come to include her as an equal partner and not as a forced consort.

Magda became ever closer with Bronisław's sister, Ewelina. They were both young, with Ewelina having some five years beyond Magda's own age of fourteen. This gulf, at first, seemed tremendous, as Ewelina had already been long married and had two children. Yet, Ewelina's recognition of Magda's education and virtuous soul seemed to shrink that gulf, and they became the closest of friends.

It was several months later, when Bronisław had come out of the mines after having been underground for a week, which was not uncommon. She found by this time that she greatly looked forward to seeing him again.

When Bronisław arrived, he extended his right arm in a position of offering. His palm was exposed passively skyward, yet its fingers were curled in a tight clench of secrecy. His skin was, as always upon his return from the mines, dried out from the salt dust. His knuckles were cracked and slightly bleeding. Shyly, he opened his clenched upturned fist, offering her from within it a dark gray object wrapped in a piece of sackcloth.

She took it tenderly from him and unwrapped it with the greatest of expectation. The shape soon emerged, and affectionately so, for her Bronisław had carved from the gray coarse salt block the image of a heart. It was round and robust, not merely a flat simple shape that was the product solely of boredom.

This heart was elegantly worked by his own hands, its lifelike fullness carefully sculpted. It bore an intricately carved cross, cut in *bas-relief*, upon its front. Magda recognized the carving as a vessel full of his own emotions for her. She smiled demurely in response.

"I offer you all I possess," said Bronisław, with great fear of rejection. "I offer you the sweat of my brow, and the love from the depths of my heart."

Magda was touched by this expressive offering and took his hand, that which had carved it, to her mouth. She gently kissed the cracked skin of his knuckles. He then knelt before her and asked for her other hand. He held both in his own.

"I ask you, young beautiful Magda to become my wife," he said tenderly. "I know I do not deserve such a gift from God Himself, yet He has sent you to my door. Come under my roof, and we shall forever worship Him together."

Magda was so touched by this man, to whom she had already been illicitly given by the Duke. Instead of Bronisław having forced himself upon her, he ignored the Duke's immoral offering, and instead asked her to give her own heart freely to him.

Magda agreed to marry him. Soon they were wed in a peasant ceremony, which despite the poverty of all who attended, became a joyous and bountiful feast. Bronisław was twenty-two years old while Magda, the peasant bride, was in the last weeks of her fourteenth year.

Ewelina, the sister of the groom, stood beside Magda bearing the greatest happiness upon her glowing face. Her eyes were alive with the twin flames of joy and pride. They joined into a singular refiner's fire, just as her once unanticipated best friend Magda and her loving brother Bronisław were forged into one within its flames.

Magda and Bronisław lived together over the next several years. To describe their life as happy would neglect the severe hardship and evident simplicity under which they lived. However, their lives were content, and they held the deepest respect for each other that flourished into a deep and meaningful love between them. Bronisław treated her with the greatest of reverence and would do whatever was necessary to bring even the slightest comfort to her.

The simplicity of their meager lives was soon to become exceptionally complicated by the Duke. For, he most envied that which he knew he would never possess: true love.

When Magda was eighteen, the Duke, who had been spying on her in the interceding years, sent for her. What he saw then pleased him very much. The insolent girl had ripened into a voluptuous young woman. Her lovely vigorous form, despite her hiding it under the loose garb of a peasant, delighted the Duke.

She had given Bronisław no children, and thus had no rigors of childbirth to have misshapen her form. Still, Magda's overall beauty surpassed even the exquisiteness of her alluring figure. Her face was more than lovely with the flower of her youth, and its radiance continued to overwhelm even the toll of the hardship of her existence.

The years had been kind to her in every way, the Duke judged. He envied her apparent happiness, yet he still intended to punish her insolence.

Duke Sdanowicz then recalled his rants the day he had tossed her into the poverty of his peasants. *She was never to come within his sight!* This vow he had already decided to break, in the disguise of being magnanimous, in reality only upon hearing of her burgeoning beauty.

She will never lay her head again in comfort under my roof! There was no need to have her stay within the manor house with him overnight, so long as his eyes could feast upon her during the day.

The Duke then ordered her to be added to his manor staff. Over the months that followed, he would come to covet her as he watched her at her chores. The wealth from the two mines was no longer enough to satisfy him. His own wife had grown plump with age, and still had not presented him with an heir. Nor even a daughter, for that matter.

After all, why should I be denied the privilege of carnal pleasures? the Duke asked himself, *for have not even my own peasant men been forcibly satisfying their malicious desires?* He had never considered that despite their crushing poverty, his peasants indeed had genuine love for their spouses. The Duke could not comprehend that these men do not have to forcibly take what is freely given to them.

One evening, during her nineteenth year, the Duke had dismissed the staff from the manor house. As they left, he asked Magda to stay behind to clean a stain from the library floor which, unbeknownst to her, he had intentionally made. The lady of the manor was shopping that afternoon in the *Sukiennice,* that is the Great Cloth Hall on the main square of Kraków and would not return for the night. Instead, she would stay with relatives in that city overnight.

So, in knowing this, the Duke sat and drank wine while Magda cleaned the floor on her hands and knees in her torn and sewn peasant dress. His eyes became heavy with illicit longings, that soon penetrated into every crevice of his being.

"My Magda, you toil in the life of one of my laborers," he said. "Your own parents had offered you up as dead to the King. I should think death would now come as a comfort to you, my peasant treasure."

He lifted the hem of her skirt with the tip his riding boot, exposing the flank of her thigh. She dared not pull it down, instead she shuddered, blushed and attempted to ignored his advances. The Duke watched her muscles enticingly flex under the still supple, smooth skin of her adolescence.

"My, my, my Magda. You are the cultured young girl who now can only scrub the stains from the floor of the library she once enjoyed so. Do not fear, my lovely child, for tonight I shall complete your education. You know, of course, that by the Polish law of *Pańszczyzna* you are my property, as are all the peasants on my land."

His leg extended higher, lifting her garb, exposing her hindquarters to his lustful gaze. She stopped her cleaning motions, and still on her hands and knees, craned her neck defiantly to respond to him. She was afraid, less for what actions the Duke may force upon her, but more for the suffering it would inflict upon her husband, should he ever be made aware of the Duke's advances upon her.

"No. We are not your property. *Pańszczyzna* only states we peasants are forever tied in labor rent to your lands. Even those who toil under your lands, as my Bronisław does. For you work these miners, such as my husband, to their very deaths..." she replied defiantly.

He kicked the hem of her peasant dress up upon her back. He then came out of the chair and kneeled over her. The finery of his riding pants rubbed against the firmness of her flank. His breath was unwanted in her ear. It was warm and intrusive as it whispered from behind her.

"So, yes, you are tied to my lands. My land is my property. Therefore, you are my property, Magda," stated the Duke in a devious logic that was generally held by the landed nobility. "As for your beloved Bronisław," he said, "did he not just leave this night for the mines? How long will he be in the darkness my dear, four, perhaps five days? Why not a week?"

"It is whatever you decide, of course," she sneered. "For only you control the lengths and depths of his laboring." There was a seed of spite in her words.

The Duke then slipped his arm around her waist from behind. "What you do not understand, my peasant Magda, is the abundance of dangers that lurk in those mines. For the ground can shift, shafts can cave, and in an instant the lives of unexacting men are crushed, if lucky."

She felt his fingers slithering across the skin of her taut belly like a brood of serpents. Soon, they tightened into the thick rope of his forearm around her waist, before the fingers snaked themselves in exploration of the exquisite arcs of her pendant breasts.

"What luck is there in being crushed?" she sneered, all the while fighting the press of his crotch against her buttocks, as his arm pulled her closer to him.

"It is a luck they would soon enough desire, for if they are not crushed in the second," hissed the Duke at the curls of the back of her lovely head, her ears ever so near his own lips, "they may find themselves trapped for hours, only to slowly consume what little air remains trapped along with them. What air they do breathe becomes warm, then hot, and finally choked with dust. They will claw at their immoveable confines, until the darkness simply absorbs their strangled souls."

Having said this, the Duke's arm slipped from her waist to hungrily grasp the fullness of her buttocks. She attempted to push him away, still upon her hands and knees, but her defiance only resulted in her pressing herself harder upon the vulgar intention of his manliness.

The wine glass still being in his other hand, the Duke then raised it to his lips and drank deeply from it. He then freed his arm by placing the crystal goblet upon the floor next to her. The newly freed hand immediately groped at the girl. As he did so, he breathed into her ear. The sweetness of the vine's press upon his breath had soured with the burning needs of his pungent, drunken lust that it also carried.

"Not all accidents are the providence of fate, my girl," he said. "Do you understand what it is that I am telling you?"

She feared he was moving closer up to her ear to bite its tender skin as he forced himself finally upon her. Yet he merely brought his lips closer to it. Then, she could not only feel the heat of his words, but also the flutter of his parsing lips across its tender creviced skin and soft full lobe.

"Tonight, you will give me what I desire, or your Bronisław will draw his final breaths in the blackness of his own terrifying fear."

She knew then, beyond all his other actions, that his vile and depraved desire for her had accumulated to the point of evil and immediate issue. She then knew it would be exhausted upon the pearl of her innocence.

Yet, if Magda resisted, she feared her sweet Bronisław would likely never breath the chill of the Polish morning frost again. She also was sure that the Duke would take her by force regardless of the exertions of her resistance.

Magda then, with the greatest reluctance, under a shroud of shame that would forever wrap itself around her nakedness, gave herself to the Duke.

It was surely at this moment, beyond all the others, that Magda had come to realize the Duke's heart was etched much deeper in darkness than any of the shafts beneath them in which her husband was then held hostage.

As the Duke imposed himself on her, she thought only of the carved heart that her Bronisław had once offered her. It was whittled from the same gray salt-stone of the mines in which he was now imperiled.

She thought of the beauty and goodness that her Bronisław had been able to produce from the depths of darkness in the form of that carving, that offering, that heart.

As the Duke hungrily drove himself within her, she could only visualize the very beauty that was her untainted liaison with her husband, as being forever dropped into the deepest and darkest recesses of obscurity. As the urgency of the Duke's needs increased, the shame of Magda's violation overpowered her.

Though she resisted with all her might the urge to do so, she feared she would degrade into a hysterical wailing given her debasement from his exertions. Since she could not defend his physical advances, she direly wished to deny him this conquest over her emotions. She would find this desire to be only that: simply a desire.

For despite her intentions, heavy, salted tears did indeed form in her eyes. She could taste their bitterness in the back of her throat. Just as the Duke achieved his physical satisfaction, a pervasive and morose wave of mourning welled up from deep within her being. It was then that she broke down into a weeping, uncontrollable wrenching of shame and sorrows.

In her wailings, young Magda had overturned the glass next to which she had kneeled. Its remnant red lifeblood drained from the soon emptied crystal vessel, and It became nothing more than yet another stain.

For even though the tenderness of her virginity had long ago been given lovingly to her own husband, Bronisław, it was in that covetousness moment of the Duke's illicit craving that he had ripped away what she had long most revered. The intimacy in which she had found comfort and succor from her eternal life of hardships. The solace of those silent moments in the embrace of her loving peasant spouse was now forever tainted.

For in the darkness of the Duke's desires, he had desecrated the innocence and purity of the marital bond between man and wife.

5

TRANSITION TO EMPIRE

AUGUST 1772

During the summer months, the troops of Austria peacefully entered the lands south of Kraków, just below the Vistula River. At the same time, Prussian troops entered from the north, and Russians entered from the east. On August 5, the three powers signed the treaty ratifying the lands of Poland to be divided to each empire.

The Austrian Envoy thereafter met with King Poniatowski in the southern Polish city of Kraków. Afterwards, Duke Cyprian Sdanowicz, as the area's predominant landowner, and administrator of the royal salt mines, was to be formally visited upon by a representative of Empress Maria Theresa. The envoy's name was Count Maximilian Von Arndt.

The Count's presence was preceded by a delegation from the Austrian Army. Dressed in their all white uniforms, save for the royal blue trim of their cuffs and their colorfully plumed military headgear, they reminded Duke Sdanowicz of the toy soldiers with which he had played as a boy. They lined, with great military precision, along the crushed gravel drive that accessed his manor like decorative road-posts awaiting the ornate carriage that was surely to carry the Envoy Von Arndt.

Before the Empress' Envoy could be received, the leader of the military unit, Colonel Erwin Hundstedt, had insisted on conducting a thorough review of the manor grounds and the surrounding structures. It was not until they entered the manor house, into the Duke's study - the very room where Duke Sdanowicz was to receive the Envoy - that Colonel Hundstedt became somewhat less condescending with his host.

"Duke Sdanowicz, does this case contains what I think it does?" asked an amazed Colonel Hundstedt as he spied a set of armor the Duke had enclosed in a beautiful glass cabinet.

Figure 3: Winged Hussars on the charge (above) and their armor (right)

"Yes, it indeed is genuine, if that is what you ask, Colonel," said the Duke.

"My God, there can't be many of these still in such wonderful condition," he said appreciatively as his eyes seemed to be arrested by the contents of the large upright cabinet.

"It the armor which was worn by the grandfather of my own grandfather in the defense of Vienna just over a hundred years ago," said the Duke.

The Duke was a man in his early forties, and he could see the Colonel doing the generational mathematics in his head, as his eyes peered upon, with the greatest of respect, the nearly pristine armor of the famous and long-feared Polish Winged Hussars.

Although considered heavy cavalry, the armor itself was relatively light. It needed to be to allow the horse warrior the dexterity and agility to manage the leveling of their signature long lances from their saddles. The pair of wooden half-arches extending from the armored body of the garment were curled high over the back of the Hussar's head and were lined with the feathers of eagles. This created an illusion of both imposing height and great strength.

The Winged Hussars were among the most feared horse warriors of Europe in 1683, when they had descended from the heights overlooking the city of Vienna to drive off the besieging Ottoman Turks. That cavalry charge was led by no other than the Polish King Jan III Sobieski. This was not an unknown position for King Sobieski, for before being elected as King of the Commonwealth, Sobieski had held the next highest position of honor in the country as *Hetman*, or Field Marshall of all combat troops.

"It is said that my ancestor rode astride King Sobieski, and the Winged Hussars struck fear into the ranks of the Turks. The Turks had threatened that very day to breach the city's walls," said Duke Sdanowicz. His words held a mild hint of protest over the fact that the descendants of those once rescued by his own forefathers were trooped upon his own *folwark* this day.

"It is a day that every schoolboy of Austria is taught," said the Colonel. "Your countrymen saved not only the city of Vienna, but the Christendom of Europe itself. It is said that the Ottoman Grand Vizier Kara Mustafa is to have said, *'Why do the trees move so?'* before realizing what he saw were the wings of the thousands of Polish Hussars on the attack."

"And for having saved Vienna, we are now to become part and parcel of the Austrian Empire?" asked the Duke.

"There is no greater honor, my Duke!" said the Colonel, snapping back into his role as leader of the invading forces. "But let us not forget the great glory of your past King."

"Nor the sniveling weakness of our current King," added the Duke in his native Polish tongue, knowing the Austrian Colonel would not understand it, as they had been speaking in the German language.

Colonel Hundstedt excused himself to send off a messenger to the envoy, letting him know it was safe to travel from Kraków, where he had been hosted by King Poniatowski at Wawel Castle the day prior.

The Colonel then returned, along with a youthful Austrian soldier. The Colonel informed the Duke that he was then free to wander about his home, except not his grounds. *So, I am forbidden to walk my own lands,* he thought. *My own home, however, I am so generously permitted to wander through, mind you!*

The young soldier stood at rapt attention. The Duke thought he had the look of a Slavic national. He was blond and strongly featured. The Duke knew that the Austrian army had forced enlistment from the lands they absorbed. "Is this soldier to be my shadow?" asked the Duke of the Colonel.

"This soldier is to remain by your side, my Duke, until his excellency, the Envoy, arrives. Wilhelm is quite fluent in your language, so feel free to converse to him in either Polish or German. I apologize for this inconvenience, for I simply cannot take the chance that any messages might be dispatched to any local Polish partisans. Heavens, no. The last thing the Envoy should be greeted by is a charging mount of Cossacks coming across your fields."

Duke Cyprian Sdanowicz then turned to the soldier Wilhelm.

His next statement was said in German to the soldier, although it was intended for the ear of the Colonel.

"Perhaps, young Wilhelm, you should explain to your Colonel that the Cossacks are Ukrainians, not Poles," said the Duke, sneering internally at the senior officer's lack of familiarity with the local cultures. "They are from the eastern regions of that land, where all devils are bred. Of course, they are favored by the Russians, the allies of your Empress Maria Theresa."

The Colonel ignored the Duke's contemptuous comment, then left the two men alone together to assure the grounds were properly secured.

Several hours then passed as the envoy's arrival was awaited. Duke Sdanowicz entered into conversation with his Austrian shadow, who he was soon to discover was from the Czech border town of Ostrava. His Polish was passable, yet certainly tainted in an accent by his Czech tongue.

The Duke had soon learned, through the beguiling charm of convivial banter, that the young soldier's Christian given name had been Wojciech. This being too Slavic for the Austrians, it had been stripped of him by his unit commander and replaced with the more Germanic name Wilhelm. The Duke could only wonder if a similar rechristening awaited himself.

"So, Soldier Wojciech, you must know of the Siege of Vienna in 1683?" asked the Duke in a comment that was only a question in disguise.

"Yes, of course," responded the infantryman. "We all know of your King Jan Sobieski's glorious charge upon the troops of the Ottoman Turk Grand Vizier Kara Mustafa. The famous Winged Hussars of Poland scattered them into disarray, before slaying them like fattened cattle."

"And you know what became of the Grand Vizier?" asked the Duke.

"Yes. Only what which was befitting his failure," the soldier said. "Months later that year on Christmas Day, upon the command of the Turkish Sultan Mehmed IV, he was strangled to death by his own troops with a silk scarf."

"And, as for King Jan Sobieski, do you know how many statues were raised in Vienna for his success?"

"I would imagine he was given many triumphs of his incredible heroic actions in statues, paintings and all other forms," said the soldier.

"NO!" exclaimed the Duke, as he interrupted the soldier, "by order of Emperor Leopold he was given no recognition whatsoever. For the Austrian Emperor, who had fled the city in cowardice before the Turks had even arrived, was outraged that the Polish King had dared to enter the rescued city's walls before the Emperor could return. So, instead Leopold erected statues in his own honor as the savior of Vienna. Emperor Leopold had demanded that King Sobieski be unacknowledged throughout the city."

"That is incredible. The Emperor had fled in fear of the Turks, while Sobieski risked not only his own life but that of his country to repel the Muslim invaders?" The boy seemed truly astonished. "The Poles saved Christianity in all of Europe."

Duke Cyprian Sdanowicz then slipped his arm around the young soldier. He pulled him close, in a display of affection.

"Well, Wojciech, don't say that too loudly. Even though we speak in Polish, as sure as the Colonel has left you here to spy upon me, they may have another soldier just as easily spying upon you."

The young soldier looked around suspiciously. "No, Duke Sdanowicz, I am the only speaker of Polish in this unit."

"So, they would have you believe, Wojciech. Never trust the Austrians, for just as easily as they have changed your name to Wilhelm, they also have tried to change the facts in their favor. In this case, worry not, for true history is tempered by the arc of time, and today King Sobieski is still lauded as a hero, and Emperor Leopold as the coward that he was. Since then, the Austrians have gone on to do battle against the Prussians and the French, yet their army is no longer feared as it once was. Like the Prussians, the Austrians hate the Slavs. Perhaps not as much nor as openly as the Prussians do, but the Austrians certainly believe they are superior to our race. So today, Austria swallows a large sect of Polish lands, as do the Prussians and Russians. Yet, it is still true that the eventual arc of time will bring the truth to the forefront – that these lands will forever be Poland!"

The Austrian soldier was then clearly discomforted by this brazen speech of Duke Cyprian Sdanowicz. He had allowed the Duke to play upon his Slavic heartstrings, only to hear what could be construed as treason coming from the Pole's tongue. For even being caught criticizing an Austrian Emperor from the previous century could result in the most serious of recriminations. And the criticism of the empire of that day as being antagonistic toward the Poles was pure treason, for it was exactly the opposite of the words of Empress Maria Theresa.

The hours then passed slowly, and Wojciech known as Wilhelm spoke no further. The Duke waited impatiently, as he knew not what message to expect from Count Von Arndt. No advance news had come by courier from the discussions in Kraków. For, perhaps, any dispatched courier from Wawel Castle may have been intercepted by the Austrian troops stationed across and around his great estate.

As the day came slowly to meet the dusk, long shadows stretched across the russet colored fields of grain surrounding his manor home. It was at this golden hour, that the magnificently ornate carriage carrying the Empress' Envoy was pulled upon the lane leading to his estate by a team of four beautiful white Lipizzaner stallions. It was preceded by a large and well-armed honor guard.

Duke Sdanowicz ceremoniously received Count Von Arndt from his carriage, and welcomed him profusely in his best German, in which he was more than proficient. "My Count, and Envoy of the Empress Maria Theresa, it is an unprecedented honor to have you as my guest here in our modest *folwark* of Wieliczka. Please grace the humble floors of my manor house with your footsteps, its table with your leisurely recline, and its stables with your most majestic stallions."

As the Duke spoke, he bent at the waist and symbolically swept the ground with his open right palm. The Count, finely attired in the ruffled and plumed Austrian style, stood upon the top step of his elegant carriage, purveying the grandeur of the manor house as the Duke lowered himself before him.

"Well, my fine Duke Cyprian Sdanowicz, it appears your conception of humility is as overstated as the grandeur of your graceful residence. I have known kings of lesser lands who have lived in less elegant accommodations. Perhaps you would be so kind as to escort me within its resplendent walls."

"Of course, my Count," the Duke said, extending his hand to assist the Count from his coach. This was yet another intentional submission of the Polish Duke before the Austrian Count, who instead took the hand of his coachman. Duke Sdanowicz did not care for the envy in the Count's words, nor for his coveting gaze as it lingered upon the façade of his ancestral home.

The Duke also begrudged the Count's rejection of his offered personal assistance. It was noted for what it was, another way for the Austrian Count to remind the Duke of his domination over the Pole. Or perhaps, to reinforce the concept that he, the Count, represented the Empress Maria Theresa, and as the Duke would never dare touch the Empress directly, then the same respect should be afforded her Envoy.

The Count descended his carriage and the two gentlemen walked through the massive doors of the manor house. They soon recessed into the Duke's private study for their personal discussions. The wall that separated the study from the adjoining library was adorned with a massive stacked-stone fireplace, which opened onto both rooms. The flames flickered from its recently stoked bed of cherry-red embers, upon which a few fresh lengths of the very best beech wood taken from his forests had been laid.

The Count and his host settled in by the relaxing fire which had been set to take the coming chill off the overnight air. For even in these summer months, the night airs carried a cold edge in this area. The small fire was almost lost within the massive fireplace, its flames dancing alone like a singular ballerina upon a theatre's stage meant for a troop of performers.

Although it was not discussed beforehand, surely both the

Count and the Duke would agree that the most difficult conversations are best undertaken before the distracting and entrancing veils of flame of a wood fire. The hypnotic movement of the flames, the smell of the wood as it burns, the hissing and popping of its consumption would fill the awkward moments of silence that so often became an impassible gulf between two powerful men in disagreement.

"My dear Duke Cyprian Sdanowicz," began Count Von Arndt, "allow me to offer the apology of the Empress for this horrid affair. Our countries have been peaceful neighbors for many years, and she regrets Austria being compelled into this situation. Yet, at the same time, she welcomes the formerly Polish province of Galicia into the Austrian Empire."

Duke Sdanowicz noted the term "Galicia" used by the Count. For he knew that the term Poland, or Austrian Poland, would henceforth be banned within the Empire. One was either Austrian or Polish, and they could never be confused.

The Count's tone had neither been inflated with condescension nor sarcasm. He was a much younger man than the Duke had expected. Strikingly handsome with dark looks and finely groomed facial hair consisting of a neatly clipped mustache adjoining a thin beard that was expertly trimmed.

In these ways, the Count was not unlike the Duke as both were young men. The Duke was in his early forties, while the Count was in his mid-to-late thirties. They were both men of great standing, although the Count seemed accustomed to much greater finery than even the Duke could provide. The sole exception between the two men, thought the Duke, was that his own robust mustache appeared more manly than the vain grooming of his guest, Count Von Arndt.

"It is unusual to hear an Empress apologize at all, for any conduct," offered Duke Sdanowicz, having seen that the Count had noticed the surprise on his face. "Most certainly, Tsar Catherine of Russia does not share your Empress' feelings."

"The Empress Maria Theresa abhors this entire matter of

absorbing some of the lands of your forefathers, I assure you. She had been reluctantly persuaded to sign the accord, yes this is true. However, King Frederick of Prussia and Tsar Catherine of Russia distrusted each other to the point that each feared the other would grab more or all the lands of the Commonwealth. Should this occur, it well could lead to a war between these two powers, with Poland trapped between them. The Austrian Empire has little need to act as a third party to assure these lands were evenly distributed. Bringing in the Austrian participation stabilized the situation. Austria participates only to create a balance of the imperial powers and thus minimize the impact upon the Commonwealth altogether."

"Yes, that is very considerate of your Empress," said Duke Sdanowicz, somewhat mockingly. *So,* he thought, *the rumors were indeed true*. The Prussian King Frederick II had said he intended to consume the Polish provinces *"like an artichoke, leaf by leaf"*. Indeed, he had dragged the Austrian Empress into the partition to wean her Empire away from its growing alliances with France, Prussia's enemy. At the same time, Frederick II, by aligning Prussia with Austria, created a plausible deterrent to keep Tsar Catherine II of Russia from grabbing all the lands of Poland outright.

Empress Maria Theresa had indeed initially objected to the idea of a partition. She had asked, *"What right have we to rob an innocent nation that it has hitherto been our boast to protect and support?"* Ultimately, the Empress reluctantly agreed. Frederick The Great, as he was later to be called, had been quoted as saying of the Empress, *"The more she cried, the more she took."*

It was then that the Duke decided to change the tenor of his discussions with his guest. For he knew that the Count had been in discussions with King Poniatowski, and certainly the status of the Bar Confederation must have been discussed.

"And what news is there of the rebellious Confederates?" asked Sdanowicz.

"Of course, you likely have not heard. *Jasna Góra*, the monastery in the town of Częstochowa, has fallen just in the past few days. Now the only refuge of the scoundrels is in two fortified monasteries in Zagórz and Tyniec, the latter which I understand is not far from this very estate."

"Yes, of course, Tyniec. The Benedictine Monastery is less than twenty kilometers from here. It sits high on a cliff overlooking the Vistula River," offered the Duke. "So, my Count, you have said Częstochowa has fallen. Has the rebel Pułaski been captured?"

"Alas, no," responded the Count, "that rebel has escaped for now. Yet, he has nowhere to run to, has he? The Empress no longer offers the Confederates free passage in Austrian lands as she once did. He will be caught soon enough."

"He is very resourceful, I am told," responded the Duke, "yet he also has no safety in Prussia and certainly not in Russia to the east. I am sure you are correct; he will be captured in due time."

The Duke's thoughts then returned to his guest. He dared ask the question that burned in the hearts of all those in the lands to be annexed.

"My Count, what is to become of this region as it transitions to Austrian rule?"

"Do not be anxious, good Duke. I have been told by the Empress to assure you that in these Polish lands to be annexed by Austria that your people will be free to practice their culture, to speak their language, and to manage their local affairs, to an extent."

"Ahh! But to *what* extent," replied Duke Sdanowicz suspiciously, "remains to be seen, does it not?"

The Count was put off by the Duke's impudent comment.

"Are your brothers in the lands being absorbed into King Frederick's Prussia or Tsar Catherine's Russia to be treated as well? I suspect not. No, I know not!" said the Count.

"And what of my own estate, my Count?" asked Sdanowicz.

"Each man thinks only of protecting his own interests, no?" said the Count as he inspected the armor of the Polish Winged Hussars forever entombed in the glass and Alder wood case. The Duke became impatient in the moments of silence that followed. He then broke the uncomfortable silence with the following words.

"We think also of protecting what is in the common interest, just as we risked the lives of our sons, the pride of the Commonwealth, in protecting your capital from the Turks."

"My Duke, you speak of the dull distant past as if it has the sparkle of the afternoon sun cast upon it. That was nearly one hundred years ago, and your Hussars have not been the military strength of Europe for quite some time."

The words cut at the Duke, and the Austrian Count had proved himself to be a man that understood he was in control of the overall situation. The Duke then decided to attempt another avenue of conversation.

"My Count, you surely misunderstand me. I agree that was indeed another time, however there is today another common interest to protect. I merely speak of the vital resource of salt that lies beneath our feet. It is critical to preserve the foods that fuel the Empire's armies, is it not? I have the skill to effectively administer these mines, as my family has done for centuries on behalf of the Kings of Poland."

The Count then replied, "As it is, the Empress thinks very highly of your personal administrative skills, but not so much of those in general of the rest of the nobles of Poland. Yes, not long ago, your ancestors drove the Turks from breaching the walls of Vienna. Yet, she finds that your nobility, the *szlachta*, as you say, has become too empowered, and their ability to veto the acts of the legislature have stifled the progress of your political state. The Empress directed me to mention this very abuse of power in our discussions with your King Poniatowski. As your former King Sobieski had once safeguarded the culture of the city of Vienna, our Empress intends to safeguard the new borders of Poland. Austria will assure, by their participating in this restructuring, that the ambitions of both Prussia and Russia remained checked."

"So, my estate is to become the providence of the Austrian Empire?" asked Duke Sdanowicz directly. The Count responded in a diplomatic voice, almost as if he had not heard the Duke's entreaty.

"In matter of fact, your estate is already the providence of the Austrian Empire. While Tsar Catherine of Russia demands that the Commonwealth's *Sejm* approves the new borders, the Empress already considers this land to be Austrian."

These last few words disheartened the Duke. He feared his lands and the management of the two salt mines would be taken from him outright.

"And so, I am to become a landless member of the *szlachta*?" asked the Duke. "A nobleman with no land, no power and no respect?"

The Count looked at him strangely. He knew he had the Duke hoisted in a state of uncertainty and was enjoying the Pole's angst over the future ownership of his massive estate. He then decided to make the Pole squirm no longer.

"Certainly not, my Duke. As I have already said, the Empress is very fond of your abilities and your loyalty to your King. So long as that loyalty is now pledged to the Empress, you will become a member of the Austrian Empire. You shall keep your lands, and your manor, and your peasants. You will manage your salt mines, which in German will now be known as *Groß Salze*, as you have done before, with your stipend unchanged. In fact, the Austrian Empire does not intend to confiscate any of the lands owned by the current gentry. That is unless there is behavior by the landowner for doing so."

"Praise be to the Empress Maria Theresa," said the Duke aloud, his words alive with the emotions of gratitude and relief. Tears ebbed into the corners of his eyes, as he for the first time had been told he would retain his tremendous wealth.

"Only now," continued the Count, "the output of these mines are to be in benefit of the Austrian Empress in lieu of the Polish King. That is what I have been told to communicate to you, my Duke. What is your response to the Empress' generosity?"

"Praised be the heavens, my Count!" exclaimed Sdanowicz. "Wieliczka and Bochnia sing the praises of Empress Maria Theresa of Austria. I could have hoped for nothing more!"

"But you have gained so much more, my friend," responded Count Von Arndt. "From this point on, your lands, your wealth, your mines will be protected, not by the weak and internally bickering Polish State, but instead by the strength and vast resources of the Austrian Empire. Russia and Prussia dare not consider to invade these lands, that you can be assured. Under the Commonwealth, you had no such security."

Duke Sdanowicz stepped between the Count and the flicker of the fireplace. He lowered himself to one knee, took the Count's hand, and kissed it.

"This I do, not to gain your personal favor. I do this to demonstrate my allegiance to Empress Maria Theresa of Austria. She is truly an enlightened monarch."

The Count permitted only a wry smile, as he looked down condescendingly upon the man kneeling before him. He thought, *Yes, the Empress has your allegiance, but will she have your heart? Or will you always save the pulse of its beats for the country of Poland?*

6

CONTRASTS OF INDEPENDENCE

1772 - 1776

By 1776, and during the previous four years since the partition, life under Austrian rule had been quiet and uneventful. As had been relayed by her Envoy, Count Von Arndt, the Empress Maria Theresa did indeed think highly of the Duke's management of the two *Groß Salze* mines at Wieliczka and Bochnia.

However, despite the Empress' confidence in him, she had gone on to name Count Von Arndt as the Duke's overseer, responsible for setting the mines' output quotas and identifying the improvements from throughout the Austrian Empire by which these quotas could be reached.

The Duke had heard rumors from his friends in Vienna that the Count himself had petitioned this responsibility from the Empress directly, and in a most deliberate manner. It was after this that the Duke established a small but trusted network of contacts within the Imperial Court itself. This ring of paid spies then informed him of what activities in the Viennese Court pertained to his own interests. What they reported back to him was of high importance indeed, and well worth the funds Cyprian Sdanowicz paid to his secret informers.

They had informed him that the Count had called upon the

Empress, who was known to favor him, and proposed that production increases of twenty-five percent could be realized under his leadership. The Duke had heard that the Count had gone so far as recommending the Duke's land be recommissioned to him, which would had left the Duke a landless noble. The Empress, he was told, would not consider this. Instead she committed to the Count that if his improvements could raise output to the levels he promised, she would assign half of the increased portion of the Duke's management stipend to Von Arndt.

The Duke had not trusted the Count from the very first day that he had met the nobleman. If this paid information was true, and the Duke had no reason to believe it was not, then he needed to keep a very close eye upon the Count. It was from this point forward that the Duke played a cat and mouse game with the Count, for he would over the coming years feign both the interest of the cat as well as the suspicion of the mouse in dealing with the Austrian nobleman.

At that same point in time, Magda continued to nurture her dearest son. Over the previous four years, Magda had raised Marek in the peasant village upon the Duke's *folwark*. Unbeknownst to the Duke, Magda had begun teaching Marek to read and write. Although the boy was only four years old, he was taking to reading swiftly, although the writing skills were still to be mastered by him.

It was most unusual for a peasant boy to be literate, however Magda, that most unusual of peasant *matkas*, was intent on educating her son to the limits of her own abilities. And thanks to Sister Maryja Elizabeta, Magda's abilities were quite significant.

Soon, her sister-in-law Ewelina asked Magda to teach her two sons, Bartek and Andrzej, who both were several years older than Marek, to read. Magda agreed, and soon found that since he had companions with whom to practice, Marek developed even faster in his studies.

Very soon, the situation generated a problem in providing the three boys material to read. As Magda was still working within the manor house, she had access to the library. She dared not remove any of its books to her hovel, for if they would be found, she or, even worse, her son, could be flogged for thievery. Instead, Magda would occasionally copy passages from some books by hand. This was risky enough, but in this way she only exposed herself to potential punishment.

As Magda brought home the copied materials, she was quick to notice the inquisitiveness of her boy. He immediately digested everything she would bring to him, and soon his questions regarding the smuggled text exceeded her ability to explain them. His greatest love of all were maps. He begged his mother to bring him copies of any maps from the Duke's library. These were very understandably difficult for his mother to copy by hand, although she did make rudimentary attempts to do so in order not only to please her son, but also to encourage his seemingly insatiable curiosity.

Magda was very cautious not to be caught by the Duke, for she did not wish to give that most despicable man anything else to hold over her. Duke Sdanowicz was becoming increasingly desirous of another forced rendezvous with Magda, except that his continual and depraved efforts were ultimately thwarted by his wife.

The Duke's wife had taken a liking to Magda ever since she had returned to the manor house after Marek's birth. Magda soon became her favorite servant by always helping the Duchess whenever she possibly could. Of course, this was accompanied by a rich profusion of compliments designed to stroke the Duchess' ever-ravenous ego. The Duchess soon came to love her for her hearty laugh, her pleasant disposition and her penetrating smile. Yet, if there were one singular feature that appealed to the Duchess in Magda's demeanor, it was her unfailing self-confidence.

It was a little over a year after Marek's birth when the bonds between the two women were permanently fused. It was then that the Duchess became pregnant with her first child. It was through these nine months, that her friendship with, and reliance upon, Magda had blossomed. The Duchess demanded Magda be assigned permanently to her, and the Duke, who had always feared his wife's wrath, acquiesced.

For certainly the Duke had tried to separate the two by any number of excuses. Not only did the Duchess insist upon Magda's being by her side, soon she wondered why her husband was so insistent on taking the young peasant from her at all. Duke Sdanowicz feared the ire of his wife for she was herself of Ukrainian blood, and even the most noble of Ukrainians could be ferociously vengeful when wronged. For this reason, and always fearing her family had ties to Cossacks that could be dispatched on her behalf, Duke Sdanowicz ceased in his attempting to cleave Magda from his wife's side.

Early in her pregnancy, the Duchess Sdanowicz notified her husband she would be taking a trip to Kraków to procure goods she would need for the expected baby. This delighted the Duke, for he knew she would stay with her family overnight there. It would afford him his long-awaited second liaison with Magda. It enflamed within him a such a desire that he could not wait until the appointed day.

When the day of travel did indeed arrive, the lecherous Duke was surprised to learn that the Duchess intended to take Magda along with her to Kraków. The Duke protested, saying it was unheard of for a peasant girl to travel with a Duchess.

The Duchess reminded her husband that this Magda was no mere peasant girl, for she had once slept under the roof of their own manor house, and surely no simple peasant would be afforded this consideration. Also, argued the Duchess, she was from a noble family, although her parents had disgraced themselves. The Duke was perturbed, for it was only then that he had realized his wife had grown boastful of having a nobleman's daughter as her personal servant.

When he claimed he was not able to get a pass for Magda to cross the border from Austrian Galicia into Poland (for Kraków was still within Poland, although only across the river), he thought he had outwitted his wife. She then simply said he was right, so she would still take Magda, however instead they would travel much further to the town of Prague, which was officially within the Austrian Empire. This would be a most expensive trip, and after he admitted to himself he was defeated, a border pass for Magda to travel to Kraków was found. And in doing so, his libidinous intents upon Magda were defeated.

Magda went on to become the Duchess' servant, confidante, and friend during the pregnancy. A pregnancy that Doctor Olszewski declared was to be a boy. His professional opinion was based upon the height in which the Duchess carried the child in her womb.

This news from the doctor so delighted the Duke that the cavorted around the estate with the arrogance of a peacock. His chest ballooned as he did so, that one might think his runaway pride would burst the stitching of his garments. For the doctor had assured the Duke that his heir was soon to be born unto him.

Magda helped the Duchess through a very difficult pregnancy. No chore was too low for her, no assistance requested by the Duchess was ever denied. In this way, the two became one, or as close as a servant can become to the woman she serves.

It was then, one night In the Duchess' quarters, that the Duchess asked Magda why her husband was always seemingly trying to take Magda away from her service. The question was one that Magda had suspected might be coming, having been privy to overhearing some such discourse between the Duke and Duchess. Yet, it was a question that, as much as she wished to, Magda could never answer directly. For Magda was sure once the Duchess knew of the liaison between she and her husband, the Duchess would take her husband's explanation as the truth: that Magda had tempted the weak man and he succumbed to her.

Instead, she simply said to the Duchess that the Duke feared you would feel sympathy towards me after the way my parents were exiled to Russia.

"Well, of course, I sympathize with you on this," said the Duchess, "but that is not the doing of the Duke (*for she did not know it truly was*). We discussed your coming to live with us and were pleased when you did. Later, the Duke told me of how you had fallen in love with a peasant named Zaczek, so who were we to stand in the way of your heart's desire?"

"Then truly the Duke's fears are unfounded, my Duchess," said Magda, forever closing the issue. However, it cleaved open anew the wounds in her memory of what the Duke had once forced her to do.

The months ahead were tiresome for the Duchess. She had put on significant weight over the years, which only complicated the pregnancy further. When the child was delivered, Magda was in the room to soothe the Duchess, as Ewelina had once soothed her. Doctor Olszewski delivered the child with only a singular complication: it was born without a penis. For the boy he had so outrightly promised the Duke turned out to be a healthy baby girl.

The Duke was deflated and enraged at the same time. In his fit of anger, he ordered the small wooden cabin on his property that was even then used as an infirmary to be enlarged to add a primitive living quarter for the doctor. Upon its completion, the doctor was removed from his spacious and well-appointed rooms in the manor house. He would spend the rest of his days on the *folwark* in the log structure. As a result, since he shared quarters with the sick and wounded, the peasants were often released before their infirmities were properly healed.

After many months, the doctor would eventually be invited back to the manor house for meals, and to linger in the library afterwards, although he would never be invited by the Duke to sleep under its roof again. For the Duke had been quoted as saying, "For so long as I shall go without the comfort of an heir, you, *Pan* Grzegorz Olszewski, shall go without the pleasure of a comfortable night's sleep. For you have robbed me of my dream, and I, in return, shall rob you of yours."

The girl that was born to the Duke and Duchess was named Maryja, the Polish form of the name Maria, in honor of the Austrian Empress. The Duke would not waste even the naming of his own child as an opportunity to flatter the Empress. However, the family would come to know her simply as Maya. It was the Duchess, the girl's mother, who began calling her this, even though the typical diminutive name for Maryja in Polish was Manya. The Duchess preferred Maya, because she had become aware that in Greek mythology Maia was the goddess of fertility. And so, the girl became known to the family as Maya.

After the sting of losing his heir eventually subsided, the Duke came to love his Maya very, very much. The year was then 1774, and for the second time in two years, the Duke had fathered a child. Yet, he never forgave the doctor for his previous mistake in predicting the child would be a son.

It was a long, arduous process of rehabilitation before the doctor was eventually welcomed back to the table of the manor house. At first, even when the doctor came to sup at its table, the Duke would take his meal in his upstairs chambers. Eventually, in the fall of 1776, the Duke welcomed the doctor to dine with him. It was more that the Duke missed the banter of the doctor's dialog over the meals than it was of forgiving the man's incompetence. After all, the doctor had made a fool of him, the Duke continued to think.

After their initial awkwardness at the dinner table, they slowly engaged in a conversation of the events that had unfolded in the New World.

"So, you have heard, *Pan* Grzegorz, that the English Colonists have declared their independence from the King this summer past?" asked the Duke.

"Yes, I received a letter from my brother in Paris. It is so very exciting. Their Declaration of Independence is so well written, it embodies the very essence of the Enlightenment. *We hold these truths to be self-evident, that all men are created equal...*"

The doctor was then interrupted by an emphatic Duke Sdanowicz, "That is exactly the rancid tripe that will get them all crushed. Can you imagine King George III of England allowing them to separate from his Crown? All men are not created equal, for if they were there would be no monarchies on earth. No noblemen, either. Could you imagine the day a peasant counts as much as a Duke? It will never happen and should never happen if there is to be any order among the masses, or even the sovereign states. All men created equal? These are just florid words, more delicate than the flowers themselves. Watch as the King's sabers cut them all down."

The doctor was not surprised that their discussion had taken less than a few minutes to fall back into the ruts of the tracks they had always followed.

"They have a name and a cause, my lord," said Doctor Olszewski. "They call themselves Americans now, no longer just Colonists. They fight against the excessive taxation of the Crown, especially since they are not represented in Parliament. It is my experience that when men have a cause, a homeland and a name to rally round, the results can be unpredictable."

"I don't give them until next spring," retorted the Duke. "Who will lead them? They are merely farmers and merchants, the only army they have known has been the King's."

"I suspect the King has trained the leaders of his own rebellion," said the doctor. "What is most dangerous is that those who will rise to lead this rebellion will most likely never have even lived in their *home* country..."

The Duke's vitriol exploded once more. "That is exactly my point, *Pan* Grzegorz. Here we had the Confederation of Bar. These were men from Poland who fought for their homeland and were crushed by the Russians. How can the Colonists have any chance at all, when they have never even been, for the most part, to England?"

Doctor Olszewski was enjoying once more in their discourse, as always, with each man having nearly the exact opposite view of the other. He could see the Duke had missed this interaction as well.

"My dear lord, forgive me if I should bring you to anger, still I fear you miss my point. The Americans fight for the only homes they have ever known. They know now, after their declaration, that there is no turning back. For if they do, they shall imperil all that they have."

The Duke stared at his dinner companion. "Yes, this is for certain. I have never been to the New World, yet I am told it is abundant with opportunity. Vast forests and fisheries, great tracts of land to be gained. Such treasures that the European Empires fight wars over, and in numbers far greater one can find on our continent. Yet these fools are willing to risk it all for the words of a few idealists."

"Perhaps for merely a single word, my lord," said the doctor. "Freedom! The very same ideal for which the Confederates of Bar were stirred to action. Freedom from Russia! Freedom from England! Freedom from the overlords!"

The Duke looked once again painfully at his guest, "And like the Confederates of Bar, these Colonists will also be crushed."

7

THE BARGAIN

APRIL 1777

As Marek grew, he became more and more interested in where his *tata* went off to for days on end. He was always excited to welcome Bronisław home, especially since the miner always had a small carved figure of an animal for the boy. A hen, a pig or a fox, always intricately carved, would be presented to the child each time the nearly exhausted Bronisław returned to his hovel after days of exhausting labor.

As the boy's obsession in his *tata's* work bloomed, his true father's obsession in the child did as well. Duke Cyprian Sdanowicz would seemingly find Magda in the manor house, whenever she strayed from the Duchess' side.

"Bring the boy to me," the Duke would demand, "so that I may assess him. I wish to understand if he has the traits of his family's intellect. Bring him to the manor house over the next four days, and I will spend time with the child."

"The Duchess will understand your sudden interest in a peasant child?" Magda replied, having buried a threat within her question.

"I will merely tell my wife that I am considering the boy as a playmate for our own Maya, for she is three and the boy is five. The Duchess will understand."

Magda knew that the Duke was uncertain that she would. For he greatly feared his Ukrainian wife. She had initially thought it was because of the wild savage winds of *The Steppes* that had generations ago become infused in the Duchess' tempestuous family blood. Yet, Magda had come to think that the Duke's fear of his wife was more closely tied to the transition of her womanly form, thickening with each passing year.

The Duchess had progressed from a slim, lithe girl, full of energy and *bon vivant*, to a menacing matron of a woman. Although she was by then sloppily large, her frame carried beneath its fattened flesh enough musculature to risk the threat of physical punishment upon the triggering of her explosive temper.

Magda had witnessed this many times, yet always aimed at other servants and never at herself. She had even, once or twice, noticed the Duke's flinching when his wife exploded upon a peasant servant.

"I will not bring Marek to you," Magda said boldly to the Duke. "I know not what vile thoughts you would leave within him."

In reality, Magda knew that Bronisław would be outraged should she do so. He already was jealous of the many hours she would spend away from him in the service of the Duchess. To have Marek spend days with the Duke while he was away in the mines would surely outrage the otherwise gentile Bronisław.

"I will see the boy," demanded the Duke. He drew Magda by the hand, pulled her close and whispered in her ear, "He is my son and I will not be denied!"

"Perhaps the Duchess would love to learn of your insistence!" Magda whispered in response. The Duke released her hand and stepped away from her.

"You would be extremely foolish to do so," threatened the Duke, "for your husband still toils under extremely dangerous conditions." He then softened his voice and coaxed Magda. "There must be something that you desire that I could make available to you in return. Perhaps some meat for your family?"

Meat was very rare indeed for a peasant family, unless they

were fortunate enough to catch a rabbit, or other small vermin, from the fields or forest. Even this was risky, as it was considered as stealing from the Duke, who owned the lands and all that dwelled upon them, be they peasants or other creatures. Besides this, the Duke was unaware that the Duchess had been allowing Magda to take scraps of meat and other excess foods from the manor house to Marek and Bronisław.

"There is perhaps something that I would trade for the boy's time," said Magda, already feeling a great guilt as soon as the words had left her mouth. "Marek wishes to see the mines where his *tata* goes to work. He is obsessed with this."

"Then it is decided," stated the Duke triumphantly, "bring Marek to the manor house tomorrow."

Magda, having had agreed to the Duke's request, was only then told that they would not be allowed into the mine itself. However, it could be arranged for the boy to wait outside the garrison that protected the mine's entrance for his *tata* to emerge. Magda considered this acceptable.

Over the following four days, while her husband labored in the mines, Marek spent extensive time alone with the Duke. Magda made Marek promise to keep his time with the Duke as a secret from Bronisław, telling the boy to do so if he ever again wished to return to the manor house. She knew that the great structure fascinated the child, with its many rooms, its oil paintings of horsed warriors, and especially the cabinet which held the famed armor of the Winged Hussars of earlier years. Magda knew the boy's imagination was lit afire by all these trappings, and so he promised to keep the secret from his *tata*.

So, for the second time, Magda kept a secret from her husband. Of course, Bronisław had not known of the abuse of his wife at the Duke's hands. Magda was wise to hide this molestation from her husband, for the gentle miner would have exploded in a torrent of rage. A rage that would have consumed them all, for if Bronisław attacked the Duke in revenge, he surely would lose his life. Marek would then lose the only father he knew and so deeply loved.

It had by then been nearly six years since that attack, and, perhaps thanks to only the Duchess' newfound omnipresence on the *folwark*, as well as her having taken a considerable preference to Magda, that the Duke had never attempted to exploit his position over her again.

Deep in her heart, although Magda knew herself to have been the victim of his outrageous advances upon her, there was still a heavy guilt of complicity that bore deep into her being.

Magda thought, *I did not resist the man as I should have. When he forced himself upon me, I should have fought back, even with the threat of my husband's life held over me.* She realized that should Bronisław have returned home from the mine to have found her bruised and battered, that he would not have rested until he had found and taken his revenge upon the one who had dared to assault her.

Magda knew her husband well, and she knew it did not matter if her attacker was the Duke himself. She knew Bronisław would revenge her even if it would mean his own death.

Bronisław would have undoubtedly revenged her, and in effecting this revenge, the only thing she had left in this world, her peasant family, would be sacrificed for her honor.

Her guilt was that of a survivor, which she had come to know from Bronisław himself. He had nearly been crushed in a mine shaft collapse years before they had met. He was only an apprentice then, and the two men he worked with died that fateful day. Bronisław, the youngest of the three miners, had fortunately been sent back at the last moment from the very face of the shaft to find a pickaxe. Had he not, he too would have perished. While it had been many years in the past, he still was prone to the most severe melancholy whenever anything reminded him of that darkest of days.

Magda also was prone to a dreaded remorse regarding the crushing memory of her night with the Duke. She shook with revulsion anytime the Duke touched her, even innocently upon the arm, during her duties in the manor house. Often, when they were known to be alone in one of its many rooms, the Duke would grab her by the waist. She would snap her head around only to find him smiling vilely. "That day will come again," he would whisper into her ear, and then gently laugh, "and I will once more enjoy it so!"

The only person to whom Magda had ever revealed the details of her secret was her dear sister-in-law, Ewelina. Years earlier, when she was still pregnant, Magda had desperately needed to unburden the crushing weight of the guilt that she carried along with her unborn child. She had made Ewelina promise, weeks before the birth, that whether the child be a boy or a girl, it was to be committed to the religious order to atone for her sins. She was driven by an unshakeable premonition that because of the great sin forced upon her, that God would not allow her to survive the birth of this child.

Ewelina had argued with her that there was no sin, only the shame she imposed upon herself. Since the Duke had threatened her with the life of her husband (*my one and only brother*, Ewelina thought in revulsion), Magda had no choice but to submit herself to the Duke's advances. Therefore, there was no sin on her part, only on the part of the Duke.

By that logic, Magda had no sin for which to atone, and Ewelina attempted to console her fears.

"The Lord will not take you in childbirth," she had told Magda, "and you, yourself, will one day hand over this child to the Church."

However, Magda tended to more readily agree with the only other person to whom the secret had been shared. In the days before the childbirth, Ewelina had been loose tongued around the old midwife, *Pani* Urszula. She was as devout a Catholic as there was on the *folwark*, although typically all the peasants were very religious. Sunday was always reserved as a day of worship and rest, and services were held by priests throughout the hamlets on the *folwark* at the wooden chapels constructed by the Duke. In these modest structures, *folwark* priests had heard Magda over the years confess her sins regularly, except that Magda could never bring herself to confess her shared sin with the Duke.

Magda, driven by her guilt, believed as *Pani* Urszula did. That despite the circumstances, both she and the Duke had committed adultery, and thus both had sinned. Even had Magda vigorously fought against the Duke in his attack upon her, so long as he defiled her, they both had committed adultery and thus sinned. *For even as a soldier drops another in battle, has not a man's life been taken unjustly in murder*? Urszula had reasoned that to murder is a sin, no matter under whose flag it is justified.

Magda had by then lived with the shame for these nearly six years. Much to her relief, the secret had been held by only the three women. For Magda knew that Ewelina dared not tell the secret to her husband Jacek, who her sister-in-law thought to be an idiot. Ewelina kept Magda's secret from him out of fear that Jacek would ultimately share it with Bronisław. As for *Pani* Urszula, she had died three years earlier from a raging fever. On her deathbed, she told Magda that she had never divulged her secret.

It was likely that the old woman had not done so, for the old midwife had always treated the facts surrounding each woman's delivery as a sacred covenant entrusted only to the mother and herself. It was a vow held so sacred that even the portending shadows of her own death could not tempt *Pani* Urszula to violate it.

The secret had been safe these many years, although Magda soon found herself trading her son's time with the very man who had molested her. Her guilt was unbearable. And from this point on, it included keeping a second secret from Bronisław.

Then came the dawn that was the product of Magda's agreement with the Duke. The sun was bright, yet there was a chill to this cold April morning. Marek was now of the age of five years, and he waited, along with his mother, for his *tata* to emerge from the salt mines of Wieliczka.

The day was special to the boy, for Marek had been asking for some time to see where his *tata* went off to work, and for such long lengths each time. As the town of Wieliczka was a restricted area for the peasants who worked the fields of the Duke's *folwark*, Marek was normally not allowed to see where his *tata* worked. For in this simple town was where the shafts of the mines soared to the surface, like demons escaping from the underworld.

"*Tata*, where do you go?" the innocent youth would ask.

"Into the ground, my Marek," had always been Bronisław's response. Yet, this morning, Marek's eyes looked not on the hole, nor even a cave that he had pictured in his imaginative mind's eye. Instead, the boy's actual eyes had this morn been opened to so much more that he had never seen before. He stared in amazement at the *Rynek Główny*, or main square, of the town of Wieliczka. This was the boy's first time being off the expansive fields of Duke Cyprian Sdanowicz's *folwark*. The town and its colorful square amazed him.

What soon would really astound the child was a few minutes' walk from the main square. There, he saw for the first time the massive brick garrison of the royal salt mines, or as they were by then renamed by the Austrians, the *Groß Salze.* With its protective ramifications, the garrison appeared as a fortified castle in the eyes of the boy. Indeed, this child was bright, for the Wieliczka's garrison had been built in the fourteenth century by the Polish King Casimir the Great. Its wealth funded his court, as well as the establishment of the Jagiełłonian University in Kraków, and the overall emergence of the Polish State in Central Europe. Given its being the source of great wealth, the King had ordered it to be protected. As testimony to his decree, thick brick walls, complete with turreted towers, enclosed the mine's shaft.

That frigid morning, the sun was still rising when Marek first saw his *tata* walking towards him. Its brilliant orange rays sliced through the brick castellations of the parapets adorning the garrison's walls, which in turn cast massive sawtooth edged shadows. It was in this darkened obscurity that Marek first recognized his *tata*. It was not from the familiar features of his face, which, at first, were still awash with shadows, but rather by the exhausted gait of the miner's walk as he exited through the immense archway that separated the inner garrison yard from the open space where Marek and Magda waited. Bronisław was clad in his leather miners' frock, although he had already removed the leather cowl from his head.

"*Tata, Tata*, over here," screamed the boy, waving his free hand so violently that Magda felt the zeal of his welcoming gestures in his other hand, which she held tightly.

The child had recognized Bronisław's exhausted and clipped stride, as he had seemingly dragged the shell of his fatigued and spent physique away from the mine that had so thoroughly consumed his energy. Yet, when Bronisław heard Marek's excited, youthful voice, it imparted a vigor into his being that instantly revived him.

"What a wonderful surprise, my Magda and our Marek," yelled Bronisław. "Come to me, my son!"

At this point, Marek pulled his hand out of his mother's grip, although she was readying to release him. Marek shot off like a bolt of lightning toward Bronisław. Magda watched as the boy threw himself upon his kneeling *tata*. A cloud of gray salted dust gently exploded from the miner's garb as a result of the boy's impact.

"*Tata*, I missed you so," said Marek.

"But have you been a good boy for your *matka*?" asked his father.

"Yes, of course," Marek responded. "Do you have a gift for me?"

At this, Bronisław rose and stood above the boy. "You are certain that you have been a good child, Marek?"

The boy nodded so vehemently that his mother feared for the muscles of his neck.

"All right, my child, I have carved something for you," he said, and gave his son a small cloth sack that his sister Ewelina had sewn just for the occasion of his giving these whittled gifts to the boy.

Marek greedily took the cloth sack and loosened the string binding it tightly. From inside it he anxiously drew out an intricately carved wolf, complete with the unfinished body of a prey dangling from its jaws.

"*Tata*, it is wonderful," said Marek, "but what is the animal in its mouth?"

"What do you think it should be, Marek? I have not finished carving the prey, so what should it be? What do wolves like to eat beside bad little boys?"

"I would not know, *Tata*, as I am only a good little boy," responded Marek in this playful game between the miner and the boy he thought to be his son. "Perhaps it is a beaver. Wolves eat beavers, don't they?"

"Yes, Marek. Wolves do indeed eat beavers. When I get home and after I rest, I will finish this and make the prey have the long, flat tail of a beaver."

"How do you make these?" asked the boy. "The wolf is so real, and I know that the beaver will be also when you are finished. How do you do it, *Tata*?"

It was then that Bronisław responded to his son, as he had done many times before by saying with a shrug, *"Nie ma za co"* which is Polish for "It is nothing."

By then, Magda had walked up to the two of them. She leaned over her son to kiss her husband on his cheek, which embarrassed Bronisław.

"So, you are both off from the fields of the *folwark*," he said. "You have permission?"

"Yes, the Duke agreed. It is how we knew when to expect you, my husband," she said. What she had intentionally failed to tell him was of the deal she had struck with the Duke.

She heard Marek ask him, "*Tata*, why has the salt mine been placed so far away from our home? Why do you have to leave us for days at a time?"

"Well, my Marek," Bronisław replied, "it takes a great effort to go down into the mines, and to return to the surface as well. To come home every night is nearly impossible, for all we miners are exhausted after digging at the salt all day. Still, we are better off than the horses that are sent down into the mines. Once they are sent underground, they are never returned to the surface. I am told that to bring them back to the surface after many years below would kill these animals."

"There are horses underground, *Tata*?"

"Yes, my boy, but not the fine animals of the Duke's stable you seem to be forever dreaming of. No, these are beasts of burden, work horses, who pull the ropes that lift great weights."

The boy seemed amazed that such great undertakings were

being carried out beneath the very ground upon which he stood. Bronisław then addressed his other question.

"As for where the mine is placed, we will have to ask Saint Kinga."

Marek looked quizzically at Bronisław. "Who is Saint Kinga?"

"You have never heard of Saint Kinga? She is the patron saint of all salt miners. I cannot believe you do not know of her!" Bronisław stated with mock disbelief.

"Tell me about her, *Tata*," Marek said excitedly.

"Well, she was a beautiful princess from Hungary," Bronisław started...

"Where is Hungary?" asked the inquisitive Marek.

"It is a land south of here, on the other side of the mountains..." resumed the father.

"Someday, I will go there..." interrupted Marek.

"Yes, my son, someday you will go there and beyond. You will see many places. In fact, you will see the entire world. Then, you will come home to tell your *matka* all about the magnificent places you have visited."

Magda smiled broadly at the boy. She was enjoying the warmth of the conversation between the two who knew each other as father and son. Then it crept into her thoughts, *How could a child of such innocence be the result of such an indecent act?*

"So," Bronisław continued, "Princess Kinga was to be married to Prince Bolesław The Chaste. He ruled Kraków then. She was asked by her father the King of Hungary what should be her dowry."

"What is a dowry?" asked the young boy.

"It is what the father of the bride gives the man to take his daughter as his wife," said Bronisław.

The boy's face enlarged, with his eyes taking a disproportionate share of his expression. "You mean like a prize?"

"Yes, my Marek," said the dusty miner, "Like a prize..."

"What did you get, *Tata*?"

"I got the greatest gift of all. I got the smile of the most beautiful woman in the world. It is a treasure unlike any other, my child," Bronisław said.

Magda smiled dearly at her husband. *Would he think her such a treasure if he knew of the evil she hid from him?*

"Then, I guess Princess Kinga was not so pretty if her *tata* had to give Prince Bolesław *the Chased* some other gift to take her."

"Marek, I am sure she was very pretty, but not as pretty as your *matka*," responded Bronisław, eager to finish his story. "The Princess told her father that Prince Bolesław was rich and had many jewels, so these were not considered. Then the King said that he would take Princess Kinga to a very special place. He took her to a salt mine in Hungary. She was very excited, for at that time there were no salt mines in Poland. Her only problem was how would she get the mine to Poland."

"She surely couldn't dig it out of the ground, *Tata*. What did she do?"

"Princess Kinga prayed to Our Lord, who told her to take off her ring and drop it into the deepest shaft of the mine. She did this, before she walked away from the mine."

"How did that help?" asked the boy.

"Well, my son, when the princess travelled to Kraków, she stopped the procession of travelers at a location very near here. She told the miners to dig in a certain spot, and when they did, they found a clump of gray stone, which they handed over to her. Princess Kinga tasted it on her tongue, and immediately knew it to be salt. Then she crumbled the soft salt stone in her hands. Guess what she found inside?"

"I don't know," said Marek as he extended the tip of his tongue to taste the salt stone wolf his father had carved.

"She found the very same ring that she had thrown down the shaft of the salt mine in Hungary. Poland now had a great deposit of salt, thanks to Princess Kinga."

"It was magic?" asked Marek.

"No, Marek," answered his father. "It was the work of God. He had told Kinga to drop the ring. For God can do anything, and those of us who believe in Him and have faith in Him can accomplish anything at all that He wills."

"You said that Princess Kinga was a saint?" Marek asked.

"Yes, for after she and Bolesław the Chaste wed, she became a favorite of the Polish people. Many miracles were accomplished by her."

"You mean besides the miracle of the mine?"

"Oh yes, my son. For she was favored by God and all her people raised thanks to God for giving her to them, just as all we peasants give thanks to God for having given us your *matka*."

Magda blushed at the compliment from her husband.

"I know what God said when all the people thanked him," said Marek.

"And what did He say, my son?"

The boy smiled broadly, before responding, "He said, *'Nie ma za co'*, of course."

Bronisław laughed aloud. "Yes, Marek, for everything, no matter how impossible for us, it is nothing for Our Lord to accomplish."

Bronisław lifted Marek above his head, and holding him high above him said, "You are a very bright boy, my Marek. Will you be a miner like me someday?"

The boy dangled above his *Tata* like the unanswered question. A hesitant shyness overcame the child.

"It is all right, my son, if you wish not to be a miner," said Bronisław, hiding the hurt of his son not wishing to follow in his profession.

"*Tata*, I wish to be a great rider of horses when I grow up. I can be one of the Duke's couriers, carrying messages to foreign lands. I will see the world, and all on the back of a great stallion."

Magda thought of the Duke's rider that carried the message from her own parents exiled in Russia. To think of her son one day carrying such dreaded news distressed her greatly. Then, she calmed herself knowing that she would instead give her son to the church. He would become the priest who would one day absolve her.

"You have great wishes, my Marek," said Bronisław. "It is better yet! When you are older, I will have your Uncle Jacek teach you to ride. For if you are to be a great traveler, you will need to know how to stay in the saddle."

Bronisław laughed heartily as he lowered the boy to the ground. Marek giggled with the innocence of a child.

Magda once more smiled at the tenderness between Bronisław and Marek. She had forgotten, for only the fleeting pulse of an instant, that Marek was not his but was actually the Duke's son. She immediately felt great guilt for having secretly bartered away the many hours, even days, of her son's life for the minutes of pleasure in which the three of them had shared.

It was the weight of those discussions between Marek and the Duke that crushed what spirit was left within her. Despite Marek's joy in seeing Bronisław emerge from the mines, Magda realized that she had only created yet another secret to be kept from her loving husband.

Magda at that point realized that she had not bartered a gift for the boy at all, but rather only another dagger of betrayal against Bronisław. A dagger that the devious Duke Cyprian Sdanowicz would surely one day hold over her.

"Come, my family, let us all walk home together on this fine morning," chuckled Bronisław, "for life gets no better than this, than a man being blessed with a loving wife and an ambitious child, under the bright glow of the rising sun."

8

A CHANGE OF STATE

DECEMBER 1780

The child Marek Zaczek had grown into a strong, and inquisitive eight-year-old youth. His blond features were not uncommon among the peasant children, yet his hair seemed finer, and purer in its luminescent golden intensity. His eyes were blue, and bright with wonder. His disposition was generally happy and content.

He was not a child of great need. He seemed never bored and was always intrigued by the workings of the manor. On the few occasions when he was in the vicinity of the manor house, his attention seemed always to be drawn to the stables where his Uncle Jacek, Ewelina's husband, toiled. Marek loved to be around the horses, whether they be quartered in their stalls, or roaming free in the great pasture. Their stately elegance pleased him. To the young boy, only men of substance rode these animals. Great men. Marek Zaczek knew, even as a young boy, that his future was tied to his ability to master these magnificent beasts.

The Duke enjoyed watching, from afar, as the young boy grew. He took great pride in the peasant boy. The child that he thought only he and the doctor, and of course the mother, knew was his own.

The Duke thought the boy resembled himself in his youth. He was too bright a child to be merely of peasant stock. Marek Zaczek was destined for greatness in some form, the Duke was convinced.

Marek had become his secret pride. The Duke also by then had his daughter, Maryja. She was two years younger than Marek. Her father called the girl by the tender name of Maya, and he loved her deeply. But, it is true that the Duke had expected a boy, an heir to his vast fortune, who would have become a young man of substance to run his *folwark* and the mines when old age overcame him. Despite his love for his daughter, her birth had been a tremendously bitter shock for him to accept.

While the birth of the daughter was a terrible disappointment to the Duke, it was not that he did not love the infant. After all, how could even the cruelest of hearts turn against its own delicate and defenseless progeny.

It was just that not having a lawful heir became only the latest deflation of the boastful pride that ached within him. First, his *folwark* had come under the rule of the Austrians. Then, not having a legitimate son to inherit his wealth, his estate and his possessions dangled along with his own life, susceptible to the whims of the Austrian Empire.

The Duke wondered if there was any appeal possible to the Austrian Empress herself. For surely, in a domain where a woman ruled an empire, there must be some mechanism by which to leave his wealth to a daughter. Of course, a bastard son inheriting it was out of the realm of the possible. *However, what of a daughter? Could this not be possible? After all, the Habsburg Empress had herself inherited her family's title and wealth.*

As she had promised, the Austrian Empress had been true to her word over the previous eight years. She had administered the lands that she had annexed fairly and had been the most generous of the three Empires in allowing the Polish language to be spoken, as well as the Polish customs to be honored.

Yes, it was true that German was the official language of the Austrian Empire for conducting state business and that of the royal court. Despite this, however, there was no hostility to the peasants, nor, for that matter, to the former Commonwealth nobility, of speaking Polish between themselves.

This was not the case in the Polish lands annexed to Frederick's Prussia or Catherine's Russia, where public use of the Polish language was strictly forbidden. In short, the Prussians continually tried to "*Germanify*" the Poles. The Russians demanded the "*Russification*" of their Polish subjects.

Despite the Austrian leniency, all was not entirely as it had been before the partition. There had been intentional incursions into the Duke's business. Count Von Arndt had retained, after petitioning the Empress herself, the position of overseer of the production from the Duke's salt mines. He had inserted himself in the chain of command between the royal court and Duke Sdanowicz.

The Count had promised the Empress that the output of the very valuable salt could be increased by twenty to thirty per cent under his oversight. To support his claims, the Count scoured the Austrian Empire for improved mining tools and methods which could be brought to bear in the Polish mines. The Duke was soon forced to implement foreign cutting tools and other unfamiliar mining methods.

One such invention brought to the Polish mines was the Hungarian Horse Treadmill, which greatly increased the animal's utilization of its tremendous power within the confined spaces of the mine. It increased not only the rate at which the shafts could be mined, but also the efficiency with which bulk salt was removed to the surface.

The net result of this and other improvements was that it increased efficiency and reduced required manpower simultaneously. Needing fewer peasant men in the mines worried the Duke, as these men had to be employed actively, lest idle hands foment the seeds of rebellion.

Rebellion had not been a concern of the Count. He kept pressing for implementation of more improvements and demanding an ever-increasing output of the precious salt in return. The Duke secretly feared that under the increasing production, the Count was absconding with a greater and greater percentage of the mines' output with which he was lining his own pockets. Certainly, this was done at every level of administration, and was almost expected, the Duke thought. Although with the Count increasing his take, it became harder and harder for the Duke to hide the small slice of illicit bounty that he retained for himself. The Duke also feared the Count's actions could invite an inquiry that would prove to be detrimental to them both.

On a bitterly cold December night, the Duke shared a brandy with the physician of his estate, Doctor Grzegorz Olszewski, in front of the fireplace of his library. It was once more a common enough evening, after their both having adjusted to the doctor's having been outcast from his quarters in the manor house. The Duke and doctor had resumed dining together, which included after dinner drinks in the library. They had once passed many a night leafing through the volumes they both knew they would never find the time to read completely.

This night they resumed their conversations, which the doctor greatly appreciated, for the manor house was much warmer and much more comfortable than the humble infirmary residence to which he had been exiled.

The doctor reasoned that a few hours of enjoyment could be stolen from the dread loneliness of a winter's night even if it meant having to play the role of supplicant to the man who had so grievously expelled him.

The two men conversed of the latest world events known to them. Foremost among these, was the rebellion of the British Colonists in the new world against their English King. They also often discussed the ongoing ebb and tide of alliances between the European powers of England, France, Austria, Russia and Prussia.

They spoke in the Polish tongue each man longed to hear. They detested the German language which they were forced to use in doing business with the crown.

"The Empress certainly has been true to her many promises, *Pan* Grzegorz," began the Duke.

"Yes, I suppose that she has ruled us benevolently," said the doctor, "but I can only hope one day soon we will return to the Polish Commonwealth. *Na drowie*!" The doctor raised his snifter of French cognac in recognition of his host.

"*Tak, tak, na drowie*! Still, beware for what you wish, my friend," responded the Duke, elevating his snifter less dramatically than his guest. "That country that was once our own is now only a shadow of what it once had been. Frederick of Prussia, having taken all the lands in the North, has connected the East Prussian lands with those of Brandenburg. He has cut Poland off from the sea. He assaults the Commonwealth with punitive tariffs for its Polish grain shipped along the Vistula to the Baltic, crippling its trade."

"And this only further weakens the position of the King," agreed the doctor, "but he remains upon the throne?"

"Only because this is exactly the position where the Tsar Queen Catherine wants her old lover," answered Duke Sdanowicz. "Yes, King Poniatowski, after all these years, is still only a puppet of the Russians. The same pack of devils who continue to manipulate the remaining *szlachta* in order to have their way in the *Sejm*."

"But as you yourself have stated many times, my lord," said the doctor, "we are now Austrians here in Galicia, and should not concern ourselves with what goes on across the river."

The Duke was perturbed at the doctor using his own words against him.

"Nevertheless, we must stay aware of all the moves of our neighbor states, should they one day dare to assault even Austrian Galicia. Catherine had once sent her troops into the *Sejm* to force it to formally accept the partition. Even after she steals Poland's land, she rubbed salt into that state's wounds by forcing it to approve the crime perpetuated upon them! Sometimes, I think all hope was truly lost in the fall of the rebellion of the Bar Confederation. It is only a matter of time before what is left of Poniatowski's Poland falls completely."

"My Duke, you speak of the Confederation of Bar as having been the country's last chance, yet you yourself did not join in this rebellion, did you?" asked the doctor.

The Duke glanced harshly at his guest with the insolent tongue.

"Of course not, as it was doomed to failure. Why should I have thrown my own wealth away? Look at what happened to so many of those rebels," said the Duke. "Thousands, including the pompous Duke Sroka, were exiled to Siberia."

"Well, not all were shipped off to Russia," said the doctor. "Look at Kazimierz Pułaski and Tadeusz Kościuszko who escaped to France, only to be selected by Benjamin Franklin to fight alongside the Marquis de LaFayette in the new world. They still fight for freedom, and rebellion of a foreign throne, only now in the rebellion of the Americans rising up against the English King. It is inspiring."

The doctor drew heavily from his snifter, rolling the fragrant cognac upon his tongue, reveling in the penetration of its vapors throughout him. The Duke watched him contemptuously.

"Do not be too inspired, my friend," eventually responded the Duke, "for I have been following news of your rebellious idol, Count Kazimierz Pułaski. I do have to admit he was always the greatest of Poland's horsemen. It is alleged that he taught the Colonists how to organize a cavalry and taught them the very formations and strategies which he had used in Poland. And to great effect, I must admit. Word has it that he even saved the life of their commander, George Washington, in the Battle of Brandywine."

The doctor seemed delighted, as he had not heard of the heroics of Count Pułaski at Brandywine. The Duke allowed him his moment, before crashing upon it with the impending burden of further news which he had withheld from his guest.

Figure 4: Kazimierz Pułaski, Tadeusz Kościuszko and King Stanisław II August Poniatowski

"Alas, however, for the so-called father of the Continental cavalry, died last year in a charge upon the British in a place called Savannah in the Southern Colonies. Riddled with grapeshot from the British cannons. Well, eventually the rebel got what he deserved. I suppose God's vengeance is meted out on His own timeline. You look surprised, my doctor. Had you not heard of this?"

A look of shock had indeed exploded across the doctor's face upon hearing for the first time of Pułaski's death, then faded into ripples of concerned reflection, much like the aftermath of a rock splashing upon a calm pond.

"No, I had not yet heard of this, my lord. I must say that it saddens me greatly," said the doctor, still wrestling with a weighty apprehension of the Duke's long withheld news. "Pułaski must be viewed as a hero among them. The man spent his life fighting in rebellions and gave it in full to the cause of liberty. Alas, however there is still Kościuszko! No harm has befallen him, I pray."

"Yes, Kościuszko, the military engineer," said Duke Sdanowicz, "he is still very safe in the New World. He has built many fortifications for the Colonists."

"It is my understanding, my lord," said the doctor, "that Kościuszko himself designed and oversaw the installation of the defenses to the most important protective fortification along the west point of the Hudson River known as Fort Clinton. It was the plans of these defenses that were taken by the traitor Benedict Arnold to be delivered to the British. Kościuszko also, I have been told, taught these rebels the proper use of artillery. He is most definitely a hero to their cause."

The Duke scoffed at the doctor's suggestion. "The man was hardly a hero at all, *Pan* Grzegorz. Did you know that before leaving for the British colonies, just after the uprising of the Bar Confederation, Kościuszko fled to Paris like a coward? Some two years after the first partition, long after the Bar Confederation had failed, he returned to Poland to tutor the *Hetman* Józef Sylwester Sosnowski's daughter. The fool fell in love with the girl and requested her hand in marriage. Do you know what the *hetman* told him in response?"

The doctor looked upon his host with great suspense. "I would not know, my lord. I do not routinely find myself in the circles of any *hetman*, as these warrior magnates of the *szlachta* are only one level below the King himself. What did *Hetman* Sosnowski tell Kościuszko in response to asking for his daughter's hand?"

"He told the coward that, *'turtledoves are not for common sparrows, and magnates' daughters are not for petty nobility',* before he sent the presumptive and petulant man away," answered Duke Sdanowicz.

"So, Kościuszko then left for America?" asked the doctor.

"No, this timid, weak man then decided to elope with the girl. Imagine, taking a *hetman's* daughter against his consent. Of course, the *hetman's* thugs caught up with them, and thrashed Kościuszko within inches of his life. The wretch crawled back to Paris, without the girl, where he was convinced by the American Benjamin Franklin to join the rebellion of the Colonists. It is my opinion that he left for the American colonies just to get as far away from the *hetman* as possible."

Doctor Olszewski imagined the sequence of events. "That is certainly a very determined man. It would appear to me that he not only knows what his heart wants from this life, but he has the conviction to go after it with great fervor. Forgive my disagreeing with you, my lord, still he does not sound at all like a coward to me. He sounds like the type of man the Americans, as they now call themselves, need so very badly."

"Of course, I do not mind your disagreeing with me, my Doctor. Yet, what good is one man assisting those hugely unorganized Colonists? What difference will it possibly make? They cannot overcome the might of the English Army, not to mention the power of the British Navy."

The doctor pondered the Duke's statement, not wishing to anger his host too greatly, who had provided such an excellent brandy.

"My Duke, I have heard that the French are also assisting these rebellious Colonists. They have sent their Marquis de LaFayette, as you had mentioned, at the Colonists' request. And they have committed their ships, as well, to blockade the English. The French Navy is still formidable, is it not?"

The Duke looked at his doctor scornfully, as his guest always seemed to be taking a contrary position to his own in these discussions. He decided to acknowledge the doctor's point, if only to go on to make another of his own.

"Yes, my Doctor, I suppose the French are always formidable upon the seas. They certainly hate the English. They have fought with the Indians for seven years in the wilderness there, only to be beaten by the British. So, they do only what will heal their wounds of defeat. The French continue to pour their ever-dwindling resources into supporting the rebellion of the English Colonies. I suppose King Louis XVI remains the only hope of the Colonists," said the Duke. "Those American rebels have managed to hold on for some four years since they have declared themselves independent of the English. That alone is quite impressive. Here is to the spirit of rebellion in the New World, let us salute it before it is finally crushed, as all rebellions are, by the reigning powers."

"Here, here," joined the doctor, even though he did not join in his host's sour assessment of rebellions. He again raised his glass to the Duke. "But let us not give up all hope! They just may surprise us all and inspire further revolutions."

"Remember," warned the Duke, "it is only a revolution if they win. For when they fail, it is merely a crushed rebellion, like that of the Confederates of Bar."

The two men seemed engaged in mutual disagreement. One failed to see the ember of hope resident in the midst of all rebellions. The other ignored that even the most fervent of any revolts' flames could be snuffed out by a greater might.

After both men imbibed, the Duke said to his companion, "This discussion reminds me, *Pan* Grzegorz, that I wish to begin my young Maya's tutoring in the French language this spring. You speak the French tongue, I am told. Do you think this would be good for her?"

Maya was the diminutive name for Maryja, his daughter. She had proven herself bright to her father, and he wished to test her intellect in a more formal setting.

"Yes, I do speak French. To be a physician, one needs to. All the greatest physicians are French, are they not? You know of the chemist Antoine Lavoisier? The man possesses a truly brilliant mind. French is the language of modern Europe, of the Enlightenment, and much more elegant than German, I think. Yet, I am ashamed to admit I have not the skill to teach it."

"*Pan* Grzegorz, I ask of my daughter Maya only, *Do you think it wise to teach her the French language?*" repeated the Duke.

"Most certainly, my lord. Forgive my digression. However, do you not think the girl too young at only six years old?" asked the doctor.

"No, not at all. The child's mind is a sponge. In addition to her native Polish, she already speaks German as well, with no instruction whatsoever. Even some Czech. The children learn much more rapidly than we do, for they have a clean slate with which to work."

"*Tableau rosa,*" said the doctor in French. He could see the Duke did not understand. "Yes, a clean slate indeed, my lord. Well, given she has a demonstrated talent for tongues, then I think it is well advised. Who do you have in mind to tutor the child?" asked the doctor.

"There is a nun, still quite young herself, and well educated. She is at the convent in Kraków. I will arrange to have her travel here once a week," said the Duke.

"Her Mother Superior will allow her to leave the convent for this purpose?" asked the doctor.

"I am certain. Her Mother Angelica is in dire need of funds. They are dependent on the money I contribute. They will comply, or my generosity will suddenly dry up like a summer's creek bed."

"But Kraków is across the border. It is still in Poland, while we are on the Austrian side of the Vistula. You can get this nun documents to cross the border that regularly?" asked the doctor.

"My dear *Pan* Grzegorz, you underestimate my importance in this new empire," the Duke said boastfully. "I am in high favor with the Empress. She greatly values my administration of these mines. It is within my political means. I can well assure you that it is."

At that point a great tumult was heard outside the manor house. The solitude of the frigid night air was pierced like the veil of the temple by the commotion of a horse rider bearing imminent news. The Duke and the doctor left the comfort of the library, just in time to see the rider coming to a halt before the doors of the manor. He attempted to catch his ragged breath, yet only managed to choke on the icy air burning deep within his lungs. His nostrils' exhalations fogged in wisps of platinum mist as it hung in the night's frigid chill.

"What is it, rider?" cried out the Duke, annoyed at being kept waiting outside the manor house in the freezing cold.

"I was dispatched by Count Von Arndt forthwith to hand deliver this message to you, my lord," said the rider in a raspy voice as he fought against his physical pains from the long journey. He handed the Duke a letter, folded upon itself and sealed in wax bearing the Count's signet imprint.

"Yes," said the Duke, as he had taken the dispatch, "Take your horse to the stables, I will send out a servant to assist you."

The rider did so.

The Duke and the doctor returned inside the manor house, and Sdanowicz then adroitly used an opener to fillet the letter's wax seal, as one would a small fish.

The doctor watched as the Duke read the contents of the letter which was in the script of the Count's own hand in German. Doctor Olszewski's observed the pain which collected in the recesses of the Duke's face, and which seemed to intensify with every word which arose from the unfolded page.

"Terrible news, *Pan* Grzegorz," said the Duke.

"What is it, my lord?" he asked.

Sdanowicz raised his eyes to the doctor's. His face was colorless. He said simply, "Empress Maria Theresa of Austria has died in Vienna!"

9

REVERBERATIONS

JANUARY 1781

The death of the Austrian Empress had two immediate effects upon the Duke. First, it created a great uncertainty in him, for the Empress had stated repeatedly, albeit indirectly, that she admired the manner in which the Duke had administered the functioning of the salt mines at Wieliczka and Bochnia. By then both were renamed *Groß Salze, or Great Salt* mines in the German vernacular. With the Empress' death, and thus, naturally, with her no longer championing the Duke's management skills, an opportunity was provided to Count Von Arndt.

The Count would have much earlier taken a far more direct role in the overseeing of the mines, had his petitions to do so not have been rejected by Maria Theresa. Duke Sdanowicz remained concerned that Count Von Arndt might now be emboldened to attempt to take control of the mines from him all-together.

The second effect of the Empress' death was that all of Austria began to take on an even more militaristic footing since the Emperor Joseph II had taken over as the sole monarch. Joseph was the son of Maria Theresa and had jointly ruled with her in the years prior to her death. He considered himself an Enlightened Despot, having been educated on the teachings of the French philosopher Voltaire.

Ironically, Voltaire was the same theorist of the Enlightenment who had for a brief period taken up residence in the Sans-Souci Palace of another self-proclaimed Enlightened Despot, Frederick II of Prussia. Voltaire had promptly become disillusioned with the Prussian King. Their relationship soured when Voltaire wrote biting satirical works after only a few years of residence in both Berlin and Potsdam.

Frederick would become both friend and rival to Joseph, as he had been to Maria Theresa. Of her, Frederick the Great had said after her death that although Prussia and Austria had fought multiple wars during their overlapping reigns, he never considered the Austrian Empress to be his enemy.

So, Joseph inherited the lands of Galicia, which Austria had annexed from Poland in the First Partition of 1772. Indeed, Frederick of Prussia and Catherine of Russia had intentionally solicited Maria Theresa to join in that partition in order to distance Austria from its growing alignment with France. Also, neither Prussia nor Russia trusted the other, and bringing in a third empire stabilized the situation.

As for Austria's coming close with France, just two years before that first partition, Maria Theresa had agreed to the political marriage of her youngest daughter, Marie Antoinette, at the tender age of 14, to France's Dauphin, Louis-Auguste, the heir to the throne who would then become King Louis XVI in 1774.

The marriage was intended to be the golden thread that would tightly stitch the seam of friendship between the two pre-eminent European powers of Austria and France. Instead, it would become the garrote that would strangle all of Europe.

As Joseph's sole rule of the Austrian Empire effectively started in January 1781, the partitioned elements of Poland had been part of the Empire for over eight years. The Austrian Army had been depleted after decades of European wars. Thus, all regions of the Empire were called upon for the conscription of foot soldiers.

Duke Sdanowicz had noticed a more forceful call from the Count for young men from his *folwark* to be taken into the army.

Sdanowicz had previously become quite adept at getting the men of the estate exempted, due to their labor being needed in the mines. After all, the Imperial army needed salt in great quantities for the preservation of the food with which they would feed their soldiers.

With the blessing of the new Emperor, Count Von Arndt tightened his grip over the Duke. He had promised the Emperor that the improvements in mining methods which he had forced the Duke to employ would not only increase salt output, but would also free up miners for potential conscription. While they would not be professional infantry, they could be trained to march, and if nothing else, would be effective cannon fodder for the guns of the enemies of the Empire.

And the enemies of the Empire were ever shifting. Austria had fought and lost a war with Prussia over the mineral rich territory of Silesia and had disputes of its own over the decades with Russia. By the time of Emperor Joseph II's reign, the three empires were by then allies, tightly bound by the criminal conspiracy that was that First Partition of Poland.

As his reign began, Emperor Joseph turned his attention to the increasingly desperate situation in the realm of France. For even with his sister as the sitting Queen at Versailles, Austria's many miles of borders with the debt-ridden power would ultimately prove to be a tinder box awaiting only a spark.

Joseph would only reign until the end of that decade. During which, he would watch France continue to deteriorate, such as it threatened his very family. The Habsburg family losses would potentially include not only Marie Antoinette, who the French populace saw as the embodiment of their destitution, but also the Austrian holdings of the Netherlands, with their access to the sea, as well as the critical lands of Lombardy in Northern Italy, would eventually be lost.

Joseph would die in 1790. He lived long enough to witness the mayhem in Paris the earlier year. He planned for the rescue of Marie Antoinette, yet never was able to enact it. However, it was those Austrian lands in northern Italy that he had failed to reinforce that would become the initial loose threads of the Empires' eventual undoing. For here would rise an enemy who would cast a pallor of death across the continent.

10

THE SECRET LANGUAGE

SPRING 1782

As the decade progressed, the children of the Duke continued to grow in good health. Of course, this included his beloved daughter, Maya, but also his bastard son, Marek. Marek had always been a challenge for him, for while he took great delight in watching the child mature, the boy constantly reminded the Duke of the heir he seemingly would never have.

The Duke had been successful in negotiating with Mother Angelica to have Sister Maryja Elizabeta come to the estate and tutor young Maya in French. What had been unexpected was that the process of procuring an open border pass for the nun to travel unhindered out of Kraków took nearly eighteen months to arrange. The delay had been caused, he was told, since Kraków still resided on true Polish soil. Allowing the Sister to cross the Vistula River and into the Austrian territory of Galicia to visit the Duke's *folwark* regularly required bureaucratic approval from Vienna. However, the Duke thought that the delay might have been nothing more than the mischief of Count Von Arndt at play.

Maya, who by the time the lessons started was eight years old, forged an instant personal bond with the Sister. Despite this, the young girl proved initially slow to pick up the language. She did well during her sessions with the nun, however her skills seemed to degrade afterwards in the interim between Sister Mary Elizabeta's visits to the estate.

"Sister, I do not understand," complained the Duke to the nun one day, "the child is very bright. She excels when she is with you, yet fails to later retain her skills. How do you explain this?"

"It is quite understandable, Duke Sdanowicz" answered the nun, "as the child has no one with which to practice her skills. I suggest you have another child sit in with the girl, and together they can practice the language together."

"My *folwark's* physician, Doctor Olszewski, speaks the language fluently and can make time for her," offered the Duke.

"It is my opinion that the girl will be intimidated by exposing any language flaws she may have with a figure as respected as the doctor," said Sister Maryja Elizabeta. "It would be much more effective if there were another child with whom she could learn the language. I can teach two children just as easily as one. The two will draw close, having their own secret language. It will be enjoyable for them."

"Sister, my Maya is the only child here," answered the Duke. "She has no sisters or brothers."

"Yet, I see children throughout the estate!" said the nun.

"These are peasant children. I cannot have the daughter of a Duke receiving instruction with a peasant child, Sister!"

"Then her skills will not sharpen," answered the nun boldly. "We may well be wasting our time without her having another child of her own age with which to practice their conversations. They must use the language, not just memorize the drills. It must drip from their tongues like honey."

The Duke continued to argue with Sister Maryja Elizabeta, until the nun responded with some edge of frustration in her voice, "Are these not all the Lord's children?"

The Duke finally relented and called for Magda to bring Marek to study the language alongside his Maya. Up until this point, the good Sister had not seen Magda at the estate. When Magda entered in her shabby peasant attire, hand-in-hand with her ten-year-old son, she spotted the Sister who had tutored her in the convent. Immediately Magda's head dropped in shame. She blushed in her uneasiness.

It had been a dozen years plus four since Magdalena had left the convent at the age of fourteen. At this point, the former nun's pupil was a beautiful woman of thirty years, but her once vibrant smile had long since left her.

Sister Maryja Elizabeta was shocked to find the daughter of a *szlachta* Duke in the rags of a peasant. She had been told by Mother Angelica that the Duke had taken the girl under his own roof. The Sister recognized that the shame which had come over Magdalena upon seeing her was not simply that of having been forced to live the poverty of a peasant's life. It was much deeper and of greater agony than merely the loss of physical comfort. The Sister knew it immediately was the loss of something much more cherished. The Nun had nearly instantly discerned the nature of Magda's shame, for Sister Maryja Elizabeta, herself, had lived under its mark since her own defilement at the hands of the professor years ago.

Sister Maryja Elizabeta exclaimed, "Magdalena, it is so good to see you once again. I have missed your astute wit and pleasant smiles so much, my former pupil." She embraced the girl, only to find that the young woman was shaking intensely. Yet it was not cold, for these shivers were nothing more than the rattle of nerves. Sister Maryja Elizabeta attempted to calm her, saying, "It has been so long. What a lovely young woman you have grown to be..."

"This is ***Magda***, my good Sister," interrupted the Duke. "She chose to marry a peasant by the name of Bronisław Zaczek. He works in the mines. I have provided for Magda's good fortune by assigning her work on the staff within the manner. It is one of the choicest assignments upon the *folwark*." The Duke resonated with pride, as if he truly had gifted the former daughter of a *szlachta* member with a prized appointment.

"Yes," responded the good Sister, "I can see she has had great fortune bestowed on her since leaving the convent. It will be a pleasure to teach her child."

The Duke did not rise to anger over the Nun's sarcasm. "One must be careful in providing free choice to even the brightest of children, Sister. She has freely chosen the life of a peasant, and now must live out her preferred existence."

Sister Maryja Elizabeta ignored his obvious dishonesty. Instead, she turned to the beaming face of Marek.

"And who is this delightful young man?" asked the nun.

"He is my son, Marek" answered Magda, her head still hung heavy in shame. "He likes to watch the horses, so I am allowed to bring him to the stables of the manor house from time to time."

"Now, Magda, your son will take instruction in the French language from Sister Maryja Elizabeta," boasted the Duke. "My Maya needs a partner, and Marek, being so close in age to her, has been so chosen."

"I understand," said Magda, as if a sentence had been passed upon her son. She recalled learning the language herself from the nun long ago, as if it were in another lifetime.

"Do not worry, Magda, I will be as gentle with your Marek as I am with the Duke's daughter," said Sister Maryja Elizabeta.

"Yes, of course," said Magda in response, "I have only the greatest respect for you, Sister."

"Young Marek," said the nun, "would you like to learn another language from me just as your mother once did?"

"Yes, I would, Sister," said the boy with great enthusiasm. "Then, I can speak with my *Matka* and even my *Tata* will not know what we are saying."

"Marek, I am afraid that I have forgotten much of what I was once taught," said Magda in a loving tone to her son. "But you can teach it to me all over again."

"Enough!" shouted the Duke. "You forget you are but peasants and chitter like monkeys in front of your lord! Now let there be silence, so that the good Sister and I may discuss what is to be done."

The nun looked at her former student with pity. She remembered, as had Magda, the nun's instructions within the convent to guard against the men that were respected most. They passed a look that shared not only the dislike of the Duke's overbearing nature, but also the indignity that Magda suffered under it.

From that day forward, Marek and Maya were instructed together in the French language. They soon reveled in the fact that they were the only two souls on the entire estate that understood the tongue, for the Duke had never learned the language himself. The Duke's wife understood some phrases, yet the children rapidly surpassed her skill level.

Marek and Maya were not aware that Doctor Olszewski spoke French fluently, for he had never needed to engage in the language within the confines of the *folwark*. Of course, he would not have had anyone with which to converse.

The two children learned the tongue and eventually became quite accomplished, although a far cry from fluent. In doing so, they became very close, one would say nearly inseparable, and were ultimately allowed to even play together.

The Duke and his wife both noticed the effect that the friendship had upon their daughter. While she had always been bright, her demeanor became more joyful. Her outlook became more optimistic, which for this bright, but shy child was very notable, in that she had not always been quite so expressive, or had so outgoing a personality. Maya became more gregarious than the quiet and shy child she had previously been.

This her parents had accredited to the friendship she had enkindled with Marek. The boy was kind to her, and she responded in opening up her previously guarded personality. Over time, the Duke suppressed his concerns over what others might think of his child playing with a peasant boy. After all, he knew the boy was no mere peasant.

It was on Marek's eleventh birthday that he was assigned his work duties upon the estate. According to the law of *Pańszczyzna*, every peasant must provide work to the *folwark* upon to which his life is tied. Duke Sdanowicz decreed that young Marek would be assigned to the stables, under the direction of his Uncle Jacek, who had just been named stable master.

The Duke would later explain to Magda that this had been done also as a favor to her. After all, the boy enjoyed being around the horses, and showed no fear whatsoever of them. The child was overwhelmed with joy in hearing of this assignment. In reality, the Duke had done a favor for himself, as Marek's work in the stables would allow Maya routine access to him.

Several years more passed, and Marek and Maya would continue to be found in the company of each other whenever possible. Often, Maya would be found shadowing the boy in the stables. This was unusual for a daughter of a Duke, still Cyprian Sdanowicz and more importantly, his wife, the Duchess, saw no harm in it, and so it was allowed.

11

ANOTHER TOLL OF THE BELL

AUGUST 1786

By the high summer of the year 1786, the Duke's daughter, Maya, was twelve years old. His bastard son, Marek, was fourteen, and the two had become very close through their joint tutelage under Sister Maryja Elizabeta. Their French skills had developed significantly over the years, and quite often the two could be heard conversing in the foreign tongue. Occasionally, the Duke would have Doctor Olszewski eavesdrop on their dialogue, just to assure everything was proper between the two children. Doctor Olszewski assured the Duke on multiple occasions that all was as it should be, that their dialogue was merely the banter of childhood friends. Of course, the two children had no idea that the Duke had sent the doctor to spy upon them.

Maya had also taken great joy in watching Marek as he exercised the Duke's stable of horses. She would plead with her father to walk with her along the carriage path as Marek, atop one or another of his magnificent stallions, blew like a gusting breeze through the high stalks of the summer fields.

Even the Duke had become, by this time, impressed with the boy's exceptional horsemanship. Marek had always been something of a dichotomy for him. For while he took great delight in watching the child mature and his skills develop, the boy was a constant reminder to the Duke of the heir he thought he would never possess.

On this hot summer's day, the Duke and Maya walked along the crushed gravel path as they watched Marek gallop across the fields upon one of the Duke's most prized Arabian stallions. The Duke's family had studded a long line of Arabians, the original stock of which had been captured by his ancestors from the Ottoman Turks at the Battle of Khotyn in 1673.

In that conflict, his forefathers had served under *Hetman* Jan Sobieski, a full decade before they served once again under the same man, by then King Jan Sobieski, in the relief of the Ottoman Turks' Siege of Vienna. It was held within the family that his great-great grandfather rode in that charge of the Winged Hussars atop one of the very same Turkish stallions he had pillaged as spoils from the Turks ten years earlier. It was this very warrior's armor, complete with the fabled arching wings, that were encased within his manor house.

"Your friend rides wonderfully atop my Arabian, Maya," the Duke said to his daughter.

"There is nothing that Marek cannot do, Father," she responded.

The Duke signaled to the boy to come to them, which Marek did. The Duke and Maya were, at this point, upon the outer edge of his great field, and away from the manor house and its stables. Marek had slowed the great stallion as he came upon them. Maya instinctively drew back as the horse and her friend, the rider, sauntered over to the carriage path.

Maya looked up at Marek in a gaze of infatuation. She noticed the glistening of the sweat upon his brow in the afternoon sun. She tried to capture forever in her mind's eye the rose-colored blush of his boyish cheeks.

"*Cześć*, Maya," he said, smiling broadly.

"*Bon jour*," she answered playfully.

"Marek, you ride that fine horse like a *Hussar* ready to engage the Teutonic Knights," said the Duke in a loud, robust voice.

"*Cześć*, my lord," said the boy, still atop the Arabian, his voice huffing with the labors of his riding. Marek was embarrassed that he had not addressed the Duke in the midst of focusing his total attention instead to his daughter. "Thank you for your compliment, however I am told that there are no more Teutonic Knights."

"But of course, there are, Marek," corrected the Duke. "Who fills your young head with such bad information?"

The Duke was testing his illegitimate son's knowledge of Polish history.

"Were they not defeated at Grunwald?" asked the boy. "Were they not crushed in that battle? Was not their Grand Master killed that day?"

Indeed, King Władysław Jagiełło had obliterated this Order of warrior monks in 1410 with his joint Polish and Lithuanian forces. The Battle was called Grunwald by the Poles, and Tannenberg by the Germans. By either name it was a decisive victory for the Commonwealth of Poland-Lithuania.

Maya tugged at her father's sleeve, as if to say to him to leave her friend alone.

"All that you say is correct about Grunwald, my boy," the Duke responded, "but that victory merely defeated the Teutonic Knights for a time. For a very long time, in fact. However, that Order returned like the plague upon these lands. Only today, these knights are known as the Prussians."

The boy looked confused, as he drifted with the footsteps of the restless Arabian. "I was taught that the Teutonic Knights were brought to Poland to defeat the Prussians."

The Duke was very impressed. Marek had all the right facts, he just needed to understand how they were interrelated. He turned to his young daughter. "Maya, your Marek is very well taught. Over four hundred years ago Duke Konrad of Masovia welcomed in the Order to defend against the raids of the pagan Prussians. This was after these Knights had been thrown out of the Holy Lands and later expelled from Hungary. The Teutons defeated the pagan Prussian peoples, annihilating them completely over the years. They then laid claim, in the service of the Holy Father in Rome, to the Prussian lands. It was not much later that the Teutons assumed the name of Prussians, so as to continue to control these conquered lands. They retain both the lands and the name to this day. It was they who stole these lands from Duke Konrad, he who had initially invited them to Poland. It is they who stole the rest of Poland's northern lands in the heinous crime of 1772 – the Partition."

"If they were defeated, then why do they still rule today?" asked Maya.

"Because, my lovely daughter, life is a war made of many battles. Even a great battle won upon the field may not turn the war, and over your life you will live to see this. The Teutonic Order was strongly aligned with the Church and used their alliances like the devil's own trickery to expand their grip upon Poland's northern lands."

The Duke laid his hand gently upon her shoulders. He looked upwards at Marek and continued.

"The Knights were defeated at Grunwald, yes! Still they used their alliances with the church and other powerful nations in Western Europe to force a peace which left them with some of their holdings in the eastern part of Poland. Then slowly, over decades and even into the next century, they regained their power and expanded their lands in the east. These were separated from their other holdings in the German states, including the cities of Berlin and Potsdam in the Brandenburg province, by the large holdings of northern Poland that reached all the way to the Baltic Sea. The Prussians waited well over three hundred and fifty years, before their Emperor righted what he believed to be the mistake of Tannenberg. During this time, they grew strong with a vast army, yet even then they feared the Commonwealth. So, they joined with Russia, and together in their combined malice for the Poles, devised the theft of the Polish border lands. With the Partition of 1772, the Prussians were finally able to bridge their lands in East Prussia to Brandenburg, taking over all the North, cutting Poland off from the Baltic Sea."

"They sound like they were very devious foes," said the boy from his saddle.

"That they were," said the Duke, "and that they still are. One can never truly trust the Germanic peoples."

"Does that include the Austrians who rule us?" asked the girl.

"Well, Maya," stammered the Duke, "Austrians are not Prussians, my girl."

"But they both speak German. Does not that make them the same?" she asked.

"Well, no, not precisely," the Duke hawed. He was concerned that should this discussion be overheard it could cause him great disfavor in Vienna.

"The Austrians do indeed speak the German tongue. However, they are ruled by Catholics, as is the country of Poland. The Prussians are fiercer, and their Protestant hearts have no sympathy for the Poles. It is the generous rule of the Austrians that allow those of us here in Galicia to speak Polish and honor our Polish customs."

"Why do the Prussians hate us so? Just because we are Catholics?" asked Marek from his vantage point mounted high above them both.

The Duke thought on Marek's last question. "Simply because we are Slavic peoples. We are different from them. Our language is of a different root than theirs. They believe we are beneath them. Deep in their hearts they believe they are better humans than we are. They feel the same of the Russians, however they suppress this because Russia is growing strong. Mostly, the Prussians hate us because we have these beautiful lands with all their great abundant harvests that they covet for themselves."

"Why doesn't the Polish King simply tell the Prussian King they cannot have our lands? That we want them back," asked Maya.

"For three reasons, my daughter," answered the Duke. "First, they are aligned with Russia, and as such are much more powerful than Poland. The second reason is that it has been fourteen years, and the Prussians have displaced the Poles from these lands, and replaced them with their own peoples. The third reason is the simplest of all. I have just learned from the Count's courier that the Emperor of Prussia, Frederick II, died in just these past weeks. This is very good indeed, for he hated the Poles more than anyone."

"Why do you think he hated the Poles so, Father?" his daughter then asked.

The Duke looked upon them both, and in an attempt to teach them what must never be forgotten said, "Frederick once said, '*All these people with surnames ending with -ski, deserve only contempt*'. He thought us as stupid, even referred to our countrymen as '*slovenly, Polish trash*". And since our *szlachta* forefathers shaved their heads except for a strip down the center, he considered us Europe's version of the North American savages - the American Indians. As I have said, it is best that he is gone, but the scornful nature of his words live on in other Prussian hearts."

The boy sat upon his mount and looked down at the Duke and Maya. He felt comfortable with Cyprian Sdanowicz, even though all the other peasants feared him greatly. He knew that the Duke would have made any other rider dismount from his horse, so as not to be seen in a superior position above him and Maya. Yet this was a privilege that the nobleman allowed Marek this day. Perhaps as a gift to his daughter, who continued to gaze upward at Marek.

The Duke then continued, "Frederick once said, '*Every man has a wild beast within him*,' and one cannot argue that he was ever so observant. His own wild beast hated the Poles, perhaps because of his forefathers' loss to us at Grunwald. Will we ever really know? We do know that he has coveted our lands, and wished to drive us from them only so that the Germans could cultivate them. Yet, Frederick only lived long enough to take some of them in his forty-six-year rule. Today, he lies beneath the soil, like the potatoes he so loved during his life. I am told he is buried next to his beloved dogs. Marek, allow this tale to be a lesson for your own life, for no matter how powerful a man may become, all men will eventually succumb to Father Time."

"And bow to the will of God," added Marek.

"Yes, and bow to the will of God," agreed the Duke. "Even

Frederick, King of Prussia, no longer accompanied by his armies or his wealth, bows to the will of God, the Deity that he denied ever existed. May our God have mercy on his soul."

The last comment drew looks of great surprise from Marek and Maya. This the Duke noticed, and thought he had confused the children's young minds.

He then scowled and added, "but perhaps not too much mercy!"

12

THE GUEST HOUSE

SEPTEMBER 1786

Duke Cyprian Sdanowicz had his hands full in dealing with his overseer, Count Maximilian Von Arndt. The Count would call upon the Duke each spring and fall for several days to review operations at the mines. Between these two visits, the Count pummeled the Duke with demands by way of couriers.

The mining improvements forced by Von Arndt upon Sdanowicz had continued to create tremendous efficiencies. Such that production was nearly continually increased and so much so that fewer and fewer men were required for brute labor underground.

The Count having knowledge of this, continually compelled the Duke for idle men to be pressed to service into the Austrian army. The Duke could no longer shield his peasant boys and their fathers so easily. He had reluctantly begun to identify those who could be conscripted into the Austrian Army. This included mostly the miners who had been displaced of their work.

Magda feared that her husband Bronisław would soon be relieved of his duties in the mines. She more greatly feared that he would then be inducted into the Imperial Army. It was known that the Austrian officers would shrewdly place their peasant conscripts closest to the front lines. In some cases, so close that they came within the fire of their enemy's artillery.

Count Maximilian Von Arndt's twice-yearly visits to Duke Sdanowicz's *folwark* created a great commotion in preparing for his stays. For the Count was never satisfied with his accommodations in the manor house. It became his joy to mock his host over the limits of his hospitality.

The Count complained of the *accoutrements* of the quarters. Their appointments were never satisfactory enough to his refined tastes, despite the guest chambers having been refashioned after each of the Count's previous stays. His tastes for wealth and luxury were seemingly insatiable.

The Count had also made disparaging remarks as to the restrictive nature of his accommodations. No matter how the Duke tried, the rooms could not be made more spacious.

It was at this point that the Duke had decided to undertake addressing the Count's petty complaints by adding a very luxurious guest house adjacent to his manor house. He would commit a huge portion of his wealth and spare no expense to make the guest house as expansive and lavish as a proper Viennese villa.

Duke Sdanowicz was tired of the Count's grumbles, and the guest house would be complete with its own study for the Count and even an annex of his own expansive library that the Count seemed to enjoy so upon his visits.

Duke Sdanowicz also had an ulterior motive in his construction of the magnificent guest house. Ever since their first encounter, the Duke had longed for another tryst with Magda.

Of course, it had not come to pass. The Duke still greatly coveted Magda, however the close proximity of his ever-present wife meant that no such liaison could be undertaken within the manor house. The Duke was too cautious a man to take Magda in the stables, or elsewhere upon his *folwark* for fear of being found out. So, the guest house would have an ancillary purpose when the Count was not upon the estate.

At the time of the groundbreaking for the guest house, the

Count was staying again in the existing guest chambers of the manor house.

"How were my Count's accommodations last evening?" asked Sdanowicz at breakfast the morning following his guest's arrival. He was quite proud of the most recent improvements that had been made since the Count's last complaints during an earlier visit. Decorations had been imported from the lake region of Northern Italy, which had been at that time under Austrian control.

"I can only say that I am fortunate to only have to stay in these quarters in the darkened night, my Duke," answered the Count, "as the room in which you lodged me was so small that my shadow would not have fit had it been daylight."

The Duke was irritated once more with the Count's peevish comments. "It is the largest room in the Manor house," retorted Sdanowicz.

"Not the largest, my Duke," said the Count, "I believe your chambers to be greater."

"You would have me forego my own bed on your behalf?" asked the Duke in amazement.

"It is done all the while in the country estates of Austria *proper*," answered the Count. "After all, there, a gentleman's stature is recognized."

Austria proper, thought the Duke. He became enraged. *The Count thinks of these former Polish lands as backwaters, to which he is forced to make periodic visits.*

"I suppose you'll expect me to make my wife available to you next?" asked the Duke sarcastically.

"Oh, good dear, no," responded the Count, "for what use is giving me the choice quarters if you are only going to fill it up with *her considerable volume ...*"

Sdanowicz chafed at the Count's temerity. Von Arndt was intentionally being audacious to agitate his host. The Duke bit his tongue, although his blood boiled within him.

"You do, however, have a servant here who could do nicely in her stead," said the Count, as he glanced in the direction of Magda, who was serving them at the breakfast table. Both men were aware that she did not understand the German tongue in which they conversed.

"Well, perhaps, my Count, upon one of your future returns, when the lavish guest house is completed and made available to you," said the Duke, despite having no intention whatever of making his Magda available to the Count. "In the interim, I think my rather robust wife would prefer we not turn the Manor house into a common brothel."

The Count chuckled and said simply *"touché"*. He paused before adding, "It will be of great interest as to whether you even complete the thing altogether. I would assume that even if you are committed to do so, your limits in fashionable taste will restrict your ability to achieve a residence worthy of an Austrian Count."

The last comment drew an instantaneous response from the otherwise staid Duke. "You shall see my Count," said Sdanowicz, "that when the guest house is complete it shall be a villa worthy of the Emperor himself!"

The Count laughed scornfully. They had finished their breakfast and next took refuge in the library to discuss the business of the mines. The Count was very pleased with the increase in production since his last visit. He listened as the Duke briefed him on the progress.

"Despite the increases in output, my Count, we have a very significant issue which will hamper us in the near future. You had directed us to take our mineshaft's structural timber from an Austrian source instead of the Polish source we have traditionally used."

"Yes, I recall," said the Duke quite calmly.

"The Austrian wood has been found to be inferior to the Polish wood, with many lengths received in a rotted or split condition that are unusable in the mines. We will be forced to slow production until this issue of supply is remedied."

The Count appeared to become unsettled with the Duke's assessment.

"So, my Duke, I am expected to believe that the wood taken from Polish forests is superior to the exact same wood taken from Austrian forests? How droll, how so petty and nationalistic of you..."

The Duke knew this to be the case, but wished not to anger his overseer guest.

"I beg your pardon, my Count, yet it is not the exact same wood. We have learned from centuries of experience to only take the choicest of wood from the forests. I am quite sure your Austrian forests have similarly choice wood; I only ask that your woodcutters be more discriminating."

The Count stared at the Duke. The gaze said, *How dare you lecture me on the finer points of mining. Since I have brought you improvements in techniques from throughout the Austrian Empire, production is up nearly thirty-five per cent.*

Instead, the Count answered with a single word, "*Your*?"

"I do not understand, my Count?" said the Duke.

"You said, '*your Austrian forests*' and '*your woodcutters*', did you not?" stated, more than asked, the Count coldly. "Perhaps you might have meant '*our* Austrian forests' and '*our* woodcutters' as you have been for most of the past two decades a member of the Austrian Empire, and a very privileged one at that. While I am sure you still have great affinity and affection for the country just across the waters of the Vistula, how can I be assured your allegiances are still to the Austrian Emperor?"

Suddenly, Duke Sdanowicz was flushed and embarrassed by his slip of the tongue. He became flustered and stammered in his response. "For ... , forgive me, my lord, I ... , I assure you ... , I am fully ... , that is ... , my allegiance is only to the Emperor."

The Count looked at him in a calculating manner, intentionally making the Duke as uncomfortable as possible.

"Good, because we need more conscripts to the Army," the Count finally said. "I suggest you continue production at your current levels. I will take up the quality of the wood coming from *our* Austrian forests. In the meantime, I recommend your mining engineers space the supporting timber within the mine at greater intervals, if necessary."

"I have already suggested that very solution to our mine supervisors, my Count," protested the Duke mildly, "and they have said that doing so would increase the likelihood of a collapse of the shafts."

The Count did not like being contradicted by the Duke.

"Well, my Duke, the mines are, of course, your responsibility. You may have the wrong supervisors in place, however that is for you to decide. I only know as overseer, I have set your production limits, and I will expect nothing less."

"Yes, of course, my Count," said Duke Sdanowicz sheepishly.

"Now, let us turn to the conscripts for the army. It appears you have excess laborers on your estate. After all, my Duke, the Habsburg Empire must continue to maintain the peace of Europe," said the Count. "The French are getting restless. Their peoples' minds are full of fantasies of '*The Enlightenment*'. They are hypnotized by the proselytization of Jean Jacques Rousseau and Voltaire. It is indeed a most volatile condition that exists in the streets of Paris today."

"I understand the French are being radicalized by the students and leftists," stated the Duke, attempting to impress the Count with his knowledge of European matters. "Are you concerned that King Louis XVI does not have control of the situation?"

"The situation, as you say, has been deteriorating for quite a long time. Likely ever since the King's grandfather, Louis the XV, took that Polish vagabond as his Queen."

Another caustic comment from the Count designed to insult the Duke's Polish heritage. Von Arndt referred to the French Queen Marie Leszczyńska.

"What fault does the Count find with Maryja Leszczyńska?" asked the Duke, using the Polish version of her first name. He felt a need to defend the Polish wife of the French King. "My understanding is that she was very popular with the people of France at the time of her death. Did not her own father once rule Poland as King Stanisław I? Was he not a much better King than the fool Stanisław Augustus who sits there this day?"

"Duke Sdanowicz, do not become so defensive of France's Queen Leszczyńska," cautioned the Count. "For what was her downfall was beyond her control. It was the weakness of her Polish blood. She did indeed give the King ten children, including two sons. One son died of organ failure at only two years of age. The other went on to become *Dauphin,* heir to the throne. However, the *Dauphin* died at the age of thirty-six of consumption. This left only the *Dauphin's* son, grandson to Louis XV, who went on to become Louis the XVI. All Europe today feels his weakness. Still, how can he help it when his veins are one quarter full of Polish blood?"

The Duke was by this point raging within himself, but strained not to give the Count the satisfaction of seeing him angered so.

"So, as Queen to Louis XV, Leszczyńska did nothing to please yourself or the rest of the Austrians?" asked the Duke as calmly as he could.

"Oh, quite to the contrary, for she used her influence to expel Voltaire, the rogue masquerading as an Enlightenment philosopher, when he published a poem which insinuated that her husband, the King, was having a sexual relationship with Madame Pompadour. Of course, Voltaire's accusation was common knowledge, nonetheless the Queen was so insulted that she had Voltaire banished from the Royal Court and eventually from all of France."

"And yet, despite your contention of Queen Leszczyńska's weak blood coursing through King Louis XVI, your Austrian Empress Maria Theresa gave her youngest daughter in marriage to him?" The Duke thought he was trapping the Count by his own logic.

"Yes, of course," replied the Austrian Count, "in order to stabilize the situation, and bring the nations of Austria and France closer together."

"Yet," responded Duke Sdanowicz, "it is reported that even today Queen Marie Antoinette is despised by her own French subjects. It would seem to me that she is doing exactly the opposite of stabilizing the situation, for she is antagonizing the rabble. The people have even accused her of siphoning funds from the beleaguered French treasury to her brother Emperor Joseph II of Austria."

The Count looked shocked at Duke Sdanowicz for even repeating this slanderous accusation of the French people. "You realize that any defamation against our Emperor, even if it only repetition of another's country's slander, could be construed as treason."

Duke Sdanowicz laughed off the insinuated threat. "My Count, we are merely having a discussion of the increasing instability of the French Monarchy. I seek no disfavor from either you or the Emperor. It is only of interest to me just how corrosive the writings of these great thinkers of the Enlightenment have become to the Royals. Could you ever have imagined such a deteriorating situation would have developed threatening not only the King and Queen of France, but if not arrested, all the monarchs of Europe?"

"Good God, no!" answered the Count in a disparaging tone. "These Enlightenment writings have only sewn seeds of discontent among the French masses. The French people have come to adore the very liberty and democracy that the rebellious Americans have so successfully wrenched from the British. The Marquis de LaFayette has returned to Paris a national hero for his assistance to the Americans in protecting *"Life, Liberty and the Pursuit of Happiness*". The French peasants don't realize that the triumph of the American Revolution was only possible with the supporting actions and funds of the French monarchy. Navies and military advisors cost great sums, and this is a fact that the hungry common people so hurriedly forget. It is bad enough that their King Louis cannot fill the bellies of the peasants, but now after LaFayette's success abroad, dreams of *"Liberté, Égalité, and Fraternité*" fill the heads of their students. There is no telling to where this might lead. The Austrian Army needs to be prepared to assure this brewing idiotic rebellion is never exported to countries outside of France. To assure this, the Austrian Army needs soldiers, my Duke. The time has come for you to contribute your share in meeting the responsibility of conscription."

So smoothly and shrewdly the Count had turned this discussion to his never-ending demand for conscription of the Duke's peasants.

"Yes, of course, my Count," said the Duke, "but the men from my estates are not fighters. They know nothing of war. Spare them. They are only poor Polish peasants."

"The Austrian army will train them," the Count replied with an edge in his voice. "Be reminded, while your region has been granted permission to speak the Polish language and celebrate the Polish customs, it is the soil of Austria that is under the feet of your peasants. These are not Polish peasants at all. These are men of Galicia, and Galicia is a region of Austria. Keep that in mind tomorrow when you will tell me which ones are to fight for the Empire. I will hear nothing further on this matter."

Upon the arrival of the next day, for the first time, the Duke began assigning some of the men from his estate to be conscripted into the army. Those who had served him in the mines so faithfully over the years instead had been denied returning to their labors underground by the very efficiency of the Count's improvements. These were the first to be conscripted. With time and training, and due to their quiet acceptance of hardship and their ability to take orders without questioning their validity, these men would make good foot soldiers. And in the wars that lie in the decade ahead, they would make excellent cannon fodder.

However, Bronisław Zaczek would be spared this fate.

13

THE HUSSARS' WINGS

AUGUST 1788

When Marek was sixteen years old, he had become a tall, strong child. His blonde hair had shone like the finest strands of gold. He was lean, yet not scrawny. His muscles were developed from his chores in the stables. His mother had found great joy in the wholesome boy that he had become, as well as the promise of the man into which he would soon mature.

Marek had learned from his Uncle Jacek how to ride upon the Duke's striking Arabians over the past several years. He had a natural feel for being in the saddle upon the broad backs of these spectacular animals. Gusting like the wind, together they would blow through the rolling fields of the estate. In the spring, fragrant hopes of the coming months scented the air. In the summer, the breeze whispered candied promises in his ears of things yet to come. At harvest time, the budded tips of the stalks would brush pleasantly against his legs. Marek was never happier than when he reigned over the Duke's kingdom in the saddle of one of his stallions. Uncle Jacek joked it was because he must have some Cossack blood running through his veins.

The Duke had noticed Marek's proficiency in the saddle increase with each passing year. Sdanowicz's secret pride swelled within him as he watched the progression of his furtive offspring's riding skills.

One day the Duke had called for Marek to be brought inside the manor house. He took the boy to the case containing the armor of the Winged Hussar.

"Do you know what this is, child?" the Duke asked.

"Of course, my Duke," the boy answered eagerly. "They are the wings of the angels of death, the protectors of Christianity, the most ferocious warriors in all of Europe. They are the Winged Hussars of Poland."

"Very good, Marek," said the Duke as his pride of the boy beamed, "and why do you suppose these great horsemen would wear such wings?"

"For several reasons, my lord," the boy began excitedly. "They would make the Hussars appear much larger, especially at a distance. Also, the clacking noise they made as their horses charged at full gallop, along with the eerie whistling moan of the wind through the feathers would drive fear into their enemy's mounts which were totally unaccustomed to the sounds. Finally, the wings themselves protected the Hussars backs from the lasso's used by the Cossacks and Tatars, not to mention the ravages of the Ottoman Turks."

The child's comments were not his own, but the near poetic babbling of his Uncle Jacek. Many nights by the settlement's outdoor fire, when his own father was away in the mines for days, Jacek had told tales of the Hussars' attacks upon their various enemies to the boy. There were the Cossacks, those Ruthenian horseman whose anger snarled like the teeth of the she-wolf protecting her young. Just as deadly were the Tatar Mongols, who upon their horses attacked in waves from the East like the swarms of an angered hornet's hive. Finally, the enemy most feared, the Ottoman Turks, who drew not the instinctive fears of threatened animals, rather the insidious plotting of the hearts of evil men. These were men who desired to dominate Poland's ways. If the Turks were not to emboss their Crescent moon into the hearts that once bore the Christian cross, then they were just as pleased to cut from each

Polish chest these still-beating organs until the very silence created was offered to their Allah. Jacek would share with Marek many stories of the Winged Hussars defeating these foes, just as his father had shared once with him.

"It seems you know much about the *Hussaria*," said the Duke, as he interrupted the youth's recalling of his fireside memories. "How can that be?"

"I have gazed many times upon this very set of winged armor, my lord, when I have come inside for our lessons with Sister Maryja Elizabeta. I had many questions, and it turns out your stable master, my Uncle Jacek, was full of knowledge of the Hussars. He would tell me stories while we worked in the stables. Even today he helps me in building a pair of the wings of the Hussars. It is our secret project."

The Duke was amazed at the boy. He was indeed intelligent, inquisitive, and his "secret project" would demonstrate just how resourceful he might be.

"When you have completed your wings, child, bring them for me to see," said the Duke. "If they are of a good quality, I will place them in this case alongside those of my ancestors."

Marek was excited beyond belief at the offer of the Duke. He took his leave and returned to the stables to tell his Uncle Jacek. The news was too great for the boy to keep contained.

Jacek listened to Marek with great interest. He thought it odd that the Duke was not angry at their wasting time and effort on this unsanctioned project. He reasoned that since his nephew was often a companion to the Duke's daughter, that alone was why he had taken such an interest in the boy.

At that point they had begun forming the wooden arches of the wings' frames, but not much beyond that. Jacek was teaching Marek how to coax the wooden frames to curl under water by the strategic application of weights. It was a process that took much time, and he was sure it would teach the boy patience.

They had checked the frames together. The wood was behaving itself and had begun to take shape. The desired arc was nearly achieved. Perhaps only another day or so, Jacek told his nephew.

"It is good enough, my Uncle. Let us move on to the next step, *proszę*," pleaded Marek.

Jacek placed his hand on the boy's shoulder and lowered himself so that he peered into Marek's eyes. He did not have to stoop much, for his nephew was by then nearly as tall as he was. He said nothing at first. Instead, he allowed his penetrating gaze to take effect on the boy.

"Marek, how long has the Duke been building the guesthouse?"

"Nearly two years, Uncle," answered the boy, "why do you ask?"

"And how much longer before it is finished?" Jacek asked further.

"I suspect another year, at least," said Marek.

"Does he rush to use a pine door before the oaken doors are planed? Does he race ahead with wood planking before the tiles for the walls and floors are received from Italy? Does he lay carpets of goatskin on the floor before his hunters have killed a massive bear?" asked Jacek.

Lowering his head, Marek saw his point and answered in a dejected tone, "No, Uncle, he does not."

"Of course, he does not," said Jacek smiling broadly, "for he knows the proverb *that a guest sees more in an hour than the host does in a year*. He knows that true quality requires the time that each artisan needs to perfect the skills of his hand. We must make our Hussar's wings of a quality to please the Duke, although not so well as to embarrass those of his own. For should we do so, he might become angry and send us off to the army," explained Jacek, laughing.

Jacek was only half-joking, as he had seen the Duke's rage in full bloom. For it had once been Jacek who the Duke had commanded to take the soiled and bloodied Magda to Bronisław Zaczek. If he could do that to another Duke's daughter, then he would not hesitate to assign his peasants to become cannon fodder.

"Listen to me, my nephew, and I will assure that our wings are of the best quality, Marek, still not embarrassingly so when compared to those in the Duke's cabinet. You know the proverb, *We don't want to call the wolf from the forest*, now do we?"

"No, we do not. Thank you, Uncle Jacek," said Marek, thankful for his guidance as always. The boy was slightly confused, but decided not to ask, *Why would we just not make them either as fast as we could, or as well as we could? Why do we have to worry about them not being better than the Duke's?*

"Now, my boy, grab a walking stick for I have a special treat for you this day. We go to the forest to a secret and very special place," said Jacek.

"Uncle, I am a strong young man of sixteen, I have no need for a walking stick," replied Marek.

"Yes, my nephew, you grow strong. Still, take the staff, and I will teach you why you will need it. Grab the longest two you can find from over in the stable. For I will need one also."

Marek did as he was told, and soon he and his uncle mounted two of the Duke's horses. They balanced their walking sticks parallel to the ground, like the lances of the Hussars. They rode their mounts across the gently swaying knee-high growth of the summer's fields for a great distance. They came to rest at the edge of a dense forest's tree line. There they dismounted and tied their mounts to a large bough of a barren oak tree.

"Whose lands are we upon, Uncle Jacek?" asked Marek.

"We are still upon the Duke's *folwark*, Marek," answered Jacek. "You just have not been this far north before. His lands stretch all the way to the Vistula!"

"I have heard *Matka* and *Tata* speak of that river, yet I have never seen it with my own eyes," said the boy.

"Well, young Marek, you will use your own eyes now. You see this tree that has been split by lightning," asked Jacek, "remember it well, for it marks the location to enter the forest. Take your staff, my nephew, for the forest is the most dangerous of places."

"You mean because of the wolves hiding in the timber, Uncle?" asked Marek.

"No, Marek, it is because of men," answered Jacek solemnly, "evil men and what they hide here in the forest."

"Brigands, robbers?" inquired the boy. "Do they hide their stolen bounty in these woods?"

"Worse," said Jacek, "trappers. The robbers are not fools, for they know better than to attack the Duke's peasants on his lands. They greatly fear the Duke's wrath. These traps are laid by the poachers who cross the Vistula in the dark shroud of night; those seeking to steal away with valuable animal pelts. These traps do not think at all. They will snap just as viciously upon your leg than that of a fox or a wolf. Stay behind me at all times and pay great attention, if you like having the use of both of your legs."

Jacek had the boy's full attention. He carefully entered the forest, proceeding along a trail that was not more than a deer run, all the while probing the undergrowth of its floor with the walking stick ahead of him. He taught the boy the markings along the trail, so they could find their way back.

Their progress was slow, and as they came deeper into the woods, everything became dark and cool. The light of the field where they had left their mounts and entered the forest continued to fade behind them, until it was nothing more than a luminous filament of horizon that threaded behind the sentinel trunks of a multitude of trees.

Marek had never been this deep into the forest before. His uncle advanced slowly, cautiously probing with the wooden staff, carefully and deliberately. When Marek next looked back behind him, he saw nothing, only the darkened hues of gray and green. The luminous filament must have been pulled like a loose thread from between the trees by God's own hand.

Marek had been warned by his mother about going into the forest alone, and at that moment he realized why. The woods had devoured both he and his uncle, who at that point, Marek was reassured to reach out and touch.

"Ah, we are almost there, Marek," said Jacek. "Can you hear it?"

The boy could not hear anything.

"Quiet yourself and listen to her speak to you, boy," said the uncle.

It slowly came upon Marek's ear like a trickle of a stream and grew in volume as the edge of the forest before them filled with reflected light. The trees slowly became less dense, until they were not only sparse, but the underside of their leaves rippled with a palette of colors of reflected sunlight.

The sound of the trickle had grown louder as the forest cleared and the light infused ahead of them. Suddenly, the trees reverently parted, and Jacek and Marek stood atop a large stone which jutted out over the banks of a swollen river.

Marek's eyes were still adjusting from the darkness of the depths of the forest. The light was intense, reflecting up from the surface of the river's murky bluish-green waters.

"So, you have never seen the Vistula before, my nephew?" asked Jacek.

"Never have I seen so much water in my entire life, Uncle!" said Marek. "What is that castle on the other side?"

"That is the Castle of the Polish Kings, Marek. It is Wawel Castle," said Jacek. "Before the capital was moved to Warsaw from Kraków, Wawel Castle was the home of all the Kings of Poland. It is said that a dragon lives by the river in a cave beneath it."

"A real dragon, Uncle?" asked the boy.

"I think there is more to fear from the dungeons beneath the castle than any dragon's cave. Now pay attention, Marek. Do not get too close to the river, as you do not know how to swim. The river looks calm, yet its currents can be very dangerous."

"How hard can it be to swim?" said Marek boldly. "I will learn easily."

"And will you learn to fly also, like the birds?" asked Jacek. "The fish make it look easy to swim, yet in the river it is only easy to drown. Be warned, Marek."

"Yes, Uncle," said the youth.

"Do you see, on this side of the river, those stones, much larger than the one on which we stand?"

"Yes, those that are shaped like three fingers?" asked Marek.

"Exactly, this is very important. Never go there. For it is known that is where the poachers who lay the traps come across the river. These are very dangerous men, who come under the dark of night to empty their hidden traps and lay new ones. Along with the beaver, otter and fox pelts they would be happy to catch a fine boy such as yourself to sell across the river in Poland."

"But Uncle Jacek, *Matka* says that even though we live in Galicia, we are not Austrians. She says we are all still peasants stolen from Poland. So why should I fear being stolen back?"

The boy was fast in his reasoning, Jacek thought. He had brought Marek to see the river, much as his father had once brought him. He placed his arm across Marek's shoulders and together they gazed upon the expansive Vistula.

How Jacek had dreamt of one day crossing that river and seeing Kraków with his own eyes. Although, he knew that would never come to pass. The Duke would never allow him to leave his *folwark*.

"Yes, Marek, your *matka* is right of course about our being Polish. We will always be Polish, no matter which empire claims the land beneath us. Still, the thieves who lay these traps are very bad men, and the family in Poland they sell you to may be worse than the one you have, Marek. After all, the proverb says *it's better to have a sparrow in your hand, than a pigeon on the roof."*

"We once had a stork upon our roof, Uncle Jacek. Father scared it off, so it wouldn't nest there," said Marek, still looking with amazement upon the river.

"Yes, I am glad you mentioned that, Marek, for it reminds me as to why we have come today to the forest," said the uncle. "Come, my child. The stop at the river is just a treat for your young eyes."

Jacek led Marek back into the forest, probing with his walking stick ahead of them. They proceeded along the trail from which they had come. About halfway, Jacek stopped and said to Marek, "Take note of that tree with the knot in the shape of a witch's face. Do you see it?"

"You mean this, Uncle?" said Marek, rushing from behind Jacek up to the tree, pointing to its hideous growth which was just above his reach. It did indeed look like a face, with two timbered eyes above a long knotted and haggard nose, upon the tip of which projected a wooden wart.

"STOP!" screamed Jacek. Marek stopped as his uncle had commanded. "Do not move, boy. I told you to stay behind me, child. You could have sprung a hidden trap." A tremor of panic edged his voice.

"Uncle Jacek," began Marek, "we have been in this forest for hours, moving like snails. If there were traps, we would have found them by now."

"Mind your elder, boy," said Jacek sternly, as he probed with his staff ahead of himself as he idled over to where Marek stood. Jacek calmed himself, before saying, "This tree marks the direction to the pond where the swans come. We will walk in the direction that the witch looks off into, Marek. Remember that always and always fear the traps."

They walked in the line of sight of the tree's bewitching growth knot. Soon, they came upon a small pond, which seemed to be dropped amongst the trees like a peasant's cap is dropped among the stalks of the field.

Upon the pond were two beautiful white swans, which became somewhat ruffled with the arrival of the two peasants. Scattered along the edges of the pond in the mossy growth were a number of beautiful white feathers. Marek used his own staff, being sure to clear for traps, and slowly edged toward the discarded feathers to collect them.

"The Hussars preferred the feathers of the eagle, still as we know of none on the *folwark,* we will make do with these. With some pigments, they will do nicely."

Marek had collected less than a dozen feathers, when the larger of the two swans swam toward him and hissed. His uncle had already checked the grounds around the pond for traps, double checking before the boy's search.

"Come, Marek, we are not welcome here. There will be many more days and many more feathers," said the Uncle.

"There are many more to take this day, my Uncle. Let me just ..."

"Leave them, Marek," yelled Jacek.

Marek, excited to gather the materials for his Hussars' wings, ignored his uncle once again. In doing so, he had not given his attention to the approaching swan.

Suddenly a great commotion overtook the boy. The swan was upon him, its wings flapping wildly, its beak hissing and nipping at his loin, which the boy instinctively arched away from the bird. Marek defended himself with his walking stick, but the fowl was relentless, driving the boy backward. The uncle laughed aloud as the combat ensued, and then stepped in to drive off the swan with his own staff.

Marek laid upon his back in the mossy growth. He breathed hard still, as the white bird had come upon him in a great surprise. It attacked hastily with an unfettered vengeance. Marek could only defend himself ineffectually before Jacek came to his aide.

“Did I not tell you I would show you why you needed your walking stick, Marek?” asked Jacek playfully, as he continued to laugh heartedly. “These creatures are not as peaceful as they first appear. It is best you learn to mind them when they hiss at you, boy. Come now, we need to leave the forest before it becomes dark. If we don’t get the horses back to the stable, the Duke will think we will have stolen them. We do not want that, do we?”

Marek picked up the dozen or so feathers that had become scattered during the attack of the swan, and along with Jacek they retraced their path back to the tree with the witches’ knot.

”Uncle Jacek,” asked Marek, “how did you know of this hidden pond?”

“Well, Marek, it is where my father once brought me. And before I married your Aunt Ewelina, I brought her here to see the swans. They have been coming here forever. No one knows why. Perhaps it is because...”

Then, just as Jacek uttered these words, a loud mechanical explosion was triggered in the woods. Splinters flew in all directions. Marek’s heart raced with an instant fear once again, each beat within his young chest more violent than the one before. He looked at his uncle, who also wore a look of shock upon his face. They both stood as still as the trees themselves.

Marek looked down at his uncle's feet. Between them was a heavy band of metal, wearing a sawtooth grin. The trap had snapped Jacek's staff into two uneven lengths, the shorter of the two being less than a foot long.

"So, you see, my boy," said Jacek, catching his wits about him, "the traps are like thieves, or even wolves. When you look for them, they hide from you, but it is only when you least expect it that they spring themselves upon you."

Marek was still speechless. The trap, now of no threat to either of them, lied docile in the ground beneath the tree with the witch's knot. It had been hidden in the undergrowth, only inches from where he had stood less than an hour earlier.

14

THE EVENT

JULY 1789

At this time, Maya was fifteen. She had developed an exquisiteness about her that was enchanting. Her hair was of an auburn color, unique among everyone on the *folwark*. Her long locks seemed to become highlighted into a radiant hue of chestnut as she spent time in the sun. She was a beautifully kept young girl. The fullness of her maturity was ahead of her still, but the temptation of her womanhood was already budding upon her figure.

She and Marek had become the closest of friends. Their bonding had started in their shared language lessons, yet each soon found in the other a shared persona. They were both respectful young children and grew into adventurous youths. Yet, both the girl and the boy retained their appreciation for how to conduct themselves with seriousness, reverence and maturity. The two were a matched set, it had appeared.

While they never used it to mock the others upon the estate, they had their own secret language. The cadence of the French tongue was like a strand that tied the two of them tightly together. Maya had long ago begun to develop a crush upon Marek, although she refused to admit it to anyone other than herself.

Marek had also taken a fondness to Maya. In fact, so much so, that he called her by his own secret name of fondness, Manuska. When he wanted to impart something with emphasis, he would do so by calling her "my *Maya Manuska*". He noted that she loved his calling her in this way.

One day, Maya watched as Jacek attempted to break a wild Tatar pony. Maya sat on the uppermost fence of the ring as Jacek attempted to rope the young, jittery animal. These were the small breed of horses of the Mongol Tatars that had once swept terror eastward from the steppes of Asia. These equines were extremely spirited.

"Be careful, *Maya Manuska*," Marek warned Maya in French, "it is not good that you sit so close to that wild beast. Come down from the ring's fence."

"But Marek, It is so exciting," she replied, also in French. "I cannot pull myself away. It is impossible to think that anyone will ever ride this wild creature."

"*Proszę*," he replied, sprinkling the Polish plea in with his French response, "today I must finish my Hussar's Wings. They are nearly complete. Please do not distract me by putting yourself in such peril. Your father will thrash both Jacek and I much worse than that beast should a single hair of your head become harmed."

Maya came down from the rail, and dejectedly sat behind the fence itself on an oaken stump.

Marek called to Jacek in Polish, "Do you want me to assist you, Uncle?"

Jacek did not take his eyes off the wild animal. "No, Marek, it is only a small pony. Yes, it is wild, and this will take much time, but another hand in the ring will only agitate the beast even further. I will break this animal by myself. Go and finish your wings of the Hussars. You have spent much time on them, enjoy finishing them today."

Marek, having assured Maya was safely behind the pen's railing, turned his attention to the Hussar's Wings. He had been excited for some time, as they were almost finished. The only thing left was to install the last of the painted swan feathers into the frames.

That very morning, he had collected and painted the last of the feathers. Of course, the Hussars used those of eagles, to which Marek did not have access. Marek had to settle for the fine swan feathers from the forest pond. He had only used the loose feathers he scavenged from the molting birds. This required patience, as each trip to the pond resulted in only a few useable feathers.

Marek would never think to bring pain upon them by plucking feathers for his project's expediency. Besides, as he had told Maya, he had once been attacked by a male swan protecting its mate. It was an experience he never wished to undergo again.

Marek turned his full attention to his task. He became absorbed in his concentration and forgot about Jacek's dance with the wild mare.

It took nearly half an hour before Jacek roped the beast's neck. It was as if he had thrown a lasso around a whirlwind. The animal bucked and threw itself through the ring in an uncontrolled protest. Jacek slowly worked the rope over the next hour, reeling the tiring horse ever closer to himself. Just as the animal seemed to be stilled, and nearly in his grasp, the mare reared, its front hooves slicing through the air.

Had it been an Arabian, or other large horse in the Duke's stable, he would not have gotten so close to the untamed beast. As it was only a pony, and well tired from its resistance over the last hour, Jacek had come close upon the animal. When it suddenly reared upon its hind legs, the animal's left hoof caught Jacek in the head, driving him to the ground. His forehead was split open, with massive amounts of blood pulsing from the gaping cut. He let go of the rope, which was still lassoed about the thick and powerful neck of the beast.

The Tatar pony began to react in panic to the blood in the ring. It stomped erratically, several times landing its powerful hooves on Jacek as he laid in the already crimsoned dirt of the ring. Maya screamed in sheer terror, after which she instinctively climbed to the top rail of the pen's fence in an attempt to help poor Jacek. As she attempted to climb upon the highest rail of the fence, in her great excitement, her foot slipped and the young girl fell forward at the waist, and cartwheeled into the ring, directly across from the highly frantic animal.

"*M'aidez*, Marek, *M'aidez*," she screamed desperately in French. "Help me, Marek, Help me!"

"I am coming, my Maya," screamed Marek, also in French, as he had watched this procession of events take place in blink of an eye. He could hear both his uncle and Maya calling his name, as well as the snorting of the panicked pony. He began to move to the ring, and upon seeing the frantic mare, stopped for an instant in his tracks.

Why do the Hussars wear wings? he remembered the Duke asking, as if only days ago. Marek ran back and grabbed the nearly completed wings and ran with them to the ring. He opened the gate as wide as it would allow. The pony was still circling the bloodied body of his Uncle Jacek in a great frenzy. Only a few feet away Maya was frozen in fear, her back was up against the lowest rail inside of the pen.

"Stay still, *moja Maya Manuska*," he said. "This beast is in a great terror. Do not move or you will frighten her further." Marek slowly walked to the point between the mare and his Maya. As he did so, he raised the two wings he had fashioned with his own hands. They were heavy, not intended to ever be carried by the rider, nonetheless Marek continued to extend his arms and the wings above him.

He told Maya, in French, that all would be fine and to calm herself. This she tried to do with only limited success.

Jacek was by then only groaning. Marek feared he might become weak from the loss of blood. The mare was no longer attacking his uncle, yet the boy feared the excited animal might further harm Jacek unintentionally. Marek had to get his uncle out from under the threat of its hooves, which meant getting that wild pony out of the ring.

Marek took a half step toward the wild pony as he began to slowly fan the Hussar's Wings. The beast looked up at the tips of the wings, which imposingly reached high above its head. A fine breeze animated the feathers and caught the attention of the animal. The mare took its first step backwards, only missing his uncle with one of its hooves by the length of a crow.

Marek took another half-step forward, and slowly angled the beast away from Jacek. His arms burned from the strenuous task of using these heavy wings as extensions of himself. Despite the pain of their weight, he used them to drive the mare away from his uncle, away from Maya, and toward the open pen gate.

He knew that should he lower the wings, the wild pony might sense its dominance once again, and bring harm to any one of the three of them.

Marek continued to take short half-steps toward the mare, until finally he quartered it away and toward the open gate. When he thought he could no longer support the wings with his aching arms, he rallied his last reserve of strength and began fanning the wings toward the horse. In doing so, the wild beast for the first-time looked behind itself, before it turned and sauntered out of the pen, and trotted off into the open fields.

Marek dropped the wings in the dirt of the ring. His arms screamed in pain as the burden of the wing's weight was lifted from them. Despite this, the boy turned and ran to Maya. She was still trying to catch her ragged breath, but otherwise she seemed to be fine.

"*Moja Maya Manuska*, you are scared although fine. My uncle is not. I am going to go and find the doctor. I want you to stay with Uncle Jacek. I will close the pen gate and you both will be safe. I have to leave you here, or Jacek may not survive." He had realized he had said all this in French, except his addressing Maya in Polish.

"Fly, Marek, fly," she responded to him, as well in French. "I will stay with your Uncle. Find the doctor. Together we will save your Uncle Jacek."

And fly Marek did. He located the doctor hurriedly, as the physician had been watching the last finishing touches being added to the guest house. He told the doctor, in Polish, of what had happened. Doctor Olszewski ran first to the infirmary to gather his bag, and soon the two raced back to the stable's ring.

The doctor first checked Maya to assure she was not hurt.

"I am not injured, Doctor, attend instead to Jacek. *Proszę*," she pleaded to Grzegorz Olszewski.

Having convinced himself that she was indeed unscathed from the incident, he moved to Jacek. The man had lost a great deal of blood, and by his opinion, suffered from either shock or *contusio cerebri*, a concussive head injury. The doctor attended to the stable master there in the bloodied dirt of the ring, as Maya and Marek watched attentively. First he cleaned and then stitched the wound of Jacek's head. Then, he instructed Marek to find something which could be used to bring shade upon his uncle, as in the doctor's opinion he was too injured to be immediately moved.

Marek cleverly constructed a makeshift tent of cowhide and some wooden staves that were in the stable. It was crude, however it shaded Jacek from the midday sun. The doctor elevated the wounded man's feet to assure what blood was left within him was sent to his heart and brain.

It was then that the Duke arrived. He screamed at the doctor to leave the peasant and attend to his daughter.

"Doctor Olszewski has already examined me, Father, and I am fine," she exclaimed in defense of him. "Had it not been for Marek's swift action, that animal would have killed us both. He also ran to get the doctor."

"It was Marek who gathered you?" the Duke asked, as he turned to the doctor.

"Yes, and very quickly, as there was not a moment to waste," responded the doctor.

"Marek left you with the lifeless body of this bloody peasant to get the doctor?" the Duke next asked critically to Maya.

"I assure you, my lord, that this man is indeed very much alive," interrupted the doctor, "only thanks to Marek's rapid action."

"I don't care if he would have died, Marek's first responsibility was to protect my daughter. She is the daughter of a member of the *szlachta*, after all, and he ..." the Duke said, pointing to the wounded Jacek, "is merely a peasant."

"Father!" exclaimed Maya in terror, "How can you speak in such a way?"

Marek had lowered his head at the accusation and refused to defend himself. Instead, Doctor Olszewski and Maya pleaded his case.

"He did what he had to do!" said Maya in tears.

"Suppose that beast had returned to threaten you," said the Duke to her.

"My lord, the ring was gated and bolted when I arrived," said the doctor. "Marek had made sure that Maya was protected."

"I don't care!" said the Duke in frustration. "The boy should have brought my daughter back to the safety of the manor house, not leave her there with *him*...". Sdanowicz sneered as he pointed again to Jacek.

"And *he* would be dead," responded the doctor.

"I have already told you," the Duke replied, his voice tightening in anger, "I don't care. I have too many peasants as it is from Count Von Arndt's improvements at the mines. Now, heal him, Doctor. For when you do and he is healthy, this reckless stable master will be conscripted to the Austrian Army. Perhaps he'll take better care of the Emperor's horses. At least he will no longer endanger my children."

No one caught the mistake upon the Duke's tongue of using the word children instead of child.

"Oh, Father, I can't believe you can speak so cruelly," sobbed Maya.

As the senseless arguing continued, Marek Zaczek, having not said a word, and upon hearing the Duke's command to heal his uncle, turned and walked slowly out of the ring and followed the tracks of the agitated mare.

They all yelled after him to stop. Marek merely continued to calmly walk off after the Tatar pony until he was out of their collective sight.

15

THE RECOVERY

JULY 1789

The boy Marek did not return that day.

Soon after the incident, Jacek was stabilized and moved into the doctor's wooden cabin, where he had the small infirmary. It was away from the manor house by a distance decreed by the Duke when the infirmary was initially constructed. Not so near that he would be susceptible to the fevers of those interred, or the screams of the injured as they recovered from their wounds.

Jacek made no such screams. The worst of his trauma was behind him. The doctor had treated his head wound, and what were believed to be cracked ribs from the mare's kicks. He bore only a slight fever. His bruises were many and deep, however nothing from which with time he would not eventually recover. His weakness from the loss of blood could only be treated by extensive rest.

Soon, Jacek's wife, Ewelina, arrived to look after her husband. She was accompanied by Magda. Maya had defied her father and had not left the stable master's side since the debacle in the ring. The girl had given a full recounting of the events that had transpired to Magda and Ewelina. Then, all three women prayed the rosary over Jacek, despite the doctor having told them that their beloved stable master would recover with time.

Magda had realized in Maya's retelling of how brave and chivalrous Marek's actions had been that the girl seemed to enkindle a flame of affection to her son. Maya was terribly distraught that Marek had simply walked off into the field after the Tatar pony. Magda had tried to console the girl, telling Maya that her husband Bronisław was out in the fields, even then, searching for Marek.

It was the emotion that swelled in the words of Maya that secretly terrorized Magda. For she had heard it before, in her discussions with her son, Marek, whenever he spoke of Maya. She feared this mutual affection and knew that it must never be allowed to bloom into a forbidden romance. Other than the immediate safety of her missing son, no thought was more disturbing to her.

The day dragged by with no news of Marek. After evening had fallen, Doctor Olszewski recommended the women leave his infirmary, allowing both he and Jacek to rest. The three of them stepped outside into the cool summer's air of the deepening night. The violet hues thickened into black, and the fears of the three women bore deeper into each of their hearts.

"My Jacek was so proud to have just been named stable master," said Ewelina. "Now, no good will come from this. I have nothing to look forward to, as when he heals, the Duke will surely make good on his threat to send him off to the Austrian Army."

Magda was surprised that Ewelina would speak with such candor in front of the Duke's daughter.

"Do not concern yourself," said Maya, "for I will repeat nothing to my father. I am shamed by his response to all of this."

And ashamed she truly was. Her father's disregard for the injuries of a peasant was reprehensible. To assume in any way that Marek should have stayed with her and allowed his uncle to die was a sin, nothing less. How could she have such a man as a father?

Maya feared that Ewelina would blame her for her Jacek's misfortune. After all, had Maya not been at the ring watching Jacek attempt to break that Tatar pony, he certainly could still have been injured. However, she reasoned, had I not been there, Marek would have still saved his uncle. There would have been no repercussions from her father for endangering his daughter.

Guilt had crept into Maya's thinking. *Why did I have to be there, at all? And what would become of dearest Marek?*

"I will talk to the Duke," said Magda bravely, all the while detesting the thought. "I will convince him that Jacek and Marek both were only doing their assigned tasks, and as such deserve no punishment. After all, no harm had befallen the girl..."

"That is fantasy, Magda," exclaimed Ewelina. "You will need to do much more than merely speak to that pig of a man to save them both."

"Ewelina, how sharp is your tongue," exclaimed Magda, "and in front of the Duke's daughter, no less!"

"What, the girl has already said she will not repeat what is said here," said Ewelina matter-of-factly.

"I shall not," interjected Maya emphatically.

"Do you think that she thinks all the peasants love her father?" asked Ewelina.

"I do not," exclaimed Maya.

"You think she herself does not think her father a pig?" pushed Ewelina.

The child did not respond.

"Enough of this talk, Ewelina!" scolded Magda.

It was then that along the trail came three men carrying torches. As they neared, the radiant lashes of the flickering flame lit their faces. The three were Bronisław, and Ewelina's sons Andrzej and Bartek.

"Did you find our Marek?" Magda asked of them.

"No, we have not," responded Bronisław. "But the boy will be fine. He is quite resourceful."

"He has never spent the night in the wild," said Magda, a mother's fear having come over her.

"Marek and I have spent many summer evenings under the stars," said Bronisław, "I taught him the constellations as my father had taught me many years earlier."

"The boy has never been *alone* with all the threats in the night," answered Magda, angry with her husband's attempt to pacify her. "We will take Maya home and continue the search."

Bronisław had begun to say how dangerous it would be for them to search through the darkness, before realizing this would only agitate his wife further. He knew she was thinking a thousand unforgiving fates that awaited her boy in the night. He also knew Magda would not rest until Marek was found to be safe.

"I am sorry, Magda. I need my boys to return with me to my hut," declared Ewelina. "I need to have them near me tonight."

"I understand, my *siostra*," said Magda, "you need your boys around you. Of course."

Her boys were strong young men of nineteen and twenty years. Magda knew in her mother's heart that the near loss of a loved member of the family would disguise them as small defenseless children in Ewelina's eyes. Magda knew her sister-in-law felt they needed to be protected, and Magda understood this completely.

Magda and Ewelina embraced. "Your child is safe, Magda. Remember he is soon to be committed to the church. God will not allow anything to happen to him."

The words momentarily comforted Magda, still her fear soon returned.

The three torches separated in the night, with two heading back to the humility of the peasants' hamlet, while the other one heading to the wasteful elegance of the manor house. There, Maya speedily ran upstairs to the upper hall. Through its window, she watched as the torch's flame under which Bronisław and Magda traveled, crossed the road, progressed past the stables, beyond the ring itself, and headed into the darkened fields in the direction that Marek had last travelled.

Maya watched that ball of flame shrink with the distance it traversed until it became only a point of light bobbing in a sea of darkness. Then, it was gone altogether.

The girl was exhausted. She walked to her room, but was too tired to remove any clothing, save her shoes, before throwing herself upon the down dressings of her bed. Yet, despite her fatigue, she was unable to rest. Her comfort merely reminded her of the horrific trials that Marek must be enduring. Maya closed her eyes, only to see wolves, bears and other predators in the night.

She stared at the ceiling of her room until the faint glow from the sun rising in the east splashed upon it. She then threw herself from the bed, slipped into her shoes and walked from the manor house. The crush of her feet upon the gravel of the road seemed to echo in the quiet of the early morning like the hooves of a hundred horsemen. She peered into the stables yet found no trace of Marek. She then walked to the horse ring, where she saw the splattered blood of Jacek still staining its sand. Nearest to her at the gate were the two Hussars' wings, lying where Marek had dropped them. She saw no sign of Marek anywhere, and her fear for his safety had consumed her.

The day stretched on with the weight of uncertainty. Maya again joined Magda and Ewelina at the infirmary, and the three women prayed over Jacek. This was despite his being alert this day, and although in great discomfort, he seemed on the mend.

Magda looked drained and exhausted. She was spent. At one point, Maya slipped her hands over Magda's, as the latter prayed, the girl softly said, "I'm so sorry". True to her nature, Magda interrupted her intercessions to the Virgin Mother to console the child. Magda had become close over the two days with Maya and knew that the child had a good heart. She only hoped that the life of privilege under which she was raised would not taint that heart's innocence.

For Maya, the second night was worse than the first. There still had been not a hint of Marek. Maya was herself fatigued to the point of no longer being able to stand. She changed into her bedclothes, and on her knees said her prayers to God to protect her friend Marek. Then, as she lay upon her bed, she was pulled into a light sleep, but one that was full of dreams that disturbed her deeply. She imagined finding Marek in a deep ravine, too deep to assist him in any way. She would then awaken, sweating, only to fall asleep again to dream of Marek screaming in the forest, his foot in the teeth of a poacher's trap. From this she would also awaken, only to drift once more to a restless state where her mind fill with a new bevy of fears, all concerning Marek, all in which she could do nothing to assist him.

When she crawled finally from her bed on the third day, the sun was beaming strongly upon her ceiling. She cursed herself for sleeping so late after having had such a restless night. Maya dressed, flew down the stairs and out the front door of the manor house. Her feet seemed not to touch the gravel of the road as she crossed, so great was her expectation.

She again peered into the stables, yet there was no movement there. She checked every stall in vain. She proceeded to the ring. The sun was higher in the sky and cast its yellowish red hues across the sands in the pen. Oddly though, the Hussar's wings were gone, as was the blood of the stable master. The sands had been refreshed and were raked smooth as if nothing had ever occurred there.

She left the ring and gazed out upon the open fields of the *folwark*. The vast emptiness before her spoiled her every expectation of finding her Marek. She prayed to the Virgin Mother for his safe return.

Maya's heart should have sunk, instead it became filled with hope. She searched out once more over the sea of growth in the field. Its heights of stalks were painted in hues of magenta and ochre and mauve under the filter of the rising sun. It was then when she first noticed something lumbering through the chest-high summer shoots. It was so far off in the distance, she could not discern its shape, just that it was slowly coming nearer to her.

Maya should have been fearful, for it was not uncommon to encounter great beasts this early in the morning. Yet, she was mesmerized by the creature. Finally, the being which had until then emitted no sound whatsoever, broke into a full run, and in doing so made a loud cry not unlike the yipping of a small dog caught in the teeth of a wolf.

As the beast neared, she could hear the faint rumble of hooves.

She began to discern the shape as two separate forms, one atop the other. It was then that she saw what her heart wanted most of anything to see. She saw the form of her beloved Marek riding towards her atop the Tatar pony.

In no way was he merely holding himself upon the mare, instead he was commanding the every motion of the beast. What Maya believed only a few days before she would never see, that being someone riding upon this wild mare, was exactly what now filled her eyes.

Maya's feeling of hope was instantly supplanted with an exuberant joy. Her Marek had not only returned to her, but he had conquered the animal which had brought forth the threat of death itself.

"*Ouvre la porte! Maya, ouvre la porte!*" he yelled to her. She opened the gate, and the great Tatar mare bounded into the pen at a full gallop. Marek commanded the beast to a trot, and atop it, he circled the ring several times. Maya had closed the gate, remaining outside the ring.

Marek looked gallant upon the beast's back, Maya thought. He then surprised her as he leapt from the Tatar pony and bounded over the rails of the ring's fence effortlessly.

"How is Uncle Jacek?" he asked her jubilant face.

"Doctor Olszewski says your uncle will be fine," she said, before adding, "I am so relieved to see you, my Marek. I feared for you so."

"I am perfectly fine," he said, "as is this magnificent animal."

"But you overcame that beast in the wilderness!" she said, the amazement showing in her eyes."How did you ever do that?"

Marek smiled proudly, before saying, "*Nie ma za co.*"

She threw herself into his arms and he embraced her. Then, he did what he what he knew was forbidden, for she was the daughter of a Duke, and he merely a peasant miner's son. He kissed her, for the very first time, hard and passionately.

She melted in his embrace. The kiss was more than she could have hoped for. She felt his confidence, his accomplishment, his vigor explode into her. The two were shrouded in emotion, one that had consumed them both for some time, yet one that they had never dared to act upon.

"*Je t'aime, ma chère*" he said to her.

"*Je t'aime, mon hèros*" she replied.

They kissed again in a long embrace. Tears streamed down Maya's cheeks. Her greatest fear had been transformed into her most cherished joy.

Then in her rapture, it had dawned upon her that her Marek must be starving of hunger.

"Come," she said, "and I will feed you from the bounty of our table."

Marek's eyes searched her own. He dried the tears from her cheeks. He then brushed the tender skin of her face with the back of his fingers.

"You, *Maya Manuska*," he said softly, "already are the bounty of my life!"

16

MAGDA'S REBELLION

AUGUST 1789

Marek had been welcomed home by all parties, including the Duke. Everyone was amazed that the boy had demonstrated the skills to break the Tatar mare, in the wild, no less. It was then that his skills as a horseman were recognized as being unmatched upon the *folwark*.

Two major events occurred in the following month. First, Jacek healed, although the Duke still held the threat of the army over the stable master's head. Second, the guest house was now finished, and ready for an impending visit from the Count, who was expected to be visiting from Vienna in the coming days.

These two events twisted into an unholy opportunity for the Duke. Magda, who had been serving in her usual functions in the manor house, sought out the Duke as he was inspecting the workmanship of the guesthouse one final time. She had promised to plead with Sdanowicz, on behalf of her sister-in-law, Ewelina, for the Duke not to conscript Jacek to the army as he had threatened.

Magda treaded tentatively upon the new stone walk that led her to the guest house. It was indeed a miniature of the manor house, yet in many ways it was superior. The walls she had noted during its construction were of the finest timber from the forests of the estate. They were stacked laterally, like a log cabin, intersecting and reinforcing each other in the corners. These trunks were tightly mortared at the Duke's command.

The exterior of the guest house was then smoothed with stucco, hiding the timber walls beneath. It matched the mustard colored stucco and decorative exterior designs of the manor house. Both structures were two stories in height, and their terra cotta tile roofs were steeply sloped to allow the winter's snows to readily slide free from its own weight.

The windows matched those of the manor house, although the overall size of the guest house was only half that of the Duke's main lodging. However, Magda was soon to learn that it contained only a quarter of the rooms of the main structure, and these were all of an impressive size.

Magda was amazed upon her first entering into the guest house. She opened the massive carved oak double doors, to reveal a large French style foyer with a curved staircase leading to the upper floor. Magda thought it much more magnificent than the straight stairwell of in the main hall of the manor house.

The chandelier that hung from two story ceiling was of fine Silesian crystal. It hung suspended by a beautifully decorated rope that appeared to be brocaded in gold. Its function was to lower the chandelier such that the oil lamps could be filled and lit, without need for an obtrusive ladder. Magda could only imagine how wondrous the effect must be upon coming in from the dark night to such an illuminated entryway.

The effect would surely be enhanced by the reflection of the light from the Italian marble floor that she was almost afraid to step upon, lest it should crack. It did not, of course, and was laid by master craftsman who had come all the way from Sienna. Magda was struck by the veins of green and red that flowed like arteries through the cream-colored tiles. She was engrossed in the elegance of the tiles, a product like she had never seen before, not in the manor house, and certainly not in the house that she had once been raised in on the Bochnia *folwark* of her father.

It was then that she heard his voice, and her blood ran still in her veins.

"Oh, Magda, how considerate of you to appear. I was just about to send for you, my dear," said the Duke in his friendliest tone. Come here, into the Count's den and join me. She reluctantly did so.

"So, what do you think, Magda? Will the Count be pleased?"

Magda looked upon the den around her. It was truly a work of craftsmanship. It was as if it had been a combination of the manor's library and study. There was an elegantly styled writing desk, with a recessed leather blotter which was embossed with the Count's family coat of arms. Around the walls of the beautiful room were elegantly carved bookcases which matched the desk in a Viennese style.

Workmen had been bringing in books from the manor house library which the Duke was arranging upon the shelves personally.

"My Duke, any man would have to be a fool to not appreciate all that you have done in this undertaking," she breathed almost against her will. "It is truly befitting a King!"

"Or an Emperor, perhaps?" teased the Duke, smiling pridefully. "I had a second leather writing blotter made with the embossed seal of the Habsburg House of Austria, just in case. I had the master craftsman from Vienna demonstrate to my carpenter how to change them out. Who knows when Joseph II himself may pass through this portion of his realm?"

Magda was so impressed with her first views of the guest house that she had nearly forgotten her reason for coming to see the Duke.

"My Duke," she began, "I have come to ..."

"Dear Magda," He interrupted, "I have come to notice that you refuse to address me properly as the other peasants do, as 'my lord' or 'my master'. Even good Doctor Grzegorz affords me this respect. Yet, you do not. With you it is always the more factual salutation of 'my Duke'. I have opted not to challenge you on this in front of the other peasants, yet can you not treat me with the respect my title demands?"

The blood in her veins, which had stilled at the shock of hearing his voice only moments before, then surged through her in rebellion to his arrogance. *I will never call the man who betrayed my parents to a life of hardship in the frozen north of Russia "my Master",* she thought. *Nor will I ever address "my lord" to the man who defiled me merely for his indecent pleasure.*

Magda struggled with how to respond to the Duke, for she wanted most not to anger him just before asking for leniency for Jacek. As the uneasy quiet in the room filled the awkward moment, it was then driven off by the noisy entrance of two men carrying in large stacks of even more books from the library.

"Put them here, on the floor," said the Duke, angered at the interruption. "That is entirely enough for now. You both are dismissed."

The two men dropped their load of tomes clumsily and looked upon Magda as they left the room. The Duke noticed this and assumed they were admiring her still attractive form. Magda had noticed their gaze, although from another angle, and felt as though both peasants were looking at her for forgiveness in leaving her alone with the Duke.

The Duke followed the men to the wide-open front doors, where upon their leaving, he delicately closed them and threw the oak bar which would assure no further interruptions. He then called for Magda from the den, having momentarily forgotten their discussion.

"Come, Magda," he said, "I will show you the rest of the house. You will need to learn it, for your duties will include making our guests comfortable when they are on the estate. You may be pleased to know the Count holds a special fondness for you."

She had been thankful for the interruption, and the escape from the question which had trapped her like wolves in a forest. She followed the Duke into the kitchen quarters, and through the dining room, which he explained he had installed should his guests wish to dine in a private setting. It was then that the Duke led her upstairs to the sleeping quarters.

There were only two bedrooms, however they each were massive.

First they entered the smaller of the two which bore an oversized canopy bed. It also had a settee, as well as an elegant hand-carved bureau and matching full-length mirror upon a stand. The Duke then led her to the larger of the two bedrooms, only after they passed a closet-sized room which contained a rough wooden bunk.

“For the Count’s valet,” he said, “I don’t care if his valet’s shadow is not accommodated. However, as for the Count himself...”

With having said this, the Duke swung open the double doors. Magda’s breath left her as her eyes fell upon the lavish bedroom suite. Like the other bedroom, it had its own fireplace. Still, unlike the other, the walls were paneled in the most elaborate design she had ever seen. The wood had the amber hue of honey, and the sheen as well, having been deeply varnished. The bed, even more elegant than the other, also had a canopy high overhead, with veils of lace which cascaded over it like a waterfall.

There was also a divan and table, an armoire and a small mirrored vanity, which the Duke explained could also double as a writing desk for personal correspondence just before retiring. All had been fabricated by Viennese craftsmen, and transported through the mountains with the greatest of care.

Magda then had walked over to the window to touch the silk embroidered curtains of a majestic royal blue design bearing a repeating pattern of the Austrian double-headed eagle coat of arms.

“I can see you have spared no expense,” Magda said to the Duke, who was in the act of closing the double doors to the bedroom suite. This action concerned her, as they were alone in the house, and would be, as the Duke had barred the front doors.

“I have also spared no thought of its design,” responded the Duke. “Notice as you stare out of the window how this house is elevated above the manor house. Perhaps it is so the guest will feel superior in looking down upon the main house? Certainly, this is a desired effect any host would wish for his guests to experience. But, the real genius of the design is that anyone looking up at the guest house’s second floor windows will see no more than the ceilings of its chambers.”

With this, a licentious grin uncoiled upon his face. It was clear to her that he had designed this villa with the full intent of using it as a shelter for his misdeeds of abuse against her.

Magda felt trapped. She feared that the Duke's long-promised threat of another forced encounter was about to be fulfilled. She stiffened her back. This time she knew she must resist him with every fiber within her frame. She knew if she did not do so, that the Duke would go on to repeat his injustices against her in this house at will.

"So, Magda," he asked through his intemperate grin, "what was it you came to seek from me?"

"I have come to plead for you not to deliver Jacek, upon his full healing, to the Austrian Army," she blurted out.

He walked across the room toward her. "And you are prepared to offer exactly what in consideration of this magnanimous concession?"

"Anything, my Duke," she said, the salutation raising his ire again, "except that which I know you desire most."

He walked close to her, slipping his left arm around her waist. She resisted, however, he only pulled her closer. His face was only inches from hers.

"So, you still show me no respect, my Magda," he said, "then, why should I show you any restraint?"

With this, he groped her breasts with his free hand as she squirmed from within his other arm still around her. He then forced his lips upon hers, which she in turn responded by arching her back unnaturally in an attempt to escape his mouth. Instead, he lowered his head to her chest, nuzzling the fullness of her form through her clothes.

Without a warning he wheeled her round, so she then had her back to the opulently embroidered bed. He pushed her back upon its silken coverlet.

"Magda, you are such a firebrand. Your resistance only enflames my desires all the more. I know it is but a ploy you use against me. I know you desire the same as I do, to once more fulfill ourselves of each other."

He stood over her now. His knees were then between her legs which he had forcibly splayed apart. It was then that she asked the most unusual of questions, which offset him in a strange way.

"Count Von Arndt arrives in the coming days?"

"Yes, what of it?" replied the Duke.

She did not answer. She allowed the reason for the question to stew within him.

"Do you know he desires you, also?" asked the Duke accusingly. "Has he made advances to you beyond my knowledge, Magda?"

She had struck an unexpected chord within the Duke. She knew then that deep within him he most feared losing her, along with all his other treasures, to the aspiring Count.

"Do not hope for the Count's intercession, Magda" said the Duke. "You are my peasant, and in his role as my overseer he has no bearing upon you, nor any of my other peasants. He can only set production quotas for the mines, not direct me as to which miners are to work the shafts. He can only set the number of conscripts my estate has to offer the Imperial Army; not direct which peasants are to be conscripted. So, Magda, your Bronisław, should he escape the dangers of the mines can still face the potential of fighting in the front lines against the guns of the Empire's enemies. Now, give yourself again to me, for it is useless to resist."

She was still at his mercy given the situation, but she knew his jealousy of the Count's interest in her, as newfound as it was to her, would not abate his desires. They would only intensify its flames for men most cherish those possessions coveted by other men.

She looked up at the Duke who loomed over her entrapped form. She had her elbows extended, propping the top of her arched back above the bed covering. It was then that she had decided to change her tactics.

"You are correct," she said, relieving the resistive clamping of her thighs upon his legs. "It is what I also desire. Your threats have convinced me so. For I wish no harm to come upon my husband. I certainly wish neither he nor Jacek to have to face the cannons upon the battlefields. I will give myself willingly to you. If only you will allow me to prepare myself properly. May I refresh myself, please, my Duke?"

Duke Sdanowicz was surprised by her submissive tone. He straightened himself over her, wondering if was she stalling for time? Would she attempt to escape the house? There was only one way out of the chamber, which he could readily block. The house was far enough away from the manor house that even her loudest screams would not draw attention.

"Do not try anything rash, my lovely Magda," he warned as he backed away from her. "Please, refresh yourself at the basin as you like."

The Duke walked over to block the doors, and thus her escape. He watched as Magda drew herself from the bed, rising like a flower in the spring. She slowly walked over toward the wash basin, which sat upon the vanity.

"Please allow me some modesty and turn your head, my Duke," she requested.

The Duke, a fourth time angered by her refusal to show him respect in her addressing him, denied her. "So, I should turn my back upon you only to have you attack me with the basin itself? I think not, my dearest."

Magda then took the cloth aside the basin and wet it, washing first her face and then slowly the nape of her neck. She then reached it inside the collar of her work dress and cleansed the *décolletage* of her upper torso. All under the lustful gaze of her Duke.

"That is enough, Magda," he said firmly, "now return to the bed."

"Yes, my Duke. Thank you for allowing me this remnant of my dignity," she said to him. She then removed her hand from the collar of her dress, but without the washcloth. It laid, fully saturated upon her firm bosom, soaking through her dress in a most appealing manner.

Magda then took her two hands and pinching the edges of her dress just above of her breasts, then snapped and fluttered it, over and over again, until the cloth fell under it to land near her feet.

She had the Duke's riveted attention to the point that he followed her with his eyes as she reached down to retrieve it from the floor.

What his eyes did not see, as was her intention, was her other hand collecting an object from the surface of the vanity as she rose. It was the conjurer's trick of misdirection, and as the Duke's eyes were blinded by his lust, she easily collected the other article.

She walked over to the bed, backwards, her hands behind her. The Duke followed, his gaze still upon the moistened upper fabric of her dress which clung enticingly to her form.

"I have waited for this moment ever since I first conceived of building this house," he said softly to her, "for my desire was that it would forever be a place we both could escape the realities of our circumstances: you from the hardship of your peasant life; and I from the constant intrusion of the eyes of my wife."

As he then moved to embrace her, she raised her left arm in a motion for him to wait a second more.

"This bedspread is so beautiful. All the care you have taken to match it to the drapes with the Habsburg family emblem," she said. "The expense must have been extravagant."

"Indeed, it was," answered the Duke. "I can wait no longer to lay you down upon it, my dear."

She smiled at his suggestion. Then, she flexed her arm once more for him to wait a moment.

"It must have taken months for it to be made to your designs," she sighed.

"Nearly a year," he said, "but well worth the wait for the pleasure it will bring to us both."

Her arm, for a third time, asked him to wait just a moment more.

"It is a shame it will not be available in the coming days for the Count's visit," she said.

"Whatever do you mean, my Magda?" the Duke asked.

It was then that she raised her right arm and balanced delicately in her palm over the bed dressings was the well of indigo ink she had removed from the vanity without the Duke's notice.

"No, Magda," exclaimed the Duke, "put that down immediately."

His voice's anger recognized the clever trap she had laid for him.

She held the inkwell ever so precipitously balanced over the bed. Any rush upon her would have caused it to tumble and spill. As she had earlier lain defensively upon the bed, she had judged it to be her only real weapon in the room. It had prompted her to ask the question pertaining to the Duke's arrival.

"Magda, should you spill one drop of that upon the bed, I will throttle you myself..." threatened the Duke in a terse and unforgiving manner.

"And how would you then explain my bruises and battery to your Count, who by your admission desires me so?" she asked. "Or, for that matter, to Sister Maryja Elizabeta upon her next visit? Or most of all, to the Duchess whom I serve."

"I should merely say it was discipline," stated the Duke flatly.

"Does your Count know that you have imprisoned another Duke's daughter in a life of peasantry upon your *folwark*?" Magda asked threateningly. "Perhaps it will be of no interest to him, but I sense, as you do, that your Count desires all that you possess. Perhaps he would use the news of your treatment of me as leverage against you with the Emperor."

She had lied in her last statement somewhat. She had never sensed anything lustful in the Count's treatment of her. She only had sensed the fear of it in the Duke himself.

"Magda, I warn you," said the Duke in as intimidating a manner as he could affect, "put down that inkwell and abandon your idle threats."

"Just how idle are my threats? I will make you fear for every second I am ever left alone with the Count!" she sneered. "The secrets I may share with him will stoke your demise, my Duke."

"Think of the safety of your Bronisław in the mines..." he cautioned.

"We will end this encounter today not in the way in which you have so lasciviously desired," she said softly, "but yet still in a manner which will greatly benefit your interests. You will agree that no harm is to come to my Bronisław in the mines, and that neither he nor Jacek are to be conscripted into the Imperial Army. And in return, in addition to my removing the tint of stain from above your trappings of wealth, I will share no secrets with the Count. Do you agree to abide by these terms?"

The Duke, at first, did not speak, for he refused to accept her dictating terms of surrender to him. He decided that his best course of action would be to agree with her, get her to set down the inkwell, and then he would overpower this insolent servant and have his way with her.

"I consent to your conditions," he said flatly.

"There is one other," she swiftly added.

He looked at her with a reprehensible stare that reflected the growing hatred he had for her in his heart.

"I will never again be asked by yourself in public or private as to how I address you," she said, "for you will never be my lord nor my master. These I reserve for *Jezus Chrystus* alone."

"And what favor do I receive in return?" he asked.

"That I continue to address you as '*my Duke*' in front of all others," she sneered at him, "for we both know the only Duke deserving of my affection is my father, Duke Władysław Kowalczyk, who you so indignantly conspired against. It was you, after all, who condemned him, and my mother, to their Russian exile."

For the first time, he could understand the hatred she had nursed within her heart against him for so very long. She had suppressed it so well that he had allowed himself to think she did not despise him so. In fact, it was his misconceptions of her feelings for him that had persuaded the Duke to allow her to "refresh herself". He actually thought that she would submissively offer herself to him afterward. And so, his conceit of her feelings for him lead to this predicament.

The Duke should have instead at that moment continued with his intention to take by force what the man in him had desired. Yet, once again he told himself, *that is exactly what I shall do as soon as she sets down that damned ink*.

"Magda, I agree, now put down that inkwell."

“First, you will slowly back up upon that far wall,” she demanded.

“I will not,” he said, “as I have given my word to you.”

“Your words are as useless as the breaths that carry them,” she responded coldly. “Now, stand with your back upon that far wall.”

He did not move a muscle. Instead, she did, quivering her palm just enough for the inkwell to slosh threateningly in her hand.

The Duke rapidly stepped back against the far wall. As he did so, Magda calmed the inkwell and took steps away from the bed, but still she kept it in such a position that the inkwell could instantly be tossed onto the fine bedding. She then backed further away to the double doors enclosing her in the bedroom.

“Do not rush upon me on the stairs, or I will throw this crystal inkwell upon the Florentine marble floor. If it does not crack your precious stone, its contents will seep into the virgin porous mortar that joins them. Do not be rash, my Duke.”

She slipped through the doors and hastily made her way down the curved staircase. As she reached the bottom, she looked up only to see the Duke standing at the railing. He looked down upon her as she lifted the bolt from the oak double doors, and exited the guest house.

The Duke’s last glance stayed with her for the rest of her days, for it was double edged. It was sharpened with his hatred, but also sheathed with the humiliation of his defeat. Magda also saw another cutting element in the gaze. It was the element of respect that this most powerful magnate reluctantly had for her cunning and ingenuity. She knew then, that she would never again give in to his intimidation. For the man, despite all his bluster, had proven himself weak, and the crucible of his fragility was his love for all the material belongings he possessed.

17

THE ASSUMED REPERCUSSION

AUGUST 1789

The night before Magda's encounter with the Duke, Bronisław Zaczek had walked the length of a shaft hundreds of feet below the ground. He had been joined by another miner, his long-time partner Jerzy, with whom he had worked closely over the years. This night, at the direction of the foreman, they were joined by an apprentice, a young boy named Lech. This boy of only fourteen years was upon his first excursion to the underworld.

Bronisław walked quietly through the lateral gray lifeless tunnel of salt, with Jerzy and the boy trailing behind them. Bronisław was the senior miner of the party, and in addition to his tools, carried an oil lantern, which cast its heavy stagnant glow upon the gray chiseled walls that entombed the three figures. For while the dark, ashen-colored walls were illuminated on their either side, the tomb was sealed with an impenetrable darkness fore and aft. The three miners travelled in a bubble of light that moved slowly like a dead corpse of prey in the tight throat of the serpent that was total darkness.

Jerzy carried additional tools with him, slung over his leather frock. The boy, as a courtesy of his initial journey into these unnatural surroundings, carried only a caged forest finch. Jerzy spoke with the boy to occupy his mind, such that any reservation of fear would not creep within it.

"So, what questions do you have for Bronisław and myself?" asked Jerzy, adding, "you must have many, my young friend."

"I do, *Pan* Jerzy. I have many indeed. Most pressing upon my mind is why do we carry this little bird into the mine?" Lech asked.

He had thought it to be the most unnatural of all things that he had ever seen. A bird, so beautiful in the sunlit sky, doubly trapped: first, by the wooden cage surrounding it; and secondly, by the quiet earth which surrounded them all.

"The bird is our warning, young Lech, so we should not be overcome by gas or should our air become too stale for life itself. If the bird falters, we then know to get out immediately," explained Jerzy.

"Do we take the bird with us?" asked the boy innocently.

"What, when we leave?" asked Jerzy.

"Yes, when we leave," answered the boy.

"No, we do not take the bird," answered Jerzy, his voice was surprised and tight, "we save ourselves, and leave the bird to die."

"Isn't that cruel?" asked the boy, having not yet come to grips with the miners' concept of doing whatever was necessary to insure one's personal survival.

Indeed, thoughts of self-preservation would grow over time like a clinging vine in the thoughts of all miners. They would grow to consume the seemingly endless portions of the miners' lives that were spent deep under the hardened soil. Each man knew that every time he descended into the depths of the earth that he was already half-buried. To relieve his deepest, darkest fears, each miner convinced himself that knowing what to do in the fleeting seconds of an accident might just save them from becoming eternally entombed.

"Is it cruel?" Jerzy repeated the boy's question. "How can it possibly be cruel? It is a bird, and in being just a bird, it has no capacity to sin. Thus, if it does not sin, when it dies, it goes directly to heaven. So no, it is not cruel to leave the bird to die, for you are just shortening its eventual journey to paradise."

The boy chuckled in response to his elder's explanation. Jerzy noticed Lech's response, which prompted him to ask, "So, you find humor in my words?"

"Forgive me, Pan *Jerzy*. That is silly! There are no birds in heaven," said the boy, "for everyone knows they have no souls."

"Oh, really," said Jerzy as he played along, "it is such that you have been taught? Well, you have been misled, my young friend. Allow me to teach you properly. Tell me, Lech, does the heaven you desire to reach have lush, beautiful gardens?"

"Of course, it does," argued the boy, "huge gardens, with every variety of flower that colors the earth. Just like the Garden of Eden. *Jezu* died for our sins so we could be permitted to praise God in such a paradise!"

"And what is sadder, my young companion, than a garden without birds?" countered Jerzy. "Heaven must have the sweet songs of the birds to praise the Lord along with those songs of our hearts. And since there are thousands and thousands of birds, we are doing this one a favor over his many friends. For the sooner he gets to that garden, the sooner his soul will find the choicest roost."

At that point the boy, who was of an exceptional mind, realized that their idle banter was a contest of reason between he and the miner.

"Then, under that reasoning, I assume we should make no effort to save ourselves," said Lech, "so, should we perish, we will also get to heaven faster. Once there, we will find the choicest spots to eternally rest."

Jerzy noticed how cleverly the boy had turned his own argument against him however he refused to be beaten by this child.

"Well, my apprentice, this is where you must remember that we differ from birds and all animals," answered Jerzy, "for we are men and full of sins for which we must repent. We have to save ourselves from the dangers in these mines, such that we can return to the world above us and repent for our sins before dying. Only in that way can we one day look Saint Peter in the eye and enter through the gates of heaven to enjoy the gardens and sweet songs of the multitude of birds."

The boy again smirked at the older miner. He then attacked his argument of sin being the distinguishing aspect between man and beast.

"So, you put forth that animals do indeed have souls, but not the ability to darken them with sin. Yet, the Duke works us underground all week, even on the Lord's day," pointed out Lech. "How can we repent when he causes us all to sin?"

Jerzy smirked loudly so that Bronisław would hear him. "This one has much to learn, Bronisław," he said, before turning again to the boy.

"My young helper, mining is itself the Lord's work. We have just passed the chapel. Does not the Duke send priests deep into the mines on Sunday mornings to say mass and bless us all? Of course, he does. Yes, it is a simple chapel with only a cross and some modest religious carvings, but someday we miners will carve out of the salt a grand cathedral for ourselves down here." Both Jerzy and his great imagination refused to be bested by the boy in arguments of logic.

"*Pan* Jerzy, you avoid my question. For even after mass, we still work on the Lord's day. Is that alone not a sin?" said the boy.

Indeed, Jerzy had been stalling. He had marked the chapel as they passed, and immediately threw it into his logic for one reason only: to provide him the seconds needed to form his answer. Then, it solidified within his thoughts.

"Was it not the Lord who spoke of the salt of the earth? Did He Himself not say, *'What good is salt when it loses its flavor? Is it not then to be trampled underfoot?'* Of course, he did, and we are all exempted from sin when working on the Lord's day, because after all, in mining this flavorful salt, we are doing the Lord's work." Jerzy was proud of his ability to out-reason the lad, which had turned out to be a much tougher task than he would have anticipated.

"Well, I am young and have no sins for which to repent," said the boy. "I am the same as the bird. Thus, there is no need for me to be concerned with saving myself." Lech then scoffed at his new companion in a friendly way.

"Your arguing with your elder is a sin of itself," said Jerzy. "Now enough of this talk. You are here to listen and learn, so that one day you will be the miner that Bronisław and I already are."

Bronisław had enjoyed the back and forth between Jerzy and the boy. Jerzy had always been much more talkative than he was. Often his friend's mouth said too much, and it had come back to haunt the man. Bronisław sensed he had learned from these misgivings, as with the young boy Jerzy had decided to close off the banter while he was still in a superior position.

That being said, Bronisław still thought it good that his partner should keep the boy's attention away from his fears of being underground. He remembered his first lengthy trip into the mines. The first few hours were an adventure in themselves. However, as the time stretched into days, his excitement slowly morphed into boredom, and then from boredom to confinement, and finally from confinement to the penetrating fear of never revisiting the sunlight and fresh air of the surface again.

Their walk was long, and Jerzy changed topics, as well as his discussion partner.

"Bronisław," he stated, "this is the location from where the foremen have increased the spacing of the wood support timbers. I do not like this wider spacing. We have never before worked under these conditions."

Bronisław looked at the posts that periodically lined the wall of the tunnel. Jerzy was correct in his observation, as the spacing of the post timbers, and the wooden beam that each pair supported to stabilize the ceiling above them, was now twice the length of the older sections of shaft.

"Did the managers not say that it was acceptable?" asked Bronisław. "Would they risk our lives? No, we are the very lifeblood of the mines. No salt would leave these mines without us. The salt will not mine itself, will it? So, the managers must keep us safe. Have you not considered this?"

Jerzy revered Bronisław. He was the senior miner of their team, yet still Jerzy's heart harbored concerns of its own.

"Yes, of course, what you say is true, Bronisław. I have considered all this, my friend," said Jerzy, "but with all the changes that have been made down here, there are many miners who are out of work. Sure, some go to the army, but there are still many others, of course, available to take our place. Perhaps the managers know this and are thus willing to gamble with what we hold most sacred for the sake of production."

Just as Jerzy had taken the boy's mind off his concerns, Bronisław realized it was now time for him to do the same for his partner.

"It is safe, my friend," reassured Bronisław, "let your heart be still. We have great toil in front of us. Save your energy for the salt, my friend."

They walked on only a short distance further before they came to the end of the lateral shaft and entered a massive chamber where the salt was being excavated. They stared at the smooth wall of gray salt stone before them.

Next, the two miners explained to the boy how to lay out their pickaxes, chisel bars and other cutting tools. They then used the tools to cut a ledge into the side wall of the shaft, large enough for them to place upon it the lantern such that it could cast the maximum light upon the gray salt wall. Jerzy turned to the boy.

"Remember, Lech, our Lord *Jezu* once said, *When one has a light, he does not place it under a bushel basket."*

"It is just as well," said the boy, "for we have not a basket at all."

"That is enough from both of you. It is time to get serious and go to work, my friends," said Bronisław. He took the bird from the boy and placed it carefully on a similar ledge, only cut lower to the ground nearest the salt wall where they would be working.

"Lech," said Jerzy, with great seriousness, "should gas enter the tunnel, it is heavy with poison. Any air that is good is above it. That is why we place the bird so low to the ground."

All three then donned the leather hoods which they would wear over their heads, and they soon began their work. Better said, Jacek and Bronisław worked, as Lech was allowed to watch and learn this first day.

Jacek and Bronisław worked for many hours and had freed much salt from the chamber's face. The time was not of interest, for there was no way in which to mark it. The only light they had burned constant, its shadows never changed their angles, for there was no arc of the sun to cause them to do so. The only ways to determine the length of their toils was the increasing aches of their muscles, and the amplified dankness that clung to them as the sweat of their exertions fouled the warm, close air.

It was only upon the completion of their making their quota that the men dared to bring their toils to an end for the day. The product of their labors sat in mounds of rubble piled in the shaft behind them.

"How will all this salt be removed from here?" asked Lech.

"That is your job for the second day, young one," said Jerzy to the boy. "In the morning, you will roll the wagon here, and fill it from the salt we freed today. Then, you will attempt to keep up with Bronisław and I as we free even more salt. Today your eyes learned from watching men tire of their work. Tomorrow your muscles will learn exactly how tiring the work is."

The boy had begun to play once more with the encaged finch. It seemed, even as bright as the boy was, he did not yet realize this was his entry into a lifetime of hazardous work that awaited him.

Then all three miners removed the leather hoods from their heads and the leather frocks from their chests. Their hair dripped with sweat, so much so that it would appear they had dunked their heads in the refreshing waters of an underground stream. Their chests were slick with moisture, which soon sucked the dust from the air and became brine upon their skin.

Only then was it that they rested before beginning the long journey back to the underground lodging quarters. They left the tools at the face of the shaft, yet took the caged bird with them, should they encounter any hazard along their way.

Bronisław had noticed the boy Lech had indeed become more silent with each hour that he spent below the ground. He felt compassion for the boy, who wrestled with the unnatural absence of both daylight and fresh air. He and Jerzy had so long ago become accustomed to this eternal and dank semi-darkness which was their working reality.

"Lech," Bronisław said to him, "it is not forbidden for an apprentice like yourself to be given a reprieve to go up to the surface for a break. I can arrange it with the foreman for you, if you like."

"*Dziękuję, Pan* Zaczek," said the boy. "I am truly tempted to do so, but I fear that the fresh air would only cause me even more discomfort. For what if I should determine that I have not the will to return to the depths? I would be ashamed, and I would be viewed as a failure by you all, as well as by my family."

"Do not feel ashamed," Bronisław continued, "it is only natural to wish to see the sun, the moon and the stars. It is no wonder one feels trapped this far below the earth. You will get used to it, as we have over time, and you will become a worthy miner, I am sure of this. Even to this day, the first breath I draw upon leaving the mines is the sweetest breath of all."

"*Dziękuję, Pan* Zaczek" the boy said again.

"What is it that you thank me for this time?" asked Bronisław.

"For remembering back to when you felt what I am feeling now," answered Lech. "I will make you proud of your new apprentice."

"I have no doubt that you will," said Bronisław, remembering when he had once uttered similar words to those who had taught him.

They soon came upon the underground encampment that lied nearest the vertical shaft that rose to the surface. This was where each crew returned after their day's labors. Here, they would be fed, allowed to refresh themselves and sleep, as well as mingle with the other mining crews.

"Why do we have to walk so far each day?" asked Lech of Bronisław.

"Hold out your arm, my boy. Place your palm down upon the floor. Make your palm stiff and spread your fingers." The boy bent over and did so. Bronisław said to him, "Your arm and wrist are the great vertical shaft, and the fingers are the horizontal tunnel shafts that spread out in all directions from it. Each crew walks out along their finger, until they come to its tip, which is the shaft's face. It is in these chambers where the day's mining occurs. Each shaft has many chambers, and over time there have been thousands excavated."

"Why should we not just sleep there, so in the morning we don't have to walk so far again?" he asked.

Bronisław could see the boy thought greatly about all things. He had a curious mind.

"For like the blood flowing in your wrist to your fingers," explained Bronisław, "the vertical shaft is the life of the mine, of all the tunnels. All the food, water and other necessary provisions are lowered here and provided to us. All the precious salt, as well as the waste we make here below is raised to the surface. Also, it is the community of miners that congregate after each shift here that makes life underground somewhat bearable. Now, take your hand from the floor."

Lech did so, and then raised himself. "So, I think I now understand, *Pan* Bronisław. We all come here each night, and should there be an emergency of any sort, we are close to the vertical shaft for a rapid escape."

Bronisław knew Lech to be bright, however he did not think the apprentice miner would discern the very reason for the underground encampment's position that he himself had decided not to share with the boy. Lech reminded Bronisław of his Marek, not so much by looks, but by the quickness of his mind. It was then that Bronisław had a stinging vision of his Marek and Magda. She was weeping mournfully, and a somber Marek attempted to console her. That vision was nothing more than a flash that seemed to sear itself upon his mind, and then, in a second, it was gone.

Before they ate, they washed from barrels of water which had been lowered into mine. Then ate heartily of bread and a stew that had been prepared. Then there was time, just enough time, to talk to their brother miners before the camp's lanterns were extinguished.

They slept underground on the rawhide crew cots stretched over wooden frames. All slept in an exhausted fatigue except young Lech, whose thoughts were driven by the weight of the impenetrable darkness and the mass of earth that hung overhead between them all and the surface. He thought of the stars in the night sky above them, and underneath of these he envisioned his family. He had many brothers and sisters whom he loved dearly. In his heart, he wondered if he would ever see them again.

The miners were awakened at the prescribed time by the foremen. They arose, washed and hungrily ate their breakfast. As they had slept, their lanterns had been refueled by other workers in the central underground camp. These same workers tended to each crew's caged forest finches, providing them with feed and water. After breakfast was cleared, these workers would sleep while the miners toiled, arising in time to prepare once again for their return.

Lech was very interested in the horses he had seen in the camp area. One was on a treadmill, which as the horse walked upon it, provided power for the lifting and lowering of massive loads of salt and supplies, respectively, through the great vertical shaft.

The three miners then walked again to their shaft's end, but this time with Lech the apprentice pushing a heavy wagon for the removal of the mined salt from the previous day. There was no horse available to pull it for them, so Bronisław and Jerzy thought it best to allow the boy to struggle with it. Best that he began to taste the bitterness of real work.

Some of the shafts had been fitted with rails upon which the wagon could be pushed. This was one of the many improvements that had recently been introduced, although this particular shaft had not yet been converted.

"I prefer to mine as our fathers did. These improvements are not needed," said Jerzy. And so, the boy pushed the cart over the smoothly chiseled salt floor of the shaft.

After they had begun to work for an hour or so, Bronisław called Jerzy over to him. "Does it appear that the support post has walked on us?" His meaning was, *Has the vertical timber of the shaft's chamber moved ever slowly under the vibrations of their labor?*

"I do not think so," answered Jerzy, "for it looks the same as yesterday."

"Mark it," said Bronisław, and Jerzy picked up a tool and scribed a line along the shaft into the soft, gray salt stone wall behind it.

They worked for the rest of the day. Their efforts removed the face of the shaft in large salt stones which Lech then loaded into the cart. Their production was good, and the foreman was pleased. It was a day like so many before it, however totally unlike the day that would follow.

At the end of their workday, the three of them pushed the salt-laden cart down the shaft. They pushed it until they reached about halfway along the tunnel's length, where it had been marked that a workhorse would later in the evening be strapped to it and pull it the rest of the way to the central shaft.

Bronisław, Jerzy and Lech had sweated profusely under the leather tunic and hooded shroud which covered each miner's torso and head. The boy looked like a withered reed within his garments, which hung from his frame like the skin from a starving dog.

They removed their hoods, wiped their sweated brows, and returned to the workers' camp. There they again washed, were fed and spent some idle time relaxing before it was time to sleep. Bronisław sat against the salt wall of the encampment and took from his pocket a small pouch of sackcloth. He opened it and took out his knife.

"What is that you are carving, *Pan* Zaczek?" asked Lech.

"Did I not tell you to call me Bronisław?" said Zaczek.

"I am taught to call my elders as such," said the boy.

"Down here there are no elders, just miners, foremen and horses. We all work, just the foremen not so much. So, call me Bronisław," he said with a smile.

"So, what is it that you are carving, Bronisław?" asked Lech again. "It looks like a bull, or a bison."

"It will neither be a bull nor a bison. It will be an Aurochs. Much more ferocious. They are gone forever, now only a part of the past.

My father once told me that his father had seen one in his youth in the Jaktorów Forest. Even then they were rare. This one is for my boy, Marek. He loves the figures I carve for him down here."

"I wish I could carve," responded Lech, "but I have no talent for it."

"Nor did I at your age, Lech. It comes with time. Lots of time in the mine when your muscles are too exhausted to work, and your mind is too anxious to allow you to sleep. Carving allows you to settle both. All miners carve to some degree, just for this reason. Have you not seen the chapel crucifixes and the figures of *Jezu* cut into the walls?"

"Yes, of course, I have seen these," said the boy, "for Jerzy had taken me there. They are amazingly lifelike."

"These stones of salt are like your life," said Bronisław, repeating a phrase he had heard long ago, "for you can carve from it whatever you desire."

The boy looked upon him, and said with great gravity, "Your carving is merely an escape from a thankless job."

"I prefer we miners think it is our way of saying to the Lord, *'Dziękuję, Jezu'* for keeping us safe these many hours, days and weeks underground. And thanks to our families, for we are sorry for all the time we spend away from them."

Bronisław finished his carving for the night and replaced the partially defined Aurochs in the sack cloth enclosure. The signal was given for lights out, and the miners slept upon their cots. This included Lech, whose mind still wandered, but his frame was exhausted from his day of work. He soon drifted into the restful sleep of the fatigued.

The next day, the three miners returned to the shaft chamber and began their work once more. That morning, once placed upon its low ledge, the caged bird was much more animated than the previous days. It chirped and jumped about within its cage. The finch's agitation did not escape the attention of the apprentice Lech. Nor did it escape the attention of Jerzy and Bronisław, as both men were greatly superstitious.

"Is there something wrong with our friend?" asked Lech.

"No, it is good he moves about so. He has great stamina. It is when he stops moving we should become concerned," answered Jerzy, hiding his own concerns with the bravado of his response.

Bronisław then came alongside his partner and asked a question in a whispered voice such that the boy could not hear.

"Jerzy, did you check the scribe-line last night before we went back to camp?"

"No, this I forgot to do," answered Jerzy. "Did you?"

"No, I did not either, but this day it appears the lower quarter of the line you scribed is behind the timber."

"Let us keep a close eye upon it today as we work, my friend," said Jerzy.

They worked for many hours, and soon forgot again about checking the post. Yet, this they could not forget for long, for the bird remained animated in its cage. The miners were too superstitious to ignore that.

"Lech, please come here," called Bronisław after several hours. "I need to send you on an errand. Return to the camp and have them supply you with additional lamp oil. We are running low, and it is quite difficult working in the dark. Here, take this tallow taper and light it from the lantern so that you will have a flame and can find your way. Do you understand?"

"Yes, Bronisław, of course, I understand," the boy said, "except why does the oil burn faster than during the past two days, when we had plenty enough to last us until our work was done?"

Bronisław was unprepared for the boy's question, but rapidly recovered.

"It is that they did not fill it properly overnight," Bronisław answered Lech.

"But this you did not notice before?" asked the boy. "Was the lantern not lighter than the past days?"

"Do not question Bronisław," said Jerzy in a sharpened tongue, "only do as you are told to do, young Lech. Go to the camp and get the oil, as Bronisław directs."

Having been reprimanded by Jerzy, Lech took to his errand. He lit the tapered candle, and its flame slowly disappeared into the all-consuming darkened shaft behind the two miners.

"I need to talk to you, Jerzy," said Bronisław.

"Of course, you do," replied Jerzy, "for why else would you send the boy for oil we do not need?"

"That post is shifting. I checked it a few minutes ago and now three quarters of your scribe line has disappeared behind it. We need to demand that it be replaced," said Bronisław.

"Not just replaced," said Jerzy, "but to have the shorter spans between posts restored as well."

"Yes, but for that demand we will need our miner brothers to agree. We will call a meeting tonight at the camp. For now, I suggest we leave this area at once."

Jerzy looked at his partner. "It is only a little more effort and we shall make our quota. Do you fear it that much?"

"I fear the bird," said Bronisław, "it has been chattering all day. It senses something we cannot. Now, grab the tools. We will tell them it shifted suddenly, not gradually. The foreman will have to believe us. They can assign us to another shaft tomorrow while they brace this one more strongly."

At that point the finch began fluttering its wings inside the cage in as excited a fashion as Bronisław had ever seen in all his years. It was as if the shadow of a cat had just passed over it.

"We move now," shouted Bronisław, reaching only for his pick-axe as Jerzy moved to grab the lantern. It was then that a great sound exploded through the shaft in which they stood. It was a crackling of wood, as if lightning has just struck an oak, followed by dirt sifting like flour from the beams spaced over their heads.

"Go, go, go," screamed Bronisław, who was behind Jerzy, who himself had turned to move up the tunnel of salt. Another crack of a splitting beam thundered around them, and instantly the ceiling came down upon them. They had waited an instant too long.

When Bronisław awoke, or more properly came to his senses, for he had not passed out, he lay trapped in an unexpectedly illuminated pocket under the rubble. His life was spared by his being closest to the end face of the chamber, which provided support to the ceiling nearest it. It was as the ceiling moved away from the shaft face, it became supported only by the beams held up by posts, like the one they had scribed. The timber posts had failed, and the overhead beam had come down upon Jerzy, killing him immediately.

Bronisław knew this, because he could see the crushed silhouette of Jerzy's head among the dust in the tight space. How could he even see it at all? Only because in the shock of the collapse, the lantern had been thrown from his partner's hand and was crushed, splitting its reservoir. The spilled oil immediately was enflamed from the fire of the wick. The burning wash of oil was trapped in the same chamber as was Bronisław, however thanks to the unevenness of the floor, it luckily flowed away from the miner.

Bronisław was pinned down by the fallen debris of the mine's ceiling and could not move. The light of the burning fire within the enclosed chamber was scattered and diffused by the thick shower of dust, producing an eerie glow.

Bronisław was in intense pain which seemed to radiate from his entrapped legs and torso. All he could see before him was the deformed head of his deceased partner, which protruded into the trapped chamber from the wall of fallen earthen debris that then cut Bronisław off from the main shaft.

The wounded and trapped Bronisław was in disbelief. Jerzy's skull had been crushed, with the physical distortion having stretched the skin of his friend's face into an unnatural mask. As a result of this, Jerzy's death grimace was overpainted with a macabre and haunting smile. The sickly sight seemed to float through the dispersed haze of illuminated dust like an apparition. The same dust which choked Bronisław's every breath.

Within him a panic built as he gulped chaotically for air. The sweat of the closeness of the enclosed chamber drenched him, though he knew not whether it was produced by the panic of his fear, or the product of the burning oil. All he knew for sure was that the fire produced by the oil was stealing the very air he himself needed if he was to survive until a party of miners could assemble to rescue him.

At that point, for the first time since the collapse, he heard the call of the bird that had warned him in vain throughout the day of the impending doom. It sat upon the salt-ledge they had fashioned for it earlier, just above him. When he craned his neck, seeming beyond his human limits, he could just see the animal.

Bronisław's thoughts remained as scattered as the diffused light of the chamber. He struggled to free his right arm and he was successful. However, his left arm, as well as his legs and all in-between, remained trapped under the debris. The air continued to thicken around him, and his thoughts became heavy with disorientation.

He thought of his boy, Marek. He tried to reach for the carving of the Aurochs, still in his pocket, and with a great exertion of effort was able to do so. The pain in his legs was now unbearable. He tasted salt in the back of his nose, and it drained down his throat in a thick unbearable slurry. His nerves, which still screamed in unbearable pain, slowly began to subside along with any traces of hope.

The air increasingly was pungent with the trapped smell of the burning oil. Bronisław was entombed, with only his head and right arm freed within the illuminated burning chamber. The air was hotter now, the dust thicker, when the light from the burning oil beginning to flicker wildly.

He thought of his Magda, the wonderful blessing God had given him.

Bronisław craned his neck. He heard the bird no longer. He strained with every ounce of his remaining strength to turn his head. His eyes strained, not in focusing, but in physically rotating enough to see the bird. And see it he did, just in time to watch it wobble, before falling from its enclosed perch.

His spirit fell heavily. He began to pray to God with what breaths he had left in him, and as he did, he reached out to the piece of salt stone upon which he had begun to carve the Aurochs.

Our Father, Who Art in Heaven,
Hallowed be Thy Name,

As he mouthed this, Bronisław scratched with his nail into the soft stone the letter M.

Thy Kingdom Come,
Thy Will Be Done,
On Earth as it is in Heaven,

Gathering all the control of his dying muscles that he could, he then scratched out the letter A.

Give us this day our daily bread ... Forgive us our trespasses...

He had nothing left. Neither the ability to recall the rest of the prayer, nor the strength to scratch out the next letter in the salt stone.

It was then, that the fire which burned from the oil within the chamber flashed in a last spectral surge before yielding to the total darkness. In that brief flash of light, Bronisław saw the blue haze of the morning sky, scattered with the pink and purple hues of the rising sun, above the green velvet softness of the sweet-smelling grass.

A few seconds later, Bronisław Zaczek drew his last breath in total darkness, accompanied not by the terror of all his fears, but rather by the joyous memory of his wife Magda, and his son Marek, smiling and laughing as they had waited for him on that crisp bright morning as he exited the mine. It was a precious few seconds from a dozen years ago, yet the sheer happiness of this most cherished gift carried his soul from this world as if it were cradled upon the ivory wings of angels.

18

THE UNBEARABLE GRIEF

AUGUST 1789

The news of the death of Bronisław Zaczek and his mining companion, Jerzy, seeped throughout the peasant community, hamlet to hamlet, hovel to hovel, like the spreading of the black plague. Within each hut crept not only the solemnity and utter dread from the loss of these two humble and good men, but also the residual fear - *Which of the other peasant miners would next be consumed in the unsafe chambers of Wieliczka's shafts?* The dire news affected many, if not most, of the men of the peasant community who were either currently underground or would be returning there soon. For whether they be miners, spouses, fathers or even children, all feared the devastating reality that could very easily be in store for their own families.

Ewelina was the first to hear the news of Bronisław's tragic demise. A pair of miners had slipped out of the garrison amidst all the chaos following the accident. They rushed to Ewelina to inform her of her brother's fate. They did not wish for her to have to wait until the disastrous notification eventually came from the uncaring lips of the mine's supervisors.

Even though the news of her brother's death came from the mouths of his close friends, it still assaulted her with the relentless fury of a ravenous predator. She was devastated to think of Bronisław buried deep within the mine, unable to move, gasping to draw his last breaths.

Ewelina was overcome by these thoughts of her brother's last seconds. She felt an oncoming faintness, and her limbs became numb, nothing more than useless appendages of unimaginable weight. A most sorrowful pity for Bronisław swelled within her heart. When that organ could hold not a drop more of the agony, it leaked freely through the wounds where the sharp edge of reality had gashed it.

All the while, her mind's eye was fogged with the rush of memories of her brother. First, in the pleasant moments that curled like wisps of smoke within her thoughts. Yet, even these would morph into heartbreaking visualizations of his final unendurable suffering.

Of all of Ewelina's poignant memories, foremost was that of the day Bronisław married. She had never seen her brother happier, nor more proud. Images of that joyous occasion seemed to swell within her brain, until they displaced all others. However, even these were corrupted by her unbearable distress. Then, all she could see, all that she could feel, through this day's surreal haze was his young, innocent bride Magda alone, surrounded only by a sea of turmoil.

My God, sweet Jezu! How could I have been so selfish and not thought of Magda?

Ewelina's guilt, at this point, had saved her from being completely consumed by her own torment. She braced herself and insisted on informing Magda at once. Her sons, Andrzej and Bartek, took her to Magda, supporting their mother, if not nearly carrying her outright.

Magda was in her hut, unaware of the day's sorrow. No one had the courage to be the first to tell her the bitterest of news, even though everyone by then had known. Ewelina, still bearing her own grief, went to Magda and embraced her.

In reality, it was Ewelina herself who was the most unsteady of the two women. She had trembled in such an uncontrolled fashion that Magda feared Jacek had succumbed to his wounds.

"What is it, Ewelina?" asked Magda.

Ewelina tried to respond, however only the bitterness of her tears escaped from her. Magda consoled her with comfort, stroking her face, which only made Ewelina's heart sink all the further into desolation. After many minutes, Ewelina was finally able to utter her broken thoughts.

"Our Bronisław...My dearest brother...Your loving husband... There has been an accident... In the mines... Our Bronisław is gone..."

Ewelina's words were heavy with grief. They stumbled from her lips only with a tremendous effort. They fell upon Magda and struck her like the cascade of an unyielding landslide.

Magda's hands drew back instinctively from Ewelina, and then began to tremble.

"No, no, this cannot be," said Magda. "There must be a horrible mistake in this news! Whoever has told you these things must themselves have been lied to."

Deep within her, though, Magda knew that these words were true. For she knew the heartless and vindictive nature of the man whom she had just refused. To her, nothing could be more true than the death of her Bronisław would have come from the hands of the Duke himself.

"There is no error in these words," Ewelina said through her distress. "They come from his fellow miners, who themselves carried my brother's lifeless body from below the ground. There is no mistake, I only wish that there could be ..."

The agony that was within Ewelina passed fully onto Magda, yet in no way gave either woman any relief. In their joined embrace under this darkest deluge, the two souls, already close, became one.

What was different between the two women was their response to the horror of the loss of Bronisław. Ewelina was fully consumed by her darkest emotions, and as a result her body was driven to tremors, quaking and fits of uncontrolled sobbing.

Magda, in contrast, stayed as strong as she could for Ewelina's sake. Her refusal to give in fully to her own grief only hardened the hatred for the Duke that by then had consumed her.

The most difficult thing Magda ever had to do was to tell her son Marek that day of Bronisław's death. Still ahead of her was the even more difficult task of how to tell Marek the truth about his real father. However, this day she could not steal the boy's fatherly memories of Bronisław from him.

Magda knew that she had to find the strength to tell her son the dreaded news before he heard it from another. When the difficult moment finally came, the child only looked passively upon his mother as his eyes welled up with tears. Even so, Marek fought their release. He became silent and rigid, as if in a trance.

Magda embraced him, fearing that this dark reality would drive him to the brink of insanity.

"It is as I have always feared," Marek whispered in her ear, "that one day my father would leave me and never return."

Magda clutched him within her arms all the more tightly.

"He loved you, Marek," she cried, her words muffled into the shoulder of his garment. "You were the light he carried in his heart each time he descended into those dark and dreary mines. He was always so proud of you."

The boy was still and unresponsive to his mother's words of comfort.

"Do not worry, *Matka*," Marek then said as he reached to gently pull her arms from around him, "for I will take care of you just as *Tata* would have. His strength will come to you through me."

With these words, Marek took both of her hands in his, and kissed his mother tenderly upon her cheek. Magda thought this a good sign, that the boy had empathy for her even in dealing with his own grief, until she realized it was merely Marek's way of removing himself from the captivity of her embrace.

Marek had kissed his mother, but still in a cold and docile way, before he released her trembling hands and walked away from her to be alone with his precious thoughts of Bronisław.

Marek's response hardened her, as if it were a message from Bronisław to deny herself from wallowing in the morass of her own emotions. She knew she could not travel on that low road of sorrowful commiseration that Ewelina was journeying upon. Nor could she herself tread on that high path of pained isolation as did her son. She had to deal with the reality of this loss, and steeled herself to do so.

When the foreman eventually came to Magda hours later to tell her of her husband's death, the only thing left to squeeze from Magda's shattered soul were the words, "Take me to him."

"It is of no use, Magda, for he is forever gone to God," replied the foreman.

"Take me to him," insisted Magda, not accepting his answer. "He is my husband, and you will take me to him."

"It is impossible. I would have to get permission from the Duke himself."

"Take me to my Bronisław," Magda said. "This instant, take me and my Marek so that we can lay eyes upon his crushed and tattered body."

But his body is neither crushed nor tattered, thought the foreman. "I know I will regret this, Magda," he said, "but gather your boy, and come with me."

The foreman led the mother and son to the mine. It was a great distance during which no one spoke. Magda and Marek tread their steps in a surreal state of disbelief.

Magda would, upon their reckoning procession, lapse into infrequent but sorrowful torrents of tears, which she cried into the shoulder of Marek. The boy would hold her close, but would say nothing other than that he would remain strong for her. In time, Magda would recover herself, and restrain her emotions further until they welled up within her once more. When they could no longer be ignored, they would pour forth in another outburst.

When they reached the square of Wieliczka, Magda realized it was only the second time that Marek had ever been there. The first had been his greatest joy, and now that pleasant memory would be forever overshadowed by a deeper and more unforgettable sorrow.

Magda thought that Marek's stoic response was from the shock of the news, yet in reality it was the manifestation of the anger that had penetrated him like rigid staves of hardwood. For Marek knew someone was to blame for his *tata* having been taken from him in so untimely a manner. He knew not at whom he was angry, Marek just felt its tension ratchet ever tighter within him.

They came upon the brick garrison enclosing the main mine shaft of Wieliczka. The foreman led them through the arched entry gate into the foreyard. He paused as Magda and Marek caught sight of the two bodies, which were laid out upon the stony courtyard grounds, covered with a simple rawhide.

Magda and Marek were then taken to stand over the still covered bodies. Around them rose the brick walls of the garrison, which protected them both from the gaze of curious on-lookers. The heavy gray sky threatened to fall down upon them all.

"Uncover him," demanded Magda, her hand urgently grasping that of Marek. He was her lifeline, and she held onto to him desperately, as much as anyone drowning in a river would clutch a rope thrown to them.

The foreman dropped to one knee. He gently pulled back the rawhide covering tenderly, as if too swift a movement would harm the corpse further. Of course, it was not any damage to the body he feared, only that to the eyes and minds of its surviving wife and son.

The face and chest were all that was revealed to them. Neither was crushed nor deformed. The skin was not even bruised, although it bore the unearthly hue of a grayish green pallor throughout. Even this was further tainted with an overcoating of the gray dust of salt stone. The faint but unmistakeable smell of death mixed with the murky scent of burnt oil.

"He was trapped, but not crushed," said the foreman. "Jerzy, his fellow miner, was not so lucky, for his body was mangled in the first seconds of the collapse."

Marek cast an incriminating eye at the foreman for his thoughtless and disrespectful use of such descriptive words in front of his grieving mother.

Yet, Magda was lost in her thoughts from years ago, when she was so young and naïve, at the hands of the Duke.

"Jerzy was the lucky one..." she muttered, as if from deep within a trance. "How long did it take for my Bronisław to die?"

The foreman felt the weight of the question upon him as soon as it left Magda's lips. He knew he should not answer, however, he could not bear the burden of the question's massive weight.

"Not very long," he answered, "for there was a fire in the chamber he was entrapped in. It burned rapidly, but away from your husband. He was not even singed by it, yet the air he needed to live was consumed by the flames very swiftly."

"Until his soul was merely absorbed into the darkness that surrounded him..." Magda repeated aloud the words of the Duke from long ago, as if they were from another life. She turned her head again into the shoulder of her son and cried from the guilt of her initial submission to the Duke so many years ago. And only for this, its ultimate result.

Marek could not help but feel the distraught and wretched emotion roiling within his mother. She heaved with agony. She clutched at his garments desperately. All the while she clung to him, to the strength that he had become for her. He understood that he was all she would have in her life going forward.

"This was found near his hand," said the foreman. "The young apprentice, Lech, said that he was carving an Aurochs for you, Marek."

"I have long told *Tata*," Marek stated aloud, as if to no one, "that I was too old for such things..."

Tears collected in the corners of Marek's eyes. That was when Magda collected herself and raised her head from her son's shoulder.

"What happened to this boy, Lech, that he was not killed?" asked Magda through her tears. She had recalled the story her Bronisław had told her of his once being an apprentice.

"He was fortunate. Bronisław sent him back to the encampment for oil. For certain, it saved the boy's life," said the foreman.

"He saved the boy," said Magda, stepping forward as her husband's heroic act dawned upon her. "It is just as he, as a boy, had been saved so many years before..."

"So, *Tata* knew their lives were in danger," said Marek. His mother having removed herself from his embrace, Marek then took the partially carved figure from the foreman, who still knelt next to the body of Bronisław.

Marek inspected the unfinished work. He then pointed out to his mother the letters MA scratched upon its unfinished surface. "He was either trying to scratch out your or my name, *Matka*."

Magda recalled teaching Bronisław to spell both her name and Marek's. It was all the literacy her husband possessed. He could not even spell his own name. Only those of the two loves of his life, so he could cut their names into the expressive gifts that his hands would carve. Except, now, these hands would never carve again.

"He was thinking of us both," Magda said through her tears, "I am sure of this."

In the moments that followed, Marek once more held his mother tightly as she again slipped into an uncontrollable sorrow. Her body shuddered with grief as she stood over the corpse of her loving husband. After a few minutes, she collected herself as much as was possible. She dried the tears from her face, and the calm of a great resolve overcame her.

"It is time," she said simply. This the foremen took to mean it was time to go, but actually what she had referred to was her son. It was time to commit her Marek, the product of her forced liaison with the salacious Duke, to the Church of *Jezu Chrystus*.

The foreman, still on his knees, began to cover the chest and face of Bronisław with the rawhide covering when Marek defiantly yelled out the words, *"Stop! Move away!"*

The foreman, although taken back by the boy's audacity, obeyed Marek's command. He stood and then moved away from the body, yielding the precious space to the mother and son.

It was then that Marek helped his mother down to her knees before he himself knelt alongside her. Then, mother and son, wife and child, prayed over the bodily remains of Bronisław Zaczek to the Virgin Mary to intercede for the salvation of his soul.

Magda then leaned forward and kissed Bronisław gently on the lips. When she had finished, Marek kissed his father on his forehead. Marek then helped his mother to her feet, and without a word between them, they began their walk back to the peasant village as the sun set in the west. They journeyed through a falling shroud of dusk, and arrived at their empty home amidst the deepening hues of darkness.

19

THE COUNT'S RETURN

SEPTEMBER 1789

Weeks later, on the twenty-first of the new month, Count Von Arndt arrived at the Duke's *folwark*. It was typical of him to stop at the estate for a day or two on his trip to the provincial capital of Lemberg, another several day's ride further east. Lemberg was the Austrian name for the old Polish town of Lwów, and here the Count would carry out provincial business matters on behalf of the Emperor.

The Count made this journey twice each year, in the spring and the early fall. It was not lost on the Duke that the Count, who was himself a citizen of the resplendent city of Vienna, considered the Galician province, including its capital of Lemberg, as worse than just the backwater of the Empire. Indeed, Von Arndt considered it a cultural desert.

The Duke had welcomed his overseer to his *folwark* once more. This time the Duke was eager to see the Count's reaction to the newly completed addition of the opulent guest house. However, the Count seemed to be very anxious upon his arrival, pre-occupied with another matter. After settling into his new quarters, the Count demanded a rapid engagement with the Duke to discuss the shifting demands of the Emperor.

"What does my Count think of the *accoutrements* of the newly completed guest house?" asked the Duke.

"It is very fine, my Duke, however this we can discuss later," said Von Arndt. "There are great on-goings in Paris we must discuss. Emperor Joseph II demands more conscripts to the Imperial Army. He fears war with France is imminent." The Count's face visibly wore the very same concern.

"War with France," asked the Duke incredibly, "but is not his own sister King Louis XVI's Queen?"

"This the Emperor regrets very much, at this point," responded the Count. "In fact, he is calling for an effort to rescue Marie Antoinette from the French, yet her husband is refusing to abandon his country."

"Abandon his reign? It is incredible that the King would even be harboring this thought," said the Duke. "What could have gone wrong so abruptly in France?"

"The French are rebelling against their monarch's rule. After the costly war with Britain supporting the Americans, the King needed once more to raise taxes. The starving peasants, driven by severe food shortages, revolted and demanded representation in a lesson they had learned from the Americans. That was when King Louis thought he could appease them by convening the Estates General, an advisory convocation, for the first time in over one-hundred and seventy years."

"Yet, I take this did not pacify the peasantry?" asked the Duke.

"Not at all, for they soon saw what the King already knew: that the Third Estate, that is the peasants' representatives, would merely get outvoted by the other two estates, those being the clergy and the nobility," explained the Count.

"And this only enraged the peasants all the more?" asked the Duke.

"Yes, the peasants rebelled at this injustice," said Count Von Arndt. "It was then that King Louis, the buffoon, responded by locking the representatives of the Third Estate out of the convention altogether. Instead they then met on a nearby tennis court, where they took an oath to continue to represent the people. They formed what they called the National Assembly. Two months ago, in July, on the fourteenth, masses of peasants revolted and attacked the city fortress and prison known as the Bastille. Those horrid creatures began to tear it apart, brick by brick, stone by stone. Can you imagine?"

"And what of the King and Queen?" asked the Duke.

"They are still in the Palace at Versailles, however they are virtual prisoners there. For the King and Queen to leave its gates, they subject themselves to attack from the people. The masses have swallowed the concept of '*popular sovereignty*' as put forth by the Enlightenment. They refuse to accept that the reigning monarchs have any authority over them whatsoever."

"This National Assembly, do they hide behind the discontent of the peasants?" asked the Duke.

"Not hide, Duke Sdanowicz," the Count continued, "for the *Jacobin* leaders, as they are called, are as clever as the jackals that they are. They agitate the masses only to gain even more privileges for this rabble with their promulgations. This month alone they have issued proclamations to abolish serfdom in France and eliminate the requirement of a one-tenth tithe to the church. The world has turned upside down. Even now, I am told they prepare to issue a '*Declaration of the Rights of Man*' that will all but eradicate the preferred rights of the nobles and clergy alike. Can you imagine where this may lead?"

The Duke could only think of how dangerous these thoughts and actions would be if they were extended to the peasants of his *folwark*.

"Yes, this is extremely serious," said Duke Sdanowicz. "I can see where the Emperor must fear that this rebellious contagion will spread to Austria."

"To Austria? To all of Europe itself!" proclaimed the Count. Von Arndt began to nervously pace the floor as if his mind alone comprehended the utter gravity of what was occurring in Paris. But, the Duke, himself, was quickly absorbing the importance of the moment. He understood that this malignancy would be quick to spread eastward.

"Do you think that the Emperor will attack France to save Marie Antoinette?" asked Duke Sdanowicz.

"No, not at this point. However, that is exactly what the peasants and the National Assembly of France believe," answered the Count. "They prepare for an invasion, and at some point the Emperor believes they will attack their neighboring states in the name of spreading this unholy Revolution. For this eventual war, he needs more conscripts. Massive amounts of new conscripts."

"Yes, of course," said the Duke, as he continued to think through the scenario. "One must assume that Prussia and Russia are also reacting in this same manner."

The Duke had never seen the Count in this agitated of a state before. The concern for the survival of all the monarchs of Europe was alive in his eyes.

"With the passing of Frederick II only three years ago," said Count Von Arndt, "one would think that his successor, Emperor Frederick Wilhelm II, would be greatly concerned with this revolutionary thinking spreading east to Prussia. As far as Catherine of Russia is concerned, she must feel her country is so far removed from France physically that revolution will never reach her doorstep in the Royal Courts of St. Petersburg. But I tell you, this is a false security."

"I think Emperor Joseph is wise to be concerned," said the Duke. "These things tend to spread swiftly if they are not promptly and forcibly put down, and it does not appear King Louis XVI has the fortitude to do so. He has waited too long to act, if indeed the masses are destroying the fortresses of Paris with their own hands. I do have conscripts available for the Emperor, including my own stable master and his two sons, all of whom I would think would be of high value in maintaining the horses of the Austrian cavalry. I also have several excess miners to conscript as well, perhaps as many as twenty in all."

"Excellent! Excellent!" said the Count, "This will please Emperor

Joseph. We would like to think the worst of the situation in Paris is behind us, yet it may not be at all. Now, let us discuss the disaster that recently befell the Wieliczka mine."

The Duke noticed how quickly the Count was to change the conversation once his conscription concerns were addressed. Sdanowicz anticipated that the Count wishes to assure even with these miners becoming soldiers that the mine will still meet its output quotas. For all the Count is concerned with is fulfilling his promises to the Emperor.

"Hardly a disaster, my Count," answered Duke Sdanowicz. "Only a simple shaft collapse. These things occur ever so infrequently. Merely two dead miners. But do not be concerned, for even with these conscriptions I still have many replacements to select from. This accident is merely an inconvenience, nothing more."

"Therefore, you will still make your monthly quota?" asked the Count.

"Yes, but of course," answered the Duke. He had decided not to raise the issue of the inferior Austrian timber as being the source of the collapse with his guest, as the Austrian suppliers had recently improved their quality. Besides, the Duke was certain that the Count would only lay the issue of the collapse, caused by the timber's extended spacing, at his own feet.

"Then, I presume there is nothing more for us to discuss before dinner," said the Count, "so, why don't you have that lovely peasant, Magda, from your staff assigned to my service in the guest house quarters while I am staying here?"

The Count had an impish smirk upon his face. He had clearly remembered Magda with great fervor.

"I am sorry to disappoint you, my Count," said the Duke, "but that will not be possible at this time."

"Please explain to me as to why, exactly, this is not possible, my Duke," retorted the Count. "I do recall you promising me her services once the guest house was completed. Did you not?"

"Your recollection is correct, as always, my Count," Sdanowicz responded deferentially. "However, fate has intervened. She is in the clutches of mourning, my lord, for her husband was one of the two miners lost in the accident we just discussed."

The Count looked away dejectedly. "Yes, I see. She would not be of much value to me in that state, now would she?"

20

THE LAST FRENCH LESSON

SEPTEMBER 1789

The next day, just after the Count had left the Duke's estate, Sister Maryja Elizabeta arrived to tutor the children in their French language lessons. The Duke, having received her into the manor house, was explaining to the Sister that Marek would not be joining them due to the death of his father.

"How horrible for Magda," said the Sister, "I must go to her and help her through this terrible loss. It is a friend's embrace, as well as the touch of the Spirit, that gets one through an ordeal as trying as this."

"Yes, Sister, we will arrange for you to see her on your next visit. Magda has asked to be left alone with her thoughts and family at this time," lied the Duke boldly.

It was just as Sister Maryja Elizabeta was recovering from the initial shock of the news when the clearly heartbroken Marek appeared in the entry hall of the manor house. Young Maya, who had been greatly concerned for her grieving friend, rushed forward upon seeing him and flung herself in his arms. The Duke, after gently but physically peeling his daughter away from his bastard son, put his hands upon the boy's broadening shoulders.

"Marek, it is so good to see you here with us," said the Duke warmly. "We were all so very sorry to hear of your father's accident in the mines. How is your *matka*, my boy? She must be bearing a burden we cannot imagine. Tell her not to worry, that I will take care of you all, for it is the least of what I can do as your Duke."

Sister Maryja Elizabeta knew he had said all this only for her benefit, not Magda's. She knew this from the pain she had seen in Magda's eyes during her earlier visits, and from the disregard for the Duke's words that she read at that moment even in young Marek's eyes.

The Duke left them in the library, and the good Sister taught the children. More precise it would be to state that she attempted to teach the children, for Marek was greatly distracted, as one could only expect. Maya, on the other hand, seemed to be totally engrossed in the quiet suffering of Marek.

The nun realized the affinity that had grown over time between these children. She also knew, that if her suspicions were correct from reading Magda's pain earlier, that the Duke had fathered them both. As such, any flame of attraction between the two had to be expeditiously and thoroughly doused.

They struggled through their studies for another hour, before Sister Maryja Elizabeta decided to cut off the lesson. It was then that Marek moved forward to the nun, embracing her. He palmed her a note in French which read, *"I urgently need to see you. Please allow Marek to bring you to me."* It was signed, *"Your pupil Magdalena, who needs your help most at this dark hour!"*

21

ESCAPE FROM THE FOLWARK

SEPTEMBER 1789

Sister Maryja Elizabeta followed Marek to the stables, presumably to have the boy prepare her horse for the ride back to the convent in Kraków. Unexpectedly, the Duke's daughter followed them. It was then that the nun turned to Maya and explained that she had to go to Marek's *matka* and console her. It was then that the Sister mounted her horse, Marek another, and the boy took a third in lead by the hand.

They arrived at the hut that was home to Marek and Magda. The nun rushed into the hovel and embraced her former student. She could see that Magda's eyes were red with the abrasion of constant sobbing. She saw something else in Magda, a weariness that came from carrying the weight of a burdensome secret for many years. It was a secret she was no longer able to conceal.

"My darling Magda," said Sister Maryja Elizabeta as she embraced her former pupil, "how your heart must break with your loss."

Magda merely turned to her son and said, "Marek, I need you to allow me to speak to the good Sister alone. Please go outside, but do not go far, for as we discussed we have a great journey ahead of us."

"Yes, *Matka*," answered the boy obediently, "but I will be very close, as you request, should you need me."

After the boy left the hut, Sister Maryja Elizabeta continued her attempted consolation of Magda. "Although it breaks our hearts, we can never understand the moment that the Lord takes our loved ones."

Magda then turned to the nun. "The Lord did not take my Bronisław, good Sister. His death is at the hands of the Duke. We do not have much time. I can explain as we ride."

"Ride where?" asked the nun.

"I need you to take Marek and myself to the convent in Kraków. There I will commit the child to the church."

"Of what child do you speak?" asked the Sister.

"Why, Marek, of course," said Magda.

"And he knows of this intention?" asked the nun.

"He knows he loves his *Matka!* He is a most obedient boy, he will do what I ask of him."

"Can you be so sure, Magda? Are you aware the Duke's daughter has grown so greatly fond of him?" The Sister could see this comment sparked an eruption of angst in Magda's face.

"Yes, and this can never be allowed," said Magda sternly.

"Who is the boy's father, my child?" asked the nun, as delicately as she could.

"He has no father," Magda said, as she dodged the direct question. It was a ridiculous response, yet these were the only words her fragmented mind could think to pass to her lips.

"Magda, do not speak blasphemy to me! You can tell me anything, and I will never judge you, child. All children have fathers, and if I had read your eyes correctly since I have come to the *folwark*, then I must conclude that Marek is the Duke's issue, is he not?"

Magda blushed at hearing the words she wished were not true. She lowered her head. "Yes," she said, "and my shame consumes me. It was a sin forced upon me, please believe me."

Sister Maryja Elizabeta moved forward to take Magda in her arms, "Oh, my poor Magda, of course I believe you. I recognized the grief in you from my first visit here, only because I too once was taken against my will. It is his sin, child, not yours."

"You, Sister? This sin has touched you also?" asked Magda incredulously.

"Men only know force, Magda. For this, they will one day meet the force of God's judgement," said the nun. "So, the Duke forced himself upon you?"

"Yes," she replied, her tears welling within her.

"And you resisted?" asked the nun.

"Not enough, and I am very ashamed for this," cried Magda as a fresh cascade of tears began to flow. "He threatened my husband's life with an accident in the mines. Even then, so many years ago, he described it just as it has occurred now. It is my sin that I did not fight that evil man with all the strength my body possessed."

"And you would only have been bruised and possibly disfigured," said Sister Maryja Elizabeta. "Nothing else would have changed. Yet for this 'sin' you wish to commit Marek's life to a destiny his heart may not desire?"

"Yes," Magda said, "for I have committed him in my prayers long ago, since his birth, to the service of the Lord."

"You know God forgives you, my Magda," said Sister Maryja Elizabeta. "You realize this offering of the boy's life is not necessary."

"No, but it is, good Sister," explained Magda, "for now the Duke has taken my Bronisław exactly as he had once threatened."

The Sister noted that this was the second time Magda had said this. There was more that the young woman wished to tell her.

"Why would he wait eighteen years to take your husband's life?" asked the nun, quickly calculating the age of Marek plus the nine months of her pregnancy with him.

"Only three days ago, I rejected the Duke's advances once again. He was emboldened as he attempted to force himself upon me once more. However this time I resisted him, and for this boldness of mine the Duke has taken my husband's life." Magda then began sobbing inconsolably.

Sister Maryja Elizabeth took her deeper into her arms. "You

did the right thing according to God, my dear," she comforted Magda. "It must be only a coincidence."

"It matters not," Magda said, choking upon her own emotions. "Whether it be by the Duke's hand or by fate itself, I am responsible for Bronisław's death. I have two mortal sins now for which I must be absolved: one as the result of yielding to the Duke's treachery; and the other for resisting it."

At this point, Magda broke down and shuddered with despair. Sister Maryja Elizabeta attempted to comfort her, yet immediately realized the only consolation would be to take both her and Marek to the convent, just as Magda had requested.

"It is all right, my lovely girl," said the nun as she stroked the hair of the thirty-seven-year-old Magda, whose head was bowed in shame. "I will take you to Mother Angelica, and she will decide your fate. There you will be freed of this evil Duke. Come, let's get on."

Magda's tears and heaviness lifted somewhat, and she then called upon Marek to assist them. They mounted the three horses and departed directly to Kraków without returning to the manor house.

They rode for some time before coming upon the bridge that crossed the Vistula into Kraków. As they approached the river, Sister Maryja Elizabeta said to Magda, "Allow me only to speak, even if the guards ask questions directly of you or Marek."

"Yes, of course," Magda said. She thought of Marek and realized that he had never been across this river. He had never seen the great sights of the remarkable city of Kraków that awaited them on the opposite bank. How exciting this would have been for Marek, had he not been wallowing in the depths of mourning for his father. Instead of the great excitement that it should have been for the boy, the crossing would be lost in a deluge of immeasurable sorrows.

The three riders came to the Austrian border guard. The barrier had been lowered, stopping anyone from crossing the bridge.

"My good man, please allow us to pass. I have my papers in

order and this woman and her son are under my care, *en route* to the convent in Kraków."

The border guard looked at the nun, measuring her with his gaze, as if determining how sternly he would admonish her. He decided he did not need for her to register a complaint against him to the Bishop.

"Many apologies, Sister, however the border is closed. No one passes in either direction, upon command of the Emperor's Envoy, Count Maximilian Von Arndt."

"But I am engaged in the Lord's work, sir. Dare you intercede in its completion? Would you bring the wrath of God upon yourself and your family in doing so?"

"I am sorry, Sister. I have my orders. Absolutely no one is to cross this border. I have all respect for Our Lord above, and wish not to enrage him in any way, but I must execute the Envoy's order, lest the Emperor decide to execute me for not carrying out my duties."

"Why is the bridge closed?" asked the nun, unsure if the guard would even respond. "What event has caused the Count to even declare it be so?"

Once again the border guard assessed her, as to how much information she was entitled. He then thought once more of the wrath of God, or at least his high clergy. He then decided a brief explanation would be in order.

"There has been an attempt on the Count Von Arndt's carriage. He is unharmed. It is merely another futile attack by simple petty highwaymen. The Count's guards are in pursuit of the bandits. They wish them not to escape into Poland. Thus, until we are directed otherwise, this bridge into Kraków and all the border crossings into Poland are closed."

Night was beginning to fall. Sister Maryja Elizabeta's head was running through many scenarios at this point. What would they do if they could not cross until the morning? Would the Duke's daughter tell of Marek's taking the nun to their hovel with two other horses? Had the Duke already sent a party to track them down? If so, how far were they behind them?

Turning back to the young woman, Sister Maryja Elizabeta said, "Magda, I have another idea, please allow yourself and Marek to follow me."

With having said this, the nun led them to the road that followed upriver alongside the Vistula. As the sun set behind the trees, its pale reflection upon the river's waters seemed to float just beyond their collective reach. It was as if their destiny was being denied to them, although it was held teasingly near, as if to draw them all into the enticing depths of the river's deadly waters.

After a long ride, the three wanderers came upon the walls of the fortress of Tyniec. This was the Benedictine Monastery that had once been the refuge of some of the last remaining rebels of the Bar Confederation many years ago, in the months following the birth of Marek. The monastery at Tyniec was as strong a fortification as one could hope to survive within. It was situated high on a point of land atop a limestone cliff overlooking the Vistula. Here they would be safe for the night, and once the border crossing was opened, they could sally forth to the convent in Kraków.

What they did not realize was that, despite his daughter Maya having said nothing, the missing Arabians were noticed. Soon enough, it became known that Marek and Magda were also missing. Indeed, the Duke had sent out a party to recover the nun and his two peasants. The Sister was accused of providing them an escape from his *folwark*. They were, at that point, off of the estate without his permission, and by law, any force necessary could be used in ensuring their return.

Sister Maryja Elizabeta was granted entrance to the monastery. There she described Magda's intention to commit her son to the order. Upon hearing this, the evening watch of the monastery deemed it appropriate to open its doors to the refugees that were Magda and Marek.

Just in time, one might conclude, for the party of guardsmen sent forth by Duke Sdanowicz had arrived in less than a half hour after Magda and Marek entered the sanctuary.

22

THE SIEGE AT TYNIEC

SEPTEMBER 1789

The next morning, word had come to the fortification that the border between Austrian Galicia and Poland was once again open. This no longer mattered, for the Duke's horsemen had blockaded the entrance to the monastery. Any attempt to leave its walls by Magda, Marek or Sister Maryja Elizabeta would have resulted in their capture and immediate return to the Duke's *folwark*.

The Benedictine Monks cared for their guests in the most welcoming of manners. The night before, all were fed, and provided humble quarters for their rest, although none of the three would rest that first night at all. The next morning, Sister Maryja Elizabeta had called upon Marek and Magda to attend the sunrise service in the Church of Saints Peter and Paul, which stood proudly within the confines of the walled monastery. There, Magda prayed for the repose of the soul of her dearest departed Bronisław. Sister Maryja Elizabeta prayed for the Lord's comfort to come upon her former student and vanquish her misery. Marek prayed, with the selfishness of young love, above all else, to be safely and promptly reunited with his beautiful *Maya Manuska*.

As Magda, upon her knees, prayed for the salvation of Bronisław's soul, the combination of her devout belief intensified by her lack of adequate rest drew her into a somber trance. Her mind was already perforated with confusion, for the entire night before she had slept not in the least. She had a clutch of worries weighing upon her, stealing any hope of respite.

During the morning mass, the repetition of Magda's silent prayers to the Virgin Mother calmed her somewhat. She became disassociated from the physical world around her. And then, impossible as it may appear, Magda experienced a religious intercession like none she had ever known before.

Figure 5: The Benedictine Monastery at Tyniec

Triggered by the first aromatic whiffs of the burning incense and accompanied by the rhythmic chanting of the assembled monks, Magda was lulled into a reverie, where she alone was primary, and all else within the massive church faded into oblivion. She then felt a presence come upon her like a touch of tingling fever which soon spread through the whole of her physical being, until she surrendered herself to it. She then felt as if her entire body were immersed in the heat of a dazzling white light, from which she heard a voice speak to her.

The voice of the presence said clearly unto her, ***"Magdalena, daughter of the szlachta once betrayed, suffering child of God, give your son, by his own will, unto me."***

The voice reverberated through her as does the shudder of a great fear. Yet, it was just the opposite of foreboding. This spirit quaked within her, and its every resonance seemed to not only calm the dread within her, but slay her every concern. Like the smoke of the incense, it spread slowly, but deeply through her entire being. The voice was one not known to her, although it seemed to carry familiar sub-tones within its timbre. The most evident of these were the touch of love in her mother's call, as well as the subtle lightness of Bronisław's laugh. Magda found this spiritual intonation to be so very reassuring. It eased her anxieties, and for the first time, she felt the blessing of serenity. She then knew exactly what she must do.

She knew she must stop allowing herself to be called by the name that was the result of the Duke imprisoning her upon his *folwark*. She was christened Magdalena to a noble *szlachta* family, and it was by this name the Spirit had called her. While she was not ashamed of her peasant life, from this point on she would answer only to the name Magdalena.

She also knew that it was her duty to God to have her son, Marek, commit his life to the Church. So it was said clearly by the Spirit's voice. Unsaid, but felt nonetheless by Magdalena in the Spirit's touch, was that her failure to complete this tasking would result not only in the damnation of her own soul, but also would lead her son astray upon a very treacherous path of sin.

Then, as passingly as she had attained this enlightened state, it was taken from away from her. She had the sensation of falling back to reality. She tried with all her might to recover its calm, yet with no success, as it dispersed like the vapor of a dream upon waking. The more she attempted to clutch onto the voice and all of its manifestations, the more abruptly they had been driven from her.

Magda looked up to find several monks, Sister Maryja Elizabeta, and Marek staring at her, for she had risen to her feet in the portion of the mass when everyone else around her kneeled. It was then that they all began to wobble in her sight, before a cloak of darkness overtook her.

Magda awoke to discover them all hovering over her. Sister Maryja Elizabeta was stroking her face. She was lying in the main aisle of the church, her back flat upon its tiled floor. The service had been interrupted for the brothers to attend to her. Having realized after a few minutes she was regaining herself, they gently carried her to the narthex. Sister Maryja Elizabeta told the brothers that she would care for the woman and that they should return to the service. This they did, and the service was continued.

"*Matka*, are you injured in any way?" asked Marek with great concern, "you look so pale."

Sister Maryja Elizabeta was holding the woman's hand in her own. With the strain of apprehension in her own eyes, the nun looked into Magda's. There, all the good Sister found was the tranquility of the ages.

"Marek, please get some water for your *matka*," said the Sister. She wished to speak to the child's mother alone. Marek went off in search of water.

"Magda," the nun began, "what has happened?"

"*Magdalena*, Sister" the woman began. "My name is *Magdalena*."

The good Sister looked upon her with such a tremendous empathy, one that truly only these two women could share. The Sister was worried that her one-time student had struck her head upon her fall. She worried that Magda had incurred a loss of the cerebral, when in fact she had gained a touch of the celestial. Or so, she would discover, the young woman thought.

"The Holy Ghost came over me, Sister," Magdalena said upon noticing the Nun's confusion, "and told me I am not, and have never been a peasant. It is all right, Sister, I know what I must do. We are here today not by accident, not by the coincidence of the bridge being closed to us, but rather we were guided here by the Spirit's hand. I must meet with the Abbott. Tell him of the Duke's treachery. Then, I must convince Marek to commit his life to this order. I must convince both my son and the Abbott that Marek's life is to be committed to God."

"My child," replied the nun, "you are exhausted. Your guilt is playing tricks upon you."

"No, Sister," Magdalena said calmly, "I have no longer have any guilt. For I am sure of the path forward. It has been shown to me by the Spirit."

Sister Maryja Elizabeta looked once more into the eyes of the young woman. The solace she found there was immovable and pervasive. It was complete.

"You must think of your parents in Russia, child," said Sister Maryja Elizabeta, "for if you declare yourself their daughter, after they had declared you once dead, how might this affect their lives further?"

"I could feel the love of my own *Matka* in the voice of the Spirit, telling me it was proper," said Magdalena.

"What will Marek think of you abandoning the name by which his *tata* had always called you?" asked the nun.

"I could hear the laugh of Bronisław in the Spirit as well, telling me that he approved," said Magdalena. "All is clear to me."

Just then, Marek arrived with a cup of cold water. He held it to his mother's lips, and as she drank from it she stroked her son's still-boyish looking face. He would become a man soon enough. A man committed to God.

Afterwards, when Magdalena was stronger, the three of them were for the first time brought before the community of monks again to join in their providence and good fortune. A simple breakfast was shared with them. They were seated at the bench of the utmost authority within the monastery, that being the Abbott named Dawid. The Abbott was a simple man, dressed in the same plain brown sackcloth robes with modest rope belts as his monks. The small amount of hair that he allowed to adorn his head was as silver as the gleaming altar chalice from the church. His years were not as advanced as his appearance would indicate, but his responsibilities were great, and these had over the years produced many worries which gnarled at the Abbott faster than time itself.

The food was brought to them, and they ate. All except for Magdalena who continued only to look upon the Abbott with a passive, knowing smile.

"I am sorry for your collapsing in the service, my child," he said to Magdalena, gauging her state of being. He found her to be calm, peaceful and relaxed.

"Do not be sorry, Reverend Father, but rather be joyous," said Magdalena, "for the Spirit of the Holy Ghost has touched me."

Abbott Dawid was inwardly shocked at this statement yet affected not to let this be known. Instead, he attempted to draw more from her.

"That is truly joyous, child," he said, "for each of us to experience the Spirit is God's greatest gift. We shall speak more of this after we breakfast. Please eat, my guests. "

Abbott Dawid finished his food quickly, and then explained as his guests ate, all once again except Magdalena, that the Benedictine order had been installed in this location since the year 1040 by Kazimierz the Restorer. It had undergone many sieges, he explained, and he was quite confident it could withstand the small party of the Duke's horsemen encamped outside its walls. These walls, after all, had harbored some of the last of the Confederates of Bar within this compound, with much greater adversarial forces kept at bay.

There was so much more at stake during those earlier confrontations than some petty squabble with the Duke over a peasant woman's treatment. The Abbott knew and explained to his guests that neither the Duke, nor his men, would attempt to enter the monastery by force for two reasons. The first was the time-honored concept of all Holy Churches as being considered as sanctuaries for refugees. For had the Duke's men even attempted to breach these walls, the issue would become one between Duke Sdanowicz and the Holy See in Rome. This would also bring the Duke into an improper favor with the Austrian Emperor, Joseph II.

The second reason the Duke's men would make no attempt to enter the monastery would prove to be even more of a dissuading concern for the Duke. For despite the monastery having been on the Austrian side of the river, it was legally considered to be an extension of the town of Kraków. The same consideration extended to the town of Debnicki, just outside the monastery's walls. This town was officially a suburb of Kraków, even though it was seven miles away from the Polish city, and across the river that generally separated Poland from Austria.

Certainly, the Duke would not risk an international incident by directing his men to attempt to forcibly enter the monastery. On the other hand, the monks could do nothing other than acknowledge the line of the Duke's horsemen outside their walls. The guards were evenly spaced, and as the monastery was situated on a point in the bend of the river, this short line of horsemen was indeed effective in restricting any of the three refugees from leaving the monastery compound.

After breakfast, Abbott Dawid escorted Magdalena into his private quarters. She requested, and was granted by the Abbott, permission to have Sister Maryja Elizabeta join her. Marek was not present. As the Abbott sat down at his private table to begin the discussion, he mentioned that he had allowed the three of them entrance into the monastery the previous night only upon the good Sister explaining briefly the nature of their situation.

"I am told, Magda, that you wish to commit your son's life to the monastery?" the Abbott asked more than stated.

"*Magdalena*, Reverend Father," she corrected him, "Please call me *Magdalena*. It is the form of my name by which the Spirit has called me."

"I see," said Abbott Dawid as he arched his eyebrows at the request. He thought the name too glamorous for a peasant woman yet decided to accommodate her request. Nonetheless, he decided he would shock the woman with a very direct question.

"So, Magdalena, why is it you wish your vibrant, young son to serve God? Is it to atone for his sins or yours?"

"Mine alone, Reverend Father," she responded without hesitation, "for you will forgive me in being so coarse, but my son, Marek, was not of my husband. He is the result of an attack upon me by Duke Sdanowicz."

The Abbott once again raised his eyebrows in response. "This is a very serious allegation for you to be making, my child. And if proven true, why do you consider this your own sin against God?"

"Oh, most Reverend Father, it is true, I assure you! It is my sin, for I did not resist as I should have when the Duke forced himself on me." Magdalena did not lower her head in shame, as she was full of the Spirit.

"And from the age of your boy, Magdalena," the Abbott stated, "that was a long time ago. You have waited this long to address your sin, my child? Did you not confess this to the priests on the *folwark*?"

"I could not bring myself to do so, Reverend Father. I feared that the shame of the secret would become known. I know now it was wrong to do so. I also know that God has forgiven me."

The Abbott looked at her, judging as to whether she was fabricating all of this for the purpose of punishing the Duke for general ill-treatment of herself or, perhaps, even her peasant friends. He asked himself, *Was this child simply confused as a result of her swooning during the service? Of course, there was always the possibility that the devil himself had taken refuge within her soul, was there not?*

That is when Sister Maryja Elizabeta interjected, "Reverend Father, long ago Magdalena was a child of a *szlachta* Duke who was entrusted to my tutelage at the convent in Kraków. She left the convent after her parents were exiled by the King to Russia. She departed under the care of Duke Sdanowicz. The Duke then betrayed her and cast her into the peasantry. She was married to the peasant man who recently was crushed to death in the salt mines at Wieliczka. Most Reverend Father, she was married to him for five years and bore him no children. It was not until the Duke expended his lust upon her that she conceived Marek. And for the seventeen years of Marek's life, she has laid faithfully with her husband, as a good Catholic wife, and attempted to bear his children with no results. Surely, this is proof of her truthfulness."

The Abbott was carefully listening to what amounted to testimony from the two women with skepticism. "The ways of the Lord's Sacred Heart in granting the gift of children cannot be understood by mere mortals, my good Sister. After all, Abraham and Sarah were denied this gift until they achieved the oldest of ages, were they not?"

The nun looked in a conflicted manner at Abbott Dawid and his twisted logic. *Why were men so slow to believe of the incredible cruelty that resided in other men's hearts? Were they fearful to acknowledge it, lest they should acknowledge that it was within all men, although perhaps buried more deeply in some than others? Did each man fear that in admitting another man's lust, that he might loosen that sinister yearning in his own heart?*

"Reverend Father, what you suggest is true, however even Abraham had not fathered a single child until God so blessed him and Sarah late in life. Of course, before that, he had impregnated Sarah's servant Hagar and produced a son, Ishmael, who was cast off when Isaac was born. We all are aware that Ishmael went on to father a long lineage of non-believers in *Jezu*, the Son of God. Magdalena, sitting here before us, has no reason to lie. Yes, like Hagar, she is a servant with whom the master has lain and was forced to bear him a child. Yet, she willl never cast off her son, Marek, as Abraham did Ishmael, to the cruel hardships of the world. Instead, she has come to offer his life to the monastery in dedication to our Lord! For Magdalena still loves her son so much that despite his being the bastard issue of the Duke, she seeks to commit his life to God. For only God can purify Marek of the sin that produced him."

The Abbott was impressed with the shrewd wits of this nun. She had used his own Biblical reference, in which he had attempted to undercut the allegation against the Duke, to indeed reinforce her belief in Magdalena's tale. What the Abbott did not realize was that she was, in a major way, arguing the case of her own molestation so many years ago.

"Sister Maryja Elizabeta, there is still the situation of Magdalena's not having come forth for so many years. How can this be explained?"

"Reverend Father, Magdalena has continually been under threat of the Duke taking her peasant husband's life. The Duke recently attempted to thrust himself upon her again, and this time she resisted forcibly and denied him. This occurred only for her husband to die days later in the Duke's salt mine where he worked, precisely as Duke Sdanowicz had once threatened."

The Abbott's eyes had peered at Magdalena while the Sister spoke. His face, like his overall appearance was lean and hard, and the sharpness of his long nose between these peering, penetrating eyes threatened to cleave any untruths she might be contemplating to issue forth from her lips. He directed his questions once again to Magdalena.

"Do you think the Duke killed your husband? Or for that matter had him killed?" the Abbott asked stoically, as if he did not believe the accusation of murder.

"It does not matter, Reverend Father," she said simply. "For whether it be his doing or not, by Bronisław's death the Duke has lost his power over me. I fear always for my soul, but I will never fear that vile man again in this life."

"It matters most greatly, my dear," said the Abbott, "for you are his peasant."

The last five words lashed at her like a cat-o-nine-tails.

"I am not a peasant," exploded Magdalena. She went on to explain the entire story of her parents having been betrayed by Duke Sdanowicz and the conditions of her having been forced to live as a peasant upon his estate. She reminded the Abbott that it was her parents who had sent her to the convent to be tutored by Sister Maryja Elizabeta.

"That is indeed a very different set of affairs than those set forth by the communique from the Duke that we received only this morning. He claims that Magda, as he calls her, is nothing more than a peasant, who has with your assistance, Sister Maryja Elizabeta, run off from the *folwark*. There is also the matter of the stolen horses as well."

The blood in Sister Maryja Elizabeta pounded within her veins. "Only this corrupt man would equate a woman's freedom from her imprisoned life with the value of a couple of his horses. He is nothing more than greed in all its forms, including lust!"

"Nonetheless, good Sister, we shall return his two mounts this morning. Please tell the monks which is yours, so it is not returned alongside," cautioned the Abbott.

"Yes, of course, Reverend Father," the nun replied. "Please forgive my outbursts."

"Good Sister, there is one other question that I have for you. Will you attest that this Magdalena who sits before us here and now is indeed the same woman as was the child that Duke Władysław Kowalczyk entrusted to you within the convent for the purposes of imparting an education?"

"Yes, my Abbott," the nun responded, "before God, I do so attest."

"In that case," said the Abbott, through his hands which made a steeple with the apex just covering the tip of his aquiline nose, "this will likely take a few days, if not longer, to settle out. I will need to travel to Kraków and question Mother Angelica, to assure the accuracy of the facts. Then, I must elevate this decision beyond my own level. For if everything you both have told me is true, and I have no reason to question it other than to assure to my superiors that I have made every effort to authenticate your claim, then we have a very complex situation on our hands."

"I am sorry, Reverend Father," interjected Sister Maryja Elizabeta, "but this appears to be a very clear situation of a Duke abusing the child of another *szlachta* brother."

"Well," the Abbott began after several seconds of deliberation, "its simplicity is complicated in that *szlachta* brother was later expelled from the noble ranks. His sins against the Polish King, no matter how righteous his intentions were, marked him as a traitor, and the expulsion was legal and just. However, by the Duke

Cyprian Sdanowicz's own words, he removed the child from the convent to raise her as his own. One may certainly make the case that, either as his own adopted child, or that of Duke Władysław Kowalczyk, Magdalena was not a peasant. Even the *Golden Rights of the szlachta* do not, to my knowledge, allow a man as prominent as Duke Sdanowicz to make a peasant girl from a Nobleman's daughter. As I have said, this will take a little time. Relative to the boy, once I have this situation under hand, I will need to talk to him, to see if his heart is set truly upon serving the Lord within these monastic walls. Please prepare him for this discussion, which will take place upon my return from Kraków." He then dismissed the two women.

Magdalena and Sister Maryja Elizabeta left Abbott Dawid's private quarters and headed to return to Marek.

"The time has come for you, Magdalena, to tell your son the truth of who his father is. I see no path forward that does not hinge on this. Failure on your behalf to do so will lead everything to the devil's doorstep. It must be done."

Magdalena's nerves cringed at the thought. She knew such a foundational shift in her son's life would devastate the boy. She could not envision herself mouthing the words of such a wicked reality to his ears. Despite this, she said to Sister Maryja Elizabeta nothing more than, "Yes, Sister, it must be done."

While this discussion was ongoing, back upon the *folwark* of Cyprian Sdanowicz, Ewelina had learned that not only her husband, but also her two sons were to be conscripted into the Austrian Army by the Duke's authority. This news seared her heart just as a hot stoked ember singes tender flesh. Life without her Jacek, even as silly a man as he could be at times, would be intolerable. Life without their sons Bartek and Andrzej would become a constant torture of never knowing if their spines grew strong with valor, or if they lay mangled upon the blood-soaked battlefields of Europe. Her three greatest treasures had not left Wieliczka yet, but they had been sequestered with the other conscripts in the garrison quarters of the salt mine. In a few days they would be marched to Vienna.

Ewelina had been tasked to assume the position that Magda's absence had created within the manor staff. She had decided to use her close quarters with the Duke to plead with him to spare her husband and sons. She realized that this was forbidden, however she had nothing left to lose, so she pressed on with her ill-advised plan.

"Please, my lord," Ewelina begged one morning as she surprised the Duke after breakfast in the forecourt. He was strolling from the manor house on his way to the riding stables. "My husband and my sons are all I have in this life, please do not take them from me. Jacek meant no harm upon your beautiful daughter."

"Jacek!" exclaimed the Duke upon hearing the man's name spoken. "So, you are married to that irresponsible stable master. After the harm he allowed to threaten my family, he deserves not to live upon these lands. It is an honor to serve the Empire, indeed an honor of which neither he nor your sons are deserving. So, you should be thanking me for having triply honored your family so."

"But my children, my boys, my lord," she pleaded, dropping to her knees, "Can you not spare them? Without them I have no family at all."

Her pleading then became physical as she wrapped her arms around the legs of the Duke. As she said these last words, she cried hysterically at the thought of living the rest of her life alone.

"I have done you a great favor, woman" said the Duke stiffly, not having been accustomed to having a peasant pleading directly to him, let alone in physical contact with his body, "for how would you raise two boys without a man about?"

"But my children are already grown men themselves, my lord. They can both read and write, and would be of great service to you here upon the *folwark*. Please spare them, my lord," again pleaded Ewelina.

She clutched even more tightly at his legs. The Duke was in a state of shock, for never had a peasant dared to touch him so directly. His efforts to free himself from the sobbing woman only resulted in her sliding lower until her face rested upon the polished blackened leather of his boots.

“Read and write? Peasants reading and writing? Surely such a thing will only allow them to bring discontent to the other peasants, and the shadow of rebellion to our doorstep. Since you have taken great care to educate them, let them serve the Empire!” said Duke Sdanowicz.

“Oh, please have mercy, my lord,” Ewelina cried, her tears streaming down upon the high polish of his riding boots. Her face was soon smudged with its blackness, and her tears channeled darkened rivulets through the stains upon her cheeks.

It was then that the head servant of the manor staff came out from the house. She immediately saw Ewelina, her newest charge, head down, sobbing at the feet of the Duke and was instantly aghast. The Duke motioned contemptuously to her, and violently pulled his legs in a jerking motion, one after the other, from the hysterical Ewelina’s clutches.

It was when the pitiful Ewelina raised her face to the head servant, that a twinge of compassion rippled through the latter woman’s heart. Blood was by then mixed with the water of her tears, as the buckle of the Duke’s riding boot had ripped open her no longer youthful, but otherwise smooth face. She held her palm to cover it, but the mixture of blood and tears merely flowed through her fingers, just as her sons and husband were soon to do. The Duke paid her no further attention, and addressed only the head servant.

“I want this woman to never again set foot upon the manor house and to never again come within the arc of my sight. Let her rot in the fields, if you will, only remove her from even there on the days that I choose to ride. Do you understand me, woman?”

“Yes, my lord,” said the head servant meekly, “I will make it so.”

Ewelina, lowered her head in defeat, and continued to sob uncontrollably upon the ground. No longer having the Duke’s legs upon which to steady herself, she then laid prostrated in the crushed gravel court. The Duke walked away from this hysterical wretch toward the stable of his much valued horses.

23

THE DEATH OF MAREK ZACZEK

SEPTEMBER 1789

Abbott Dawid departed the Tyniec Monastery to consult with Mother Angelica in Kraków. Magdalena stayed in her room which she shared with Marek, however the boy merely peered out the open window downwards on the cliffs below the monastery. They dropped precipitously to the Vistula River.

As the day passed into night, above the cliffs, torches were lit. They flickered in the deepening darkness, casting an eerie illumination upon the monastery's walkways. Far below, the flames' reflections danced seductively in the river. Softened, they appearing as enticing sirens swaying just beneath the surface, calling out to Marek to come join them in the Vistula's waters.

Magdalena had indeed attempted to discuss the boy's father that evening with her mourning son, but she could not bring herself to do so. Marek was severely depressed, and he moped in the window, pre-occupied with both the loss of his *tata* as well as his being denied access to his Maya, from whom he felt he had been forever separated. When the boy did speak to his mother, it was of her. "*Moja Matka*," he would say to his mother, "what do you think my *Maya Manuska* does at this hour?"

Magdalena decided to use Maya's name as an entry point into a much broader discussion.

"Do you suppose that Maya loves her father?" Magdalena began.

"Of course, she loves the Duke, as much as I love you, *moja Matka*," said the boy. "I only wish she could love me in that same way."

"What makes you think that she does not?" asked Magdalena.

"I know she has feelings for me, *Matka*, still they can never be acted upon," said Marek.

These words caught Magdalena's attention as fiercely as a hawk dives upon a sparrow. How much did her son already know?

"Why is that, my Marek?" asked his mother.

"For I am merely a peasant," he said dejectedly, "and she is the daughter of a *szlachta* Duke."

The boy still does not know the truth of his father, Magdalena thought. It came as a relief to her, even though she struggled to tell him exactly this.

"What if you were not a peasant at all?" asked Magdalena.

"It is more than I could possibly wish for," he said, "not that I am unhappy to be your son at all, *Matka*, however, as the son of a peasant I too am a peasant. A peasant who has run away from his *folwark*. I fear the Duke is enraged and will never take either of us back onto its grounds. I fear I will never see my *Maya Manuska* again."

The words broke the heart of his mother. Her son had been completely obedient of her in their flight from the Duke's estate. Marek had never questioned his mother's reason for it. Certainly, while they both were still in the depths of mourning Bronisław, when his mother asked him to gather the horses and bring Sister Maryja Elizabeta to her, he simply did so without question. However, when it was revealed that they would flee to Kraków, his heart must have sunk with the thought of departing, perhaps forever, from his *Maya Manuska*. Still, Marek did not complain. Even when they had been rerouted to the monastery at Tyniec, and surely his heart sank deeper within his chest because Marek knew the nature of their disappearance from the *folwark* would ignite the fury of the Duke. Even then, her son did not complain. But Magdalena was certain that Marek had fully convinced himself that his separation from his *Maya Manuska* was by then permanent. The despondency this created within her boy was obvious.

Magdalena could see the despair in her son's physical composure. His shoulders were uncharacteristically slumped, his head held low, and his eyes reflected the hollowness of his heart. Magdalena knew her son mourned the loss both of Bronisław and Maya, and his pain reverberated through his mother's heart.

"Why are we even here, *moja Matka*?" Marek sighed.

"Do you realize that you have never asked me about my father, Marek?" blurted Magdalena. "I cannot remember you asking even when you were young, my son. I always supposed it was because you never met, or even laid eyes on him. Yet, he is still your *dziadzia*, is he not? And you have never thought to ask of him?"

"I must have," responded the boy, "for you told me that he was in Russia."

"You merely heard me telling that to ..." she paused, for she was readying to say, "your father."

"You merely heard me say that to Bronisław," she repeated.

Marek found it odd that she referred to his *tata* in this way. She had never before done so.

"Marek, let me tell you tonight all about my father," she said.

"*Matka*, my heart both breaks for my own father and aches for my *Maya Manuska*. I do not feel like listening to you talk of your family at this time," he said.

"This discussion will lift your heart high," promised Magdalena. "You will see. You will see it is important regarding Maya as well."

"How can this be so?" asked the boy.

"Well, my son, how is it you know how to read and write?" responded Magdalena.

"Because you taught me so, just as you taught cousins Andrzej and Bartek," Marek replied.

"Besides the three of you, how many peasants do you know who can read and write?"

Marek thought on the question, and it became clear only then to him that the answer was none. He was amazed that he had never made this observation before, still he could not recall another single peasant, not even his Aunt Ewelina or Uncle Jacek, who knew how to read or write. His own father, Bronisław, could barely spell his own name. Bronisław could spell Marek's or his mother's simple five letter names only because his wife had taken great care to teach him to do so.

"I know of none, *Matka*. I see your point, it is uncommon for peasants to read or write," Marek said. "So how did you learn to do so?"

"My father taught me when I was very young, and when I was older, he sent me to the convent to gain more education. That is where I first met Sister Maryja Elizabeta."

"Yes, so Sister Maryja Elizabeta has mentioned, but how could your father send you there? Peasants do not become nuns," Marek said.

"My father was not a peasant at all, Marek," said Magdalena. "He was a *szlachta* Duke who ruled over the Bochnia *folwark*."

"But Bochnia is part of Duke Sdanowicz's *folwark*," scoffed the boy, as if catching his mother in a lie.

"Yes, you are right, Marek. Today it is, but before you were even born, it was a separate *folwark*, with its own salt mine. My father was the Duke who ruled over it."

"Then how did you become a peasant?" asked the boy.

"I never really did. I just married Bronisław, who was a peasant and was very proud to be so. He wanted us to live as peasants do. I have always been the daughter of a *szlachta* Duke, and this why we are here, to have this recognized, now that my Bronisław has been taken from me."

The boys face registered disappointment at her last comment.

"Of course, I should say taken from us," she corrected herself.

"So, if you are not a peasant," said Marek as he reasoned aloud, "then neither am I !"

In an instant, it had dawned upon the boy that he was of *szlachta* blood, although he still did not understand then that it was not only by his mother's lineage. For he had in his veins the blood of two *szlachta* lines. Magdalena intended to break this news to him in the following moments.

"This means I can ask the Duke for *Maya Manuska's* hand in marriage," he said triumphantly.

Magdalena's heart sank upon hearing these words. This could never be allowed to happen, for him to marry Maya was to wed his own half-sister. It was then that Magdalena realized that should she tell him the full truth, her son would once again be heartbroken knowing that he could never consummate his love for the Duke's daughter.

Magdalena watched the boy, who acted as if the fresh winds of life had been blown into his lungs. Where he was earlier morose and listless, he now was energetic and optimistic. Magdalena had no desire to steal from the energy that at that point revitalized her son, so she told herself that she would tell him of his father's true identity the next day.

It also saved Magdalena from having to fulfill her duty when her own body was so exhausted. Tomorrow, after she had rested, but before the return of the Abbott, she would take up this dreadful, but necessary, task.

She would explain then to the boy his need to commit himself to the Church, as she had long promised the Lord.

Magdalena then laid her head down to rest upon her bed. She was herself despondent, stemming from her mourning for her lost love, Bronisław. Yet, that was not all, as she found herself fretting over the situation she had come to find herself in. She had to break the heart of her son to prevent him from an unwitting incestuous relationship with his loved Maya. She had to steal from him the father that had been the rock of his happy childhood, as well as his best friend. She had to break that rock by explaining to Marek that he was born of her great sin. Not only could her son not marry his beloved *Maya Manuska*, but because of her sin, his life must be committed to the church in order to absolve it.

Marek was still at the window when Magdalena gave into an exhaustion she could no longer resist. She had not slept the night before, and her fatigue then swelled within both her body and mind to overcome her. Yet, she gained no relief, for her angst only transitioned from her conscious thoughts to her dreams. She dreamt of Marek and herself going to the beautiful basilica together in Kraków. Just as they approached its door, three demons appeared and stole her son from her. She was separated from Marek by them, but Magdalena could still see the beasts clawing and tearing at Marek's tender flesh. Just then, an eagle, much more ferocious than the demons, swooped from the sky to rescue her son. It clutched him in his talons and carried Marek ever higher into the sky. At a perilous height, the great eagle itself was attacked by a convocation of smaller eagles. As they fought over its captive prey, Marek was then dropped, and he fell towards the rocks upon the banks of a great river.

In a panicked sweat, Magdalena awakened to a darkened room. The dream's terror unsettled her, and she found that she needed to touch her son, to wrap her arms around him. She felt through the darkness, her heart beating wildly, only to find Marek's bed empty. It was then that she noticed that the door to their chamber was still closed, and the small wooden table she had placed against it was undisturbed.

Where had he gone? Was he taken? If so, by whom? How long could have passed since he was taken? How could the table have been restored to its place against the door afterwards? A dread arose from deep within her.

Magdalena had placed the small wooden table against the door, which had no lock, the night before so they might not be disturbed. Upon seeing the table had been undisturbed, she understood that the door had not been opened.

Magdalena could not get the image of her son falling towards the rocks out of her mind. Magdalena then moved to the window.

The very same window that Marek had been looking out all evening.

There was no moonlight, however, the torches' flames instead told her that everything was peaceful. The river flowed, still and silent, through its bend towards Kraków. The solitude of the night, however, could not displace the terror that still gnawed within her.

She then lowered her head, looking down onto the rocky cliffs that the monastery was perched upon. Immediately her fears flared like dried grass thrown upon a fire. She made out the image of her son clinging to the sheer cliff walls. "Marek," she screamed aloud in a hysterically high pitch. The shriek pierced the night as a dagger does unprotected flesh.

The boy looked up to see his *matka,* far above him, leaning dangerously out of the chamber's window. She pleaded pathetically to him, "Come back to me, my son."

The plaintive words cascaded through the black night, sinking to him upon the weight of her fallen hopes. He could feel the heartbreak in the tremors of her voice, and its frantic utterance, but knew he had no choice but to continue upon his perilous escape from the monastery. He wanted only to soothe his mother's broken heart.

He answered with a single word, for his expended strength could afford nothing more than for his brief response of "Maya".

The word rose to Magdalena like the curse it had become to her. She knew not what to do.

"Come back to me, Marek" she cried over and over again, ever more fervently, ever more excitedly. When it seemed that her fears had completely overcome her, she would think of the dream and the dread it had instilled in her. Then, her voice would tighten even further, rising in pitch, until it became drenched in the bile that rose up from within her gut. Her panic undulated within her like a serpent, readying to strike.

Magdalena was at that point giving in completely to her emotions. She could not then understand that her son had reasoned that he could scale the cliff to its base, and scurry to the adjoining copse of trees along the river to make his escape. She could not comprehend that her Marek was sure to return to the *folwark* to tell his Maya of the wondrous news that he was not truly a peasant after all. *To tell Maya that they could be married.*

Magdalena could not think of any of this, only of the terror within her as she thought of the danger to her son's life. She continued to call out to him, as he worked himself down the cliff. She prayed his life would somehow be spared. The serpent of her fears coiled within her, its head wavering, awaiting the opportunity to strike at her soul.

My God, Magdalena then thought, *Marek will ask the Duke for Maya's hand!* She knew that Sdanowicz would do whatever was necessary to keep his bastard son from marrying his daughter. Magdalena knew that wretched man's vengeance could indeed be lethal. Her face cringed in anguish, her brow threatened to buckle from the ratcheting tension within her. "Marek, do not go to her," she wailed.

His mother's words struck him like a fatal blow. Marek was only a short distance from the safety of the trees when suddenly his footing upon the cliff gave out. A spray of small rocks preceded his leg lunging downward. Marek reacted and tried to steady himself upon the near vertical ledge, but his sudden shift in momentum acted as a claw that dragged him from the cliff. It was fortunate that he was near its bottom and had not far to fall. His reaction of trying to catch himself actually drove him outward from the cliff and soon after a great splash was heard of Marek falling into the quiet but strong flow of the river.

Magdalena watched in terror as the serpent of fear struck at her. She screamed in a voice she did not think she even possessed, one of unadulterated horror. The splash of her son upon the river's surface was a shock that pulsed like a venom through her. She knew he could not swim. The very worst thing that she could have fathomed had come to pass. She was screaming incoherently by then, and nearly fell from the window as she watched her son thrash in the river's waters.

It was then that she felt the hands of Sister Maryja Elizabeta on her shoulders. The nun was wrapped in bedclothes, and had rushed from her room next door. Magdalena had not heard the door to her room open, nor the sound of the small wooden table sliding across the floor. She heard only the splashing upon the river's surface as it threatened to swallow her son. The commotion made by her in the window had by then awakened not only the nun, but also the monks, who were just beginning to gather upon the path below the two women.

Marek continued to thrash wildly in the river. The currents took him away from the shore into deeper waters. He rose and fell like great claps of thunder during a storm. His arms clutched in panic at the air each time he returned to the surface only to find nothing to grasp. He would then go under again, sinking beneath the river's silted surface. Each time his face descended into a watery blur, new fissures were struck with the most unrelenting of force into Magdalena's already broken heart.

The nun clutched with all her might at Magdalena to keep her from throwing herself out the window as she watched her son drown in abject horror. The boy, thrashing erratically as he was, drifted downstream towards Kraków. The terror of Magdalena's dream had descended fully upon her. The demons of the watery depths pulled at him to his demise.

"The devil is stealing my child," she screamed inconsolably, "the beast is taking my Marek."

The night had come alive with a desperate, uncontrolled chaos. Sister Maryja Elizabeta watched as the monks below had found a rope, and lowered one of their own down the cliff to the river to attempt to retrieve the boy. All the while she fought the wrangling of Magdalena, whose body was thrashing wildly as she cried into the night in a heartbreaking, tormented unending wail.

Unnoticed to all were two of the Duke's guards hidden in the copse of trees toward which Marek had been traversing the cliff. Once alerted by the frantic screams of Magdalena, they realized they had not anticipated this escape route. However, they at that point were sure to have apprehended Marek had he safely made the woods. Yet, neither seemed even remotely interested in risking his own life to save the boy from the perilous waters of the river.

Neither the tethered monk nor the Duke's horsemen had even the slightest chance of saving the boy. For Marek's frantically flailing body sunk below the river one last time. It was then that the Vistula became smooth once again having consumed its prey. Its mirrored surface returned, bearing only the slightest of ripples from the subsided wake of Marek's struggle for life.

Magdalena howled in an unending stream of sorrow like a wolf at the moon. Everything she had ever feared had not only come to pass, but was burned forever in the irrepressible vision of her memory. First she had lost her husband, and now just a few days later she had been forced to watch the joy of her life, her only son, tragically drown.

Magdalena clutched at Sister Maryja Elizabeta in her unconsolable anguish. Every ounce of hope had been drained from her through her tears. Every corrosive drop of bile churned within her. Every breath had been stomped flat within her exhausted lungs. Nothing was left for her save her own tormented, continuous cries into the darkness of the night. The viper's venom spread through her slowly now, unstoppable in its horrid course. She knew, even as despondent as she was, that the lethal reality of her son's death would spread through her, until it would mercifully cause her to take her own.

24

THE RESCUE

SEPTEMBER 1789

When Marek awoke, he felt the sting of the cool night's air upon his face. As his awareness returned to him, he was surprised to find that his arms and legs were bound, and his mouth gagged. He then remembered the desperate fight for life he had been engaged in. He was in the midst of this returned panic when he felt the boney hand of an old man upon his chest.

"Easy now, young one, you're safe enough with us," said the raspy voice in a hushed whisper. The hand, which initially had felt feeble to Marek, then pushed him hard into the flat bottom of the boat such that he could only look up into the night sky. "Now, boy, keep yourself silent or we'll be forced to quiet you, once and for all. These men are looking for your carcass in the river. We could easily just slip you back in there. We'd rather not, but we will if we have to."

Marek could hear great commotion in the distance, with much yelling and men on boats splashing about in erratic throes. In the further distance, running like an undercurrent of sound, came an unending drone of misery, which Marek immediately recognized as the anguished wailing of his own mother. His heart sank as its mournful, distant howl reached his ears.

Despite the threats upon him, Marek could only remember the panic of his fight for life in the Vistula. While he then found himself captive, bound and gagged within this boat, it was a much preferred situation than having his hands free only to flail at the river's surface, and his mouth not gagged only to swallow seemingly endless amounts of the flowing water.

The boy calmed himself, as he came to realize he had been saved from the river's attempt to consume him. Marek interpreted the old man's hushed words as nothing more than a caution to stay quiet. For even though his mouth was gagged, Marek knew it could still be possible to make a muffled scream whose muted sound would, in the night, carry far across the river. However, he thought, if the old man had meant to harm him, he would have simply allowed Marek to drown. Marek realized the old man who spoke to him in raspy whispers merely wished to maintain the stealth of his boat in the darkness of the night.

"It is a good thing young Tolo knows how to swim and was able to fish you from the *Wisła* " the old man said, using the Polish name for the Vistula. Marek thought at that point that he had smelled the blood of animals, yet still could not see anything but the speckled lights of stars in the darkened night sky.

He could hear the strokes of their own oars upon the water, however even these were carefully softened as much as possible as if to evade pursuers, known or unknown. Later, he would find the wooden oars wrapped in cloth to prevent their splashing upon the surface.

"I am glad to see you are back with us, my friend," said a much younger and more vibrant voice, although still only barely above a whisper. His next words were pulsed between the strokes of the oars, indicating the younger man was rowing the vessel. "You nearly pulled me under in your panic. *(Stroke)* They say a drowning man will grasp at the edge of a razor, and by your panic I know this is true. *(Stroke)* We are not accustomed to so much excitement on the river at night. In fact, we effort greatly to avoid it. *(Stroke)* It is our desire to remain as unnoticed as we possibly can."

"Hush, the both of you, we are coming upon the bank," said the old raspy voice, "and not a moment too soon. There appears an even greater number of boats heading for the bend in the river where this boy fell in."

Marek, who had figured he was no longer in danger, remained calm. The voices did not seem to threaten him, only to sooth his anxiety. He felt a final great stroke of the oars, and just afterward a shudder in the front end of the boat as it lunged up onto the shoreline.

"Come, let's make haste, for these men will be all over this river looking for his bloated body soon enough," said the old man. Then, Marek felt the four hands, both young and old, raise him from the bottom of the boat. They carefully lifted him over its side and sat him upright on the grasses of the bank such that he faced the vessel.

His first sight of the pair of men was in the darkness as they emptied and then hid the boat. The old man was a thin, leathery sort with a pronounced limp who must have been sixty years on. Despite his infirmity, his actions were well known to his body, indicating that he had been doing this for a very long time. Whatever "this" was.

The younger man, who the older one had called "Tolo", was not much beyond Marek's own age. Perhaps, he was no more than five years older. Marek knew "Tolo" was the diminutive form of the Polish name "Witold". Tolo was scrawny, but his frame knew also of what needed to be done. His clothes were soaked from head to toe. He helped the old man take goods from the boat, including the carcasses of several dead fox, otters, and beavers. Even the remains of a bloated possum was firmly in his grip.

Marek then saw that the young man had metallic devices in his other hand. It was only then that Marek realized he was being held by the trappers who crossed the Vistula during the night to poach animals from their illegal traps on the Galician side of the river. The very same trappers of whom his Uncle Jacek had once warned him.

Tolo and the old man pulled the boat from the riverbank and carried it some twenty paces inland into a dug-out recess, where they placed it neatly within. They then covered it with two large animal hides. On top of that they carefully placed brush, small tree-limbs and scattered shore grasses. They moved silently and efficiently. They then came back to Marek and cut free his legs before raising him onto the limbs.

Marek's arms and hands were still bound, and his mouth still gagged when they led him away from the shoreline in utter silence. The time from their landing upon the Polish riverbank to their walking away was less than five minutes.

The three of them walked in the darkness a great distance before coming upon a cabin set inside the edge of a small forest. Inside a small fire burned in the primitive stone hearth. The younger man carried the dead animals over to inspect their catch in its light as the old man freed Marek of his bindings and removed the gag from his mouth.

"These will all be nice skins, Miłosz," said the younger man, Tolo, as he ran his fingers through the pelts.

The older man had cut Marek free, and then looked hard into his eyes. He realized that the young boy knew both of their names.

"Yes, I am Miłosz, and this young one who saved you is Tolo," said the old man to Marek. "I am sorry we had to tie you up and gag you as we did, but we feared you would awake in a panic and scream or thrash, alerting those on the river to our location. What is your name, boy?"

"My name is Marek," the youth responded, as he stretched the muscles of his jaw after the gagging cloth had been removed from his mouth.

"Well, Marek, you are very lucky that you decided to drown yourself where you did," said Miłosz in a louder, but still raspy, voice, "for we always make our way across the *Wisła* at that bend in the river. It is out of the view from both the Kraków bridge downriver and the Tyniec Monastery upriver just beyond the turn. Between the two, we trust the monks more than we do the border guards, so we tend to cheat towards the monastery just a little."

"That was when I heard you struggling in the water," said Tolo's younger, more vibrant voice. "We thought it might have been a small deer swept from the banks and so we rowed towards the disturbance. I was so very surprised to see your hands break through the river's surface one last time. I knew you were in trouble, so I dived in with the rope. To be honest, I thought it was already too late."

"I don't remember that at all," said Marek, as his mind replayed his terrified struggle for his life in the Vistula. He realized exactly how fortunate he was to even be alive, thanks to these two illegal trappers.

"You were near the bottom when I found you," said Tolo. "Your body was already as still as a corpse, but as soon as I touched you, you grabbed me in a death grip. I had to fight to be able to tie that rope around you so old Miłosz could pull you in. After that, I was able to free myself and swim to the surface to catch my breath, before helping you. That was no easy feat, as you hacked and coughed up the river water from within you. I have never seen anything so violent in my life. You passed out as soon as we got you in the boat."

"You damn nearly got us caught," said Miłosz, his voice rising well above his earlier whispers.

"I am sorry," said Marek. "The Lord sent you to me, so that I may have escaped from the monastery."

"The monastery!" cried old Miłosz. "You jumped into the *Wisła* from the monastery. Are you one of the runaway peasants from the Duke's *folwark*?"

"Yes, I am," confessed Marek, "and my mother and the nun are still there under sanctuary from the Duke's guards."

Miłosz's face soured as Marek described the situation. Worry invaded the old man's thoughts.

"I told you we should not get involved, Tolo," screamed Miłosz. "The last thing we need is to be entangled with the Duke's horsemen. They may have seen us fishing the boy from the river."

"Relax, Miłosz," said Tolo calmly, "I had watched, and no one followed us across the river. It was very dark. And while they may have heard his hacking cough, they would just assume it was his last gasp before drowning. They never knew we were even there. We were as stealthy as the otters and beavers on the river."

"I told you to let him drown," responded Miłosz, still frenzied, "but you simply ignored me and dove in with that damn rope. Well, that same rope will be around our necks if they find us with him. For just as we trap the otters and beavers, one day your ignoring my voice will find *us* in *their* traps."

"Calm yourself down, Miłosz," said Tolo in a soothing voice. "Since when do you not enjoy stealing from the Duke? Marek here is your greatest prize. Are you getting too old for this game? Perhaps you should retire, old man."

"Why do you both risk yourselves trapping animals on the Galician banks of the *Wisła*?" asked Marek, wishing to hear no more of how he was almost allowed to drown.

"Because these skins fetch much, and the money keeps us fed," said Miłosz tersely.

"And with the city life of Kraków on the Polish banks, there is not as much wildlife," added Tolo with greater patience. "What there was has been trapped long ago. So, we lay our traps on the banks and in the woods of the *folwark*. We do nothing more than steal back the Polish animals that the Austrians have stolen from us."

For the first time since his near drowning experience, Marek returned his thought to the *folwark*, and his *Maya Manuska*.

"I need to get back to the *folwark*," said Marek. "Perhaps tomorrow night?"

"No, no, no," said Miłosz firmly. "You can never go back there. I will not allow it. You could lead the guards to our cabin. If you insist to do so, then you truly leave us no other option than to kill you."

Tolo laughed aloud, as if the thought of either of them killing anyone was preposterous.

"Miłosz, you are as rude as a Turk," said Tolo. "No one will harm you, Marek, my friend, for we did not save your life to just spill your blood. However, Miłosz is right in that you can never go back there. You will stay here until we determine what to do with you. Do not try and run, or we will be forced to chain you up like a wild dog."

"I will not run," said Marek, "as I owe my life to you both. I will do whatever you say is needed to repay you. However, once I do, I intend to go back to my *Maya Manuska*?"

"And who is this one with such a pretty name?" asked Tolo. "Her lips must taste ever so sweet for you to wish to risk giving yourself up to the Duke once more."

"She is my heart's deepest desire," answered Marek, realizing he had struck a chord with young Tolo. "She is also Duke Sdanowicz's daughter."

"*Jezu, Maryja i Józef*," yelled Miłosz, "what have you dragged us into, Tolo?"

"Miłosz, I will not tell you again to calm yourself," answered Tolo. "It was I who saved him, so I will take full responsibility for the boy. Tonight, he sleeps with us by the fire, and tomorrow I will teach him to skin the pelts from these vermin. Let us see what talents he has. Perhaps young Marek will come to assist us in our thieving."

25

THE INTERCESSION

OCTOBER 1789

The provincial capital of Galicia was the town known to the Austrians in the German tongue as Lemberg. When the town, and the province of Galicia itself, were part of the country of Poland, before the partition, it was known as Lwów. This, of course, to the Austrian's ears sounded as *"Lvoof"*, far too Slavic a pronunciation for the German speaking monarchs, and thus, after the partition, the town had been given the Germanic name of Lemberg.

Count Von Arndt represented the Emperor in this province of Galicia. He detested coming to this provincial capital twice each year. It was a long, arduous journey from Vienna, through the Czech lands of the empire, and over the mountains that earlier had formed the border with what once was southern Poland. From there, it continued across the swamps and woodlands of Galicia, infested as they were with clouds of swarming insects and bands of ruffians known as brigands, the robber-men of the by-ways.

To dissuade the insect swarms, fires infused with incense were lit and carried night and day. To dissuade the brigands, the Count always traveled with a contingent of heavily armed guards. Neither deterrent was fully effective. As he sat in his office in the atrocity upon the frontier that was the town of Lemberg, the Count was irritated by both the half-healed bites upon his skin and the memories of the attempted raid upon his traveling party. The latter was readily fought off by his guards, and after the borders were closed to their escape, the brigands were tracked down, flogged and hung. The insects were more insidious and generally escaped retribution.

The Count's travels were often marked by stays at various points with local gentry, most of who took the presence of the Emperor's Envoy, even for only an overnight stay, as a great honor to their homes. Such were his visits at Duke Sdanowicz's *folwark,* although unlike many others, these visits had a predominant business function. There were many others in the Czech lands and throughout Galicia that were merely overnight rest points along the way.

Perhaps his favorite city in the Austrian Empire, other than Vienna, was Prague, known locally as "Praha". He had been appointed as the Emperor's Envoy there before Galicia. The Count felt at home among its massive Stone Bridge and towering spires. Often these steeples had their own spired appendages that would emerge from them like fresh shoots of an aged growth. Scanning the soot blackened spires among the rooftops, the Count could easily imagine the city's uppermost layer as the floor of a recently burned forest upon which the budding regeneration of life was in process.

In some ways it had always been, as the city had recreated itself many times over. After all, Prague had been not only the ancient Catholic stronghold as the seat of Bohemia, but also the court of the Holy Roman Emperor, and the birthplace of the Hussite Bohemian rebellion that spurred the Protestant Reformation, to name a few iterations of the city. The Count felt Prague was the only truly sophisticated city within the backwaters that were the empire's Slavic provinces.

The cross currents of Catholicism and Protestant Reformation made Prague a vibrant, dynamic provincial capital. Its location along the Vltava River (known in the Count's German tongue as the Moldau), as well as its proximity to the Danube located to the south, had long made it a center of trade and commerce. From this wealth and prosperity sprung forth a love for the fine arts and classical architecture.

The Count especially loved the gothic Church of Saint Nicholas on the main square in the *Staré Město, or Old Town*, despite it being of the Hussite denomination. It's exterior, with its two square towers and roofs of metal so softly greened with exposure to the city's oft pungent air, was built only some fifty years earlier. Still, it was St. Nicholas' interior that Count Von Arndt had come to love so intensely. He did so after having been present there when his fellow visitor from Vienna, the musician Amadeus Mozart, had so masterfully played the keyboard of the church's organ of four thousand pipes.

<u>Figure 6: Winter Scenes of Prague</u>

Count Von Arndt also loved to stroll what was known as the Stone Bridge, or simply, the Prague Bridge. It was the sole crossing over the Vltava, and was built at the end of the fourteen-century by the Holy Roman Emperor Charles IV to connect the town's *Staré Město (Old Town)* district on the one bank with what was known as *Malá Strana,* literally meaning *"Little Side"*, but what many came to call *"Lesser Prague"* across the river.

Above *Malá Strana* the Count had resided many times as a guest in the *Pražský Hrad*, or *Prague Castle,* which was fortified on the hillside that overlooked the Vltava River and the Old Town that lie just beyond it.

The Count loved to depart from atop the *Hradčany, or the Castle District,* and stroll through *Malá Strana*'s narrow downward sloping streets of shops and its beautiful collection of burgher houses. He would descend the steeply inclined neighborhood until he came to leisurely cross the Stone Bridge which connected to the Old Town on the opposite bank.

One hundred years earlier, give or take, famous Czech sculptors had added the statues of saints and other figures that lined the bridge, seemingly assessing judgement upon all those who crossed its massive and wide span. Count Von Arndt had initially enjoyed examining the quality of those sculptures, but in his later crossings he ignored them altogether, just as so many of the city's residents had come to ignore the saints in their religious lives.

Five years earlier, in 1784, Count Von Arndt had been instrumental in having persuaded Emperor Joseph II to permit four of the town's five districts to be combined into a single, officially recognized *City* of Prague. Only the Jewish district of *Josefov* had not been included, a product of the antisemitism of the time. Nonetheless, the city's consolidation had markedly increased its prestige and prominence in central Europe. For his facilitation of this Imperial decree, the Count was always well received there, with the merchant's and nobles of the city often fighting for the honor of hosting him for banquets during his stays. More than once, the noblemen's daughters had been sent to him as prospects for marriage. More than once, he had sampled their wares, only to leave town once more, still formally unattached.

Yet, this fall day in 1789, Prague seemed a million leagues behind him. Galicia's capital of Lemberg was Prague's antithesis. The Count had been in Lemberg for several weeks, as the Emperor's representative. Just as Prague, in all its glory, could never quite match the opulence and elegance of Vienna, or so the Count thought, so neither could Lemberg ever hope to match Prague.

Or for that matter, even the medieval charm of Kraków, which was closer. But alas, Kraków was not part of the Austrian empire, despite sitting just upon its border across the Vistula. The

Count would eagerly have preferred to spend his time there, upon Kraków's simple, but expansive, medieval town square. Still he preferred it over this forsaken Galician town of Lemberg, where the mixed residents of Polish, Ukrainian and Jewish heritages had only one thing in common: they all detested the unwelcome rule of the Austrians.

For the past two weeks, the Count's official duties had consisted of hearing the petty squabbles of land disputes, and those of other property, such as the peasants who were tied to said lands, between former Polish and Ukrainian "*Nobles*". This gentry had been vastly diluted over time, to the point neither could even stand to be compared to even the lowest class of Viennese merchant. The Count disliked the traditional *szlachta* dress they would wear. Instead of their attire being somber and respectful, it was often far too colorful and loose fitting. Their robes and the scabbards of their ceremonial swords were often encrusted with jewels. Their dress flowed with the attributes that the Count had previously only known of the Hungarian elites, which included the manifest sign of authority, that being a knotted horse's tail, adorning their garb.

These "nobles" would call upon the Emperor's Envoy, as the Count was, with their symbolic *szlachta* sabers hanging from their waists. They would demand that their rights be recognized, even though those were rights bestowed on them by the country to which they were no longer citizens. For Austrian rule was much different from either Polish or Ukrainian rule. Yet, these rude and often ignorant nobles, many whose families were by then landless and mostly owned only slightly more possessions than the peasants, demanded that the Count bestow them with privileges from the empire merely because of the elite blood that coursed through their veins.

The Count very rarely gave them the satisfaction they wished for. Rather he educated them in the new reality of the Austrian Empire in which they existed. Despite the partition having occurred seventeen years earlier, there still was an unending line of former nobles awaiting his audience each time he came to this ignominious outpost.

Occasionally, the Count would hear a protestation from a Jewish shop owner or merchant who not only had become exceptionally prosperous but was brave enough to raise a complaint to the Emperor's Court. These complaints would most often be lodged against the very same nobles, who the Jews had in some way perceived to have laid harm upon or grievously insulted their families. The merchants were determined to be heard and pressed forward their claims despite the fact that these were nearly never adjudicated in the Jews' favor. In fact, the Jewish merchants would often face the most severe retribution afterwards by the very parties they had claimed against, be they Polish or Ukrainian. For in punishing them for even having had raised the issue to the Emperor's Envoy, the nobles very effectively discouraged future complaints from these merchants. That was until time passed, and another Jewish shop owner felt prosperous and courageous enough to defy the status quo. Then, once more was initiated the cycle of the rejection of their claim, followed by the retribution of their claimants, and the intimidation of their rights as a class of citizenry.

For all of this, the Count had detested Lemberg as nothing more than a provincial settlement, rotted like so many of its wooden structures from the slurry of the fetid mud of its streets and the rancid bile of its residents' hearts. The populace spoke only the crudest German, and the Count refused to provide interpreters for those that spoke only either Polish or Ukrainian. The Count even refused to converse in French, which he understood fluently, as did many of the nobles, for it was a very fashionable language in that time. His intent was to force these eastern mongrels of the empire to learn its proper tongue or have no access to its many avenues of recourse.

It was in the midst of this unpleasant and dreary daily repetition when a horse rider arrived in the Envoy's Court bearing an urgent message from Abbott Dawid at the Benedictine Monastery at Tyniec. The note bearing the Abbott's seal was broken by the

Count, only to reveal a discourse in the finest written German that he had seen since leaving Vienna. The message was astutely and concisely written. Apparently, this Abbott was a highly educated man, with whom the Count decided it would be a pleasure to spend a few days.

The Tyniec Monastery, as has been earlier stated, was officially considered a district of the city of Kraków, despite lying across the Vistula from the walled medieval town. As such, even though the monastery lay on the Austrian side of the river, the Abbott's issues were none of the Empire's concern. Except in one manner, for the Abbott's well-written communique implied it needed the Count's resolution of an issue dealing with Duke Sdanowicz of Wieliczka, a member of the Austrian empire. Furthermore, the issue had already resulted in loss of life of a boy, and even at the note's writing, the Duke's men continued to besiege the monastery. The Abbott asked for the Count's intervention before he formally raised the issue with the Bishop of Kraków, who would then be compelled to pass it onto the Holy See in Rome.

The message could not have been more welcome to the Count. It gave him a legitimate excuse to cut short his time in Lemberg, and also opened the door for a potential formal grievance against Duke Sdanowicz. While he was still the Duke's overseer, the Count was jealous of the Duke's massive land holdings. Even more so, he envied the Duke's right to administer the Imperial *Groß Salze* mines. He envied most, from those mines, the great wealth to which the Duke was entitled. For as overseer, the Count did indeed take his portion of that wealth produced from those mines, but this was small in comparison to the excess wealth it generated for the Duke. This was physically visible in the ostentatious and excessively ornate guest house that Sdanowicz had just completed.

The Count responded to Abbott Dawid that he would arrive in three-days-time. He requested accommodations for himself, his horses, and a field in which his guards could encamp. He immediately sent the note by return rider. Count Von Arndt then happily concluded his most pressing responsibilities and set off for Tyniec.

Upon his arrival, and after only a brief rest, the Count met with Abbott Dawid to become learned on the nature of the dispute. Count Von Arndt was surprised to learn it was a complaint that had been pressed by the servant Magda from the estate. This was the very lovely peasant woman, he reminded himself, upon which he had once set his own desirous eye.

The Abbott told the Count of his discussions with Mother Angelica from the convent in Kraków. She had confirmed to him that Magdalena, as she had called the girl, was indeed the daughter of another *szlachta* Duke. Her father had enrolled her at that tender age of ten, and she was educated by Sister Maryja Elizabeta, who confirmed the tale as well. The complaint against the Duke was that after taking the girl to raise as his own, Sdanowicz had improperly forced her to marry a peasant, and then had later defiled her against her will.

Upon hearing this, a most curious emotion befell the Count. He remembered his own lustful wishes once for the peasant Magda. Then, he recalled the Duke telling him that she was unavailable to him for she had lost her husband in the recent collapse of the mine. The Count was extremely grateful that the opportunity to have "taken" the woman for a night, as a gift from Sdanowicz, had never arisen.

Strangely, though, when the Abbott continued to tell him that she had also lost her son, Marek, who had drowned in the river as he attempted to escape the monastery, what can only be described as sympathy for the woman overcame him. When the Abbott went on to define the depth of the misery which had engulfed her since that night, the Count's sympathy transformed into a deep and unrestrained sorrow for the woman.

"She claims the boy was the Duke's bastard son?" asked the Count.

"She does," admitted the Abbott, "but there is no way to confirm this."

"Perhaps there is. Was the boy's body recovered?" inquired the Count.

"Regretfully, no," said the Abbott, "but the river ran swiftly that night. The child's corpse could have flowed downriver all the way to Sandomierz, or even on to Warsaw, for all we know."

"Is the Duke aware of the boy's death?" asked the Count.

"Undoubtedly, for his men watched him drown from the woods along the river that abut the cliffs," said the Abbott, "and they most certainly reported it back to the Duke."

They spoke in German, and the Abbott's pronunciation and vocabulary was excellent. It was a pleasure to be in dialogue with him, the Count thought.

"Reverend Father," said the Count, "I would like to call upon the Duke tomorrow to hear his side of this complaint. I will leave in the morning and return by nightfall. I would like to interview the woman Magda upon my return."

"That would be *Magdalena*," said Abbott Dawid, as he corrected the Count. "She only responds to that form of her name since arriving here. She says that Magda was her peasant name that died with her peasant husband. She suffers greatly still, having lost a husband and a son in short sequence. She also claims to have been visited by the Holy Spirit."

"You tell me this, why?" asked the Count.

"This woman has endured..., no, that's not fair," paused the Abbott, "...***is*** enduring a series of great losses. She has nothing left to lose, for she has lost the love of her life in her peasant miner husband. She has lost her reason for living in the drowning of her son. She has also lost her very self, or more accurately has had her identity and life stripped from her by the Duke. Most of all, the girl feels her very soul has been lost forever, for she had fully intended to dedicate her son's life to the Church as an offering against her sins. With his drowning, his life is no longer hers to give. She feels that she is damned by circumstances."

"Considering this," said the Count, "you recommend I use a more subdued approach than I might otherwise use in questioning her?"

"Not so much a recommendation as a warning," said the

Abbott, "for as I have already said, the poor woman has nothing left to lose."

It was then that the Count thought to himself, *Perhaps... but she everything in the world to gain.*

26

THE BURGEONING BROTHERHOOD

OCTOBER 1789

Since the night of his rescue, Marek stayed with the trappers, Miłosz and Tolo, in their decrepit cabin within the Polish woods. Yet for Marek, who had only lived in the hut made of earthen walls and a thatched roof, the cabin's shelter was a luxury he had never known. He, of course, had glimpses into the remarkable manor house accommodations in which his love, Maya, had been raised. He knew these were forever to be out of his reach. This cabin, though, was a shelter unlike anything in which he had ever lived.

Wood was not a commodity with which peasant huts were built, for it was far too valuable. The only wooden structure he was familiar with were the *folwark's* chapels to which his and other peasant families attended mass each week. This cabin surrounded him in the strength and warmth of its timbered walls and roof. Unlike his hut, the wind came only in whispers, not in cold slaps from above as the gusts of winter would part the thatch like the Red Sea. (His *matka* had often told him Bible stories to explain how their hard lives were nothing compared to the misery others had lived under throughout history. That strategy was not altogether effective, Marek would later come to think.)

While this trapper's cabin did have some water dripping into it from overhead leaks in places, Marek could not imagine it ever gushed in cold, wet penetrating fingers as it did in the hut during a summer's storm when the thatch was partially washed aside. The fire in the cabin gave warmth without filling the structure with excessive smoke, thanks to the stone chimney.

Of course, the cabin floor was speckled with rodent droppings, however this was something to which he had long been accustomed. Shoots of green forest ferns grew up between gaps in the floorboards, which themselves were rough and all too willing to yield their splinters into one's unsuspecting foot, as Marek hurriedly found out. Yet despite these hazards, Marek considered himself very lucky.

The first morning Marek awoke to a cold chill on his face. He slept under one of Tolo's blankets, actually more of a patchwork of animal hides, which surrounded him in a warmth he had never before known. Tolo would later teach him why these pelts were inferior, and could not be sold, but they were never wasted. What one could not sell to the tanners and furriers could always be put to use as blankets. Or they could always be bartered for food, drink or other necessities with other peasants, those less fortunates who would welcome the warmth of even the most inferior skins and furs.

The cold upon his face that had awakened Marek was due to the long-held routine by Miłosz and Tolo of dousing the fire before daybreak. The plume of smoke rising from the chimney was invisible in the darkness of the night, but in the daylight would instantly identify their hidden location within the woods to anyone searching for them.

Marek had, for some time, been used to rising before the sun, however after having discovered the overnight comfort of the furs, he wished not to emerge into the cold reality that was the cabin in morning. Tolo, knowing Miłosz would not accept the boy's defiance, roused Marek and introduced him to the chores of the day.

As they exited the cabin, Marek's eyes were opened to a world that been denied to him by the darkness of the night before. The wooden cabin sat within a densely overgrown forest, which broke up the morning light into angled radiant shafts which penetrated the thinning canopy of leaves overhead.

As the reddened leaves spiraled to the ground around them, like the fluttering snowflakes they preceded, Marek noticed that a large hardwood tree had fallen and partially crushed the roof of the cabin. It lay leaning like a drunkard upon the structure, the tree's roots having ripped from the soil presumably during a raging storm long since past. Thick ropes of clinging vines had grown from the forest floor and covered much of the bark of the tree as well as the roof of the cabin. Even Marek knew this took a great deal of time.

"When did this happen?" asked Marek. "Were you and Miłosz inside then?"

"By the love of all that is good, we thank the Lord that we were not," Tolo answered. "This happened long before we found this hideaway."

"It is not yours?" Marek asked.

"It is for a while. Until someone comes and drives us from it. For today, it serves us well enough."

"So, you find an abandoned house, and merely move in?" asked Marek.

"More or less," replied Tolo.

"Aren't you afraid that the Duke who owns these lands will come to drive you from them?" inquired Marek.

"Of course," answered Tolo, "but we have been driven away before. We just disappear into the forest until we find our next lodging. We are quite adept at living in the forest for as long as we need. So long as we have our knives, our traps and our boats, we are free men. All else, including the skins you slept in last night, come from these three things."

"You said boats," Marek interjected, "you have more than one?"

"Yes, we have two hidden," answered Tolo. "The one you rode in last night is upriver from the border bridge. There is another hidden downriver past the bridge. Even on the darkest night Miłosz and I would not be foolish enough to attempt to float under that bridge. For sure, Miłosz doesn't need another musket ball in him."

"Is that why he limps so?" asked the boy.

"Marek, my young friend, you ask far too many questions," said Tolo. "Now, I need to teach you how to perform your new duties, so you can earn your keep."

First, there was the skinning of the animals Tolo and Miłosz had removed from the traps the night before. This was completely foreign to Marek, for he had never caught any animal, let alone skinned it. In fact, upon the *folwark* it was a grievous crime to take even the least of the Duke's beast or fowl. Peasant men had been lashed for doing so when they were found eating from a plate of *bigos*, or hunter's stew, containing only the meat of a single hare, or other vermin, they had been fortunate enough to catch. The rule of the *folwark* was that the land was the possession of the Duke, and anything that tread upon it, be it peasants or animals, were also his possessions. For the peasants to hunt from his lands was the same as breaking into the manor house and stealing its possessions.

Tolo taught Marek first how to properly hold and sharpen a gutting knife. He then could feel Marek shudder as he pierced the belly of a dead bloated possum, which Tolo explained had been in the traps for some time. The young trapper expertly removed the innards in an efficient manner. Then he taught Marek to skin the pelt: where to begin and how to peel it free from the meat by a cutting method that took much practice to render a pelt useable.

"Of course, there is not much value in a possum's skin, however it will make good practice for you, Marek. Here take the knife and finish this," demanded Tolo. Marek did so, and after a bit of time, became somewhat proficient. Then, Tolo taught Marek to skin the beaver, and Marek did so nicely for his first pelt.

"Marek, you take to this like the duck takes to the river," laughed Tolo. Then, that afternoon, Tolo taught Marek how to handle and set the traps. He also instructed Marek in how to hide the traps in the undergrowth. After this, they collected firewood before returning to the cabin as sundown approached. Marek was starving, having had nothing all that day to eat.

"Let's see what the old man has for us," said Tolo as they entered the cabin door.

"I figured that damn boy had run off and you with him," yelled Miłosz at them both as they entered. "Should have listened to me, you should, and let fate take its course. Let the *Wisła* swallow what the *Wisła* will swallow. It'll be you and me someday, Tolo, and this one won't be around to save us, either." He pointed at Marek.

Miłosz was staggering, which Marek first thought was due to his bad leg, before he saw the jug of drink on the table. His speech was slurred, and eyes looked far off into a distant land, or perhaps a distant life.

"It's time to make the fire," said Tolo, and moved to the hearth. "It will be dark soon."

He had clearly seen Miłosz in this state many times before. Marek had only seen this once before, when his father and Uncle Jacek had been given a barrel of mead that the Duke found unsuitable to drink.

"He's drunk," whispered Tolo to Marek. "He drinks to escape the pain in his leg, but too much so."

"What's all that muttering about, Tolo," asked Miłosz tersely. "Are you going to keep this boy for company, like a goat or something?"

"I'm teaching him our trade, old man," answered Tolo, "So you don't have to go to the boats anymore..."

"To hell with you," the old man spewed angrily. "Him, I'm going to sell him to the tanner in town. If he can't be useful otherwise, he can still make the piss that bastard needs."

"Marek's not going anywhere," said Tolo defiantly, "and if you drive him off, I will leave with him. Now, what do we have to eat?"

The threat seemed to sting Miłosz. It was clear to Marek that these two had quarreled often. His presence was only the latest excuse for them to do so.

"Hard sausage, that's all. Not enough for him, mind you," said

Miłosz, pointing at Marek. "Bad enough I have to feed the both of us when you bring on a third stomach to fill."

"Just give me mine, then," answered Tolo, taking a length of dried-out, smoked *kielbasa* from Miłosz. He then turned and gave it all to Marek. Marek took only half, and returned the rest to his new friend, so Tolo himself would not hunger.

Tolo started the fire as the night enshrouded them. Soon enough, the flicker of the flames enticed the drunkard Miłosz into a deep sleep. Then, Tolo helped himself to some more of the sausage and once again shared his bounty with Marek.

"Tomorrow, we go into town with the new pelts and we will eat well. You'll see, you will not hunger for long," said Tolo.

They sat before the fire, chewing the hard sausage, moistening it with their saliva, to coax it into the twisted pit that was each of their stomachs.

"Why does Miłosz hate me so?" Marek finally asked.

"Miłosz takes a long time to warm to new people, Marek," answered Tolo, as he looked over his shoulder at the dozing old man.

"I don't think there is enough time for him ever to treat me well," said Marek.

"It is only because he knows you are the Duke's peasant. He hates the Duke. That is why we set traps upon his land. For every hide we sell is money that Miłosz thinks the Duke owes him. It's part of the payment for the life the Duke had taken from him."

"I don't understand," said Marek. "What had the Duke ever done to him?"

"Much, I am afraid," responded Tolo. "Long ago, before the partition, Miłosz was a stone mason. He was a proud and respected craftsman. Duke Sdanowicz hired him to set the foundation for his stables, which were being enlarged. Miłosz knew his craft well and came to criticize some of the existing stonework of the Duke's manor house. An argument ensued between them."

"He would argue with a Duke?" Marek was aghast.

"Not just argue. Miłosz was a proud craftsman. When the Duke bragged of how he had brought masons all the way from Sienna,

Miłosz told the Duke his manor house stonework looked the stones were laid by drunken pigs. When he went on to say perhaps the Italians were indeed drunk when they laid the stones, the Duke slapped him. They were at that time in the area where Miłosz was laying the stable's foundation, Miłosz pushed the Duke with both his hands, landing him on his *dupa* in the thick mud. In his finest riding clothes, mind you." Tolo smiled broadly.

Marek laughed aloud, envisioning the scene.

"What was not funny, however, is that the Duke saw to it that Miłosz received twenty lashes for his insubordination." Tolo's face became pained as he said this.

"So that is the reason he limps so?" asked Marek.

"No," answered Tolo, "those lashes have long since scarred over and lost their pain. The pain that did not ever go away is that the Duke had Miłosz thrown out of the mason's guild. He could no longer work in Kraków, or anywhere in this part of Poland. All because of the Duke, Miłosz lost his livelihood."

"Is Miłosz your father, Tolo?"

The question caught the young trapper off guard. "You ask many questions, young Marek. No, Miłosz is not my father. Yet, also, he is. My parents died in a fire when I was young, but I survived. No one would take me in to care for me. Perhaps they thought me unlucky, or that I had caused the fire, which I did not. I became a child of the streets, without either a family or home. Miłosz the mason found me sleeping in the yard of his work site one day, and instead of chasing me off, brought me food and clothing. Soon, he took me home and into his house to live. He cared for me when no one else would."

"Did his wife become your *matka*?"

"Miłosz had no woman, had no family at all," said Tolo, "and from that day forward we were together. When Miłosz lost his right to his trade, he soon after lost his home as well. Since then, we have been vagabonds living off whatever we can trap from Sdanowicz's lands. It is a hard life, yes, but believe me I know there are worse ways to live."

"And the limp?" asked Marek, returning to the subject.

"As I have said, you have far too many questions, my friend," responded Tolo.

"But I must know, Tolo. Please," begged Marek.

Tolo looked upon him as one would a dog that refused to settle in for the night, before he decided he could trust the boy.

"One night we were setting traps upon the Duke's *folwark*, close to the river. We heard his men coming towards us, so we took to our boat swiftly and made for the middle of the river. Sadly, we took a little too long, and one of the Duke's men fired upon us, plunging a musket ball into Miłosz's leg. It is still in there after all these years and causes him great pain. He drank to escape its soreness, but the pain of the Duke was far greater that just that of the musket ball, so he drank more, and then more again. Now he is just a bitter old man who can barely walk, and has great difficulty running the traps with me. That is why I am so glad you came along. You will be my younger brother. Together we will trap the vermin of the Duke's lands until the only thing that crawls there are the ants and worms."

"You know," Marek said, "someday I must go back there."

"You will go back, Marek," answered Tolo, "however, it will be with me at night, and not in the day at all."

27

MAGDALENA'S SORROWS

OCTOBER 1789

Each day in Tyniec Monastery was another sorrow added to Magdalena's already unbearable grief. She would stare out the window of her room upon the river where in the darkness she watched as her son struggled for his life. He had gone under the surface of the river so many times, flailing wildly, desperate to catch one last breath of air. So it was burned in her memory that he did so until the water was once again still. Even after he was out of the light of the monastery's torches, she listened to the sounds which carried across the water as if it had been frozen solid. She heard one last splash, and after that a final gasping cough, before the river became as still as a tomb. The next day, her last flicker of hope was extinguished when it was reported that no boat had rescued Marek, nor was his body found anywhere along the river.

Each day since then was like the next, as Magdalena relived the sequence again and again in her mind. It was not long before she realized that in doing so, day in and day out, she was fighting for her own life. Just as her Marek had disappeared below the surface, only to come back to it in a perpetuated terror, likewise Magdalena was being pulled under by dark thoughts of taking her own life. One day she would feel its ghastly claws drag her under as she wondered how strong were the river's currents, or how cold were its waters. Was she strong enough to climb down the cliff as her son had done, or should she simply throw herself from its peak? She envisioned being reunited with Marek, albeit always with a dead, lifeless version of the vibrant, lively son that she had loved so.

She would survive a day or two of this anguish, only to awaken on the succeeding day to think of Bronisław, who always seemed to tell her to hang on. *All is not lost, his eyes told her, do not take God's greatest gift and toss it asunder.*

Soon a day would follow when she once again re-lived Marek's death, only to contemplate taking her own. Like Marek in the river, she thought, each dive below the surface became deeper, and had a stronger pull. In this way, she knew she was in the grips of a frantic struggle, just as her son had been in the Vistula, which would result in her going under one last time, never to return to the surface.

Where was Sister Maryja Elizabeta? By her former pupil's side, day in and day out. She recognized that the devil had Magdalena in his clutches, and tried desperately to free her from them, yet unsuccessfully so.

Finally, Magdalena's depression confused her ability to reason, and then mastered the woman's mind in an unholy logic. For in her depression, Magdalena began to reason in her head the following argument:

- You have sinned against God, this sin produced Marek,
- Your recent defiance of the Duke had caused Bronisław's death,
- Your flight from the *folwark* caused Marek's death,
- Marek being dedicated to the Church was your only salvation,
- Since your soul cannot now be saved, why not end your suffering?

The hope that she had from her spiritual visitation many days before no longer consoled her. Magdalena decided that the very next morning, she would turn these thoughts into actions. She would climb down the cliff as her son had until her fatigue caused her to fall in the river. Once she fell, there would be no saving her, as there had been no saving Marek. Tomorrow, right or wrong, it would be done.

The next morning the sun rose and Magdalena, who had not slept, wearily rose with it. She prepared herself for the last day of her life. She would scale the cliff during morning service, when the entire monastery, including the good Sister, would be occupied. It was as she decided this that Sister Maryja Elizabeta entered her chamber to tell her that Abbott Dawid needed to see her before the morning service.

The nun took Magdalena to the Abbott's chambers, where she was surprised to find sitting next to the Reverend Father none other than the Count, who she recognized from his stays at the manor house. The Abbott then did the formal introductions and told his guest that she was excused from morning service as the Count needed to talk to her. Abbott Dawid then turned and gently placed his arm around the back of Sister Maryja Elizabeta.

"Come, Sister, for while Magdalena is excused from service, you and I are not."

And they both left Magdalena alone with the Count.

"*Dzień Dobre*, Magdalena," the Count said in his strained Polish to comfort her.

"*Guten Morgen*," replied Magdalena in what little German she knew.

The Count continued in Polish, stopping often to search for words. "Before we begin, I must tell you that I am here in the service of the Emperor Joseph II of Austria. I have long been in Austria's service, including in many battles and wars. Before you begin answering my questions, I want to share something that I have learned from this with you."

"Yes, my Count, and you tell me this why?" she asked.

"You will understand shortly. For what I have learned is that the corpses of dead men float."

"I do not understand," said the perplexed Magdalena.

"I am told you are as distraught over your son's drowning as a mother can be. This is understandable in every way, for does not a mother love the children to which her own body has given birth and nurtured?"

"Yes, I loved my son, Marek, and have been inconsolably distraught," she said as tears began to come to the corners of her eyes.

"When Abbott Dawid informed me that your son had drowned," continued the Count, "I immediately had two boats launched upon the Vistula: one from Kraków, and the other from Warsaw. Both have searched the river and its banks for the last few days. We have recovered no body. It is inconceivable that even a log would float further than Warsaw since your son's 'drowning'. What I am telling you, Magdalena Kowalczyk, is that I believe your son to be alive. Missing, yet very much alive."

"Please, do not do this to me," Magdalena said, realizing belatedly that the Count had used the surname of her exiled parents. "This is too much, too painful for me to carry the hope of ever seeing my son again."

Her eyes came to glisten with tears that she fought hard to keep from falling.

"Did your son have anything of value on his body, such that any peasant who found him would steal away with the corpse?" asked the Count.

"We have nothing of value," said Magdalena simply.

"My experience is that peasants run away from dead bodies, not hide them," the Count said, scoffing. "You are wrong, my child, about having nothing of value, for you have the name of a *szlachta* noble – Kowalczyk!"

"Yes, I do," she muttered. "So, you know?"

"Yes, it is a fact. Now, you do not have to join in my thinking, but without the presence of a corpse, I am of the belief your son is alive, *Pani* Kowalczyk. Perhaps you think the river's carp may have feasted upon and consumed your son's body, eh? Or that the mermaid *Syrenka* has taken him to her lair, perhaps?" the Count said smiling. The corners of Magdalena's mouth peaked into a hopeful smile for the first time. "I promise you, *Pani*, I will find your missing boy."

"Thank you, my Count, for all the trouble you have gone through on my behalf."

"Ah, but *Pani* Magdalena, I had another reason also. For a day past I met with the Duke Sdanowicz, who I had been told you say is the boy's father. Of course, he denied this upon my questioning. He claimed he took you from the convent out of goodwill, that you fell in love with a peasant, and that your husband put Marek in your belly."

The Count watched her closely as anger permeated her sorrow.

"Of course, this is exactly what I would expect the Duke to say. That the man I loved was the boy's father, even though my husband could not fill my womb in the years before Marek was born, nor in the years since. How convenient a story to be told by the man who raped me."

He had stoked her fighting spirit, and this pleased the Count. He must assure that this woman was filled with the hope of finding her son. Once so, he would continue to stoke the embers of hate for the Duke to fuel the fight ahead.

"I did not believe him, of course," said the Count, "yet, I am required to hear his side. However, it was his eyes that convinced me he was lying. For when I entered the manor house, he said he knew that your son had drowned and was sorry for that. I believed he was sorry, for while he would not admit it, I believed then, as I do now, that he is the father, and as such had grieved at the news."

"I despise him, but I do believe him to have been fond of Marek," said Magdalena. "So, how did his eyes betray him?"

"Just as I was leaving, by my intention, I shared the news of the search of the river having turned up no corpse. I told him that I believed the boy to be alive. It was then that his eyes sparked with hope, just as yours have today. It was the love of a father flickering inside him, and that is exactly why I believe you. That plus the story from the conscripts I questioned at the garrison."

"Conscripts?" she asked.

"Yes, they had been sequestered there until their march to Vienna next week. All said your story of being forced into the peasant ranks was true and accurate. Especially the stable master and his sons."

"Jacek?" asked Magdalena, "and Andrzej and Bartek, as well?" No, no, it cannot be so. Can you have them released?"

"No, *Pani* Magdalena, for once they are conscripted even I cannot have them released. That is up to the generals and military staff. Do not worry, the military will make strong men of them."

"Poor Ewelina, she is all alone now," said Magdalena. She suddenly realized it was the first time she had thought of anyone else's misery since watching her son in the river.

"There is one thing more I must ask of you," said the Count.

"Yes," she answered, "what is it?"

"I must return to Vienna to discuss this situation with the Emperor personally. It is complicated by your parents having been exiled. However, I feel I can persuade the Emperor to restore you to the ranks of the nobility. This discussion and the travel to and from Vienna will require a great amount of time. Can you commit to me that you will stay here, in the monastery, awaiting my return from Vienna, and not give up hope of being reunited with your son?"

"Yes, I can now, thanks to you," said Magdalena, hopeful once more that her Marek lived, and of being reunited with him.

28

THE APPROACHING WINTER

1789

The Count had returned to Vienna just after his discussions with Magdalena that October of 1789. He had travelled just in advance of the snows over the mountain passes that separated Galicia from the Austrian Czech provinces. Then, the Count abstained from his usual visit to Prague, which was out of the way to the west. Instead, the urgency of his mission demanded a more direct route with only short stays in Ostrava, Olomouc, and Brno, before the final push onto the resplendent city of palaces that was Vienna.

The Count had left behind in Galicia the sullen spirits of both Magdalena and Duke Sdanowicz. The cold and dreary gray clouds overhead soon gave way to clear blue skies lording over fields of pristine white snow. Both of the parents of Marek Zaczek could hold only on to the slightest fragments of hope - the Count's belief based on no corpse having been found - to use as a shield to protect themselves against the deepest of sorrows - the loss of their son.

Magdalena also still mourned her lost husband, Bronisław. In her mind's eye, she continually replayed her love's last minutes alive. Her sorrow deepened, like the jagged rut of a sharp plow in the earthen soil. Magdalena blamed herself by recalling its cause: her defiance of the Duke's advancements.

She knew her own soul to be damned, although the thoughts of taking her own life had since left her. For if the Count was right, and his men having not found any trace of her son's body along the river, then there was hope. The voice of the Spirit that had resonated through her was not an illusion, she was convinced, but an omen of the trials that awaited her. As long as Marek was alive, so was the opportunity for her to convince him to dedicate his life to God. And in his doing so, her own sins would one day be absolved.

The Duke also had found hope in the Count's words that his illegitimate son might still be alive. A deep mourning had arisen in him since hearing of Marek's death. Though he desperately wanted to recapture the boy, he could not stand to think of him as having perished.

As the siege of the monastery at Tyniec stretched from days to weeks to months, the Duke became more concerned that this intercession in his dominion over Magda would not end well. First, there was the incessant complaining of his wife, who whined constantly that she missed her favorite servant.

More importantly though, the Count had involved himself directly in resolving Magda's far-fetched claims. One thing that the Duke had long recognized in those piercing blue eyes of the Count was his desire for all that he, the Duke, possessed.

Not only had he long wanted the right to manage the *Groß Salze* mines directly, but the Count, despite all his protestations otherwise, was envious of the manor house and the guest house, as well as all the fields and forests that made up the *folwark* upon which they presided.

In fact, the Duke began to think that he had made a great mistake in building that luxurious guest house. Its finery had cost Duke Sdanowicz five years worth of his earnings, an exhaustive sum. Nonetheless one the Duke expected to recoup through his enhanced prestige. He expected for the Emperor himself to stay there upon his next foray into his Empire's eastern provinces. This would then allow the Duke a stronger trading position, given all would respect his close ties to the Emperor. The Duke was confident he could turn such favor into the *złoty* that would repay his investment many times over in coming years.

Yet, the Duke thought that the elegance of both his manor home, now enhanced by the guest house, had only wetted the envious desires of Count Von Arndt all the more. He feared that the Count in Vienna would call upon Emperor Joseph II in the Winter Palace and plead the tale of Magda being forced into the peasantry by the Duke. He saw the Count conniving to take from him all he loved most: the generous stipends for managing the imperial mines; the seemingly endless and bountiful lands; the two magnificent structures and all the possessions they contained; the stables of a multitude of fine Arabian horses; and most of all, the beguiling womanhood of the lovely Magda.

The Duke had indeed every reason to be concerned. The Count had returned from the eastern province towns of timber and rough-hewn stone to the Imperial capital that seemed to have been chiseled by the hands of God Himself in marble and granite and trimmed in gold. While the Count had missed the trappings of the city of Vienna which he loved so, he had on his mind only a singular goal: to use Duke Cyprian Sdanowicz's abuses of the besieged Magdalena against him. The Count intended him to not only forfeit her from his peasantry, but to also forego everything else that he possessed.

The Count pleaded his case before the Imperial Court, although he was no longer allowed to argue his case directly before the Emperor himself. The Count was denied that access, as he once had with Empress Maria Theresa. Ultimately, Joseph II would decide Sdanowicz's fate, and knowing this, the Count had included what he thought might be a deciding factor. Count Von Arndt had relayed his own personal discussions with the Duke where Sdanowicz had made accusations against the Emperor as having taken payments from the French treasury at the insistence of his sister, Marie Antoinette, the reigning Queen of France.

As this case was slowly considered in Vienna, with the very fate of his mother in the balance, Marek continued to learn his new trade at the hands of Miłosz and Tolo in the woods outside of Kraków. Tolo taught the boy the skills he would need in working the trap lines, as well as those of skinning hides and most importantly, before the *Wisła* froze, of swimming. This last skill Marek learned at only a rudimentary level in the icy waters of the river that had not yet frozen over.

In fact, it was after the river froze that the most contentious events arose. It was a harsh winter, and the old trapper Miłosz had become seriously ill. The rotting cabin in the woods was good shelter, but Miłosz, still drinking heavily, refused to light a fire during the day, wishing not to give away their hiding place. Tolo pleaded with him to stop his reliance on the jug, yet the old man ignored him. Instead, Miłosz relied on a patchwork cape of furs to keep him warm.

It began as a simple cold in Miłosz's head. Tolo urged him to allow a small fire to be built for warmth, but the old man was adamant against any such action. The cold had penetrated through the cabin, not as a wind or even a breeze, instead as an all-pervading icy stillness which seeped into one's being, especially those whose resistance had been weakened by age, alcohol and inactivity.

"My chest is warmed by these hides, I will be fine," said Miłosz, who continued to drink from the jug of grog. While his chest was indeed warm, it was the inescapable winter air that pierced his being through his exposed head each day. By the time the fire came alive each night, its smoke hidden under the shroud of darkness, the mucous of the old man's sinuses had progressed first to his ears and throat, and ultimately deep into his chest. As the winter weeks passed, the old man was drawn deeper and deeper into sickness. Marek had hand-carved from wood a large rough bowl, and every day Miłosz would cough and hack the phlegm and spittle of his sickness into it. As Marek dutifully would discard it into the woods, he thought of the pale green discharge as the very life being drained from the sickly old man.

It was one day when Marek emptied the bowl that he noticed the pale green phlegm laced with red iridescent ribbons of blood.

By this point, Tolo had disobeyed his elder and ran the fire around the clock. Even this would not drive the chill from Miłosz, who suffered and withered in great pain.

With the river having frozen, there was no trapping to be done. The two young men, Tolo and Marek, became full time care givers to Miłosz, although they soon came to realize that he would not survive. As he slowly slipped into the throws of death, Miłosz increasingly asked Marek about Duke Sdanowicz. Marek spoke of his great wealth, and of his beautiful daughter, Maya, and how they had been raised together. He told of the incident with the Tatar pony, and how great was the Duke's concern for his daughter.

"Marek," Miłosz wheezed, "each time you speak of her, the spark in your eye outshines the fire of the hearth. Boy, it is certain that you love this girl."

"Yes," said Marek, "I truly love her, still it can never be. For you both have saved my life, and that life I owe to you both."

Then, Miłosz, surprised them all by his next statement. For the man who once threatened to sell Marek into slavery said in a breath that seemed to be pulled from him in a garbled friction, "Only *Jezus Chrystus* can save life. You are free to live your life, and pursue your Maya..."

It was too much for the old man who had been burning with fever. He began to hack uncontrollably, before he reclined into what would be a restless sleep. Just before he did so, he waved Tolo over to his bedside and whispered something to him that Marek could not hear.

That night both Marek and Tolo watched over him. At three in the morning the death rattle began. Marek had never heard such sounds, which Tolo said was the spirit of Miłosz being ripped from his emaciated body, back into his soul. Soon his soul would rise to the Lord on the lightness of its having shed the burden of suffering. By the time the dawn broke, Miłosz had departed from them, and only what had been the sickened shell of his misfortunes remained.

Marek and Tolo prayed over him. Then they carried him from the cabin, and with only the flinty edge of large stones, dug a grave for him until their hands bled. They laid his corpse in the shallow grave, with the animal hides still wrapped around him, and prayed once more before covering him with the loose, disturbed soil of their own tormented effort. Marek fashioned a cross from staves of the limbs of fallen wood and the cord of a thick, thorny ivy. His hands bled again as he set it deep into the soil at the head of the grave. The makeshift cross, Marek's blood stained upon it, rose above Miłosz's grave, marking that this fallen man held his belief in God that until he drew his final breath.

"He was the best of men, like a father to me," said Tolo, his eyes teary, but their heavy drops had not yet fallen. "For all that had been taken by the Duke from him, he freely gave all he had left to me."

"Perhaps," Marek said, "you were all he had left."

"Yes, perhaps," said Tolo, his tears then streaked down his young face.

"He was a forgiving man," said Marek, attempting to ease Tolo's pain.

"Perhaps not," confided Tolo, "for the last words he struggled to utter to me were these:

'Tolo, like a son to me, promise me to do all you can to see that Marek takes the Duke's daughter from him.'

How he loved to trap and steal the animals of the Duke," said Tolo. "This is only the highest form of that. It is as if I promised the thrashing beheaded snake that I would inject his venom into the enemy he can no longer reach. But, promise Miłosz I did, and assist you I will."

29

THE ERMINE PELT

DECEMBER 1789

Miłosz had been in the grave for less than one month. Tolo and Marek lived through a surreal gloom, mostly staying close to the cabin and surviving off what meager stores that had been left from Tolo's last trip into Kraków. Marek still had not seen the great city, except from a distance, although soon his luck would change.

There came an unexpected warming, and the Vistula yielded her covering of thick ice. It could not have come at a better time, as the stores of Tolo and Marek had become precipitously low. Tolo said it was the work of Miłosz, who looked out for them even then.

On the next moonless night Tolo and Marek recovered their boat and set off across the river to run their traps along Duke Sdanowicz's shoreline. They were fortunate that although the river had not completely thawed, its icy waters ran thick like syrup with great clumps of ice floating upon its surface. It would not be long before the river would once again freeze, as the spell of warming had come to an end.

They came upon the three fingered rock in near total darkness. In utter silence they emptied and reset the traps. Without saying a word, they were soon back in their skiff with a tremendous haul of multiple beaver, several fox and, most prized of all, a singular rare ermine.

Both Tolo and Marek were jubilant with the bountiful catch, although they would remain silent until they reached the far shore. Tolo rowed upon the river, gently dropping the cloth-covered oars into her waters without a sound. It was a perfect night, and both boys thought to themselves that they had Miłosz's blessings cast down upon them.

After stowing the boat in the hiding place in the tall grasses, they walked back to their cabin. Tolo was the first to speak.

"This is a catch of pelts as we have rarely had," he said. "Old Miłosz is thanking us for the care we gave to him. And he is very generous, for only twice before have I ever trapped the ermine."

"That animal's coat is so beautiful, so much finer than the others," said Marek, as he had never seen an ermine before. "With the monies it will bring we will feed ourselves for the winter, Tolo."

"You have much to learn, my friend," said Tolo, a wicked smile upon his face, "for we shall feast off of the pelts of the others, but we will live like Cossacks off the ermine pelt."

The conversation then changed to all they would need to do before taking the pelts into Kraków for sale and barter. Marek grew excited in that Tolo had agreed to take him along, and for the first time the boy would enter into the walls of the great city.

The animals were then skinned, and the pelts were prepared. Over the next several days, the furs were meticulously hand-brushed, and the skins were allowed to dry. Then, after a certain point determined by Tolo, the skins were treated with animal fats, which were rendered from the remains of the skinned carcasses, to stop the drying process. The skins could not be allowed to become either hard or cracked. The final product was a thick pelt of warm fur on a supple skin, which a master furrier could readily then turn into coats, hats, stoles or even the trim for exotic boots.

Of these fine fur pelts, the ermine pelt was the most luxurious.

It was over a week later when the two boys took the pelts to Kraków. They waited until just before the hour when the gates of the town were locked down at night. Wrapped around their waists, under their shabby coats, were the contraband pelts.

Both boys were hungry, as their stores had run out. They had lived off the land for days, and their bellies by then greatly craved smoked meats and *Kluski* noodles to nourish them. Yet, they would have to wait a little longer still.

"Why did we come to town so late?" Marek asked as they approached the walls of the city. "All the vendors are gone for the day. We will have to wait until tomorrow to sell our pelts. We do not even have funds to buy a meal."

"Do not doubt me, Marek," said Tolo sternly, "as I know what we are to do. This way, tomorrow morning we approach the fur traders early, when there are fewest eyes about. Especially those of the devious tax collectors."

"But where will we sleep tonight?" Marek then asked. "When do we eat?"

"In bliss, my friend, tonight we sleep in bliss," said Tolo, "and tomorrow we eat and drink on the riches we will reap."

Kraków had once been not only one of Europe's most lovely cities, but also one of its most prosperous. The very source of that prosperity, the city's proximity to the exotic Eastern trade routes, was also a potential source of attack. Over the past millennium, Kraków had withstood attacks from the Huns, Tatars, Turks and even the Cossacks during their frequent rebellions.

To protect the city, a defensive wall was built to encircle it, to the point where it adjoined the battlements of Wawel Castle in the city's south along the Vistula. While the castle was defended by the Royal Guards, the defense of the city was the responsibility of the merchants who prospered within its walls. Not only did the various guilds pay for the manning of the defenses, they also had to pay for the building of the wall and its forty-seven towers. The result was that nearly no two towers along the walls appeared to be alike, as they were all built by different merchant guilds.

The two boys entered the barbican, the massive brick double-gate on the north side of the city. It was the outer entry to the

Brama Floriańska, or Saint Florian's Gate. Above it loomed a great tower of stone. At the outer portal of the barbican, they were stopped by the guard, as his hand rose briskly and was thrust into the chest of young Tolo.

"The gate is closing," he said, eyeing the two boys suspiciously. "You both seem to be up to no good, arriving here so late. Turn around, and do not come back."

Marek began to sweat at the rancor of the guard. As they had agreed, only Tolo would talk to him.

Figure 7: Krakow's Barbican, Furriers' Gate and Floriańska Street Today

"Most generous sir, we are here to take care of my sister, who has fallen ill upon her visit here. We fear for her life, as she has no one to administer to her health. By tomorrow morning, we fear she may pass from this world."

"Your sister?" the guard snarled. "Where is she staying in Kraków?"

"The good Sisters of the convent have taken her in. We were invited by Mother Angelica to come to her aid, to lift her spirits."

"Boys in a convent?" quipped the guard. "It does not sound like such a thing would be permitted."

"We are only children ourselves, sir," answered Tolo in his sweetest voice.

"And you there," the guard said to Marek, "why does it take two of you to assist her?"

Tolo began to reply when the guard abruptly cut him off, saying that he wanted to hear directly from his friend's mouth. Marek was frightened and stuttered, once he gained the courage to speak.

"To, to, to be truthful, sir," Marek replied, "I have never been within the walls of Kraków, and I simply wanted to see the elegance of this city. So, I joined my brother."

"Such an unbelievable story," the guard said, although it was clear that Marek's truthful tale had touched him somewhat. "What documents do you have to make me believe this rash of lies?"

As the guard said this, he extended his hand rubbing the tip of his thumb along his fingertips. It was then that Tolo knew he would allow them entry for a small bribe. Tolo pulled from his pockets a wad of printed notes and secretively placed them in the guard's palm.

"What is this rubbish?" the guardsman bellowed. "What can I possibly do with this?"

"They are French *Assignats*, sir," replied Tolo, "very valuable to the merchants here. They will buy you many, many treasures."

"Be gone," bellowed the guardsman, "you two have tested my patience long enough, be on your way."

As Marek prepared to turn away from the city, the guard suddenly stood aside, turned his back, and allowed them to pass. As they cleared the barbican, and then passed through Saint Florian's Gate in the wall itself, Marek looked back at the guard to see him inspecting the French paper notes. He thought he could envision the man calculating their worth.

"That is why we came so late in the day, my friend," said Tolo. "These guards always want a bribe from whoever they can coax one from. Never from the wealthy, who will report them, only from the poorest of us, who have nothing at all to give. It is why we hide these pelts under our clothes, for they would take one or more of them. Instead, I gave those *French Assignats* which I recovered from Miłosz's things. He kept them as a souvenir, but with the revolution in France, they are practically worthless. As it is late, and with all the merchants having finished their trading for the day, that greedy gateman has no one to ask as to their value."

"But he will soon, no?" asked Marek.

"He will soon, yes," replied Tolo, "so best we be off the street. For when he finds that they are worthless, and further finds we are not at the convent, he will surely look for us. We have little time. First, I must show you the tower under which we just passed."

Tolo turned Marek around to look back on the inner wall of the city and the great stone tower. It was illuminated by the city's lamps, and their flicker licked along the edges of its stacked grayish-brown stones. These were topped by a cantilevered covered turret for the archers. Atop the turret was a metal decorative medieval structure greened with age and exposure.

"Each tower is from a different guild: carpenters, masons, and so on. This tower is the finest of them all. And it is only appropriate that we came into the city under its shadow, for, my friend, that is the Furriers' Tower."

Marek found the irony delightful, and could not suppress his laughter, when Tolo promptly spun him around and marched forward. "Come now. That oaf will think we are laughing at him! We do not need him chasing us just yet."

They walked down the main thoroughfare, which Tolo explained was Floriańska Street. On either side were the shops of merchants that had been closed for the night. The street's oil lamps had not yet been extinguished, and their light seemed to crackle upon the cold night air. Both boys were beginning to sweat from the pelts around their waists.

"Floriańska Street is a part of the Royal Way," Tolo explained to Marek, "as it is the route long taken by the Kings of Poland as they entered the city to arrive at Wawel Castle. Warsaw is the capital now, although Kraków is the home of the Kings. They are always crowned and buried in Wawel Cathedral here."

The street led directly to the north side of the great Medieval

Square or the *Rynek Główny* and its famed Cloth Hall. "You see those towers ahead?" asked Tolo.

Ahead of them, hovering above the end of Floriańska Street were two massive brick towers, adorned with elaborate medieval spires.

"Yes, of course, how could I miss them?" said Marek as he thought they looked like something from the fairy tales his mother had told him as a young boy. "Are those the towers of Wawel Castle?" he asked.

"No, they are the towers of Saint Mary's Basilica," answered Tolo. "That is where we are heading to get out of the cold. Once we are within its doors, though, you must be reverent and pretend to pray."

"I will not have to pretend, Tolo," said Marek, "for I have so much to be thankful for, and yet so much more to ask of our Father."

The street soon opened up upon the square. Marek's heart raced within him on his first viewing of its expansive elegance. It was one of Europe's largest open squares, and Marek could envision it full of troops to be mustered against the barbarian invasions over many years.

In the center of the enormous open square stood the mammoth Cloth Hall, or *Sukiennice.* It reminded Marek of a great vessel upon an open sea, even though he had never laid eyes on a true ship or an ocean in his entire life. Its soaring clock tower was of what he thought a ship's mast might look like. The vaulted windows of the upper floors and their ornate roofline could, within his mind, almost be seen to rock upon the shifting tides of the masses in the square's expansive open space.

Closest to them in the northeast corner of the square stood the King and Queen Towers, as Marek thought them to be, of Saint Mary's Basilica. This was one of the largest brick houses of worship in all of Europe. The unmatched towers loomed impressively over the square, and even over the city itself.

From the northernmost corner of the square, these tower's dominated the town. The taller of the two towers consisted of eight tiers of windowed floors which transitioned into an octagonally shaped edifice. Upon this was a massive crown of spires, with a central peak that threatened to grasp the very heavens above. This was rimmed by numerous lesser projections that seemed to rise in praise of the central pinnacle. This was the King's tower.

Figure 8: St. Mary's Basilica and the view from its towers of the Sukiennice Cloth Hall in Krakow's Rynek Główny

To the south of it was the Queen's Tower. While it was similar to the other tower in construction, its facades were notably different. First, there were only seven tiers of windows. The octagonal edifice was much smaller than that of the King's Tower, and if not inspected closely could be thought to be missing altogether. And in lieu of the crown of spires, the tower was topped with a rounded baroque summit surrounded by four smaller complementary rounded domes. Overall, the Queen's Tower stood a respectful height shorter than that of the King's, but their combined effect was truly regal.

Just then the mournful call of a trumpet laced through the open square. Its melancholy tune undeniably demanded one's attention. Then, in mid-progression it stopped unexpectedly.

"It is the *hejnał*, the warning call of the trumpeter," explained Tolo. "Legend has it he discovered the Mongols advancing on the city's walls five-hundred years ago, and sounded the alarm, only to be shot in the throat by an arrow. That is why it stops so suddenly, always on the same note. It is played every hour from Saint Mary's highest window, once in each of the four directions so that all Poland can hear it and remember."

Then the *hejnał* began again, and even though they were close to the basilica, Marek could differentiate that it was coming from another direction.

"Come, we are early yet," said Tolo, "let us wait in the shelter of Saint Mary's."

They entered in a respectful silence. Marek had never before been in such a cavernous space. They found a wooden pew and knelt, although Marek found he could not lower his head. Instead he raised it to take in all the works of the artisans that engulfed him.

After a short time, Marek lowered his head and began to pray, as Tolo was already pretending to do. Marek prayed first for the soul of Miłosz, then prayed for his father Bronisław's soul, then next for the safety of his mother and Sister Maryja Elizabeta within the besieged Tyniec Monastery, and finally, and most fervently, for the love of his *Maya Manuska* to stay true to him.

He had been deep in prayer for some time, when Tolo tapped him on the arm and rose to leave. Marek followed him.

"I thought we were to spend the night there?" asked Marek as they departed the church out onto the square, which by then had become deserted.

"No, only to warm our souls there," quipped Tolo, "for as I said, we rest tonight in true bliss."

He led Marek through the darkened streets of Kraków a few blocks west from the square until they stopped under an oil streetlamp, just outside a boisterous tavern. A huge smile creased Tolo's face, as he said, "This place is lively at all hours, Marek."

The tavern was tucked inside the shadows of the town's western wall. It appeared a place for drunkenness and debauchery, the boy thought, merely from the ruckus that emanated from within its frost covered windows.

"We have no money to pay for drink," Marek said, hoping this would prevent them from spending the evening in such a rough and wild place.

"We are not going inside," said Tolo with a laugh, "tonight we climb the stairs to heaven above." With Marek following, Tolo went around the side of the tavern, and ascended the exterior wooden stairs to a second-floor door upon which he knocked.

"Yes, who is there?" came a youthful woman's voice from inside.

"It is I, Tolo, and I have something very elegant for you," said Marek's companion.

The door opened to reveal the dark, lovely face of a woman, still herself young, although years older than even Tolo. She wore only a flimsy silken robe, with an exotic pattern unfamiliar to Marek's eyes. Beneath it, he could discern her wearing nothing else, except for the voluptuous curves of her femininity, the likes of which Marek had never before seen. He was instantly affected by her, and could not look away.

"Tolo," she shrieked, in an almost melodic sing-song voice, as she threw herself around him. With her bosom pressed to his own, and her chin resting upon his shoulder, she looked past Tolo at Marek. Her eyes washed over him with curiosity, and a wry smile unfurled on her lips.

"Tolo," she said as she continued to press herself upon him, "who is your gallant young friend this evening?"

Releasing her, Tolo turned to face his friend. "This is Marek. He drowned in the river. There I found him and brought him back to life."

"Sounds like the devil's work," she scoffed in her thick accent. Then she turned to Marek.

"Hello, Marek," she said with a radiant smile as she extended her hand. The boy, still captivated by her every movement, was confused and began to grasp her hand to shake.

"Kiss her hand, you feeble child," Tolo barked at him. Marek seemed in a trance, and did not respond to his friend's direction.

As if to demonstrate, Tolo himself took the girl's hand and kissed it most tenderly. Afterwards he said, "Marek does not know these things, my apologies."

"Everyone has to learn sometime, Tolo," she said, smiling broadly as she again extended her hand to Marek. He then kissed it as Tolo had. "Reka welcomes you. *Witamy*, Marek. Please come inside, my young boyish visitor."

Marek was in a daze, awe-struck. Reka's skin was bronzed in a way he had never before seen. It smelled of a foreign fragrance that he could not place, somewhere between the sweetness of wild berries and the sacred spices of a chapel's incense. On her wrists she wore pewter bracelets that that seemed to curl like wisps of smoke. Her face was beautiful, framed by a delicately curved thin, black brow and wavy, dark locks that seemed to drip with a subtle mystery. Her eyes sparkled like the gems adorning a *szlachta's* scabbard. They were set a bit closer together than he thought was possible, but the bluish-purple powder that adorned them seemed to pull them outward and away from the bridge of her nose. The overall effect was mesmerizing. Marek thought her to be a gypsy. A beautiful, entrancing gypsy, whose spell he was sure he was already under.

"Reka is Hungarian," said Tolo, as if reading his mind. In reality, he did not need to do so, having had noticed the boy's uninterrupted gaze cast so intently upon her. "Do not stare so, Marek, it is rude."

Shame was then layered upon Marek's infatuation, for she had become a craving that his eyes seemingly could not satisfy.

"I am sorry, *Pani* Reka, I do not mean to stare," apologized Marek as they stepped inside. "It is just you are so different from the other women I have known."

"Ah, so Marek has known many women?" she asked with a laugh in a sultry, devilish voice. "Do not apologize, for Hungarian women love to be stared at by strong young men like yourselves. Call me only Reka, save your *'pani's'* for the women you know outside these doors. Reka is no *pani*, you will see. And you will know." Again, she laughed.

Everything about her entranced Marek. Her Polish words, which were simple and demonstrated her lack of command of the language, were infused with unusual vowel sounds as Marek had never heard before. The resultant accent was exciting and mysteriously decadent, and only added to the boy's intrigue.

The noise of the tavern below resonated through the floorboards, although greatly muted. "Reka's home is modest but is open to you both," she said warmly.

It was nothing more than one large room, with a table in its center upon which burned a single oil lamp. It was not overly warm, although it was in no way frigid, either. Marek realized that the tavern below was kept invitingly warm for its patrons, and a benefit of living over it was the stolen heat, carried upward by the brouhaha of sounds from below. Projecting out from behind a worn dressing partition decorated with painted peacocks upon fields of grass, Marek could spy the foot of an unmade bed.

"So, my Tolo, you have something for Reka?" she asked seductively.

"Something that will bring you great joy, Reka," Tolo answered. From around his waist he pulled the pelts and dropped the pile on the table.

"*Oohhmm*," she purred, as she moved forward to immerse the ringed fingers of her hands into the sea of furs.

"Only one is for you, of course," said Tolo.

"Why, of course?" she objected, "Why can't Reka earn them all?"

"Because, like Reka, we also must eat." Tolo then gestured to Marek to add his pelts to the table, which Marek did.

She looked at Tolo, her eyes ablaze, saying only, "Reka will make you both forget that you hunger for food."

"You choose which pelt is to be yours, Reka," Tolo said, ignoring her risqué comment.

She rummaged greedily through the pile of furs. "Ah, beaver, this is for peasants who steal from their masters, no? And this, this is fox? Better for a merchant's wife. But, is this what I think it is? Is it a sable?"

"Better than sable, it is ermine, much rarer," answered Tolo.

"And what does Reka have to do to earn this?" she asked provocatively as she wrapped her arms around Tolo's neck. She began placing light kisses upon his face, making Marek for the first time very jealous of his friend.

"Reka only has to let us spend the night here, this night," said Tolo into her ear as she continued to nuzzle him.

"Of course," she purred into his neck.

"*Both* of us," Tolo said, denying her any chance of claiming to misunderstand.

"Of course," she said again, "Tolo and Marek. Reka knows..."

She stepped away from Tolo and returned to the ermine pelt upon the table. As she bent over to inspect it carefully in the lamp's light, her figure was silhouetted to Marek's view, as he was behind her. Marek had never before seen a woman dressed as indecently as this Hungarian, and it continued to evoke a strange response in him. Her curves, although fully covered by the thin silken robe, drew in his eyes to the point he could not look away. With every shift of her weight from one foot to the other, and the alluring flexure of her hips, he was spellbound. It was then that she looked back over her shoulder at him.

"Marek," she said with a wry smile, "you have known many women, but you have never really seen a woman like Reka before, have you?"

Marek could do nothing except blush. Yet, it was as if his entire body was blushing, for he could feel the blood pulsing through his temples, his wrists and in areas he wished it not to.

"Sit here, Marek," she said as she guided him to a dilapidated chair on the other side of the partition from the bed. She sat him in the in the chair, leaned at her waist and lowered her mouth to his ear.

"Relax," she breathed warmly in a whisper into his ear. "Do not worry. Reka will take care of you, my sweet. A boy's first time must be special, and alone. Allow me now to put Tolo to sleep. Here, undo this for me."

Marek felt as if his entire body would explode. His breath

seemed to stop and hung stagnant in his chest until he thought again to exhale. As she leaned away over him, Marek could not help but to stare at the sight of her breasts as they hung tightly from her. He did not understand exactly what was happening to him, except he knew he should not be there.

Reka then rose to fully present herself before him. She reached out to drag his leaden hands to the robe's bow around her waist. She intentionally allowed his fingers to brush firmly against the silken fabric, and her skin beneath. She then guided Marek's fingers so that they took hold of the bow's ribboned ends. Then it would slowly untied itself as she tread backward, seductively away from him.

The two ribbons of the silk bow became as taut as everything within him. The knot of the bow slowly was sucked inward, like a collapsing flower, as she walked backward from him. Soon she had taken enough slow, softened steps to make the bow "pop". Marek then held the two ribbons lengths like the reins of a beautiful mare he had never before ridden. A mare that he did not know how wild was her spirit.

She slowly, teasingly held open her arms. A strip of her naked skin only a few inches or so wide from her neck to her knees opened to his gaze. She let his hungry eyes search over her for a second or two, before she cocked her lovely head, as if saying, *This is a woman. Marek likes?*

Instead of mouthing these words, Reka took one more step backward, and the ends of the silk ribboned belt became even more tensed. The two draped curtains of the front of her robe began to draw away from each other, opening in mirrored arcs from her shoulders, revealing the fullness of her beauty for the first time before his eyes.

Marek's heart was pounding in his chest as his eyes moved over her form, from her ringed toes and bracelet adorned ankles, up through the sloping thighs and curvaceous hips, across her flat belly, and came to seemingly affix upon her firm lovely breasts. She allowed his gawking for only a second or so, which seemed like an eternity to Marek, before saying in a snappish manner, "Enough."

Her open arms rapidly came in, like one of Tolo's metallic traps, and crossed over her abdomen, as if she had instantly regained a sense of modesty. Reka laughed, not coarsely, nor vindictively, but softly, in a coaxing manner.

"Reka is saving you for later, young Marek," she said, with a devilish desire rolling through her words.

As she turned toward Tolo, who sat patiently awaiting her at the foot of the bed, Marek could see Reka holding her robe loosely off her skin. She then peeled it back over her shoulders, before allowed it to drop to the floor. Reka timed this just before she walked, totally unclothed, past the edge of the partition that separated Marek's chair from the unmade bed. The split-second image of the silhouette of her fully naked body burned itself into Marek's mind, never to be forgotten.

She then extinguished the lamp upon the table, and Marek, along with all his imaginings, were cast into darkness.

"Here," Marek could hear her say to Tolo, "you must use this pelt as a glove and rub all over Reka's body with it." Despite the muted cacophony of sounds from the tavern below, Marek could clearly hear Tolo disrobing, and then the sound of both of them together lowering their weight onto the smallish bed.

"*Ooohhmm*," Marek could hear Reka purr just over the ragged partition, "Reka loves this ermine fur," she said just before breaking into uncontrolled laughter.

Marek could smell her intoxicating perfume, hear the sensual inflection of every sound she uttered, which rapidly deteriorated from words to moans of increasing comfort. Over the next several minutes, the animalistic noises of their voices entwined, and the combination of their breaths quickened. Soon, Tolo began to grunt, as if undertaking an arduous task, only to be answered by peals of delight from Reka. This call and answer hastened, only to further stimulate Marek yet again. The smell of Reka's perfume in the air was soon mixed with the unexpectedly satisfying smell of the sweat of them both.

She was speaking now, between her moans and ever quickening draws of breath. The words were foreign, Marek could not understand their meaning. But what he did know, only from the seductively frantic pacing and desirous nature of their delivery, was that Reka was ardently urging Tolo on. Whatever it was that they did beyond the partition, Marek could not know for sure, but having grown up amongst the stable of animals on the *folwark*, he was not altogether without his own imaginings.

What Marek could not understand was what was happening to himself. It seemed that as their mysterious sounds thrashed at an ever-higher pace, so did his own pulse. He realized that a light perspiration was dripping from his own brow. His heart was still pounding within his chest. His mind seemed to race in four directions at once, although towards what he did not know. For centered within its great commotion, burned the momentary images of Reka's nakedness.

It was as if his eyes had passed these sights, before they could fade, on to the safekeeping of his brain. His thoughts then seemed to dash off to and fro' in a swirling liquid fluidity from one image of her to another, as if to defend them from being forgotten. Marek could think of nothing else, only her. He was fixated on the nakedness of her beautiful body, the intoxicating mixture of her exotic oils melded with the enticing allure of her fragrant sweat, and the blend of her ever-increasingly paced pleasured moans, gasping breaths and her foreign guttural dialect. These sounds, smells and images filled Marek's senses in such a way that it created a pressure within that made him sure he would burst.

Just then, Tolo's grunts and Reka's answering moans seemed to coalesce into a single loud, rapidly repeating drumbeat, before it suddenly came to an arching pause. Marek could hear his friend breathing hard, attempting to catch his breath. Then he could hear Tolo sigh deeply, after which Reka let loose a softly giggled laugh. For the next few minutes came only relaxed sounds from the both of them, which Marek interpreted only as satisfaction. After a few moments more, he could hear her speak.

"So, my Tolo," she whispered, although Marek could still clearly hear her words, "Did Reka earn the ermine pelt?"

"You were amazing, as always," Tolo said as he struggled to catch his breath, "but don't forget Marek. That was our deal..."

"Reka has not forgotten young Marek," she whispered to him, "not since she has laid eyes on him. Now, sleep my Tolo, rest, and Reka will take care your young friend."

She laughed gently, and after a few minutes more, Marek could hear her softly singing the simple tunes of her distant land to him. She would stop only after the gently sawing breaths of Tolo overlaid her rolling voice. As Tolo drifted to a deep slumber, Marek could hear Reka rising from the bed, followed by the silken *whoosh* of her flimsy robe as she pulled it loosely over herself.

She came directly to Marek, and in the darkness knelt before him. The only light in the room was that of the oil lamp from the street outside that diffused through the single window's covering of frost.

Her face looked up at his. A sultry smile creased her lips. Her brow was beaded with a light sweat, and its effect in the dim light of the room was tantalizing. Her hair, so perfectly brushed before, was entangled in a tempest of disarray like that of Medusa. Her hands reached up to stroke the tops of his thighs. Her silken robe hung loosely from her as Marek gazed down. Her dark, exotic face at first seemed to hide in the night before it glowed up at him. Below it, her breasts hung between his legs, which Reka's hands had playfully splayed open.

"Marek like listening to Reka pleasure Tolo, yes?" she asked in her devilish accent.

He could not respond. Her hands glided forward over his thighs, coming together at his crotch.

"Oh, no! Marek like listening too much, yes," she said when her hands found only a wetness there. "It is not a problem, as you are so young and virile, and Reka knows well how to make you ready again! Such a sweet boy, Reka will make you know the wants of a man!"

Marek, who until that moment had not realized the extent of his own condition, rose to his feet, and in one motion pulled the lovely Hungarian up to hers.

"Reka, I am not a boy. I already am a man of seventeen years," Marek protested.

"And such a strong young man you are," she said, pursing her lips as she stroked herself against him, awaiting for the effect which she was sure she could coax from within him once more.

He gently but firmly grasped her upper arms and pushed her away, which was against every desire that stirred within him at that moment.

"I am in love with a girl," he mumbled, "no, a woman."

"Then I will teach you how to please her, young Marek," her eyes were like beacons in the darkness, inviting him further into its depths. He dropped his gaze from hers, only to have it fall on the fullness of her bosom. His will teetered on the edge of a precipice.

"No," Marek said forcefully.

"Reka has promised Tolo," she said, pursing her lips, "and Reka wants that ermine pelt for herself."

"We will tell Tolo that you pleased me," Marek said firmly. "You will get your pelt, I promise."

"How sweet you are, young Marek," the temptress said. "Your girl's gain is Reka's loss," she again paused, "for now. When she breaks your heart, come back. Reka will make you forget her."

With this, Reka moved her hands, slowly grasping and pulling his own onto her robe until they cupped her ample breasts through it. She sensed his hesitation and decided to try to engage the youth one last time. She could feel him clumsily grope her, before his hands, on their own, slid down to her hips.

It was her resulting devilish smile that snapped him from her enchantment.

"No, I must be true to my *Maya Manuska*," he muttered aloud, clamping his hands around her waist and pushing her back with more force than he intended.

Reka seemed surprised by his physical rejection of her.

"Yes," she said to him, with an anger that replaced her seductive tone, "you are still only a boy. Reka offers to make a real man of you, yet you fight every desire that slithers within you. Your youthful heart yearns for your girl, but the craving of your loins cries out for Reka's flesh. When your girl teaches you that these are two separate yearnings, you will return to Reka."

She laughed tensely and pushed Marek back into the tattered chair, before stepping away from him, and in the fullness of his view, she once again dropped her robe. With no shame, she ran her hands over the fullness of her breasts and down to her swollen hips, all the while gazing at him as he was staring at her. Then, without a word, she passed behind the partition and laid once more in the bed next to the dozing Tolo.

Marek sat in the chair, listening to every sound that she made. They were relaxed and inviting. He cursed himself for having not pursued her, and soon found himself forcing the image of Maya's pale milky skin into his mind as a distraction. Even then, *Maya Manuska's* innocence was seemingly driven off by the seductively fresh memories of the Hungarian who lie just beyond both the peacock decorated partition and the limits of his will.

Just when Marek would be tempted the most, for after all, he merely had to walk around the partition and embrace her, he would conjure once again the pure and wholesome image of his *Maya Manuska*. He would imagine her being distraught, no, destroyed, at his having been with another woman. Especially, this woman.

And so, the conflict raged within him that night, until he drifted off into a light sleep, where his frustrations followed him into his dreams. He dreamt of being with Reka in a tight sensual embrace, but just when he was willing to surrender fully to her seduction, Maya would discover them and cry out to him in disgust.

Marek was awakened in the morning light by Tolo. "You slept in this chair all night, you fool," he said unto Marek. "Come, it is time to sell the pelts and feed our starving bellies."

Marek only then remembered he was hungry for food. The room was much colder in the morning, as the tavern below was quiet, its hearth no more than a bed of embers. Tolo dressed speedily, and as he did so he noticed Marek gazing down on the naked Reka covered only by a light blanket.

"It was your first time, no?" Tolo asked him.

"Yes, it was," Marek lied, before adding truthfully, "she is so very beautiful."

"Let's take one last look, yes?" said Tolo as he pulled back the coverlet exposing her full, ripened body. She was completely naked except for the ermine pelt she clutched tightly in her right hand like a purse of gold coins.

"What likes the body will lose the soul," said Marek, quoting an old Polish proverb he had learned long ago from his Uncle Jacek. He then replaced the coverlet over the sleeping temptress.

"Then we are both long lost," replied Tolo as he collected the other furs from the table. "Come, Marek, we have business to attend."

The two then slipped out the door into the bitter morning. A light snow had fallen overnight, and all sound of the still sleeping city was absorbed into its silence. Tolo then taught Marek the art of bartering the pelts, and they replenished their stores to the point they could barely carry off their spoils.

It was then that Marek had a request of Tolo. With one of the lesser remaining skins, he wished to barter for two rings of amber from the merchants along Floriańska Street, as they were just opening their stalls. Tolo did so for him, buying not only the two amber rings, but also some jewelry he could later barter for food.

As they walked to their cabin outside the city once more, Marek had another request to make of Tolo. Could he help Marek deliver one of the rings to his mother in the monastery at Tyniec? Marek wished for her to have it as a Christmas gift, assuring her that her son was still alive.

"I have no papers to cross the river," said Tolo, "but I do always have the wood of the skiff."

And so, one cold night soon after, they crossed the Vistula, and Marek climbed the cliff of the monastery only to leave a small sackcloth enwrapped package bearing his mother's name.

30

THE UNEXPECTED GIFT AT CHRISTMAS

DECEMBER 1789

A few days before Christmas, a crudely wrapped package was found on the wall of the monastery by the monks on their morning devotional procession. It had a small note attached, which read, *"For moja Matka, Magda Zaczek."*

Taken directly to their besieged guest, Magdalena immediately recognized her son's handwriting. Her hands trembled as she untied and spread open the sackcloth, to reveal the lovely amber ring through which another handwritten slip of paper was stuffed. It read:

Matka, I love and miss you so. I wish you to have this ring to remind you that your love for Tata will last longer than it took the sea to make this bead of amber. Love always, your son, who still lives and adores you, Marek.

Magdalena's shriek of joy was heard in the next room by Sister Maryja Elizabeta, who came rushing in. Thinking that she was sobbing in sorrow, she consoled Magdalena, whose face was awash in a stream of tears.

"No, No, Sister, it is good. A gift from God. Proof that Marek lives still. The Count was right."

"Where was it found?" asked the nun.

"On the wall of the walk atop the cliff," Magdalena replied through her tears, "this morning by the monks on their sunrise walk."

"Then Marek had climbed the cliff to do so, only to descend again afterward. What a risk he took to get it to you!"

"He is close, I can feel him," said Magdalena. "He has brought me this wondrous gift. My most fervent hopes are confirmed."

"God's hand is truly at work here," said the Sister.

"Now, if only the Count will soon return with the Emperor's ruling in my favor, then I can bring my son home," said Magdalena.

"But to where? What home shall you have for yourself when this is all resolved?" asked Sister Maryja Elizabeta, although she instantly wished she had not.

"It matters not, my good Sister," said the boy's mother, "for the good Lord will provide to us."

The two women embraced, before hurriedly rushing off to the Church of Saints Peter and Paul to thank the Lord above for this most generous gift.

31

THE REBIRTH OF SPRING

APRIL 1790

Marek spent the remaining nights, as well as the idle portion of his days, thinking of his encounter with the Hungarian, Reka. The image of her naked body would invade his thoughts and overcome all of his mind's resistance. Like the drunkard, he knew the intoxicant, even though it was exhilarating, was the poisonous seed of his demise.

As he would think of the rousing visions of the Hungarian, he would feel a despair in that he was being untrue to his Maya. He would concentrate on the pure pale form of the Duke's daughter, only to have the exhilarating curves and seductively dark tinge of the Hungarian temptress return. The battle between the once singular desire of his heart and the seemingly overpowering yearning of his body overtook him for the rest of the winter's days.

Soon, the thaw had come upon the Vistula, which flowed freely once again. The sun had coaxed the barren branches of the trees of the land to bud into what all knew was a pretext to an explosion of green rebirth. It was a time of great hope, the greatest of which budded in the mind of Marek Zaczek. He was determined that he would focus his mind solely upon his most urgent quest, returning to the *folwark* to be rejoined to his Maya.

The first moonless night of the month of April, Marek and Tolo worked their way across the river in the many folds of secrecy that is the night's darkness. They came aground upon the Duke's *folwark* at the very three-fingered rock of which Marek's Uncle Jacek had once warned him.

Marek assisted him in setting the first traps of the season. He marked their number and locations in his mind, as Tolo had taught him.

"Remember, we always set them in a line," Tolo had instructed him, "so use the greatest of caution in crossing that trapline. Everywhere else in the woods you may move freely but give the trapline your greatest attention. If not, it may reach up and demand it of you!"

After the traps were set, Marek and Tolo spoke at the skiff that had carried them across. Tolo climbed into the boat, Marek stood in the shallow water aside it.

"Marek, my brother," said Tolo, "I will be here waiting for you in three nights' time. Remember, I must make it across the river before the sun's earliest rays appear in the east, lest I be caught. So, make your way here no later than this very hour of the night. If you do not come to me by then, I will be forced to depart without you. Then, you will have to wait until the moonless nights of the following month for me to return."

"I will be here, and with my Maya" said Marek. "Upon these waters you shall free us both. Either I will have the Duke's consent, or you will carry Maya and myself to the freedom of the Polish shore, where we shall marry."

Tolo's face carried a grave concern. "I am bound by my promise to the dying Miłosz, and I will fulfill that promise. However, you are not so bound, Marek, and I fear for the wrath of the Duke, who I am sure you will be forced to defy. If he does not kill or imprison you, here, upon his *folwark*, then he surely will send his ruffians across the border to punish you and recover his daughter."

"Tolo," replied Marek, "I am bound only by my love to Maya. I only hope she has not given me up for dead long ago. The Duke may punish me, yet he will not harm me, I know this in my heart. Your only concern should be as to how best to whisk his daughter and I across the *Wisła*."

"So be it," said Tolo, and they embraced firmly, before Marek reached down and pushed his skiff off into the blackness of the river's night. "May God be with you always, Marek."

"And, so, with you, my brother," replied the boy. He watched the boat until it vanished into the mist that parted to swallow both the skiff and his cherished friend.

Marek turned and cautiously made his way through the trap-line. He selected a spot he knew to be equidistant between two traps, yet still he carefully probed in front of himself with a limb until he was certain he had cleared the line. Then, he worked himself more quickly through the forest, still clutching the limb should he need it to fight off any animals he might encounter. He had heard the howl of the wolves in the night. While he did not see any of these creatures, he knew this was only because they wished not to be seen. He knew they were near.

Marek reached the tree line, where the forest met the fields, as the first lights of dawn cast in hues of violet and pink across the sky. In the emerging light, he could make out the barren, lightning-struck oak which was only a short distance away. He had his bearings and rested briefly before beginning to cross the open fields toward the hamlet where he had been raised.

It was noon before he reached his destination. From a distance in the field, the huts appeared to be nothing more than a series of crouched beings, squatting close to the soil, their thatched roofs like brawny shoulders, huddled in groups, as they sowed the seeds of a future harvest into the land.

He picked a location at the edge of the field where he could watch without being himself observed. He had often done this as a young boy, marking in his mind the movements of the unsuspecting peasants between the hovels that were their homes. It had been a game to him then; now it was an altogether serious endeavor.

Marek watched the hut in which he had been both born and

raised. He saw no movement there. He hoped this meant that his mother was still within the monastery, or perhaps, by then, even at the convent in Kraków.

Marek did see movement in his Aunt Ewelina's hut, but none other than that of his aunt alone. No signs of Uncle Jacek, or cousins Andrzej or Bartek. It was late afternoon, so perhaps they were fulfilling their duties around the *folwark*.

Marek waited until the sun began to set. He dared not enter the hamlet in the day's light, for anyone who might recognize him could unwittingly err, divulging his presence upon the *folwark*. He knew his only hope of obtaining Maya for his own was based upon his total secrecy. He decided, he would patiently wait for nightfall.

As he waited, his idle thoughts welcomed distraction. Soon, he once more could smell the fragrance of the woman Reka. He could see her, kneeling before him, her smile inviting him to mischief as she stroked the tense upper skins of his thighs. He attempted to vanquish her by recalling that he had not given into her, and he coaxed thoughts of Maya to drive her off. Yet the temptress always seemed to return, luring him to entertain her seductions once more. *After all, you denied me once. So, what harm comes from only having Reka in your thoughts?* she seemed to ask of him.

He waited until dusk had fallen before cautiously making his way into the hamlet and to the hut of Aunt Ewelina. When his aunt saw his face inside her door, she broke into tears of joy.

"Oh, Marek!" she exclaimed, as she rushed into an embrace of the lost soul, "We were told you had perished, drowned in the river." She squeezed him hard. "It is so good to wrap my arms around you. I have been so lonely, so very alone. You are a gift sent to me by God from heaven."

It was then that Marek noticed the nearly healed scar across his aunt's cheek. It bore a puffy red halo shadowing the last remnants of a hardened scab that had not yet fallen free.

"*Ciotka*, what has happened to your face?" he asked.

"It is nothing, my nephew," she said, embarrassed. "I was working in the manor house and took a fall in the kitchen. The Duke had

Doctor Olszewski tend to it for me. He tells me it will be fine with time."

Marek could tell from the awkwardness of her response that she was lying to him. He knew the Duke had no sympathy for the wounds of the peasants, especially the peasant women. He decided not to press her for fear of embarrassing her further.

"Where is Uncle Jacek?" asked the boy. "Please do not tell me he died of his wounds."

Ewelina, whose cries of joy at that moment became mixed with the bitter tears of regret, lowered her head to the ground. "I fear it is even worse a fate that he knows now, for he has been conscripted into the Austrian Army, along with Andrzej and Bartek. Each day, I awake without knowing whether each breathes the reviving air of life, or lies, no longer in need of any breath at all, face down in the soil."

His aunt began to sob softly, before her fears overcame her and she then cried hysterically in his arms. He consoled her, although he only wished to ask of his mother's fate. When she finally brought her grief under control, he did so.

"Your mother," replied Ewelina, "from what we hear from those who serve in the manor house, is still besieged in the monastery. She awaits the return of Count Von Arndt, who has taken her case before the Emperor. He should be arriving soon, or at least as soon as the thawing mountain passes will allow him to transit them."

"Does she still think me dead?" asked Marek.

"I must assume so," said the aunt, and when she noticed his disappointment, added, "but we do not hear much from the monastery. I doubt she has ever given up hope. Come, Marek, you are nothing but bones. Let me feed you, child."

Marek thought it possible that his mother received his gift, and that his Aunt Ewelina was unaware of it. Or so he hoped.

Ewelina had noticed her young nephew was lean, and perhaps painfully so having barely survived the harsh winter. Still, she also noticed that the playful boy she had once remembered was by then hardening into manhood. His body bore no fat, and his muscles were rigid and strong. His face, which last she had seen, was awash with the innocence of youth, was now speckled with the tease of desires emerging from his adolescence. His eyes no longer had the wonder and amazement of a child but bore now the expectant fulfillment of his adult dreams. With the passing of the month of February past, Marek had attained eighteen years of age, and stood upon the threshold of becoming an adult himself.

"Come, tell me of how you survived both the river and the winter," said Ewelina. Then she fed Marek, and he told her between gulps of her soup the tale of his survival. Yet, he did not tell her of his plans for the next few days, nor of his intentions regarding Maya.

Marek slept that night with a comfort of mind that he had not felt since the autumn. He was back among family, true family, and felt the safety which had eluded him across the river.

Ewelina kept watch over him that night and was saddened. For every pleasant thought that came to her in looking upon her nephew only pulled forth the discomfort of worrying for the safety of her two boys, and her silly, lovely Jacek.

32

SPARROWS AND TURTLEDOVES

APRIL 1790

Marek awoke the next morning long after the sun had risen. His rest revived his once weary body, and his energy needed to be discharged along with his expectation of the day that lie before him. He cleansed his face and hands from his aunt's wash bowl, ate once more, and then set off to the manor house, where he once again hid himself in the woods such that he could view all the activities going on there.

It was mid-afternoon when Maya emerged alone for a walk along the crushed gravel path. This had been a habit of hers, and Marek had hoped she would still abide of it.

Marek watched from the woods behind the manor and guest houses, and in its shadows paralleled her walk along the path. She was as lovely as he had remembered her, and the mere sight of her walking in the sunlight shot through him like bolts of pure energy. He could feel the pulse of his heart banging against the taut, muscled skin of his chest. He wanted so to run to her but knew that time had not yet come.

He followed her, stalking like a predator in the shadows, until she turned to begin her way back. They were a good distance from the manor house at this point, and here he risked calling out to her.

"Maya Manuska, mon petit chou," he called, the last three words being the French term of endearment, meaning literally "my little cabbage".

Her head instantly snapped to the direction of his voice, her eyes enlarged in disbelief. She saw the lean, muscled figure of Marek emerge from the shadow of the woods. Her heart swelled, and she instantly ran to him, throwing herself into his awaiting arms.

Together, they merged into a frenzied realization of bliss. Nothing else mattered than that each soul was enwrapped with the other. They kissed deeply, and forgot the world around them, for it mattered not.

Marek could feel her feminine form pressed warmly against him. It made him feel swollen, with every inch of his being flushed with the blood which his racing heart pumped wildly. That heart was beating like the battle drum of a Tatar. Fast, yet disciplined at first, until as he kissed her again and again, it grew faster, missing beats, like the hastening pulse of an exuberant wedding dance.

Maya also could feel this joy. It charged through her like a line of her father's stallions, driving off the desperation and despair that had besieged her since he had left.

"Father said there was hope you were still alive," she said jubilantly, "and I never gave up hope, Marek."

"I fell in the river trying to make my way back to you, Maya," he said, still holding her tight.

"I know," she said, "we all feared you drowned."

"I have such wonderful news to tell you..."

"Yes, yes, my love," Maya said, "Tell me. Tell me everything."

Before he did, he took Maya's hand, and from his pocket slid onto her finger the second amber ring which he had bought in Kraków.

"I love you, *Maya Manuska*," he professed to her. "I have come to take you away from all this."

Her heart rose upon his profession of love and then sank like a leaden weight.

"This ring is beautiful! And I love you also, my Marek," she said, "but I am tormented that our love can never be. We are from two different worlds. It cannot be..."

He squeezed her tightly, even more so than before. "That is the best news of all!" he exclaimed. "We are not different at all in that respect. The last thing my mother told me is that her father was a *szlachta* Duke just as your own is. We are both children of the nobility. There is nothing to stop us from being married. It is why I have come, to ask for your hand, with your father's fullest blessings."

Maya seemed greatly confused. She knew she loved Marek, although throughout her entire life she also knew it could never come to pass. He was a peasant. His parents were peasants. She wanted his news to be true, but feared his hopes had leapt beyond the boundaries of possibilities for their future. Her father would never allow her to marry Marek, she was sure.

"Oh, Marek," she cried, "if only this were true."

"It is true, my sweet," he said, "and I have survived the cruelest of winters only on the hope you would be happy to be my wife."

"Oh, Marek, my Marek!" she said, stroking his strong face with her hand, "I desire to be nothing else but your wife. It is my greatest wish."

"Then this is what we shall do," he said. "Tonight, after dinner, have your father walk to the stables with you. There, I will await you both, and there I will ask him for your hand."

"It is so sudden, my love," she replied, "why not allow time to be our ally? Let my father, the Duke, rejoice at your return before you make this plea. We are young and have all of the time of the seasons." She stared at the amber ring, wanting to keep it and Marek's love forever.

"No, my love, it is tonight. For if the Duke rejects me in my request, then tomorrow night I leave the *folwark* never to return here again."

"You cannot. I cannot survive without you," she pleaded. Agony had invaded her blissful angelic face.

"Then, if your father does not grant me your hand, we shall

elope," Marek explained. "If you do not join me, you will break my heart, which I will take myself far away to heal from this bitter sting."

Maya was torn. She had in only seconds gone from the invasive angst of not knowing for sure if Marek was even alive, to the soaring elation of being rejoined in the flesh with him. Now, amidst this euphoria, her Marek presented her a conflicted decision between her love and her family.

She agreed to his demand to bring her father such that Marek could ask for her hand. Soon they separated, she walking excitedly, skipping like a child upon the finely crushed gravel path to the wealth of the manor house. He melted back into the shadows of the forest, his steps falling on the carpet of its undergrowth.

The evening came and Marek awaited in the darkening shelter of the stables. He had missed being around the many horses housed here. These were wonderful creatures that for so long had been a central part of his life. They were more than merely friends to him. Certainly, these majestic mounts were engrained in the very fiber of his being. They were a part of him, as much as was the hamlet of the *folwark* in which he was raised. Deep within himself, he knew his fate was to be found in the saddle.

After several hours, Marek heard the sound of feet shuffling across the forecourt of the manor.

"What is this great surprise you have for me, Maya?" asked the Duke.

"Patience, my father," Maya replied, "you must have patience."

They turned into the open end of the stables and without entering its shadows, Maya said, "Father, I have found something dear that you have lost."

Upon that remark, Marek stepped out from the shadows of the stables into the open night, saying only, "Good Evening, my Duke."

Duke Sdanowicz stepped back, as if he had seen a ghost. The color drained from him for a second, before he realized that his son - indeed, his bastard son, Marek - had been returned to him.

"Marek," he said loudly, after composing himself, "I am overjoyed to see you again. We thought you had drowned in the currents of the river." The Duke took his hands into his own.

"In some ways I did, my Duke," he explained, "but I have come back with a purpose."

"I should have suspected so," he said to Marek, releasing his hands. "Do not bother to plea on your mother's behalf. It is too late for that. I am told the Count is en route to us to reveal the Emperor's decision. Your mother's folly is about to come to an end."

"I come not to plea for the heart of my mother," Marek said, "but rather for the heart of another woman."

"Your Aunt Ewelina has disrespected me, Marek. Waste not your breath on her behalf. Be satisfied that I have suppressed my justified anger with her."

Marek drew a deep breath upon hearing this. He looked at Maya, who then stepped backward from the two men.

"I have come to ask for your daughter's hand in marriage," he explained. The Duke seemed to not understand at first, before he then exploded in laughter.

"You, a peasant, to marry my Maya?" his laughter bellowed once again in the night. "What dares you to think that this could ever come to pass?"

Marek patiently waited for the Duke to stop laughing.

"My mother explained to me that I am not a peasant, for her father was a *szlachta* Duke like yourself."

The Duke scoffed aloud. "Like myself, you say. Ha! He was nothing more than a traitor to the King. He was exiled for his actions."

The Duke wondered exactly how much Magda had told their son.

"His actions were against a Polish King," Marek said. "I have heard you say many times that we are Austrian subjects."

"You are no subject at all," said the Duke angrily. "You are a mere peasant."

"I have the blood of the *szlachta* in my proud veins," replied Marek.

Again, Duke Sdanowicz wondered if Magda had told the boy that he was his true father. He could not be sure. He sensed not, for the boy surely would not be bold enough to ask for his own half-sister's hand in marriage from him.

Marek went on to say, "I am a poor landless noble who loves your daughter, and I wish to take care of her for the rest of her life."

What the Duke said next, he did so without thinking. It was a reflex, as from deep within his memory he drew the words of another:

"Turtledoves are not for common sparrows, and magnates' daughters are not for petty nobility!"

These were the words of the *hetman* when Kościuszko had asked for his daughter's hand in marriage. They flooded from his brain like a deluge in his throat, before splaying with great force and intended impact over his lips.

Maya broke into tears and ran back to the manor house. Marek had never heard these words before, and they pierced him nonetheless like a tray of sharpened daggers. He never broke eye-lock with the Duke.

"You will be sorry for imbibing from your mother's tepid swill of lies, Marek," said the Duke. "I once had great plans for you, yet you have allowed a great digression to come between us. For I know, as you do in your heart, I am sure, that you can never be allowed to marry my Maya. Now, be off with you, boy. Go to the monastery to be with your mother. I will message my men to allow you to pass. You all will be back here soon enough when the Count returns, only to resume your peasant lives."

Having said this, the Duke turned and walked to the manor house, leaving Marek alone, enraged in the deepening night.

Maya had run back to the house, upstairs to her room. She cried into her bed linens for the manner in which her father had treated Marek. She cried until every ounce of feeling had been drained from her. It was then that she decided to make a bold move.

Still dressed, she composed herself, went downstairs and took a book from the library where her father tensely shared a brandy with Doctor Olszewski. Maya could feel the Duke's heavy gaze upon her as she did so. It seemed to scour her, as if the Duke was assessing how his daughter could have led him into what was nothing more than an ambush.

Maya took the book to a chair near the door, where she pretended to read it. When the Duke and the doctor's discussion had waned, she waited until the doctor put on his coat to walk back to his modest rooms at the infirmary.

"Dear Doctor," she said to him at the door, "would you be so kind as to chaperone me to the stables?"

The Duke was still in the library, and did not hear this request, as it was given in the softest of tones.

"Of course, lovely Maya," the doctor said through a broad smile. He walked her across the forecourt and near the stable entrance. Marek was still there.

"Could you allow me to talk to my friend while you watch on behalf of my father, good Doctor?" asked Maya. She knew it was inappropriate to be in the stable with this boy alone in the darkness.

"Most certainly, Maya" said Doctor Olszewski, as he stopped, allowing her to take the final steps to come face-to-face with Marek.

In the French tongue, she said to him, "My love, I am so sorry for the manner in which you have been treated this night."

Maya had used French, not knowing that the doctor had command of that language. While he stood many paces from the pair, he could clearly hear their discussion. And he understood it in its entirety.

"The toughness with which my request has been met only stiffens my resolve, Maya," answered Marek. "My love for you does not bend with the wind, nor does it cower under threat, even from as powerful a man as your father."

"The Duke is a heartless beast," Maya said of her own father. "I have known this since his treatment of your Uncle Jacek. He has made the walls of his own tomb of misery, for as the Polish proverb says, '*Roughness must be met with roughness*'. Tomorrow evening I will come with you, away from this place."

Marek exploded in joy upon hearing her words. He wanted to hug her, but her hands came up in a motion to prevent him from doing so in front of the doctor. Instead he said to her, still in French, "There is great truth in another proverb, *'for the heart sees further than the head...'.* Until tomorrow, my love."

At this point, Marek walked back to the peasant hamlet to spend the evening with his Aunt Ewelina. The doctor escorted Maya back to the manor house, before walking on to the infirmary alone. As he entered its humble door, he had still not decided if he would tell the Duke that his daughter planned to elope with Marek, her half-brother, the next night.

33

THE ELOPEMENT

APRIL 1790

It was on the fourth moonless night that Marek came for her. He knew that Tolo would be awaiting them at the rock of three fingers that jutted out upon the Vistula. Marek would meet her in the woods behind the manor house. She would be wearing her riding clothes, as he had requested. All Marek had to do was take one of the Duke's Arabians, ride them both through the night to the barren, lightning-struck oak, and then lead her through the woods to Tolo and his awaiting skiff.

As Marek crept through the blackened stables, he concentrated on which Arabian he would take for their midnight ride. It was only then that he noticed a form emerging from the shadows. His heart sunk as he knew he had been caught, before he could even collect his lovely Maya.

"Marek?" a hushed whisper crackled through the silence.

"*Maya Manuska*!" Marek answered, unaware that the delight in his voice had projected it to a louder level than was reasonable.

"Hush!" she replied. "My father's guards are gathered in the woods behind the manor house where I was to meet you. They are hiding in the darkness and waiting to apprehend you."

"How could they possibly have known?" asked Marek.

"I have no idea," Maya responded, "but I was able to sneak out of the front of the manor house to warn you."

He looked upon her, in the tight riding britches and black boots. Even though her blouse was covered by a heavy frock to protect her from the night's chill, he could still make out the shape of the curves of her hips in the dim light.

"I am so sorry we cannot proceed with your plan," Maya said to him.

"And I am sorry you do not love me, *Maya Manuska*," he responded, in a voice that sounded as injured as his feelings.

She appeared shocked. It was as if a Tatar's arrow had pierced her heart, for she had never expected him to utter those words.

"How can you say this, my Marek?"

"You are here with me. We have a multitude of horses to choose from. If you loved me, you would not be sorry and tell me how our plan to be together had already failed! You would simply say, 'Marek, let us be gone.' And thus, we would."

"I only fear we will be caught, Marek, now that they know of our intentions," she explained. "They will do nothing to me, of course, except return me to my father. I fear only for what these men would do to you. I fear they would kill you upon the commands of their Duke."

"Your father will never allow us to marry, that is clear," Marek said. "This night remains our only chance to elope. Your father's men are in the wrong location, thanks to your actions in coming here. They are on the other side of the manor house. Now, if you truly love me, come ride with me and tomorrow we will awake across the Vistula under the rising sun together for the first time."

Marek then put out his hand, and she laid her trembling palm in his. In the darkness, he could not see, although he could feel, the amber ring upon her finger.

He pulled her close to him, and wrapped his arms around her, and kissed her passionately. She melted in his embrace. After absorbing the very scent of him, after feeling the strength of his arms, and after feeling the passion upon his lips, Maya pulled herself free to say, in the most simple way possible, "Let us go, my love."

A smile of complete happiness creased Marek's face. "*Dobrze bardzo*. We go now, for we have not much time. We have to make the river before the first rays of dawn paint the sky, or Tolo will be forced to abandon us."

"The river?" Maya said in a terrorized voice. "I do not know how to swim, Marek. And it is so far from here."

"As I said," Marek continued after he reassured her with his kisses, "we do not have much time. We will have even less once those in the manor house discover you are missing."

Marek took her hand and led her to a mount which he knew to be gentle yet swift. The horse was large enough to carry them both, and in seconds, the couple were on its back and upon their way in the dead of night.

They exited the stables and soon were upon the open fields. Marek did not see the three men on horseback who awaited at the edge of the field in the shadows of a copse of birch trees. Soon, two of the riders were following Marek and Maya, while the third rode back to collect the horsemen waiting in the woods behind the manor house.

As Marek and Maya rode across the darkened fields, they soon became aware of the two riders following them. Marek knew he could not outrun them, as his mount bore the weight of two riders, even as small as they both were. Their pursuers had each their own mounts and would surely close on them before they made the barren oak, which was still a far distance off in the night.

Marek knew that even without his pursuers, time would be tight. He hoped he had enough time to try and lose these two shadowy horsemen.

Marek diverted his Arabian to a creek which fed into the Vistula. He knew it would have been a swampy bog with all the recent spring rains. He also knew that in the middle of the bog was a thin stretch of elevated soil that formed something of a natural bridge. It had been a childhood diversion for many years after the spring rains. He, Bartek and Andrzej had played upon it as children, jumping off the span of dry soil into in the thick sea of mud. He knew the swollen creek well. Marek thought that this night, his only chance was to lure his pursuers into the marsh and hope they could not find the strip of soil which would offer their escape.

Marek found the marsh and worked towards its center. The footing of the Arabian soon transitioned to a mud-thickened slop. Marek knew if he had strayed in either direction left or right, that slop would become an entrapping quagmire. He guided his Arabian at a very slow pace, working its footing from his own memory, and hoping the darkness had not led him astray. It was then that he felt the animal's footing become more secure, and then he was sure he had found the rise of the natural bridge.

Just before crossing the land bridge, the two horsemen closed on them from either side, at a distance of some twenty or thirty paces. The first yelled out to him.

"Give yourself up, boy. We have you trapped like the lowly swine that you are in this swill."

At this, Marek spurred his horse onward, and whipped its reins in a frenzy. The Arabian responded by pulling itself higher upon the rise, before breaking into a full gallop once upon the dry land in front of it. Behind them, Marek and Maya could only hear the yelling of the two pursuers, soon followed by their cursing. They had come to realize they had been trapped in the bog, and even if they freed themselves, the boy and the girl would be long gone.

Marek and Maya then rode free of their pursuers in the night. After a long ride, they came upon the tree line where Marek searched the darkness to find his landmark, the barren lightning-struck oak.

Just as Marek had identified the landmark tree, the rumble of perhaps a dozen riders preceded the approach of these horsemen. Marek dismounted and helped Maya from the Arabian, before swatting the horse, sending it off along the tree line. The approaching party of riders split, several following the horse, the rest rapidly approaching the location where Marek and Maya stood. Soon enough, the others would find the riderless horse and return here as well.

Marek knew their only chance was for them to make the Vistula River before Tolo pushed off with the skiff. The night was still black, although subtle hues of indigo could be just made out along the horizon of the fields that they had just traversed. It would not be much longer before the skies were speckled alight with ribbons of violet and pink, reflected upward from the river's mirrored surface. Marek knew that before this would happen, Tolo would have been forced to push off in the last cloak of darkness. Then, they would be abandoned.

Marek turned to Maya and took both her hands into his, squeezing them so very tightly. "My *Maya Manuska*, this is most important. As I lead you through the forest, you must only step where I step. Nowhere else. Do you understand?"

"Yes, of course, Marek. I will only step in the shadows of your footprints," she replied.

Marek squeezed even more tightly upon her hands to emphasize his next words.

"No, that is not close enough. Only *in* my very footprints, it is that important. Do you understand?"

"Yes, yes, I understand," she replied. Her heart was beating like the thunder of the riders pursuing them. The first of the Duke's men advanced briskly upon their position, and dismounted his horse only a short distance from the two fleeing souls. Marek turned, released only one of Maya's hands and then pulled her through the forest at a rapid pace.

They were perhaps fifty paces within the woods when rest of the Duke's riders dismounted at the tree line. Marek and Maya could hear shouting from them to stop, which only hastened their pace. Soon the riders entered the forest on foot, as the limbs of the trees were too dense to allow their horses access.

Marek pulled Maya with great speed through the sea of branches and pine boughs. He struggled to remember the placement of the trapline, all the while he feared he also could not be sure of his own exact location. The chances of becoming ensnarled by one of Tolo's traps grew with every hastened step that they took as they came closer to the river. Only the adrenaline pulsing though his veins pushed him forward when all sanity said that he should stop and give themselves up. However, Marek knew that so long as Maya placed her steps exactly where his own had fallen, that while he might be struck by the razored teeth of the trap, she would not.

They came then to be only a short distance from the edge of the forest where it bowed to meet the waters of the river. Two of the Dukes guards were almost upon them. Soon it would not matter, for Marek and Maya would simply clamor aboard Tolo's skiff and push off into the darkness of the river and safety.

It was then that the resonant ***crack*** of a mechanical device split the forest like a raging fire. Rising from the flame-like teeth of the metal trap was the unnatural guttural howl of agony escaping from the injured beast. Marek felt something ripping through him, as if it could be the blade of a bayonet, although he soon realized that was only the sharp pangs of an irrational panic. He turned to see Maya was still moving forward, as was he. Just beyond her shoulder he could make out the thrashing image of one of the Duke's guards, as he fell to the ground in inescapable pain. His foot had landed directly upon the trap hidden in the darkened undergrowth. His lower calf was ensnarled in a ghastly metallic jaw. Marek could not see the rider's injury in the darkness, but knew that man's blood would have been flowing like a cascading scarlet waterfall.

Marek kept pushing forward, nearly dragging Maya behind him. The second of the Duke's guards had become frozen in place in the forest, in fear of springing another of the traps, after his howling companion had fallen prey to its danger.

Marek and Maya came upon the three fingered rock that jutted out upon the river. Marek's heart sank only to find no Tolo, and thus no boat, at the river's edge. The sky above the river had faded from the deep hues of indigo to a palette of lighter shades of blue that hung over its water. Soon, morning would break in earnest. Marek knew that Tolo had waited as long as he could, but had been forced to abandon them in the lateness of the hour.

They were trapped, as much as the unfortunate guardsman of the Duke. Pinned up against the river, they had no where to further flee. Marek and Maya could only await the rest of the guards to build their courage to come across the trapline and apprehend them.

It was only then that both Marek and Maya heard something above the droning wail of pain from the injured guard behind them. In front of them, they heard a voice call from out of the woolen blanket of morning mist that settled upon the river's surface. And the words were in the voice of Marek's newfound brother, Tolo.

"Marek, swim," the voice said, "it is your only chance."

Just then, emerging from the parting vapors of the mist was the skiff, Tolo bent over at its oars.

"Swim, Marek, it is not far..." he yelled to them.

Marek, whom Tolo had only recently taught to swim, knew he could make it to the boat. He turned to Maya, who had a great panic in her frightened eyes.

"Marek, I cannot swim," she cried, "but you go and save yourself, my love."

The remaining guardsmen had by then worked their way through the woods and would soon be upon them both. Marek and Maya stood upon the flat, three fingered rock, trapped against the waters of the Vistula.

Marek remembered thrashing for his life in the river's waters. He could not subject his Maya to such a disabling fear. Besides, this time the drowning victim might not be lucky enough to be saved.

"I will not leave you, my *Maya Manuska*," declared Marek.

He then turned toward the boat. "Tolo, come and get us, the girl cannot swim!"

Tolo cursed under his breath. He knew he should have been long gone at this point, but he also knew if he did not return to Marek and his Maya, the riders were sure to pounce upon them. He reluctantly rowed towards the edge of the river to rescue them.

It was the morning light that cursed the three of them. While the sun itself had not yet risen, the darkness of night had given forth to a sky painted of purples and pinks in the palest of hues. Even this most beautiful unveiling of the dawn gave enough light for one of the guards to take aim upon the boat with his pistol from the depth of the woods.

The shot rang out with a bang whose echoed tail was heard to whiz between both Marek and Maya.

"You idiot! I gave directions no one was to fire upon the girl or the boy!" said a commanding voice from the forest.

"I was not aiming for either of them, but for the boatman," said another voice in self-defense.

"You are so confident in your skill," said the leader, "that you would risk all of our lives should you hit either of these children against the Duke's command? No one is to fire another pistol!"

Marek then turned again to look out upon the river, where the skiff now drifted downstream with the water's flow. The body of Tolo was lifelessly slumped over its side. Both oars were awkwardly angled into the air. The skiff drifted slowly into the open veil of the morning mist as a great sadness overcame Marek. The veil of mist then closed around the boat, and Tolo was gone forever. Marek realized he had lost the only brother he had ever had.

The riders came upon Marek and Maya. They were separated from each other, after which the man in charge violently backhanded Marek across the face, breaking his nose. He was then dragged over to the injured guardsman, still writhing with his leg in the jaws of the triggered trap.

"Look at what you have done, boy," said their leader. "See how the teeth of your entrapment shreds his flesh? Hear how he suffers in unbearable pain? You are a curse, child, nothing more than a curse of pain and misery."

As the blood from Marek's nose flowed down onto his clothes, he realized that his own discomfort was nothing compared to the man in the trap. Marek then released him from its clutches, as he had been taught by Tolo. The same Tolo whose lifeless body continued to float in the skiff downriver. Marek then looked up to see the tears flowing from Maya's eyes.

In his mind, he agreed with the verdict set upon him. *I am truly nothing more than a curse of pain and misery,* he thought, *and I have brought these plagues upon my Maya Manuska.*

34

REVERSALS OF FORTUNE

JUNE 1790

Several months passed before the Count Maximilian Von Arndt notified Duke Sdanowicz that he would be returning to the *folwark* with Magdalena. The message came in the hands of the Count's private courier and concluded what had been nearly a ten-month ordeal since his Magda had fled the estate.

"Doctor Olszewski," said the Duke, "today is a great day. The Count returns my Magda to me, or so my spies in Vienna have told me. It is unfortunate that I have had to suffer so much during this time, however, I appear to have won the favor of the Emperor, so it was not in vain."

The doctor responded to him only with questions. "What will you do with Magda? What is to become of her fate?"

"I do not know," said the Duke, "except that she will never be given to the Count. I have heard from Vienna that he had pleaded an unjustified case to the Emperor against me, just as he had once done with Maria Theresa. Luckily, the Emperor realizes the importance of my hand upon the helm of the royal salt mines."

"Will you tell her of the fate of her son?" asked Doctor Olszewski. "Does she even know that her son is alive?"

"She has lived for all these months only with the hope that he is, I am told, but never really knowing for sure," said the Duke, who was not aware of Marek's gift to his mother of the amber ring. "I am sure she has not heard of his return here and his attempt to steal my daughter from me. I will allow her to get accustomed to the misery of her continued peasant life here on the *folwark* before I share with her Marek's fate. Just when she thinks her life can get no lower, I will throw the news to her like a leaden weight."

It was then that a procession of carriages, led by the Count's, trundled up the crushed gravel road to the manor house. The Duke, accompanied by Doctor Olszewski, went outside to receive their guest and take back his peasant Magda.

The Duke was not surprised when the most opulent carriage door opened and from it emerged the Count. Duke Sdanowicz was, however, shocked when Count Von Arndt then assisted Magda from that same carriage. She was dressed in a beautiful gown in the most stylish Viennese fashion. The Count took the greatest pleasure in watching the face of the Duke as he looked upon her and wondered what this finery could mean. The Duke was not aware that the Count himself had personally selected the outfit for Magdalena in Vienna, and brought it along just for this occasion.

"*Pan* Sdanowicz," said the Count, "you know Duchess Magdalena Kowalczyk."

"I do not understand," said the Duke, "this is my peasant servant Magda."

A smirk flashed upon the face of the doctor, who had come to understand that the Duke's spies in Vienna had been terribly wrong. Or perhaps they had been bought off, the doctor calculated.

"Let us step inside the manor house and I will explain everything," said the Count.

Then, from the second carriage emerged Sister Maryja Elizabeta. The Count invited her to join the proceedings, as well as Doctor Olszewski, to act in the role of witnesses.

The five of them entered the manor house and took positions at the end of the long table of the great hall. The Count sat at the head of the table, and his secretary entered to hand him a parchment from the Emperor, bearing the Imperial seal. The secretary then joined them at the table to act as scribe of the proceedings.

"Before I break the seal of the Emperor, allow me to say that we all regret the loss of our beloved Emperor Joseph II this February past. This came as a great distress to us all, as His Excellency was so young at only forty-eight years. Well before he passed, however, he personally decided this issue. What has held up this presentation of the decree to you, *Pan* Sdanowicz, was its review by the Court of his brother, our new Emperor, Leopold II. That has recently been concluded, and the Decree was determined to be valid as approved by our late Emperor Joseph II."

The Count enjoyed dragging out the drama, thought the Duke. Yet, all of this was known to him from his spies in the Court at Vienna. Joseph II had decided in the Duke's favor months before his passing in February. The Emperor had died broken hearted that he was never able to extract his sister, Marie Antoinette from the revolution ongoing in France. Now, it would be up to his younger brother Leopold, who had been called back from the Austrian possessions of northern Italy, including Tuscany and Lombardy. Leopold's Court reviewed all recent decisions of the previous Emperor to insure they concurred in their validity. The Duke knew this additional review was what had held up the presentation of the final decree. This second imperial review, as well as the melting of the winter snows which allowed Count Von Arndt to travel over the high mountain passes to Galicia, were the causes for the delays that had so aggravated the Duke.

"Let's get on with this, my Count," snapped Duke Sdanowicz.

The Count smiled broadly and responded, "Everything in its time, *Pan* Sdanowicz. Everything in its time."

Then, using an overly ornamental dagger, the Count broke the seal of the decree. He then handed the decree to his secretary to read, which the Duke thought to be somewhat strange.

"The Court of Emperor Joseph II has decreed," read the secretary in his loudest, most heavily projected voice, "in the case brought forth by his Envoy for Galicia regarding the status of the woman besieged in the Benedictine Monastery at Tyniec, the woman known as Magda Zaczek is the rightful daughter of the former *szlachta* Duke Władysław Kowalczyk, who has been long since exiled from the Bochnia *folwark* by the Polish King Poniatowski. The Emperor's Court, under its authority over these lands, has invalidated the actions of the former Polish government which awarded these lands to Duke Cyprian Sdanowicz. This Decree thus bestows upon Magdalena Kowalczyk the title of Duchess of Bochnia, and herein restores all lands of the Bochnia *folwark* rightfully to her claim. Also, she is entitled to the stipend amount which had accumulated over the years of her unjust detention as a peasant upon the lands of the *folwark* of Duke Cyprian Sdanowicz."

The Duke slammed his fists upon the table in rage. "What is the meaning of this mockery? I am already informed that both the Emperors have found favor with my claim."

"Well, *Pan* Sdanowicz," said the Count smiling in such a manner as he could not contain the joy within him, "it appears that your secretive agents within the Emperor's Court have been played against you. If I were you, I would demand the return of any monies I had paid out to them, for when the decision of retaining their positions or of feeding you false information arose, they were only too happy to forward to you the misleading information, it would appear."

The Duke could not control his anger.

"You take great joy in this, don't you, Von Arndt? Damn you man, I will not allow this to pass without an appeal."

Again the Count could only smile. "That is the greatest beauty in this matter, *Pan* Sdanowicz, for it has already been reviewed and has no higher appeal possible than to the Court of our new Emperor, Leopold II."

"How dare you, Von Arndt, to come here upon my own *folwark* and not even have the courtesy to address me by my proper title as Duke! That is the fifth time you dared address me as *Pan* Sdanowicz."

The anger displayed by the Duke drew only a sinister smile from the Count. Maximilian Von Arndt was surprised that his intentional use of the salutation *Pan* in lieu of Duke took this long to raise the ire of Cyprian Sdanowicz.

"Well, perhaps I overstated when I said the lack of appeal was the best of aspect of this decree. In reality, there is more, so much more to share with you, *Pan* Sdanowicz."

The Count gave a rolling hand gesture to the secretary who continued to read the decree.

"In the matter of the wrongful detention of the Duchess of Bochnia as a peasant, the Duke of the Wieliczka is hereby stripped of his title, lands and manor house at the direction of the Emperor Joseph II. All lands and holdings are hereby assigned to the Count of Galicia, Maximilian Von Arndt. The former Duke Cyprian Sdanowicz is herewith to be recognized simply as a citizen of the Empire of Austria."

The blood then drained from the face of the Duke. His demeanor was of a man who was in shock. His face bore the stunned look of a combatant who had just received a mortal wound and knew there was nothing he could do except allow the passage of time to bleed the very life itself from him.

The Count, who was enjoying this unfolding of inequities upon the Duke, then spoke.

"*Pan* Sdanowicz, in keeping with this decree, I will be taking up residence immediately here in the manor house."

Sdanowicz was stunned. Not only was he to lose his estate, and the rights to manage the salt mines, but would be immediately vanquished from his manor house as well.

"Then, I shall prepare immediately to move my family to the guest house this evening," muttered the Duke in a flat, defeated voice.

The Count then replied, "I am afraid, *Pan* Sdanowicz, since you have not seen it fit to maintain the manor house at the Bochnia *folwark* since it was added to your possessions nearly two decades ago, and as it is currently unfit for residency, I will be allowing Duchess Magdalena to live in the guest house until further notice."

"Then where shall we live?" asked the Duke of himself, his wife and his daughter.

Only then did *Pan* Sdanowicz, at that instant stripped of his Ducal title, allow the ramifications of this unholy hour to sink in. He had invested much of his wealth in the building of the magnificent guest house over the past three years. Now, this peasant, Magda, would live in its opulence. What funds remained would barely be enough to pay the many years of stipends he owed to her, as demanded by the Imperial decree.

Pan Sdanowicz had become, within the time it had taken to read aloud this decree, effectively insolvent without a roof over his family's head.

"Well, *Pan* Sdanowicz," said the Count with unabashed glee, "I am a magnanimous man. I would not throw you out amongst the wolves. Even I would never think to take a man of a *szlachta* bloodline and expect him to live as a mere peasant."

The Count then looked up at Doctor Olszewski, who himself was trying to restrain his exuberant smile which was engendered from fate's immense tickle of irony.

"I am afraid, dear Doctor, that this next action will displace you physically. For I am moving *Pan* Sdanowicz into the living quarters attached to the infirmary. I am sure that you, being the refined gentleman that you are, have never complained to *Pan* Sdanowicz about its meager space being barely large enough to accommodate a single adult. However, fate smiles on you this day, for I am in need of a resident physician upon my new property, and I invite you to move once again into your former accommodations in the manor house."

Doctor Olszewski was elated. He had been confined to that ragged wooden shed of a building for years and was overjoyed at the prospect of regaining residence in good standing within the manor house. He thought there was justice in the former Duke being forced to taste the exile of his own design, but the doctor was more concerned for the former Duke's wife and their daughter, Maya.

"Dziękuję," the doctor said, who then paused. "No, I mean *'danke schoen'*, my most generous Count, but as you have noted there

is not enough room within the infirmary residence to house *Pan* Sdanowicz's wife and daughter. Where shall they be expected to lodge?"

The Count then affected the air of a most generous man. "I would not dream of having them abide within the infirmary, even had it the necessary room. Far too many wounds and too much disease for them to abide to so closely. No, my good Doctor, they will reside within the manor house with you and I until a more permanent arrangement can be settled upon."

It was then that all in the great hall realized exactly what was the purpose of the Count's intentions: to treat *Pan* Sdanowicz in accordance with the way he had treated the others while he held the reins of Ducal power within his hands. He had displaced Magdalena from the manor house to destitution, and he was being treated so by the Count. He had in his anger cast Doctor Olszewski to live effectively among the afflicted, and the deposed Duke was, in turn, being so treated by the Count. *Pan* Sdanowicz had stolen all the wealth and lands of the Bochnian Duke Kowalczyk. By this decree, the former Duke was made to return these to the newly made Duchess Magdalena, while the Count stole what lands that had previously and rightly been Sdanowicz's own.

It was then that *Pan* Sdanowicz asked to speak. He was a defeated man grasping for at least a remnant of dignity. This he could not muster. In its place he decided to wield a dagger of revenge, as small as it might be.

"Count Von Arndt, I am reduced to nothing by this decree. I am humbled. But, being of noble *szlachta* blood, I accept this new reality. True, there is not much else I can do, as the Emperor Joseph II, God rest his soul, has signed off on this judgement. It has been reviewed and permitted to stand by the new Emperor, Leopold II. It is a harsh fate to accept, but what recourse do I have?"

Pan Sdanowicz then turned to look accusingly upon Magdalena. Despite the finery of her clothes, he still saw her as a peasant. *Pan* Sdanowicz realized the Count had not raised the issue of her defilement within the letter of this decree. However, he knew that it must have been raised to the Emperor himself for so severe a punishment to have been levied upon him. *Pan* Sdanowicz knew that everyone at this table, perhaps save the secretary-scribe, knew that his Magda as peasant had given birth to his child, Marek.

"Duchess Magdalena," Cyprian Sdanowicz said tenderly, "I must apologize. All I have ever wished to do was to protect you. To provide you a life that would make you both happy and fulfilled. I only hope that your happiness survives the burdens of your newfound prosperity."

Magdalena's eyes were ablaze at this outrageous statement. Before she could utter a response, the Count held up a hand to her, indicating her silence was her best recourse. *Pan* Sdanowicz decided to press on.

"I also must apologize for the actions I was forced to take upon your son, Marek..."

"My Marek is here? He is unhurt? Please tell me..." pleaded Magdalena urgently.

The Count was caught by surprise at this utterance. "That is enough!" he said, slapping his hand harshly upon the table.

"No, no, no," pleaded Magdalena, her heart pierced by the joy of this news, "please I must know what has become of my son." Turning to Sdanowicz, she said, "You did not harm him, did you?"

"The boy tried to elope with my Maya after I told him he could not have her hand in marriage. Would you have preferred I allow them to wed, Duchess Magdalena?" asked *Pan* Sdanowicz.

"No, no, no," she cried aloud, "what has become of my Marek?"

"My horsemen tracked them both to the river," said *Pan* Sdanowicz, "where the miscreant attempted to steal my Maya across the Vistula in a poacher's vessel. The poacher was shot dead and Marek was captured unharmed, except for a bloodied nose."

"Where is he, I must see him, I must," insisted Magdalena.

"You cannot," *Pan* Sdanowicz stated with the bitterest of refusal.

"Why not? Have you harmed him, you beast?" screamed Magdalena.

"He had to be punished for his actions. One of my men lost a leg to a trap he had laid. However, worry not, Duchess Magdalena, for I have protected him. He is unharmed."

"My God, my God, where is he?" sobbed Magdalena, overcome with not knowing what was her son's fate.

"He is currently being marched to Vienna, along with all the other conscripts," stated Cyprian Sdanowicz with a hissing breath. "Marek Zaczek has been conscripted to the Austrian Army. It was the best way to keep him away from my daughter, Maya."

Pan Sdanowicz grinned as his words of retribution stabbed at her like a soldier's saber.

"What have you done! My God, what have you done!" screamed Duchess Magdalena Kowalczyk, mother of Marek Zaczek.

35

VIENNA

JANUARY 1791

Vienna was beautiful as it lay quietly draped in the winter's snow. The air was fresh and crisp and the sting of it in his nostrils excited Marek. After the forced march of the conscripts, including himself, over the summer months took them through the mountain passes of the Galician border and across the broad, rolling plains of the Czech lands, Marek's eyes had been opened to all things which he had never before experienced: the cool, fragrantly herbal rush of the summer wind as it climbed upwards on the slopes of the border mountains; the bustling cities of Ostrava and Brno that they travelled through before reaching Vienna itself. A final exciting last leg of the journey, albeit brief, was aboard the transport barges crossing the beautiful and serene Danube River.

The river was the lifeblood of Eastern and Central Europe during this time. Originating in the rise of the Black Forest in the southwestern German states, and emptying into the Black Sea, its waters meandered for over seventeen hundred miles. It was anything but black in between the forest and the sea, instead it seemed itself to absorb the bright orange-yellow European sun and re-radiate it through the vibrant blue hues of its depths. At the end of their journey, the conscripts' barge had sidled up to the expansive grassy plains outside of the walls of the great city of Vienna. Here they would encamp, complete their registration of conscription, and be assigned to infantry units.

Upon the great river's grassy plains, Marek could for the first time envision the legends he had so greedily consumed as a boy. The tales would come alive in his mind as he could see around him the very site where the Battle of Vienna was fought over a hundred years earlier. He could see the Eastern Turkish hordes of Grand Vizier Kara Mustafa encamped on these very fields, encircling the *"Golden Apple"*, as the Ottomans had referred to Vienna in 1683.

The Turkish objective was to overcome all of Europe, and with that, all of Christendom. Kara Mustafa had bragged about the end of his campaign being completed only when he would stable his horses within St. Peter's Basilica in Rome. Vienna was just the opening objective for him.

Each day that his regiment drilled on the fields outside Vienna, Marek could envision these Turkish siege troops in their elaborate encampments, just outside of the city's enormous walls. Tents so lavish they challenged the ability of words to describe their riches. Elaborate silks and broadcloths painted in every color of the peacock's plumage. Adorned with the finest gold *accoutrements*, all bejeweled with gemstones, some never before seen upon this land. Each tent filled with the fragrantly tantalizing smoke of the Muslim incense burning within. The furniture brought along was of the finest Oriental workmanship, and sat atop the most splendid handwoven carpets, carried overland from Constantinople.

Massive harems of exotic Turkish beauties were brought along to satisfy the desires of the Grand Vizier and his leadership during their two months encamped outside of Vienna's walls. Even the most-stunningly beautiful of Christian women, captured from lesser battles fought along their journey, were enslaved as concubines. Marek could see it all, every detail, every Oriental blend of exotic color, Eastern culture and vivacious curvature under the pinnacles of the crescent-adorned tents.

Despite their ability to carry all these comforts among their army of some seventy-thousand warriors and supporting units, the Turks had made a critical mistake in failing to bring the heavy artillery needed to penetrate the walls of Vienna. In some places two-hundred feet high, the city had been built up as a fortified arsenal bearing the unmatched power of heavy, immovable cannons which pointed outward in every direction.

The might of these weapons easily overpowered the light artillery carried by the Turks. Time had taught the Austrians that Vienna's location along the Danube River, as profitable as it had been for merchant trading, had enabled a ready transport of potential pillagers from the Ottoman East.

Previous attacks upon the city had demanded the highest level of protection and defensive cannonade along Vienna's fortifications. These massive walls were first built with the ransom monies from the imprisonment of the English King Richard the Lion-Hearted, and had nearly given out in an earlier siege in 1529 by the Turkish Sultan, Suleiman The Great. They had long since been reinforced, and just over one hundred and fifty years later Kara Mustafa would prove their most potent foe.

Mustafa was a patient leader. Given the mismatch of artillery favoring the city, the besiegers had no other option than to surround Vienna while their excellent sappers, or military engineers, tunneled beneath its walls. There, they would plan to ignite enormous explosives, breach the walls, and into the breach flood the Turkish forces along with their Crimean Khan warrior allies. The city's garrison, famished and weakened by two months without adequate supplies, were expected to be easily overcome.

However, there was another course of action afforded by the invaders' two months of tunneling. That time allowed the forces from across Europe, under the Holy Roman Empire, to assemble to repel the Ottoman Turks. These included, beside the Austrians, the Saxons, the Bavarians, the Bohemians and even the Venetian forces, although unfortunately all in numbers inadequate to lift the siege. Marek could envision them assembling atop the *Kahlenberg*, or "bald mountain", that rose beyond the city, looking down upon the Danube River, Vienna, and the open fields full of Turks outside its walls.

As Marek drilled as a member of the Empire's infantry, he could see the entire battle unfolding in his mind. The Ottoman sappers had tunneled under the city's walls as planned and were even able to breach one location on September 11, 1683. Hand to hand combat ensued along the crumbled wall, with the garrisons inside the city barely able to repel the initial assault of Turks and their allies under the leadership of the Crimean Khan. Surely the city would have been lost, had not another event occurred that very day upon the *Kahlenberg* hills, high above them.

This was the arrival of the Polish King Jan III Sobieski and his thousands of horsed Winged Hussars as well as the Ukrainian *Zaporozhian Cossacks*. Also brought atop the Bald Mountain, with the greatest of effort by the combined forces, were massive heavy guns which would rain down cannon fire upon the Ottoman Turk forces for the next day and a half. Then, just before the tunneling Turks could ignite their greatest charge of explosives under Vienna's walls, King Sobieski personally led the harrowing charge of his Wing Hussars, accompanied by their allies from the eastern Ukrainian provinces of what was then Poland – the *Zaporozhian Cossacks* - propelling themselves into the ranks of the Ottoman infantry with devastating effect. The Winged Hussars attacked directly with their deadly long lances piercing the ranks of the Turks' lines, while the *Zaporozhian Cossacks* swarmed like a mass of angry hornets armed with the bite of flesh-slashing swords. They also shot off mortally accurate arrows from their skilled bows on the full gallop of their devilish horses.

Marek knew the rest of the legend by heart. The Crimean Khan turned away his forces and refused to fight the overwhelming invasion raining down upon them. He was later blamed by the Grand Vizier for the loss and the Kahn ultimately lost his position as leader of the Crimean Horde after that battle. The Turkish troops were completely routed, and the treasures of the Orient, including their stable of battle-trained Arabians, became the spoils of the Polish Winged Hussars and the *Zaporozhian Cossacks*.

While the Crimean Khan lost his title, the Grand Vizier lost his life. Kara Mustafa was condemned to death by the Ottoman Sultan for his failure to take *"The Golden Apple"*. This verdict was carried out in Belgrade that year, appropriately on Christmas Day, by the method prescribed by the order of the Sultan – strangulation by a long silk scarf in the hands of several of his own surviving elite commandos, *the Janissaries*.

Marek's thoughts left the battle in 1683, and returned to 1791. He had been in Vienna for six months and was only then becoming accustomed to the elegance of the Austrian capital. After much training over the months following his arrival, his regiment was marched into the still walled city of Vienna. Since 1683, much growth of the city had occurred outside these walls, including the building of the Habsburgs' summer palace, *The Schönbrunn*, as well as the *Belvedere Palace* of Austria's famed Prince Eugene.

The walls of Vienna would stand for another sixty or so years after Marek's arrival, not being dismantled until the 1850s. Then, the famously wide boulevards of the *Ringstrasse*, or Ring Road, would be built in the razed wall's footprint. Vienna would at that point become a city of impressively open and beautiful thoroughfares, carrying splendidly dressed citizens on so many vital daily activities.

However, in 1791 the old city was still surrounded by a massive open space, designed to deny any cover to attackers approaching its walls. Any growth beyond the city's wall had to also be outside of this secondary cordon used to preserve these open grounds. In times of peace, these were used as drilling grounds for the city's troops.

Marek felt the pride surge within him the first time his unit had been deemed worthy enough to even cross these beautifully maintained drilling grounds. As they marched toward the walls of the city, these level grounds gave way to *glacis*, or sloped ramparts, outside the walls. The combined effect of all this was an ever-increasing anticipation of what greatly protected treasures lay within the city.

Marek's first impression of Vienna's *Innerestadt,* or city within the walls, was of a tight confluence of streets and structures, constrained if not choked, by the shadows of the towering walls. Yet, packed within this relatively condensed space was perhaps the most elegant town he had ever laid eyes upon. Even when his friend Tolo, the trapper, had taken him within the walls and through the streets of Kraków, Marek had seen a new level of sophistication, although even that was not of this scale.

True, Marek had not yet seen any open central space to compete with Kraków's massive *Rynek Główny,* or Main Square, with its prominent *Sukiennice*, or Cloth Hall, where merchants from the East traded from their bolts of material in great quantities. Vienna, however, even within its restrictive walls, conducted merchant trading on another level all together. All the treasures carried upon the Danube were sold within her walls. As a result of this level of trade, the elegance of the Hofburg Palace, home of the Habsburg Dynasty, arose in all of its marbled majesty.

Marek's infantry unit had passed under the mixed Gothic-Romanesque towers of Saint Stephen's Cathedral. It reminded Marek of that night that Tolo had taken him before the heights of the towers of Saint Mary's Basilica in Kraków, even though Saint Mary's bricked towers looked like those of a medieval castle when compared to this elegantly soaring Viennese stone cathedral. Marek could not believe his eyes, for it was as if the masons of Europe had simply taught the stones to defy their massive weight and fly. He could not help but wonder if Miłosz the mason had ever even seen such a beautiful work of stone.

Marek tended to think often of his friends Miłosz and Tolo. The two trappers had not only saved his life from his death-throes in the waters of the Vistula, but both men then cared for him afterwards. Each man taught him valuable lessons as how to live out that recovered life to its fullest. Their greatest teachings were in their own deaths. Miłosz taught Marek not to give in to the darkness of his own temptations, as Miłosz had done in his weakness for drink.

Tolo in life had taught Marek much. He taught him to trap, to skin, to barter and even to swim. However, he also introduced Marek to a weakness of his own, by taking him to the intoxicating Reka. Marek could not shed his thoughts of her, naked and vulnerable, laying upon the bed, clutching only the ermine pelt. His thoughts of her sounds and smells continued to haunt him. He found himself looking at the young women of Vienna completely differently by then, wondering how they looked stripped of their finest garments, and if their natural allure could match Reka's sensual charm. He greatly doubted so, for these women were too refined, too dignified, too respectable.

As was his Maya Manuska, he thought. Within him, the battle ensued, pitting the wicked desires of his flesh, renewed afresh by his vulgar recollections of Reka, against the unassailable purity in which he held his Maya. Most of all, he feared, through these recurring intrusions of the lustfully vivid memories of the Hungarian, he would slowly come to fail to appreciate the modesty and purest charms of his ever so distant *Maya Manuska*. Marek was determined that he would not allow this to occur.

Tolo had also taught Marek not to value a friend's life above his own, as Tolo himself had by returning his skiff in his attempt to rescue Marek and Maya. Doing so had cut short Tolo's own young existence. Marek could not look out upon the blue waters of the Danube without seeing his friend, slumped over that skiff, its oars so awkwardly pointing upwards, as it drifted out of sight on the gray waters of the Vistula. He felt the immense guilt of not only survival, but of having lured his friend to his death.

As it was, Marek had viewed the waters of the Danube often. His first several months in the city were spent training with the Imperial Army in infantry drills along its banks. The river's swift flowing waters often carried his thoughts back eastward to his days past spent with his two trapper friends. His heart would sink when his fond remembrances were interrupted by the reality that they had both, under Marek's own eye, passed from this world.

After his unit had been transferred to permanent barracks near the Hofburg Palace inside the city, Marek had been taken aside by his regimental commander, who had informed him that he was being transferred to the annex of the Imperial Riding School, for assessment as an entry level officer in the Austrian cavalry.

At that point, his German was rather rudimentary, and much weaker than his Polish, or even his French. He had questioned what he was hearing from his superior. How could he be chosen for such a respected duty?

"Your appointment to the cavalry is at the behest of Count Maximilian Von Arndt," his instructor had told him, "who carries great favor with the Emperor. It appears that your mother has been recognized as a Duchess by Emperor Leopold II, and as such your place in the infantry is not proper. Yet, do not allow your pride to overwhelm you, my young Polish conscript, for you will be serving in the cavalry alongside proper Austrian noblemen's children. And while the province of Galicia is indeed within the Empire, these men will only see you for what you truly are: a conquered Pole vying for the same appointments as they are. At least you'll be outside the city walls. You will not be at the Spanish Riding Schools in the *Innerestadt.* No. These are swiftly becoming nothing more than preparations for the show horses of the Empire. This new riding school is in the open fields, under blue skies, not far from the Belvedere Palace. You'll get plenty of open riding and fresh air. I wish I could join you, my friend. The air in this city is stagnant with greed and reeks of the rancid smoke of commerce."

The officer made a face of disfavor at being sequestered within the confines of the city walls. "If I am to smell smoke, let it be that of the artillery, in the fields of honor upon which battles are won." The officer rose, extended his hand to Marek to shake, and having done so gave the lad a hearty slap on the back as Marek turned to depart.

Marek was shocked by what he had just heard. However, what he could not then know, was that his *matka* had pressed the Count hard to have his conscription reversed. She had pleaded with him daily, sometimes many times a day, to have her son returned to her side.

"Duchess Magdalena, even I cannot do this as you request," the Count had told her in response. "The Imperial Army will make a man of your son. The boy is only of eighteen years. It is an excellent experience for his transition into the nobleman he must become. At this point, having him released from his conscription would only bring shame upon Marek. The request would have to go before the Emperor himself, and I wish not for my name to be tied to too many requests before His Excellency. Besides, why bring the boy back to continue his pursuit of the Duke's daughter? Do you realize the scandal that could become for you?"

The Duchess realized he was right. Keeping a distance between Marek and Maya was advantageous. However, living in such close proximity to the Count, Magdalena soon pleaded in an unrelenting manner for him to intervene in her son's being trained to be a common foot-soldier. She was convinced as a Pole he would be of the first to be tossed as fodder for the artillery of the enemies of the Austrian Army.

The Count was all too welcome to intervene in this request. He had come to covet Magdalena's newfound wealth and land holdings, even though they were only a fraction of those he had stolen from the former Duke Sdanowicz. He had decided he would do whatever was necessary to obtain them to add to his own. Count Von Arndt decided to please Duchess Magdalena, such that she would look favorably upon his later request of marriage.

"What I can do, and will do so proudly," explained the Count, "is to make the case that as the son of a Duchess your Marek should be trained in the ways of the cavalry. You have told me many times of his prowess in the saddle, have you not? Well, most noble's sons serve their time in the cavalry, and I am quite certain that this can be arranged."

And through the intercessions of the Count, spurred on by the pleadings of his mother, Marek was transferred to train as a light cavalryman. The Austrian Cavalry was made up of different classes of riders, and generally these classes of riders were taken from different provinces of the empire. Poles and Hungarians were recognized as excellent riders, as their ancestors were regularly pitted in battle against the fast-moving horsemen of the Turks, Tatars and even the Cossacks when they rebelled. As such, the Poles generally were selected to make up the class of light cavalry known as *Uhlans* and the Hungarians as *Hussars* (although not winged like those of the Polish horsemen of Sobieski). The more prestigious Austrian cavalry units known as *Cuirassiers, Dragoons*, and *Chevaulegeres* (or *Light Dragoons*) were generally reserved for the Austrian and German conscripts.

Marek had reported to the Imperial Riding School for an assessment of his riding skills before being assigned to an *Uhlan* cavalry unit. This military school was little more than an encampment on the southeastern plains outside of Vienna, along the broad expanse of fields adjacent to what soon would become the boulevard *Ungargasse*. Here, Marek was trained for months in the basics of cavalry tactics and warfare. It was also here that Marek, whose riding skills were already advanced beyond his peers', was taught to wield a sword on horseback. It was here that Marek was taught to kill the enemy.

As exciting as all of this was for the Austrian Cavalier in training, Marek was even more excited to discover the ground's other secret. For after being at the Imperial Riding Academy for several days, Marek soon learned the school had an unexpected benefit. Working in the stables as no more than a muck-hand was his Uncle Jacek. It took two more weeks before they could arrange time to spend with each other. So, on a cold winter Saturday afternoon, they shared a meal together in the warmed, but nearly empty, mess tent of the encampment.

"Uncle Jacek," said Marek as they sat to eat their meal, "my heart lifted with joy when I discovered you were here. What a blessing from God to bring us together here in Vienna."

Jacek, who looked thinner and frailer than Marek had ever remembered, was always quick with a Polish proverb. "So, young

Marek, *we gnaw the bones that fall to our lot*. This day our paths cross, but tomorrow, who can know?"

"Have you seen your boys, Andrzej and Bartek?" asked Marek.

"Only once, when I was allowed to watch their unit march down the parade grounds outside the city walls. I saw them both, although neither saw me, for I was but a face in a crowd. The next day they marched off to Lombardy, in the Alps above Tuscany. It was the last I had heard or saw of them. Such sweet boys," sighed Jacek, as many sorrows lined the muscles of his face.

Marek could sense the loneliness and isolation that had descended upon his uncle. They ate, and soon a heavy silence settled over them. Marek was adamant that he would not allow it to steal away his rare time with his kin.

"What is the best part of your assignments here, Uncle Jacek?" asked Marek, attempting to restart the conversation.

"The best part? Well, I would have to say first that every blessing can be a curse in disguise. But, if there is one thing I appreciate about my hours mucking the stables here, it is that each rider who passes through Vienna brings with them news from across the continent."

"How can this be a curse, my Uncle?" asked Marek.

"We have many emigres from France, those royalists who do not care for how the Revolution progresses there. They tell of the King and Queen as captives in the Tuileries Palace in Paris. They were chased out of Versailles by a mob holding the heads of their guards on the points of their pikes. They tell of the revolutionaries there who are eager to free themselves from the monarchy entirely, as well as from the church and God himself. What they describe is utter chaos. It will only lead to war between France and Austria, and my boys will be on the front lines, with the French cannons aimed upon their heads."

Marek was eager to change the topic. "But, Uncle, what do you hear of our homelands?"

"If you mean Galicia, only that your mother is a Duchess by decree of the Emperor, and lives in the fine guest house of the Duke.

The Duke himself has been thrown to the wolves by the Austrian Count, who has stolen all his wealth. My wife, my lovely wife, Ewelina, sends letters written in your own mother's hand that I must beg others to read aloud to me. She has been assigned to the Duchess' personal staff, at your *matka's* own request. I am most thankful that the Duchess Magdalena looks after her so."

Marek thought it most unusual to hear his uncle refer to his mother as "*The Duchess Magdalena*".

"There, so very far away," further said Jacek, himself gazing distantly, " the Duchess and my Ewelina shed tears together for their lost husbands, and for their sons cast off to learn the sins of war."

"Uncle Jacek, you are not lost to Aunt Ewelina," said Marek, "only separated from her."

"One is the same as the other," said Jacek. "Now then, if you are asking of our true homeland, Poland, then there is much to tell. You know of Tadeusz Kościuszko?"

"Yes, the Pole who became a Brigadier General in the Army of the Americans?" said Marek. "He is a hero to all Poles."

"Well, we will see how much of a hero he remains. Kościuszko returned to Poland when the war in America was over. He is now a General in the Polish Army. However, what is of great concern, is that he had brought with him the idealist notions of the Americans - *Freedom* and *the Rights of All Men*. The same devil's tripe that infects and threatens to destroy France, Kościuszko has now brought to Poland. I hear of his working with King Poniatowski's Court, as well as the powerful Czartoryski family with whom the King is aligned, to pass a constitution in Poland based on the constitution of the Americans. It would strengthen the monarchy, restrict the rights of the *szlachta*, and free the peasants from their attachment to the lands."

"These are all good things are they not, my Uncle? Certainly, you and Aunt Ewelina would be freed from your slavery to the lands of the nobles."

Jacek looked at his nephew in disappointment.

"Perhaps," Jacek said, "if we lived on the other shore of the

Vistula. But even if we were truly still Polish and not Austrian peasants, I would remain very leery of these propsed changes. I have lived many years, my nephew, and one recognizes patterns throughout his life. Every time I have heard of changes such as these, as sweet as they may sound to each peasant's ears, it has always preceded the rank, sour smell of war. Catherine still sits upon the Russian throne, and she will not allow such changes in Poland. There will be war, the blood of many innocents will be shed, and if these so-called *liberties* are allowed to fester, all of Poland may be imperiled."

Marek had at that point recognized exactly how defeated his Uncle had become. Every glimmer of opportunity was hidden as a further vanquishing, as another opportunity for his life, and those of the people he loved, to be crushed under the heels of the oppressor's boot.

Marek felt exactly the opposite. His young life was on the ascent. He had seen great sights, and had, as he once told his father, begun to see the world outside the *folwark*. He was being trained for what had always been his greatest ambition, to become a warrior on horseback. While he had a setback in taking Maya's hand in marriage, the Duke's own difficulties might afford him another opportunity. For while the debased images of Reka still burned within him, Marek knew his future was meant to be spent with the chaste and pure Maya.

Marek had decided first to become the successful *Uhlan* cavalryman, and only then return home to the *folwark* to claim his Maya. Together they would build a world of their own. *Who knows,* he thought, *perhaps we will leave the province of Austrian Galicia to live our new life together in the still Polish lands across the river near Kraków? In that land, our rights as well as those of the native Poles would be protected under the new constitution of King Poniatowski, the Czartoryski's, and most of all, General Tadeusz Kościuszko.*

36

THE DUCHESS MAGDALENA

APRIL 1791

Magdalena, the reconstituted Duchess of Bochnia, only heard sporadically from her son, Marek. The boy wrote her only the briefest of letters, often focused not on his missing her, but instead telling of his admiration for the glamorous city of Vienna. He would always end these briefest of communiques inquiring about Maya and asking his mother to write to him about her.

Magdalena heard more frequently of him from Count Von Arndt than she did from her son directly. She knew from the Count's retelling of his own correspondence from his many contacts in Vienna that Marek had completed his training and was dispatched to a regiment of *Uhlan* cavalry, and that they were soon to be stationed in the Czech lands between Brno and Olomouc. She thought to herself, *he is halfway here. If only I could see my boy's face once more.*

Magdalena had inherited a great deal of wealth. Along with the rights to take residence in the guest house, she had reclaimed the lands of her father from the former Duke Sdanowicz's estate. She had a regular income from the salt mines at Bochnia, which amounted to more than she could ever hope to spend, even if she were to have suddenly taken on the uncharacteristic habits of a spendthrift. On top of all this, the former Duke had been forced to repay her for the nearly twenty years of stipends he had illegally claimed for management of the mines. She had inherited a world of riches, yet despite this carried only the sorrows of a woman who had lost both her son and in doing so, any hope for her immortal soul.

Magdalena also still mourned, of course, her husband Bronisław, and still carried the guilt of his death as a burden of her own sins. Worse yet was that the man who had forced these sins upon her, Cyprian Sdanowicz, still lived upon his former lands, even if only modestly so. He was a constant reminder to her of all her suffering, of the permanent loss of Bronisław and the even more devastating loss of Marek to the Imperial Army, all of which she attributed to the sinful actions of the former Duke.

Magdalena would, however, even in the midst of her veil of agonies, never forget that had that man not forced himself upon her in the manor house, she would have no son at all. For this reason alone, there was a part of her heart that felt compassion for *Pan* Sdanowicz's newfound suffering. This empathy beat alongside the part of her heart that detested the man. Magdalena was conflicted and from this conflict grew angst, and from her angst spawned her own suffering.

Duchess Magdalena donated generously to both the Tyniec Benedictine Monastery as well as to Mother Angelica's Kraków convent. Sister Maryja Elizabeta had returned to the latter and was held in great favor, due to the Duchess' most unselfish patronage.

Magdalena came soon to detest the wealth she had inherited. It was a burden upon her. Count Von Arndt had taken up permanent residence within the *folwark's* manor house, with only occasional travels to Lemberg, Kraków, or more rarely to Prague or Vienna itself. He seemed satisfied to be managing the estate, as well as the mines. He had volunteered to manage the Bochnia mines on her behalf, in addition to his own mines at Wieliczka. The Duchess was still awarded the stipend, although the Count graciously managed the operational affairs. Little did Magdalena know that Count Von

Arndt was taking his own cut in selling the excess salt produced beyond the quotas on the black market, which had turned out to be a very profitable situation.

The lands of the estate had become the Count's foremost pride. Although he had come from a noble family, they had possessed no lands of their own. His own father had squandered the family's wealth, leaving only a modest fortune to his son: a Count's title, a few thousand Thaler coins, and a home within the shadows of the Hofburg Palace in Vienna. Von Arndt had built upon that inherited sum rather nicely in the service of Maria Theresa, Joseph II and now Leopold II, although his calculated action against Duke Cyprian Sdanowicz was the first which afforded him the addition of vast tracts of land to his budding fortune.

If there is one constant throughout history, it is that to give a man a taste of wealth only wets an insatiable desire for more. The Count, in having taken to the soil, soon looked for opportunities to add to his holdings. In fact, he did not have to look far, for living in the opulent quarters next to his own manor house was the lovely Duchess Magdalena. Of course, this had been of his own doing, as he had pleaded on her behalf in the Emperor's court. Having restored unto her the rightful lands of her father, she had, thanks to him, great tracts of property of her own.

The Count's every intention was, when the time was appropriate, to change her title from Duchess to Countess. By persuading her to marry him, he would thus come to legally own her property also. In doing so, he would become as wealthy as Cyprian Sdanowicz had ever been, that is, until the Duke was undone by his own ill treatment of the girl once known as the peasant Magda.

The Count had invited her to his dinner table each evening, to accompany him and his physician, Doctor Olszewski. Cyprian Sdanowicz was allowed to eat together with his wife and daughter in the confinement of the infirmary house, although the two women were allowed to return each night to lodge within the manor house.

After dinner, the Count, the Duchess and the doctor relaxed at table, when the doctor spoke first with the oddest of news.

"*Pan* Cyprian Sdanowicz confided in me today that his wife and daughter will be leaving soon to live in the Polish village of Maciejowice."

"They do not appreciate my hospitality here in the manor house?" asked the Count. "I would presume that they leave to secure a place for *Pan* Cyprian to follow later?"

"Strangely not," answered the doctor. "They are very appreciative of your generous lodging of them in their former home, my lord. However, *Pan* Cyprian's wife is disgraced by the loss of their social standing due to *Pan* Cyprian's boorish actions. She is humiliated by her loss of servants and title. She has been offered to live with her widowed brother on his farm in Maciejowice."

"I am not familiar with this place," whispered the Duchess Magdalena, as if fearful someone might be listening.

"It is a small village halfway between Sandomierz and Warsaw, just off the Vistula River," stated the doctor. "I have passed through it once."

"How far up the river from Kraków to Warsaw?" asked the Count, who still could not place the village in his mind.

"About three quarters of the way to Warsaw," responded the doctor. "It is an uneventful place and will be a good setting for *Pani* Sdanowicz and Maya to start anew."

"Why would *Pan* Cyprian not accompany them?" asked Magdalena.

"He shared with me that he is not welcome," said Doctor Olszewski. "Her brother and most of her Ukrainian family were against her marrying a Pole, even a vastly wealthy one as was Sdanowicz, long ago. There have been many revolts of the Ukrainians against Commonwealth rule, and much bad blood between the Poles and these people."

"Does his wife know about Marek?" asked the Duchess in an even quieter hush than before. She knew that the three of them - herself, the Count, and the doctor - were all aware of *Pan* Sdanowicz being the boy's father.

"*Pan* Cyprian assures me that neither she nor Maya knows," stated the doctor with confidence. "He sees no reason to share the fact of his having fathered the boy with either his wife or his daughter at this juncture."

"So, my lovely Duchess Magdalena," said the Count, "what actions are we to take with *Pan* Cyprian once his wife and daughter leave from here? Shall we cast him off the *folwark* altogether?"

The thought of losing access to the Duke, even given his illicit treatment of her, brought upon Magdalena a tremendous and immediate sorrow. It was as if a part of her would have died, that part being the creation of Marek. As shameful and humiliating as it had been for her, it had strangely created her life's most satisfying joy - the birth of her son.

"I see no reason to not allow him to continue to rot in his own shame within the infirmary's quarters," she replied. "Let him wallow in the misery of being poor. Let the sour taste of his own actions salt his tongue for the rest of his life."

Magdalena said this despite herself remembering the hardships of her former life fondly. Still, she said this boldly, not hushed at all as were her earlier words. Despite this boldness, she secretly feared that *Pan* Cyprian Sdanowicz might just depart from the *folwark* on his own, and away from her. One day, after she garnered enough courage to tell Marek the whole truth, just possibly, their son might hold her responsible for the fate of his true father.

37

THE THIRD OF MAY CONSTITUTION

SPRING 1791

Although it started with some semblance of order, 1791 was a transitional year into anarchy. In America, the fledgling government of the United States was in its third year of its constitution, under the leadership of President George Washington, and Vice-President John Adams. Their Cabinet initially consisted of only four members with Secretary of Treasury Alexander Hamilton, Secretary of War Henry Knox, Attorney General Edmund Randolph, and Secretary of State Thomas Jefferson (although Jefferson was actually preceded by John Jay in an acting capacity. Jay would go on to become the first Chief Justice of the United States Supreme Court).

The United States Constitution, with its division of power among three co-equal branches of government, and its provisions for personal liberty and individual freedom was seen as a watershed event in the establishment of a democratic republic. It was an experiment in government, with all power based in the populace. Established in September 1787, and ratified in June the following year, the world waited to see if this country without a monarch of any kind could effectively rule. It was widely acclaimed as the first constitution of any nation-state, although two others would soon rush to emulate it and adopt their own widely different variations.

One of these was the nation of France, where the seeds of America's revolution had produced a disastrously different result. Whereas the American nation declared their freedoms as being secured under God, France was using the Enlightenment themes of *liberté, égalité, et fraternité* as tools to strip away every remnant of the Church, as one does a strangling ivy from the bark of a healthy tree. The revolutionaries enflamed the starving public to the point of the masses acting out in a far more incendiary reaction.

Given the instability of France, in late June of 1791, the French Royal family slipped out of house arrest from the Tuileries Palace in Paris. They were dressed as servants (who had in turn been dressed as the royals) and attempted to flee the country. They headed east toward the Habsburg ruled Netherlands with their coach stopping to rest their horses in the French town of Varennes. Here, King Louis XVI was recognized by the locals, purportedly because of his resemblance to his image appearing on the coined currency then in use. The Royals were arrested, returned to Paris, and charged with attempting to flee the country as the madness of the revolution escalated.

On 3 September 1791, France drafted its first constitution. It was a short-lived document, replaced later in 1793 by the *Constitution of Year I* drafted by Robespierre's far-left *Montagnards*. By then, the seeds of the Reign of Terror had been sown, and much of the civil liberties enacted by the first French Constitution were severely restricted.

Exactly four months before the first French Constitution was adopted, on 3 May 1791, the Polish-Lithuanian Commonwealth adopted the first constitution in all of Europe, and only the second in the history of the world. Drafted during the rule of King Stanisław II August Poniatowski, and under the influence of the powerful Czartoryski family, it was unabashedly based on the United States document. While for some, like the revolutionary Tadeusz Kościuszko, it came up short of abolishing the Polish monarchy altogether, but the constitution was still welcomed for its provisions which defined a monarchic republic with the elected King heading the executive branch, the *Sejm* as an independent legislature and a truly independent judiciary with sweeping powers.

This document not only banned the *liberum veto*, it also brought a more equal distribution of rights between nobles and peasants. While it did not ban serfdom outright, it did eliminate many of its most onerous abuses. Peasants were protected by the government under this new and radical document. It was ratified on the third day of May establishing what would become formally known as the First Polish Republic.

Like the French Constitution, this document too would be short lived. Its radical provisions so threatened its neighboring states of Russia to the east and Prussia to the north and west, that a calamitous series of events soon began to unfold. The chain of events over the next three years would ultimately wipe out not only the 3 May Constitution, but also the monarchy, and eliminate Poland as a political state of Europe altogether.

38

CATHERINE OF RUSSIA

1791

The Polish Constitution of the Third of May 1791 was an affront to Catherine II, Tsarina of Russia. She had maneuvered ever so carefully over the decades to keep Poland as a weak vassal state, nearly unable to manage its own affairs. It was she who had placed the ineffective and indecisive King Stanisław II August Poniatowski, her former lover, on the throne in 1764. It was she who was forced to intercede and put down the rebellion of the Confederation of Bar only a few years afterwards. It was she, along with the late Frederick of Prussia, who had conceived of the resulting Partition of Poland. It was she who encouraged Austria, who had been reluctant to be added to the Polish dissection, even though the Austrians would go on to grab the largest jewel of the Commonwealth by annexing the Galician lands.

Catherine was intent on keeping the declining Commonwealth as a buffer-land between her Russia and the West, most notably her current ally, the militant Prussia. Prussia and Poland had signed a military alliance in 1790, and as a result she had to tread carefully, lest Russia would find itself coming into conflict with the Prussians on Poland's behalf. The Tsarina could not allow this to occur.

Catherine, Tsarina of all the Russian lands, was actually not herself of Russian origin. She was born in Stettin, Pomerania, as Princess Sophie to an aristocratic German family. Ironically, these lands would much later in history become part of the Polish homeland. Yet, while her family was of Germanic nobility, their fortunes had turned and left them with titles and not much more.

At the age of sixteen, Princess Sophie was married off to the son of the reigning Empress of Russia, Tsar Elizabeth. Reportedly, young Sophie despised the man who would later become her husband and later still Tsar Peter III. In the years before her husband became Tsar, the young princess had aggressively learned the Russian language, converted to the Russian Orthodox religion, and taken the name *"Yekaterina"*.

Soon both husband and wife had multiple liaisons outside their marital bonds. Catherine, as she then became known, had included a tryst with the Polish courtier Stanisław Poniatowski. Catherine would go on to give birth to his illegitimate daughter, Anna Petrovna in 1757, although the child would live for only three months.

In early 1762, Tsarina Elizabeth died and her son became Tsar Peter III, Emperor of the Russian Empire. This resulted in Catherine becoming the Empress Consort, which would not prove enough for the ambitious thirty-three year old woman.

Over the next six months, Tsar Peter III came into contention with the Russian nobility, most particularly over his close affiliations with Frederick II of Prussia. Peter alienated the nobles, while at the same time his wife Catherine not only courted them, but also made great efforts to remain in the good graces of the Orthodox clergy. She had adopted all things Russian since she had arrived in Saint Petersburg, and despite her speaking their language with a German accent, she soon became a favorite of the Russian people. In June of 1762, only six months since her husband had become Tsar, Catherine, along with a group of powerful conspirators, enacted a coup which dethroned Peter and secured her place upon the throne of Russia.

Only two years later Tsar Catherine, through her manipulations of the Polish *szlachta*, placed her former lover Stanisław upon the throne of the Polish-Lithuanian Commonwealth. She knew that he was a weak and indecisive man. Catherine was certain that she could control him in guiding the actions of this neighboring nation. What she had not anticipated was the resistance of the Poles to her meddling in their affairs, resulting in the Confederation of Bar in 1768, and the Polish Civil War it sparked.

By 1771 Poniatowski was at risk of being dethroned. He had been kidnapped by the rebels in Warsaw that year, but through their incompetence, he was allowed to escape. Catherine's Russia had no choice then but to continue to intercede militarily on behalf of the Polish King. Over the next year, with the overwhelming strength of the Russian forces, the rebellion was put down. This opened the door for the partition of the Commonwealth's borderlands to the three empires of Russia, Prussia and Austria.

To say that all had been quiet over the next twenty years would be a considerable understatement, but the borders of the Commonwealth remained stable over this time. Catherine's co-conspirators in the partition, Empress Maria Theresa of Austria and King Frederick II of Prussia, were by 1791 both deceased. Catherine remained upon the Russian throne in Saint Petersburg, as she approached the thirtieth year of her reign.

The 3 May Constitution of Poland in that year was the act of defiance that would break the limits of her forbearance. Whereas earlier, she had been acting against Poland by keeping the *szlachta* powerful in forcibly defending their *Golden Rights*, she thus had rendered the Polish King's power to be severely limited. This new constitution was itself a more direct threat than the Confederation of Bar to the Russian Motherland, as it began the process of unshackling the serfs from the Polish lands.

This had the potential of creating a massive revolution which would then threaten to cross the border into the Motherland. Once within the Russian territories, the peasants would demand the same liberties. As a response, Catherine would be forced to once again act militarily. Russia would declare war on Poland and once more there would be fighting along their borders. All that was needed was a justifiable reason to do so.

A small confederation of *szlachta* nobles were dissatisfied with the constitution's "democratic contagion", which they claimed had been "imported from Paris". They requested assistance from Empress Catherine. This became the rationale for military intervention. In 1792, that intervention was launched upon Poland from the east. In the north and west, Prussia would ignore her defense treaty obligations to the Polish King and would once more attack her neighbor in conjunction with the Russian army.

39

THE POLISH-RUSSIAN WAR

1792

The events of 1791 created vast reverberations in 1792, on the scale of an earthquake's aftershocks. The three events most notable were the Royal Family's failed escape from Paris, the subsequent Declaration of Pillnitz by Austria and Prussia, and the ratification of the 3 May Constitution by the Poles.

The first two events of 1791 were directly connected. The June flight and recapture of King Louis XVI and Marie Antoinette created great anxiety amongst the other monarchies in Europe. Lest the flickering flames of Paris should cast off red-hot embers, carried upon the volatile winds of revolution, that might ignite rebellion in their own lands, Austria and Prussia were forced to act together in response.

That response was the Declaration of Pillnitz. From that Saxony castle stronghold near Dresden, the Austrian and Holy Roman Emperor Leopold II and the Prussian King Frederick William II issued the declaration which informed France that King Louis XVI and Queen Marie Antoinette had the full backing of both Prussia and the Holy Roman Empire (which included Austria). They warned that should any harm befall either of the royals or their family, severe consequences would follow. Leopold explicitly stated that Austria would indeed go to war with France yet left himself an out by insisting only on the condition that the other monarchies of Europe agreed to do so.

This Declaration was received in Paris as an impending threat of invasion, and only served to further destabilize the already fragile situation. The revolutionary forces in France had until that time been focused internally on the provinces of that country. However, after this declaration they then changed their priorities and began to prepare in earnest for an onslaught by Austria, Prussia or others along its borders. They would not have to wait very long.

In April of 1792, in response to the joint Austro-Prussian declaration, the French Revolutionary Government declared war upon Austria. A few months later, in July 1792, a combined Prussian and Austrian Army left the city of Coblenz on the Rhine and marched through the narrow mountain passes of the Ardennes to invade France. They had boldly declared their intent to march upon Paris in order to restore Louis XVI to the throne and power.

The invasion had a unifying effect on the French Army, which had been in disarray under the revolution. Earlier in 1792, units were found guilty of murdering their commanding officers for "counter-revolutionary actions". All discipline had been lost in the quagmire of events from 1789 on.

Yet, the threat of an invasion upon one's homeland has the most sobering of effects. The regiments of the forces previously aligned with the Royalists then fought for their country side-by-side with the revolutionaries, along with a swelling of the ranks by voluntary citizen militia. The invading Prussian and Austrian troops, after several initial victories, were finally defeated at the small French town of Valmy on the twentieth day of September. This is considered to be the first true battle of the Revolutionary Wars under which France would fight all the powers of Europe for most of the next quarter-century.

A second repercussion of the invasion was the final formal dissolution of the French monarchy. On 10 August 1792, only a matter of weeks after the French and Prussians had begun their march on France, an armed mob swarmed the Tuileries Palace. The rabid citizenry overpowered the Swiss Guard regiment protecting the monarchs, massacring them in scenes that were eerily reminiscent of the storming of Versailles, although even more violently so. The King and Queen were taken as prisoners to the ancient stronghold known simply as "The Temple". Clearly the flame of hope of Louis XVI regaining power was extinguished that night, and its embers were stomped out cold when the French victory at the Battle of Valmy, as we have previously discussed, came to pass during the next month. In a sealing of his fate in December of 1792, King Louis XVI would be put on trial by the Revolutionaries. The outcome was never in doubt.

The other event of 1791 that had an immense effect upon the following year was the Polish Constitution ratified on the third day of May.

A small confederation of *szlachta* nobles were dissatisfied with their loss of power. However, they masked their real grievances and instead, claimed the constitution's infection of democratic ideals would soon cast Poland into the same state of anarchy as was ongoing in France. They requested assistance from an unlikely source, Empress Catherine of Russia, who simply had been waiting for an excuse to intervene militarily in Poland. In 1792, that intervention was launched in May, just one year after the ratification of the new constitution.

The Russians attacked in two main thrusts. The first would be directly upon Warsaw, and the second in southern Poland. The Polish forces in the south were placed in the control of King Poniatowski's nephew, Prince Józef, who had been trained in the Austrian army, rising to the rank of Colonel. He had returned to Poland, where he was installed as a Major General. He proved himself more than capable in leading men in combat. In the Battle of Zieleńce in July of 1792, Polish troops under his command in the Ukraine were able to repel Russian forces in greatly superior numbers. The fighting in southern Poland would prove to be more contentious than in the north thanks to the leadership of Józef Poniatowski, and his primary strategist, General Tadeusz Kościuszko.

With the war between Russia and Poland being fought just across the Galician border, the Austrian Empire mobilized forces of their own into the province to protect the Austrian lands. These forces included an *Uhlan* cavalry regiment in whose ranks was the twenty-year-old Marek Zaczek.

It was late on a summer's evening that this *Uhlan* cavalryman cantered his mount upon the crushed gravel drive outside of the manor house. First the Count came out to receive him, but before he did so, he sent a servant to make the Duchess Magdalena aware that her son had finally come home.

"Marek, look what the Austrian Cavalry has made of you! What a pleasure to have you here, upon our *folwark* once more," said the Count, his voice booming in its welcome.

"With your blessing, my lord," said Marek from his saddle, "I would like to spend tonight with my mother. Fear not, for I must be gone upon the sun's rise tomorrow to catch up with my regiment. My commander has allowed me only this night as a gift to the Duchess."

"Marek," boomed the Count, "this is your home, although not perhaps as you remember it when you left. You are welcome here for as long as your heart desires. So long, that is, as you haven't abandoned the army. I don't want to fall in disfavor with the Emperor."

A hearty laugh then filled the air between the two men thick as a cloud of dust. In seconds that cloud was pierced like a Tatar's arrows with the joyous shriek of Magdalena. Her face instantly flooded with tears of pride upon seeing her son as she had never seen him before. In his military dress, upon the fine steed, he was the complete image of gentlemanly strength and decorum. Yet, in his smile, in his eyes, she still could see her little boy.

Marek dismounted and after handing the reins of his horse to the Count's groom, walked over to embrace his mother. He could feel her shaking as he wrapped his arms around her, so much so that he kissed her gently upon the forehead. This only increased the amplitude of her trembling.

"*Matka*, *moja Matka*, your tears will stain these fine silk clothes you are wearing," he whispered to her. "I thought I would find you happier given all the good fortune that has befallen you."

Magdalena struggled to control her emotions. This was the first time that she had laid eyes upon her child since watching him struggle for his life in the waters of the Vistula. Marek noticed, most happily, that she wore the amber ring upon her finger.

"For the longest time I feared you lost," she said, "forever gone, taken from me when I needed you most."

"Yes, *moja Matka*," he said, "that is why I risked my life to leave you the Christmas present of the amber ring."

"It brought me not only the greatest happiness, my son, but an inner peace that allowed me to go on," she said. Marek's arms remained around her as she continued, "As for my good fortunes, this ring is my only thing of true value. The rest of these comforts are merely illusions. I was never happier than when I was without anything in this world except the love of you and my Bronisław."

"*Matka*," protested Marek mildly, "you still have all the love that is in my heart."

"Not all, my Marek," she responded as she sensed her son had come back not only to see her, but also to enquire about his Maya. Magdalena added, "Not as I once had."

"Let us not stay here in the twilight," said the Count. "Come, Duchess, bring your son to table. While the hour of the meal is past, I will have the servants prepare a feast for this *Uhlan*. He must be starving after riding all day."

So, the groom took possession of Marek's horse such that it should be fed and watered. Marek followed his mother into the manor house, where they all sat having a pleasant discussion as they awaited the food to be brought to nourish the returning prodigal son of the *folwark*.

"So, tell me Marek," asked the Count, as he prepared personally to pour his finest *wodka* for them all, "What brings your regiment this far east? Last we had heard from you, you were encamped in the Czech lands, between Olomouc and Brno." The Count then raised his glass and toasted, "*Na zdrowie*!"

Then Marek and Magdalena joined the Count, as they raised their glasses and toasted to their collective health. They then drained their glasses, all except the Duchess Magdalena, who sipped from her own.

Wiping his upper lip with his right forefinger, Marek responded to the question. "Yes, we were there, indeed, but once Russia began mobilizing against Poland, we were hurriedly ordered to the lands east of here, near Lemberg, to assure neither the Poles nor the Russians cross over the border into our lands."

"Yes, of course. This war will be good for no one, and we certainly don't need to be drawn into it," answered the Count. "I am comforted to know that you will be protecting us, my young man."

"Myself, and many, many others," replied Marek. "I am only happy these circumstances have allowed me this one night to join you all once again."

"But if you are stationed at Lemberg for some time, perhaps we will have many nights such as this," hoped Magdalena aloud.

"I am sorry, *moja Matka*," said Marek, "but that will not be possible. I had to bribe my commander to allow even this, and I have spent all I have to do so."

"Well, Marek, after you eat, we will find many other treasures with which you may bribe him once more. I have never seen your mother so happy," said the Count, as if her happiness was his only concern. "In fact, bring your commander here with you next visit. Bring the entire regiment, we certainly have enough grounds for them to encamp upon. I will feed them all if it means your mother gains just another few hours with you in her sight."

The food was brought, and the Count then excused himself. Duchess Magdalena watched with great satisfaction as her son ate heartily in the comforting glow of the candlelight.

"Marek, my son," she said tenderly to him as he finished, "this cavalry has made such a man of you. You are so striking. You must have many girls who desire you."

He looked at her, somewhat skeptically, and replied, "*Matka*, I love you so dearly. However, I am no longer your little boy. I am twenty years old now. I am a man, *Matka*."

"Of course, my Marek," she answered, "I know how old you are. Was it not I who bore the pains of your birth? It was I who counted the joy of every single day that I laid eyes upon you. And it was I who bore the anguish of every day since you have been taken from me. I died even when you were lost for three days chasing that damn Tatar pony. My soul was crushed when I watched you drown! And every day since then, although I later knew you to be alive, I never knew if I would ever lay eyes upon you once again."

He could see her brows furrow with pain. Marek knew it was caused not of the things of the past that she had recalled, but of her anticipation of his leaving once more in the morning.

"As for the many girls who might desire me," he said plainly, "you know well that I can only ever desire just one girl. Where is my *Maya Manuska*?

The question impaled her, even though she had been expecting it. She took a second to catch her breath before replying.

"Oh, yes, young Maya," she stammered, "she and her mother have left for a farm in Poland owned by her uncle."

"What! She is not here upon the *folwark*? And the Duke, also?" Marek asked.

"No, *Pan* Cyprian - he is no longer a *szlachta* Duke - still lives here upon the generosity of the Count," Magdalena answered. "His wife and Maya left him in his disgrace."

"He deserves no better," answered Marek coldly. "Where in Poland is this uncle's farm where my *Maya Manuska* lives." His voice was on edge.

"It is too far across the border for you to attempt to find her, Marek," said his mother. "You must forget her, my son."

His eyes penetrated her, as if he had been expecting this vague of a response.

"You look different, *Matka*, all dressed in your splendid clothes, living in these most elegant of surroundings. What happened to the peasant woman who took the greatest joy in making her son happy?"

The Duchess Magdalena lowered her head, for it was true that the comfort and wealth which she had so hurriedly thrust upon her had indeed choked out the simplicity and happiness which she had so pleasantly cultivated as a peasant. She had learned, as her son now perceived, that to have much is merely to have much to lose.

She raised her head and answered him, "Marek, as a mother, I fear I had never taught you that all things that make you happy are not necessarily things that will lead to happiness. You must forget Maya, for she is gone, and she is not what she was before. She is not the woman for you to share your life, my son."

Marek sat quietly before her. She expected him to explode in anger, although this had never really been his way. He had always been a thoughtful boy, and in his eyes she could see he was digesting what she had said.

"*Matka*, you displease me," he said abruptly after several seconds of silence. "I can only now understand what great changes have occurred in my absence. You have gone from a peasant servant to a grand Duchess. From one of rags to one of fine gowns, from living in a hovel to living in a palace. How these things have hardened your heart! So, now, the disgraced Maya is not worthy of your presence, nor of being with your son. She merely lives in a state of simplicity as you once did. Do not be so callous to tell me what my own heart needs. For I desire, above all else, to be with my Maya, be she a peasant or the daughter of a wealthy Duke. She still will be mine."

His retribution poured out upon her, and she knew then that he could never understand the true reason that he could not be with Maya unless she told him the truth of his father. Yet, it was the brash manner in which he had scolded her that enraged her soul. His petulance resulted in her fury.

"Marek, where did you learn to speak to your mother with a tongue filled with a serpent's venom?" Magdalena rose from the table. "Your words cut at me. I did not ask to be given these luxuries. I was pleased to live that simple life."

Marek then stood to respond to her. She had shouted at him, and he responded in a similarly terse and elevated tone. "But woman, you did indeed ask for all this. No sooner was my father killed than you gathered us up and fled to the monastery. There you met with the Abbott where, as you may recall, I was not allowed to be present. Did you not ask him to recognize that you were not a peasant? Is this not true? Had we never left the *folwark*, I would not have had to try to escape the monastery, and I would not have attempted to rescue Maya, or as a result have been conscripted to the army. Yet, woman, you did flee, and you did indeed request all that you have received, all the riches this world has to offer, however, at what cost? You have lost a son."

Magdalena's rage had escalated into full blown fury. "Marek! How dare you call me woman! Not once, but twice! How rude you have become. You want your way, my arrogant son, then have it. Your Maya lives in the small village of Maciejowice on the Vistula between Sandomierz and Warsaw. She goes by her mother's Ukrainian maiden name, Polischiuk. Go ahead, go after her, see if that makes your heart full. You will come to rue the day you find her, I assure you."

And like a child who had been scolded, although only after getting what he wanted, he apologized to her.

"I am sorry to have been so harsh with you, my mother," Marek said, although he did not move to embrace her. "I let my emotions cloud my words, and for this I regret."

"You are sorry only because you have divulged the true feelings of your heart, Marek," she said, slowly calming herself from her furor. "Now, I must tell you something of your father that you are not aware."

"Yes, *Matka*," he said rather plainly, as if trying to diffuse the antagonism in their words.

She hesitated. She knew this might be her last opportunity to tell him. She did not know when she might see him next. Yet, she found she could not tell him the secret. She feared that her urge to do so was only based on her current anger. Anger, she knew, was derived from the sin of pride. At the last minute, she decided to swallow her pride, lest it should escape on the breath of her next few words.

"Our Bronisław's remains are no longer buried in the peasant graveyard. I had his remains moved to the manor cemetery. I am sure you will want to pay your respects before you leave in the morning."

She could not do it. Despite every fiber of her being knowing it had to be done, she could not tell him that he was the son of Cyprian Sdanowicz.

"Yes, of course I will," Marek said. "*Dziękuję, Matka.* I will take to my quarters now."

What the Duchess Magdalena said next came as a surprise even to herself.

"There is one other thing, Marek. *Pan* Cyprian lives in the infirmary. Despite all that has passed between us, I think it best that you should see him also before you leave, if even only for a few minutes. You should not leave on the morn without saying goodbye to your father and the former Duke."

Marek was surprised at this request, yet agreed to go along with his mother's wishes. He did not understand that her last sentence held two references to the same man. It was her way of taking a half step to telling him, but its meaning was so cleverly hidden that it was lost on the boy.

They then both retired to their chambers, both disquieted by the unexpected course of their discussion. The next morning, Marek rose early, in an attempt to visit the cemetery. In the kitchen of the guest house, he came upon his Aunt Ewelina, who was tending to the morning chores.

"Marek, I am so sorry I missed you last night," she exclaimed upon seeing him. After embracing him, she added, "I was already asleep when you arrived. It is so good to have at least one of our boys at home."

Marek had not expected her to have risen so early. But was glad to see her once more.

"Aunt Ewelina," Marek said, "it is a delight to see you also. I saw Uncle Jacek in Vienna. He said to kiss you for him when I saw you next." He embraced her a second time and kissed her upon her forehead tenderly.

"Marek," she smiled, "you lie with the grin of a wolf. You think because neither your Uncle nor I can read or write that he does not have others write letters on his behalf? Jacek writes me this way often, and your *matka* kindly reads them to me. I know that from Jacek's letters that it has been forever since you last saw him in Vienna."

"This is true, *Ciotka*," Marek said as he leaned over and again kissed her on her cheek, "but he said when I saw you next, even though it has been long in coming, he still offers you his kiss. The second kiss is from me."

"You are such a sweet boy," said Ewelina.

"My mother may no longer agree with you," he said.

"Yes, she awoke me last night, and told me that you both had quarreled. I made her something to help her sleep. I told her it was just the awkward release of so many emotions you both have had penned up for so long. Do not go away angry, Marek, for she loves you so."

They spoke a little longer, and then Marek excused himself to visit the cemetery which was in a clearing cut from the woods behind the manor house. There Marek was surprised to see a solitary figure standing over a grave. It was draped in the ancient ceremonial robes of the *szlachta*, complete with the scabbarded saber of authority. This man at first appeared to wear an unusual headdress, until Marek drew closer and realized the "headdress" was nothing more than the man's shaved head except for a several inch-wide band of short hair that stood erect, centered from forehead to nape. It was the style the *szlachta* wore in centuries past. It was only then that Marek recognized the man to be *Pan* Cyprian Sdanowicz. He stood in respect above the grave of Bronisław Zaczek.

"My boy, Marek," he said, turning to the footfalls he detected behind him. Upon his face, the former Duke had grown a full mustache connected to the scrawny beard of a goat.

"*Pan* Sdanowicz," responded Marek, determined not to address him as *'Duke'*. "I have come to pay my respects to my father."

"And so you have," responded Cyprian. "I see we both wear our uniforms, mine of the *szlachta* and your of the Austrian Army."

"Yes, as I recall it was you who had sent me off to Vienna," Marek said.

Pan Sdanowicz hacked an angry cough from deep within him in an involuntary response. He wiped his mouth with a rag from his pocket before responding.

"So it was, my boy, so it was. And look at all the good it has done you. The Imperial Army has made a man of you."

"Why do you dress like this? Shave your head like a magnate from centuries ago?" asked Marek, intending to insulting him. "Why do you cling to the *szlachta* robes of the past?"

"To remind me of who I am," Cyprian said proudly. "The Austrian Emperor has stripped me of everything, except my dignity. I am a Polish noble, so I dress like this to remind the Count. And most of all, because it annoys him terribly."

"You are not ashamed?" asked Marek.

"What is shame?" replied Cyprian. "It is to admit defeat before the judgement of others. Yes, I was angry for a long while. Pangs of it still come and go. But shame? No, never. One day I will be restored, if not in this life, then the next. Now, boy, let me look upon you."

He grasped his bear like hands upon the shoulders of Marek. "You look so grand! I'd bet all that I have already lost that you are the best rider in your unit. Is it not so?"

"It is so," Marek said, "no one rides like I do. No one ever has."

"Of course, of course," agreed Sdanowicz, cracking a smile of satisfaction. "Now, I have something to tell you, Marek, about your father."

They both looked down upon the grave. Sdanowicz slid his arm around the young *Uhlan's* shoulders.

"Your father was a good man. He did not deserve what happened to him. He was only ever looking out for you, Marek, and your mother. He wanted only what was in your best interests."

"I believe this in my heart," uttered Marek.

"Your mother sent your Aunt Ewelina to me last night, to tell me that you had come and would be here this morning. She had something to tell you, which she had not the courage to approach with you in your conversation together. She wished me to tell you it myself here this morning."

"And what is it which my mother was too weak to share with me?" asked Marek.

Indeed, Marek's mother had sent Ewelina to compel Pan Cyprian to tell Marek that he was his true father. It was necessary in order to keep Marek from pursuing Maya, the messenger said, relaying the Duchess' words. Ewelina had relayed that the boy would likely not believe Magdalena, and that he would think that it was only his mother's ruse to keep him and Maya apart.

But after the Duchess' sister-in-law and servant had left, *Pan* Cyprian thought deeply on the request. It came from the woman who, in his distorted logic, had tempted him only to steal, along with the Count, all that he built in this life. She had also cost him not only his marriage, but the loss of his lovely daughter as well. Both women in his life were forever gone from him now, lost to his Ukrainian in-law family of renegades. He decided he no longer had anything to lose. However, Duchess Magdalena had the world to lose. *Pan* Cyprian Sdanowicz would take great joy in seeing that, above all else, she would first lose her beloved son.

"Your father still loves you to this day, Marek," *Pan* Cyprian said, looking up to the dawning pastel colors of the morning sky. He was being deliberate and very careful with his words. "Bronisław was a good man, solid and true. He loved you, Marek. He would take great honor in the man you have become, as I do."

"Yes, yes. All of this I already know, *Pan* Sdanowicz," Marek said. "What are the words my mother wished so greatly that I was to hear from you?"

The former Duke waited a long second, thinking only of the opportunity that Magda had laid at his feet.

"Bronisław died not by my hand," said Cyprian Sdanowicz. "The collapse at the mine was nothing more than an accident. One day you will fully understand how great a man your father was, although it may be many years in the future."

"You are hiding something yet from me," sensed Marek. "What more is there to tell?"

The former Duke again hacked a chest rattling cough. Marek had heard this before, it was the same cough that had eventually taken his friend Miłosz. *Pan* Sdanowicz again wiped his mouth with the spittled rag, before confessing his truth to the young soldier.

"You once asked me for the blessing of my daughter's hand," said *Pan* Cyprian, "and I was too proud to have you take her for your wife. Now, she is gone from me. This day, I give you my blessing, if she will have you, to take her for your own. Follow your heart. Your mother could not say this last evening, so I tell you on her behalf today. You are free to marry my Maya."

"*Dziękuję bardzo, Pan* Cyprian Sdanowicz," said the elated Marek, "I am forever indebted to you. I swear that I shall always take the greatest of care of your Maya."

You have always been indebted to me, Pan Sdanowicz thought, *as your life has grown from my own seed.*

"Remember, my son," the fallen Duke said next, "you have my blessing only as long as she freely accepts you in her heart."

Marek heard the former Duke address him as "my son" only to think it was Pan Cyprian's cryptic way of welcoming him to what was left of his family.

Then, Cyprian Sdanowicz embraced the young cavalier, and offered his best wishes to the young man. Pan Cyprian said, *"Do widzenia,"* before turning to walk away, a sly smile upon his lips.

He had set in motion the events that he hoped would destroy the Duchess Magdalena. He did not care of its consequences upon either Marek, who still revered the peasant Bronisław over himself. Nor did *Pan* Cyprian care about the consequences that might befall Maya, who had abandoned her father in his time of greatest need. The former Duke's deeply seeded anger left him bereft of compassion for his own children.

Pan Cyprian Sdanowicz then left Marek alone to pray over the grave of the miner Bronislaw Zaczek, who the former Duke in reality considered to be but nothing of a man. Marek then knelt in the dirt before Bronisław's grave, and prayed for the soul of the man who had been nothing but a true father to him.

40

THE SECOND PARTITION

1793

The year 1793 began with the earth-shaking fall of the guillotine's blade in Paris and ended with the realignment of the borders of the Commonwealth. By comparison, the United States was relatively calm, having established its own continuity with George Washington being inaugurated for a second term.

In France, King Louis the XVI was found guilty of crimes against the people, and by a margin of one vote was sentenced to immediate execution. On the twenty-first day of January, the King was led to the guillotine in the *Place de la Revolution*. Massive crowds came to witness the spectacle, and with the release of the guillotine's blade, the thirty-eight year old King's head was severed. (Although *some* contemporaneous accounts claim that the first drop of the blade failed to cleanly separate his head from his body, and that Louis died in unbearable agony.) King Louis was later buried in a simple unmarked grave, his head at his feet. Quicklime was sprinkled over his corpse to speed the decomposition process.

What followed was the descent of the country from mere anarchy into institutionalized, abject horror. On the tenth day of March, the "Committee for Public Safety", as it was ironically called, was formed under the leadership of Maximilien Robespierre. The period that followed over the next two years was known as the Reign of Terror, where over 16,500 death sentences were handed out, of which over 2,700 occurred in Paris alone. The leftward political tilt of the country's masses gave way to unfettered attacks upon the aristocrats, the clergy and others of prominence, before eventually turning on the revolutionaries themselves.

Those beheaded included the aristocrat Antoine Lavoisier, known as the father of modern chemistry, (although he was posthumously pardoned by the French government a year and a half later); Charlotte Corday, the country woman who stabbed the Jacobin newspaperman Jean-Paul Marat to death in his bathtub; André Chénier, a poet (whose wrongly accused life would later become the subject of an opera); George Danton, himself a member of the *Committee of Public Safety*; and finally the Terror consumed the very life of its instigator and defender, Maximilien Robespierre, himself.

The Terror began in 1793 as the *Jacobin* revolutionaries separated into two factions: the more moderate *Girondins* and the even more reactionary *Montagnards*. In June of 1793, the *Montagnards* used the National Guard to physically remove the *Girondins* from the National Convention and imprisoned them. Not all the Girondins had been captured during the June purge. Some had escaped to the countryside.

The extremely radical *Jacobin* newspaperman Jean-Paul Marat had boasted that if he was given a list of enemies of the revolution, including the escaped *Girondins*, he would publish their names in his paper, *The Friend of the People,* and that *"their heads would fall within a fortnight"*.

In June of 1793, when a young woman from the country named Charlotte Corday came to him with such a list, it spelled the end for Marat. Given access to meet Marat while he bathed (he worked often at a makeshift desk over his bathtub as he suffered from a debilitating skin disease), Corday produced a hidden dagger and went on to stab Marat repeatedly until he died bathing in his own blood. Corday had been a sympathizer of the *Girondins*, and had sacrificed herself to protest their persecution.

Charlotte Corday was guillotined four days later. As a reaction to Corday's unrepentant slaying of Marat, the jailed *Girondins* were found guilty of treason at trial. Befittingly, on the last day of October, All Souls Eve, the imprisoned *Girondins* were executed, with their twenty-two heads guillotined in thirty-six minutes. Such were the extremes of the Terror.

Perhaps the most famous head to fall from the impact of the guillotine's blade was that of Marie Antoinette. She was accused of sending funds from the French treasury to Austria, conducting orgies at Versailles, and even of incest by her own brother (although this appears to have been a coordinated, trumped up charge). She was brought to the Guillotine in the *Place de la Revolution* just past noon on the sixteenth day of October, 1793.

Marie Antoinette's last words were famously, "Forgive me, sir, I did not mean to do it". These words were not directed as a response to those who accused her of the criminal charges, but rather to her executioner after she had inadvertently stepped on his foot. Like her husband before her, her decapitated body and head were placed in an unmarked grave and quick-limed for rapid decomposition.

It would not be until 1815 that both the graves of the executed King and Queen were exhumed, and the corpses moved to the Cathedral of Saint Denis, to be interred in the royal crypts with the other French Kings and Queens.

As the events in Paris deteriorated into mayhem, the monarchies in the East had once again proven themselves insatiable. Only two days after the beheading of Louis XVI in France, on the twenty-third day of January, 1793, Prussia and Russia signed a treaty agreeing to new large swaths of lands to be annexed from the Polish-Lithuanian Commonwealth. This would become known as the Second Partition of Poland.

King Stanisław Poniatowski had sued for peace the previous year to end the War of 1792 with Russia, enraging his generals, including Kościuszko, as well as his own nephew, Prince Józef. The two victorious combatant states of Russia and Prussia then jointly reduced the size of the Commonwealth by nearly sixty percent. The Second Partition of Poland came twenty-one years after the first one.

The Prussians gained only about a fifth of what the Russians acquired, although their newly annexed territory included the Hanseatic League cities of Toruń upon the Vistula River (hometown of Nicholaus Copernicus), and the prosperous Baltic seaport of Gdańsk. Toruń was renamed Thorn, and Gdańsk became Danzig. The second partition solidified the Prussian holdings, and made what little was left of Poland even more dependent on Prussia for access to the sea.

The Russian territories in the eastern provinces of the Polish Commonwealth acted as yet even more of a buffer for Catherine's Russia. These lands included much of the fertile fields of eastern Ukraine, as well of much of eastern Poland and Lithuania.

What little remained of the Commonwealth after this partition featured only two major cities, Warsaw and Kraków. Kościuszko escaped westward to the German city of Leipzig. Prince Józef Poniatowski departed for Vienna. Both would return to Poland soon enough.

41

THE KOŚCIUSZKO UPRISING

1794

In France, the Reign of Terror was at its apex. Public executions were nearly everyday occurrences throughout the country. And so, like a snake devouring its own tail, the *Jacobins* had consumed part of themselves. The purge of the *Girondins* left in place only the most radical *Jacobin* elements. The Terror ended in July of 1794 when it consumed its own creator, the increasingly radical Maximilien Robespierre.

In early March of 1794, Marek Zaczek still found himself stationed in Galicia. The area had been quiet after the end of the Polish-Russian War in 1792. Although Austria had not taken part in the Second Partition of 1793, Marek was among the forces left in place in Galicia to insure that neither Polish nor Russian troops conducted incursions into Austrian territory.

Marek had not seen his mother since that sole visit to the *folwark*. In fact, after that visit, he returned her letters unopened. Despite the conciliatory graveyard message of *Pan* Cyprian Sdanowicz, Marek could not bear to think of his mother's earlier protestations against his one day marrying Maya.

Marek thought often of his *Maya Manuska. What was her life in Poland like?* The second partition had placed this village near the new Russian border, and life would have become all the more uncertain. *What type of woman had she become?* Marek was then twenty-two years of age, and Maya would be a ravishing beauty of twenty years. Several times, Marek had thought of sneaking off to this Polish village to visit her.

There were three primary reasons he did not. First and foremost, during the war, if he, as a soldier, even a non-combatant, were caught in Poland out of uniform, he could be accused of being a foreign spy. This very likely could result in the loss of his life by hanging.

The second reason was more subtle. By 1794, he had not seen his *Maya Manuska* for many years. *Would she even remember me? Suppose she had fallen in love with another? Could my heart take this strain?*

The third reason was perhaps the most damning - his lustful memories of Reka. He clung to them desperately. Every time he attempted to expel them from his mind, a small greedy part of him seemed to say, *There is no harm in remembering her, is there? If I were to cross the Vistula and squander a second night in her abode, then I would most certainly bring harm upon Maya by my unfaithfulness. However, merely remembering her scent, the fullness of her breasts, their light sensation upon my thighs, and the sound of her lovemaking with Tolo, these are only images forever trapped within my mind, that I cannot expel even if I desired to do so.*

Marek seemed to be suffering a perpetual onslaught of these memories, and they forever threatened the purity of his memories of his *Maya Manuska*.

It was mid-March when Marek was called upon by his superior. He entered his commander's tent, only to find his commander with a second man who was well-dressed in the clothes of a prominent civilian.

"Zaczek," began his commander in German. "I have a very special assignment for you. I understand that you are from this area. Is this correct?"

"Yes, sir," Marek replied, at full attention. Marek's German was by then exceptional. His eyes shifted from his commander to the gentlemen behind him. He dared not ask directly as to whom the man might be.

The commander recognized his distracted gaze.

"Zaczek, this is Herr Schmidt from the Ministry of War. Do not allow his presence to distract you," the commander said.

"Yes, sir!" responded Marek.

"Zaczek, have you been to Kraków?" asked the commander.

"Yes, sir!" replied Marek. He dared not elaborate upon his response, as the discipline of the army demanded only the most concise answers.

"And your Polish is fluent?"

"Yes, sir!" responded Marek.

"Do you know who Tadeusz Kościuszko is?" asked his superior.

"Yes, sir!"

"Would you recognize him by sight?" asked the commander.

"No, sir!"

"Nonetheless, I have some sketches and drawings for you to familiarize yourself with," interjected Herr Schmidt, speaking for the first time. "Tadeusz Kościuszko has returned to Poland from exile in Leipzig. On the twenty-fourth day of March, we are told, he plans to make a speech in the main square of Kraków. We in the war ministry are most anxious to hear what the Polish General has to say. We would like you to be in the square to listen to his speech and report back to us the next day. We will even provide you with funds to mingle among the Poles in their taverns and restaurants afterwards to see what is their reaction to Kościuszko's speech. It is a simple enough task."

Marek said nothing. His head instantly filled with images of Reka.

His commander looked to Herr Schmidt, who nodded his approval to proceed.

"Zaczek," began his commander again, "this is not truly a military tasking, except that it does fall under the domain of military intelligence. Given your familiarity with Kraków, and the ability to understand Kościuszko's Polish tongue, we are asking you to volunteer for this activity. The information will be critical to the Austrian government, from what we have discerned from our contacts in Leipzig."

They wish for me to spy on my own homeland, he thought. *They must have a very good idea what General Kościuszko is likely to say in Kraków. They merely wish me to confirm it, and measure the reaction of the Poles.*

"Well, Zaczek, are you willing to volunteer for this assignment?" asked the commander.

"Yes, sir," answered Marek, adding for effect, "I am willing to volunteer."

"Good. We will ask you to dress in a tradesman's clothes, and be in the main square of Kraków on the day of the twenty-fourth. Listen to what Kościuszko has to say, however, take no notes. Only remember his words. Afterward, attend the restaurants and the taverns. Eat and drink with the locals. Take in the reaction of the General's countrymen. You will stay late into the evening, so report back to us the next day here in camp. Here, we will debrief you."

Very soon, the twenty-fourth day of March was upon them. Marek was given papers that allowed him unchallenged access at the border and into the city of Kraków. The city was abuzz with the expectation of Kościuszko addressing them in the square.

Before Marek made his way to the square, he wandered to the tavern above which Reka had lived. He wondered if she even still did so. Marek decided he would come to this tavern after the General's speech to gage the reaction of the patrons. Perhaps then, he would also find out whether Reka still resided upstairs.

It was here, outside the tavern, that Marek first experienced the sensation of being watched. As he worked his way through the crowds to get to the *Rynek Główny*, or main square, he sensed that he was being followed. The crowds were too large to distinguish if indeed he was or not; in reality he was being followed by a mob, itself headed to hear the General.

There was something missing from the city. He had been told

that there was a garrison of Russian soldiers stationed there, yet he saw none. He heard two men speaking near him in the square that solved the mystery.

"The Russians," said the first man, "they are gone, and have left Kraków to pursue the Polish army officers who have refused to decommission their troops in compliance with the accords defining the Second Partition."

"It is evil enough that the Russian bastards take our lands, yet then they dare tell us what minuscule number of soldiers we are allowed to keep!" answered the second man.

"There are protests breaking out in the countryside against the Russians," said the first man. "This is the time to take back what those devils have stolen from us."

Marek knew that the Russians had imposed a limitation on the Polish Army of only 15,000 men. This was barely enough to fight a major battle, let alone defend a nation. The spineless King Poniatowski had accepted this demand. The career military officers were now refusing to decommission their units, and the Russians feared an armed uprising.

"Perhaps Kościuszko will lead our country in its battle against the Russians," said the first of the two men. "It is said that in the War for the Defense of the Constitution, he did not lose a single battle. Even in America, he was covered only in glory."

Marek knew the War in Defense of the Constitution was what the Poles called the Polish-Russian War of 1792.

"May God Bless Tadeusz Kościuszko," said the second man, and many around him agreed.

It was then that Marek overheard another conversation, this time between two women. They were both fashionably dressed, and seemed to have been drawn into the square by the excitement of the event. They were very much out of place, as the great majority of the crowd were men from all classes of Polish life.

"Have you heard of General Kościuszko?" asked the first woman, a tall blonde.

"Yes, of course," said the second woman, a brunette who had

a more compact frame. "Everyone knows of this great man. He made his name in America, and he and Kazimierz Pułaski taught the Americans the bravery of the Polish heart."

"Well, Kościuszko's heart is not only brave," said the blonde, "but also romantic as well. I am told when he came back from Paris after the 1772 Partition, he was tutoring a *hetman's* daughter. He fell in love with her and then he asked for her hand in marriage. Can you imagine this?"

"A *hetman's* daughter? He asked for her hand from this great a man?" asked the brunette. "What was the reply?"

"Supposedly," the blonde woman said, "the *hetman* replied, *'Turtledoves are not for mere sparrows,'* or something along those lines. Then Kościuszko defied the *hetman* and tried to elope with her, only to have the *hetman's* men thrash him within inches of his life. Only then, did he go to America."

The words of turtledoves and sparrows cut deeply within Marek's soul. It was as if a wound that was on the verge of healing had been torn open by another saber's blow. Marek thought of that night five years ago when he had asked for Maya's hand from the Duke, when these words were the core of his rejection. They led to the following night at the Vistula, when he and Maya were trapped against the river's edge. That had been the last time he had laid eyes upon his *Maya Manuska*.

It was exactly at this point that he heard a strange whisper within his ear, loud enough such that only he could hear it.

"What are you doing here, Marek Zaczek?"

Marek turned to lay eyes upon a very familiar face, which for an instant he could not place. Then, he realized he knew it deep within his memory without the beard and mustache that it now hid behind. Marek then could not believe his eyes.

"Tolo! Is it you, my friend?" he nearly screamed, embracing his once dead brother.

"Yes, Marek, it is your Tolo, in the flesh."

"But I saw you die!" Marek exclaimed.

"You saw me act as if I was dead," said Tolo. "I knew after that first lead ball hissed past my ear that I could not rescue you. So, I acted as if I had taken a wound. I figured that was the only way those men would not attempt to follow me into the morning fog. How did you escape?"

"I did not," said Marek. "The Duke's men broke my nose, but that is nearly all. Only a few bruises more, all of which have healed, except for the crook in my nose."

"Yes, so I see," said Tolo, "your face was pretty before, like a girl's. Now it has strength. It is so good to see you, my friend. I have been following you since the tavern, although I could not be sure it indeed was you."

"Does Reka still live above it?" Marek asked.

"Oh, so Marek remembers Reka? Of course, we all remember our first time," said Tolo, not knowing that Marek had lied to him long ago. "Yes, Reka still lives there, although I can no longer afford to be with her. I am lucky enough to eat in these days."

"Well, tonight you will eat with me. I will pay. And then we will drink in the tavern underneath her room. We will celebrate being together once more, my friend."

Soon after, General Tadeusz Kościuszko entered the massive square. He wore his Polish Army uniform, complete with the four cornered military cap known in Polish as the *Rogatywka*. The hero of the American Revolution, as well as undefeated guardian of the Polish Constitution, spoke eloquently of liberty, freedom, and true Polish independence from its encroaching neighboring states. He announced an uprising against Russia and revealed that it had the backing of decommissioned regiments of the Polish army. Kościuszko then also announced his intention to free the peasants from their slavery under the nobility. He called upon the peasants to join his uprising, and to fight the Russians with their scythes, pikes and axes, if necessary. His declaration whipped the citizens of Kraków into a frenzy, and it was clear that his call upon the peasants to fight was well received.

Marek marked every passage in his mind, and these words soon infected his heart as well. Despite only having ever known Austrian

Galicia as his home, all of the province's peasants had considered themselves Polish, and had a yearning to rejoin what was left of the Polish State. Now that the second partition left only a small core of what had once been the exhaustive lands of the Commonwealth, that nationalistic fervor had intensified. Kościuszko's words had brilliantly drawn on that feeling of romanticism, and he hoped to draw peasant fighters not only from what was left of official Poland, but also from the partition lands lost to Russia, Austria and Prussia. And indeed, he would.

He called on a mobilization of all of Poland proper to provide from every five houses at least one male to fight against the Russians. He knew this would require peasant combatants, to whom he intimated their freedom from serfdom would be the ultimate reward. For this uprising was not to be, as in the past, a battle of the nobility and army alone against the invaders, but an uprising of all the people of Poland, especially the peasants.

Tolo and Marek were captivated by the General's decree. They found their way into a restaurant, where Tolo ate heartily upon the generosity of his friend. He ate with the insecurity of a man who did not know from where his next meal might come. Marek had noticed his *happy go-lucky, God will provide attitude* on life had departed him. He seemed a young man under great strain.

"So, Tolo, my friend," asked Marek, as the late afternoon gave way to evening, "How goes the trapping these days? Any more pelts of ermine?"

"All you can think of is Reka, no?" he responded to Marek. "I no longer can trap for my living. It had become too dangerous to cross the river alone at night. I tried to trap on this side of the Vistula, but was caught by a *szlachta* Duke who threatened to kill me if he found me on his lands again. Then his men laid upon me, breaking my ribs in two places. Let us just say I was discouraged to going back to the traps."

"What have you done instead?" asked Marek.

"Starved, mostly," Tolo replied, as he wiped his plate clean with the last piece of bread upon the table.

"You have no work whatsoever?" asked his friend.

"I have taken to something to survive that is no less dangerous than trapping, although much more rewarding – not in *złoty*, but in pride."

Tolo said these words apprehensively, as if he was unsure he could entrust their meaning to even Marek.

"What is this undertaking you are involved in?"

"Smuggling," Tolo replied, having decided he could indeed rely upon his friend to keep this secret. "I smuggle goods upon the Vistula."

"And this is not profitable?" Marek asked. "I always thought there would be great fortune in it, provided one did not get caught."

"Not for the people for whom I work," answered Tolo, who Marek noticed had streaks of gravy in his shaggy unkept beard.

"Who are these people?" asked Marek.

"Kościuszko and his lot," answered Tolo cautiously. "They have no money to pay for my services, although what little food I have these days is directly from them. I carry their supplies on rafts along the rivers. Mostly eastwards, toward the border with Russia. It is not for money I do these things, instead because I believe so in the General's cause."

"So you knew what the General had planned to say?"

"Somewhat," admitted Tolo.

"What will become of you after the uprising, my friend," asked Marek, genuinely concerned over the fate of the man who had saved him, who he considered to be his brother.

"Well, that depends upon how successful the uprising will be, doesn't it?" answered Tolo. "I like to think in my mind that it will be successful, and I will be in good standing with the victors."

"That is your mind, but what is in your heart? Does it perceive the same outcome?" Marek's question seemed to antagonize Tolo somewhat.

"My heart only perceives that Poland must be free. For me to do nothing, would be for me to be complicit in the consumption of our country." Tolo for the first time felt his friend's questioning to be intrusive. "You are lucky, Marek, to live within the lands the Austrians have stolen from Poland. They at least allow the Polish language to be spoken, the customs to be observed. It is not so with the Russians and Prussians, where it is forbidden to speak our native tongue, to practice our ways, to be Polish in any sense of the word."

"Forgive me, my friend," apologized Marek, "I did not mean to upset you so."

"It is just after Miłosz's passing, followed so closely by my failing you, I have never felt more alone in this world," Tolo explained. He had felt guilty for having rebuked his friend so harshly. "I was befriended by some countrymen, who instilled in me the pride of Poland. I fought with the forces defending the Constitution against the Russians and Prussians. Well, my fighting was moving war goods along the rivers, but that is as critical as killing a Russian, you know, just not as satisfying. After our timid King Poniatowski lost his nerve, abandoning us and giving another slice of Poland to these devils, I vowed to keep fighting against the Russians and Prussians so long as there was a rebellion ongoing. So once again I will serve Kościuszko and Poniatowski."

"You will serve the King?" asked Marek incredulously.

"No, he is only a traitor that sits upon our throne. I speak of Prince Józef Poniatowski, his nephew," said Tolo, "we are hearing rumors that he will come back and fight under Kościuszko, who will be commander-in-chief of all the rebellious Polish forces."

"Well, you certainly know much of these things," said Marek, feeling traitorous, as his friend unwittingly passed valuable information onto him. Marek wondered what Tolo would do if he knew his friend was, in truth, an Austrian spy.

Tolo then continued, "When you move materials along the rivers, there is much information that accompanies the goods. One learns to piece it all together, and in doing so, understand what is hidden from most."

Tolo seemed proud of his essential contribution to Kościuszko's cause. It was clear that he had never stopped serving him since the last war.

"Come, our bellies are full of food," said Marek, "let us go drink together and fill our minds of great tales."

They departed the restaurant and headed west to the tavern near the wall. This time they entered the lower establishment and drank heartily for the rest of the evening. The place was packed with men of all walks of life, and the talk of all was of Kościuszko's planned uprising. A great fervor seemed to be cast upon the collective crowd, much as a blessing is signaled amongst a congregation of true believers.

They were not circumspect, but rather gregarious in their anticipation, relishing the thought of taking back the Russian lands that had been stolen from Poland.

"What does Marek do these days?" asked Tolo.

"My mother has been named Duchess of Bochnia, and has come into great wealth," he answered, as he was ordered to not divulge his being a member of the Austrian Army.

"That explains why you look so well fed, so strong," said his friend. "How is it you dress as a tradesman, then?"

"I am uncomfortable to dress as a Duchess' son. I do not wish to show my undeserved wealth when there are so many in such great need, Tolo," explained Marek. "This way, I am still treated with respect and not the scorn reserved for the peasants. Although, I have never been ashamed as having been raised as a peasant, in fact, I take great pride in it."

"But not enough pride to be seen as one?" Tolo noted. "And you are still with your Maya?"

"No, and it is a long story, my friend," responded Marek. "She lives upon a farm in Maciejowice. Do you know this place?"

"Yes, of course," Tolo replied. "It is just off the Vistula, between Sandomierz and Warsaw. I know it well enough."

"Maya lives with her mother and uncle there," he said. "I have not seen her since that night we were captured at the river. The Duke went to great lengths to keep us separated. However, I know in my heart that I will be rejoined one day with her."

They drank through the night upon the wave of hope that rolled throughout the festivities. Marek listened intently to the discussions of his fellow revelers, almost all of whom praised Kościuszko and his declared uprising.

Then the time came to leave the tavern and for Marek to return to the room he had rented earlier. Marek invited Tolo to share his lodging, yet his friend resisted.

"I have a place to lay my head tonight," he said, with a wink of his eye. "With all your money, you should step upstairs to see Reka."

The thought had occurred to Marek, but was just as suddenly dismissed. *I shall keep myself pure for my Maya Manuska*, he thought.

Then Tolo embraced him. Marek slipped a handful of coins into his palm.

"Your stomach is full, tonight," said Marek to his friend. "Take these for whoever you lay your head next to, so that they may be free from hunger as well."

Tolo departed from him, leaving him alone in the cold outside the tavern. Marek looked up at the light in the window above, which then was extinguished from within. Marek remembered that delicious darkness, and wondered if Reka was alone this night.

42

THE ASSIGNMENT

1794

The rebellion began shortly thereafter. As expected, Catherine of Russia amassed a great force of troops against Kościuszko's patriots. Despite this, there were early victories that emboldened the Polish forces, and ignited the dreams of the Polish people.

Within two weeks, on fourth day of April, there occurred the first major battle at the village of Racławice, near the town of Sandomierz upon the Vistula. Here, just north and slightly east of Kraków, Kościuszko defended his country in a battle pitting three thousand well trained Imperial Russian troops against his forces of five thousand. However, two thousand of these were the *Scythemen* – peasants armed with nothing more than scythes, pikes or other farming implements modified as weapons. Each side had an equivalent number of cannon artillery, about a dozen per side.

Kościuszko, as brilliant as ever, attacked the highest hill on the battleground and established his artillery upon it. This gave him a tactical advantage over the attacking Russian troops. After softening the Russians with cannon fire, Kościuszko personally led a cavalry charge upon the routed Russian forces, driving them from the battlefield. However, without sufficient forces to pursue and annihilate the defeated Russians, he was unable to take full advantage of this victory.

The defeat of the Russian forces at Racławice would provide a rallying cry for the people of Poland. It inspired an uprising in Warsaw, where the populace of the capital city revolted against the Russian forces garrisoned there. The five thousand Russian troops stationed there were decimated by half during the fighting that ensued, and eventually the surviving Russian troops were successfully driven out of Warsaw.

As the Kościuszko Uprising continued, Marek was encouraged by his commander and the Austrian representative of the war ministry, Herr Schmidt, to continue to meet with his friend Tolo. Marek had briefed them on his friend's smuggling activities on behalf of the uprising. Herr Schmidt was especially keen on further exploiting this source of information on what the troops of Kościuszko were planning.

After the Battle of Racławice had been won, Marek returned to Kraków where he stayed for three days until he once again found Tolo. Thereafter, they agreed to meet regularly, each time with Marek gaining valuable insights into the rebellion.

On the seventh day of May, Kościuszko declared a partial lifting of *Pańszczyzna*, or the Polish law governing the implementation of serfdom. Kościuszko promised the implementation of protections of the peasants against the abuses of their *szlachta* masters.

Kościuszko was keeping his promise, the peasants thought, and intended to free them, just as he had freed the slaves from the lands he had possessed in the United States. What they did not realize was that even though Kościuszko had left a will in America intended to do just that, it was never enacted by those he entrusted it to. In truth, the peasant serfs of central and eastern Europe would remain in bondage just as long as the Negro slaves in America, for nearly the next seventy years.

Three days later, on the tenth day of May, the Prussians had crossed the Polish border and joined forces with the Russians once again. Kościuszko had hoped to have Prussia and Austria remain neutral in this conflict. Austria continued to amass its forces along the border with Poland, but remained out of the conflict.

The entrance of Prussia in putting down the rebellion shifted the already imbalanced resources of manpower, arms and logistics into the favor of the repressing states. In early June, Kościuszko lost his first engagement with joint Prussian and Russian forces. By mid-June, the Prussians captured the city of Kraków.

The uprising continued throughout the summer and into the fall. By November, superior numbers of Russian forces pressed upon the eastern suburbs of Warsaw, especially that of Praga, just across the Vistula River from the center of Warsaw.

It was on a peacefully warm day, the seventh day of October when Marek was called once more to his commander's tent. As usual, Herr Schmidt was present.

"Zaczek, we have a very dangerous mission for you," said the commander, "but, soldier, you have the choice should you decide to decline it."

"Yes, sir," responded Marek, "what is the mission?"

"First, Herr Schmidt will inform you of the overall situation of Kościuszko's rebellion," said his superior.

"Zaczek," barked Herr Schmidt, "we have many spies, many sources of information, yourself included. As we come to analyze all this information, we have concluded that the uprising of General Kościuszko will ultimately fail. Even with General Dąbrowski's recent success against the Prussians, there simply is no way Kościuszko can hold out against the combined forces of the Prussians and the Russians."

General Jan Henryk Dąbrowski had been successful in attacking the Prussians within their annexed Polish lands. His cavalry was extremely skilled and moved much faster than that of the Prussians who had attempted to encircle him. Instead, he had encircled them. His fame as an expert of cavalry and its tactics had already been known before this, and this early October victory over the hated Prussians had secured his legend.

"Yes, sir, I understand," responded Marek, who had long before come to the same conclusion regarding the failure of Kościuszko's uprising, as much as it broke his heart.

"Furthermore," added Herr Schmidt, "from the correspondence between Vienna, Berlin and Saint Petersburg, it is understood that the failure of this uprising will not be allowed to serve as inspiration for further rebellions by the Poles. Therefore, Poland as it is today, will exist no longer. The Prussians and Russians demand as much. Poland will be partitioned a third and final time, after which there will no longer be such a rebellious country."

This information sliced through Marek like the weapon of one of Kościuszko's own *Scythemen* warriors. It was as if his heart had been plucked from its open wound, and lay before them on the grass floor of the huge tent. It only awaited his commander's or Herr Schmidt's boots to stomp the last beats of life from it.

"Austria is likely to gain lands from this final partition, Zaczek," said his commander, "including the city of Kraków, we believe. We feel that the rule of our increased Polish holdings could benefit greatly from having General Kościuszko held by ourselves. If nothing else, it will give us a bargaining position in the negotiations that are to immediately follow this rebellion."

"Yes, sir," replied Marek, "but, if I may inquire, what makes you believe that General Kościuszko will abandon his troops?"

"Nothing makes us believe that at all," said Herr Schmidt. "Yet, even as we speak, Russian forces are moving in greatly superior numbers upon his camp. We want you to lead a raiding parting of *Uhlan* cavalry, and bring Kościuszko back to us, against his will if necessary."

"You wish Austrian *Uhlan* riders to capture Kościuszko, and return him here? Against his will?"

"He will be killed by the Russians if you fail," said Herr Schmidt, "and in either case the uprising will be crushed. You are to handpick three other Polish *Uhlan* riders and leave this evening, dressed as Polish countrymen of course."

"I have the option to decline this assignment?" asked Marek of his commander.

"Of course," answered his superior, "but the mission will still go on with a lesser leader. I suggest you reconsider."

Before them on the field table was an unfurled map of Poland and the surrounding area.

"Where is this battle to take place?" Marek asked, stalling for time in making his decision.

"Here," said the commander, pointing to the map, "I can never pronounce these foul Polish names."

Marek's eyes followed his finger. It pressed onto the map at a small village just beyond the river town of Dęblin. His finger pointed, in a most incriminating fashion upon the village of Maciejowice – the small village where his *Maya Manuska* lived upon her uncle's farm.

43

MACIEJOWICE

1794

Two nights later Marek found himself drifting down the Vistula River with his horse on a large flat raft being steered skillfully by his friend, Tolo. Marek had successfully argued that a raid of four Austrian *Uhlan* cavalrymen, even disguised as Polish riders, stood less of a chance at successfully commandeering General Kościuszko than a single swift rider. The key to the operation would be surprise and speed. One rider as skilled as himself could capture and retrieve the General and spirit him across the countryside back to Galicia. The raft would be useless for returning upon the river without a beast pulling it upriver along a towpath, and that would be expected by the Poles and Russians alike.

Marek had agreed to take on this nearly suicidal mission only if two of his conditions could be met. First, that he alone would attempt the abduction of Kościuszko, and secondly, that Tolo be engaged to take him to Dęblin by river raft. The Austrian commander and Herr Schmidt agreed, however they insisted Tolo could not be made aware of the mission. That was when Marek shared with them his intended cover story: the rescue of his *Maya Manuska* from the advancing Russians.

"This girl means that much to you, Marek?" asked Tolo as the raft drifted peaceably downriver in the darkness.

"She is my only love," said Marek. "How can I leave her there to be enslaved by the Russians?"

"But you don't even know if she is there," said Tolo. "Perhaps her family has abandoned the farm to flee the Tsarina's pillaging soldiers. If she is twenty years old, and as beautiful as you say, the Russians will surely rape her. It is what they are known for, their savagery."

"Then, we must get there all the sooner," he said to Tolo.

"The river flows as the river flows," responded Tolo, "I cannot make it flow any faster. I can only assure we do not run aground, or crash upon an outcropping of rocks, my friend. Yes, I have taught you to swim, but who has taught your horse?"

"All horses know to swim, Tolo," answered Marek, "it is their instinct. I have been trained in crossing a river to let the beast pull me along, even if by grasping his tail, as the Mongols do."

"Yes, that is good advice if the river is not swollen with rain and rages like an angry woman," laughed Tolo, "like this night."

They chatted all night as they slipped through the silvery waters of the river. Was this to be their last great conversation? One could never tell. Marek was appreciative, for it took his mind off his worries of what was yet to come.

At dawn on the tenth day of October, they embanked at Dęblin. The promise of the morning rose in the east, as did the threat of the Russian onslaught.

"Marek, my good friend and brother," said Tolo, "this is as far as I am allowed to take you. Your survival has been a great comfort to me, so comfort me more by staying alive today."

Tolo reached out his hand in which he held a map.

"What is this?" asked Marek.

"This is where you will find your *Maya Manuska*. The farm is marked here. It will save you from searching for it."

Marek felt pangs of guilt for having spied on his friend throughout this uprising. "Tolo, I have a great confession to make to you," he said.

"I already know why you go to Maciejowice," Tolo confessed to him in reply. "You will not get close to Kościuszko, for I have already warned them of your true mission. Go instead directly to collect your *Maya Manuska*. She is in need for you to get her to safety."

"You knew all along that I was spying for the Austrians?" asked the amazed Marek.

"Did you really believe it was by coincidence that I found you in Kraków on the day of Kościuszko's declaration? It is not only the Austrians who have networks of spies, my brother. Kościuszko will only abandon his troops if he is carried from the field of battle wounded or dead. So, instead, go collect your woman. For if the Russians or their Cossacks don't deflower her, there are always other rancid hearts of men who look to take advantage of a battle's turmoil."

Marek took the map, and then embraced his friend, Tolo. Then, he carefully moved ashore with his horse.

"Do widzenia," Marek said as he mounted his horse.

"Do widzenia," responded Tolo.

And with this, Marek rode off in the direction of Maciejowice, determined to carry out his primary mission, despite Tolo's warning. He hoped to beat the three columns of advancing Russian infantry. Marek knew his only chance of engaging Kościuszko was to do so. Although, as Tolo had said, he knew the General would not leave his troops.

That day Kościuszko would find himself outnumbered by twice his own count of troops, fourteen thousand Russians (including their Ukrainian Cossacks) to his approximately seven thousand. As Marek rode toward his position, he could hear the opening salvo of Russian artillery. The return fire from Kościuszko's guns was nearly immediate. All Marek could do at this point was to find a safe elevated location from which to observe the battle. He knew at that point, any hope of capturing Kościuszko was lost.

The artillery battle raged on for several hours until the Polish guns fell silent. They had run out of ammunition. Then, the Russian calvary forces, along with their brethren Cossacks, attacked

Kościuszko's positions. The General himself engaged in the hand to hand fighting that ensued. Kościuszko had three horses shot out from under him that day, before getting stabbed with a pike twice in his chest and hip. He was taken prisoner by the Russians, and removed from the field of battle. It was later reported that his words at that point were "Poland is finished".

The Russians went on to destroy the Poles in the ensuing fighting. Several thousand casualties were absorbed in the Polish ranks. Once Marek observed the deterioration of the battle, he pulled Tolo's map from his pocket, determined his location, as well as that of the Russian forces, and made off to the Polisciuk farm to find his *Maya Manuska*.

Marek knew it would be suicide to ride along the ridge-line of the hill. He descended the backside of the rise from which he had been observing the battle, or more correctly, slaughter at Maciejowice. Under its cover he proceeded to the farm. He knew that once the fighting was over, the Russian soldiers and Cossacks would spread out across the countryside looking for the spoils of war, especially local women to defile. Marek thought he was not too late, although the chance of being so only made him engage his horse all the harder.

The only weapons that Marek had been allowed to carry were a pair of pistols and a sword that carried Polish markings. He was advised to admit to being a rebel Pole if captured, and under no circumstances a member of the Austrian Imperial Calvary.

Soon Marek came upon the farm. It was a good distance from the battlefield, although not so much so that the combatants would be very far off. The first thing Marek thought to do was reconnoiter the barn, in case any troops had laid in wait for him there. He saw no activity from a distance, and then cautiously rode up to it. As Marek entered, he saw no animals, only a small enclosed carriage. Its cabin was tiny, and was centered over a single axle. There was no horse hitched to it, and it sat tilted forward toward the ground. It was then that he noticed the movement within it.

Marek drew his sword from its scabbard. He approached the

carriage cautiously, and coming near to it he could see not one, but two figures hiding within it. They were both shaking visibly with fear. Marek thought this must have been the movement that drew his eye. As he came close to the cabin, he recognized the larger of the two figures, and lowered his sword.

"*Pani* Sdanowicz," Marek said, addressing the wife of the former Duke, "do not fear me. It is I, Marek Zaczek, who has come to assist you."

"I am correcting you, young Marek," said the woman, "for I am now known as *Pani* Polisciuk."

"Yes," he replied, "names we can discuss at another time. For now, we must remove ourselves from this very dangerous location. The Russians and their Cossacks will likely be here far too soon."

"Marek!" came an elated scream from behind the woman. It was Maya, and as she leaned forward in the carriage, Marek could only see her from the shoulders up. She was more than lovely. She was radiant. Her face was full and flush with a glow of innocence and purity, he thought instantly.

Marek opened the cabin door and Maya's mother instantly filled its space as she exited the carriage.

"Where is your horse?" he asked them tersely as he helped down the mother. She said nothing. Only after he repeated his question did Maya answer him.

"Our horse got loose while we were attempting to hitch it to the wagon," said Maya, "it was frightened from all the nearby cannon fire and ran off. The artillery has also frightened mother into a dither."

"It is no problem, we will hitch my horse to it," he said, still assisting her mother. "We do not have much time..."

Marek had his back to the cabin as he helped the old woman from it, and when he turned to assist Maya, he froze as he laid his eyes upon her in its doorway.

His *Maya Manuska*, forever frozen in his memory as he had last seen her along the banks of the Vistula, cautiously maneuvered to clear the cabin's frame. Her slender shoulders turned sideways, careful to allow access for her swollen abdomen. His *Maya Manuska* was pregnant. Very pregnant, indeed.

Marek stood petrified in his astonishment. It was as if he were cast into a state of delirium at the sight of Maya. A mixture of shock and anger swam through his veins.

"Help me, Marek, *proszę,*" pleaded Maya. Marek did so, but as he did a rage boiled slowly within him.

I have waited for years for her, he thought, *through the temptations of Reka, of Vienna, and once more in Kraków. And I come to find her in this condition!*

"Marek, we do not have much time," she reminded him of his own words. "We need to hitch your horse to this carriage."

"I will do it," he said, and then without a word more, he did so. The carriage was once again level, by then having his horse supporting its front end.

Marek had been icily silent throughout the process of hitching the horse, and was so even when he helped Maya back into the carriage.

"Do you have something to ask me?" she asked quietly of him.

"Yes," he said, but could not bring himself to ask the obvious question. "Where is your uncle?"

Her face filled with blush. She paused with a curious hesitancy.

"He went off to join Kościuszko's army two days ago." She finally answered, knowing it was not the question he wished in his heart to ask.

"He left you here alone?" asked Marek angrily.

Again, another pause came over her.

"He told us to leave yesterday, but we thought perhaps the Russians would not come, so we waited until this morning. Then, all the torrents of hell burst forth."

Marek helped her mother back into the carriage, when he heard her gasp, *"Jezu, Maryja i Józef*!"

Marek turned to see two Cossack horsemen at the far end of the road sauntering towards the barn. He turned and moved toward the open barn doors. When they saw him and the carriage they drew their sabers and broke into a wild attack.

Marek yelled for the women to stay within the carriage and rushed to the barn doors. He focused on completing this simple task, as the advancing rhythm of the Cossack horses' hooves drummed into the long dirt road. Marek then completed closing the doors just seconds before the two Cossacks descended upon him. He left his sword in its scabbard, dangling at his side, and crossed his arms to either hip and pulled the two pistols that they would never have suspected him to have.

In typical Cossack fashion, they attacked in tandem from either side of him. Marek extended his arms and fired both pistols. His right-hand gun fired first, and its ball found the chest of the Cossack on that side, driving the warrior from his saddle to the ground.

He fired his other pistol a second later, but its round missed its mark. The Cossack swung his saber at Marek glancing him on the forearm. A thick wedge of skin was flayed clean, and the splatter of his own blood momentarily blinded him.

The second Cossack spun his horse around in a tight circle. He rushed forward upon Marek again, although without as much momentum as the initial pass.

Marek had dropped both guns into the dirt. They were useless now, as each would take several minutes to reload. Marek began to draw his sword, when he realized the Cossack was already upon him, the Cossack's saber was again drawn back to strike.

Marek slid his partially drawn sword back into its metal scabbard until the hilt arrested it. It could travel inwards no further. Then, in a singular movement enacted with both hands, one on the scabbard, the other on the sword's grip, he raised the sheathed weapon vertically.

The blow of the Cossacks saber came down hard upon Marek's metal scabbard. Sparks flew as metal rendered upon metal, blade upon scabbard. The Cossack's blade then slid downward until it broke cleanly in two when it violently made contact with the sword's metal hilt. Both men felt the Cossack's blade break. Both men realized at this point, in this fight to the death, chance had just delivered a defining advantage.

The Cossack had been leaning so far out of his saddle to get the momentum of his weight behind the blade, that as his saber shattered, the instantaneous lack of resistance caused him to fall free from his mount. He landed only a few paces from Marek's feet, and rolled with the impetus of his fall.

Marek moved forward rapidly and placed his boot upon the wrist of the Cossack who had just rolled to a stop. He pinned the warrior's weapon hand to the ground, which was still grasping the saber's grip, although it had a blade broken cleanly in half.

Streams of blood were raining down upon the Cossack. Marek's left forearm was bleeding where the large wedge of skin had been removed by the warrior's first blow. But now also bleeding profusely was the back of his right hand and upper chest. His hand had been upon the grip of his own sword. The broken blade of the Cossack's saber had sliced through the back of his hand, before it then gouged his upper chest as it flew clear. Marek's blood gushed from both these wounds as well.

Marek stood over the Cossack, drew his own, fully intact sword, and placed its tip over the man's heart, pinning him to the ground. Despite all his training, Marek had never killed another man before. Still, he knew if he did not, this man would surely rise up and kill him. And after Marek was dead, only the Cossack knew what he might do to the two women.

Marek then leaned heavily upon the grip of his sword, and its point felt only a moment of resistance. The Cossack cursed him in a Ukrainian dialect he did not understand before the sword's tip breached his skin. Marek's blade was then driven into the Cossack's chest, and the man screamed in a high pitched terror that rattled Marek's soul. Leaning more heavily upon the sword, the next three inches of the blade then disappeared into the man's chest, and finally the scream fell into a pit of deafening silence. Marek remained leaning upon his sword until the writhing body beneath his boot became still with death.

Several feet away, the other Cossack, who Marek had shot in the chest, watched with eyes aghast in great fear. His face was drenched in a visible film of cold sweat, no doubt brought on by hearing the excruciating sounds of his partner's execution. This Cossack's chest was already a fountain of blood. He was too weak to rise from the dirt. His saber was thrown clean of him by the ball's impact. He cried out something incomprehensible to Marek in the Ukrainian tongue.

Marek stood over him. The Cossack's wounds were severe, and would certainly take his life, if only slowly. Marek stepped on his chest, and drove the toe of his boot into the torrents of blood that bubbled from the wound. The man screamed in agony, throwing his head against the dirt. Marek moved his boot so that it pinned his chin in the dirt, and placing the tip of his sword on the Cossack's neck, and with a merciful flick of his wrist, severed the man's jugular, as he had been taught in Vienna.

Both Cossacks were soon dead. The first he had killed out of necessity, the second out of mercy. Marek returned to the body of the first Ukrainian warrior, and sliced his blood-drenched shirt from the corpse in several strips. These he used to wrap his wounds on the left forearm, chest and the back of his right hand, although these wrappings would later have to be redone by unscarred hands.

Once he had attended to his wounds, he calmly walked to the nearest of the Cossack's horses. In short, smooth steps he inched toward it and was able to take its reins. He climbed up upon it and together they trotted back toward the barn.

Maya had defied Marek's directions and had clamored out of the carriage to watch the skirmish through the crack between the barn doors. She then opened these doors wide, and he entered on horseback, covered in blood.

"You killed them both!" said Maya.

"The first would have gotten up to kill me, the second was already dead. I just put him out of his suffering." Marek felt no remorse, only relief that when the time came to do his duty, he was able to do so.

"How many people have you killed Marek?" asked Maya.

"This day? Only two, so far" he said. "You forget, thanks to your father, I have been trained to kill."

As he looked down upon her protruding belly, he noticed she still wore the amber ring he had given her to mark their engagement. It was at that time on her smallest finger, for they had swollen to the point she could no longer wear it upon her ring finger.

"What did these Cossacks say just before they died?" Marek asked of Maya.

For only the second time the mother spoke, "The last man said to you, *'I am unarmed and defenseless, you Polish pig. Kill me and I will wait for you in the bowels of hell.'* And the other, he just cursed your life before screaming."

"And now they both rest," said Marek. "However, rest is a luxury for the dead and one we do not have. We must get out of here before more Eastern devils come from these woods."

"First, I must properly dress your wounds with clean bandages," said Maya. "Come now, rest while I attend to you."

Marek responded to her in an icy voice. It was as if all the love Maya had once felt from him had been drained and replaced by an antagonistic bitterness.

"You did not rest in giving yourself to another," Marek said, his eyes darting down once more to her pregnant stomach, "and that is a wound that will never heal. These wounds will wait until we are safely clear of the Russians."

Maya's head dropped for the first time in shame from his cold, heartless rebuke. Her Marek did not know her circumstances, and at this point she felt no desire to explain herself.

From atop the Cossack mount, Marek motioned for Maya to retrieve his pistols from the dirt. With the pain from his wounds, he was unable to reload them. He instructed Maya to store them in the carriage. Before she did so, Marek directed her to hand the leads of his horse, already hitched to he carriage, to him. She did so.

Then, both Maya and her mother climbed into the carriage.

They were not assisted by the wounded Marek, who found himself, even then, too weak to dismount from the Cossack horse.

Marek took the leads of the hitched horse, and drove his heels into the ribs of the Cossack's horse. Then, they left the farm and headed south toward Dęblin. He knew he must stay ahead of the Russian troops, and that so long as he stayed on the eastern bank of the Vistula and kept in a southernly direction, he would ultimately arrive in the safety of Austrian Galicia.

Early that afternoon, they entered Dęblin, where the Wyepr River from the East flows into the Vistula. The town was in a great commotion given the advancement of the Russian forces toward it. Marek had negotiated passage on the last operating ferry to cross the Wyepr, only by having Maya hand him a pistol from within the carriage. Marek pointed it at the chest of the ferryman, who had no idea that it was not loaded. He agreed at gunpoint to take the rider, carriage and two horses across. Marek then rewarded him with one of the gold pieces that had been provided him by the Austrian army. It was worth the fare of hundreds of crossings.

"Good luck," Marek said to the Ferryman as he flipped the coin to him with his thumb. "Make sure the Russians don't end up with that small fortune."

The Ferryman looked at the coin, then back to the north shore from where the Russians would approach. He put the gold piece in his pocket, and then cut free the ferry raft from its ropes.

Good, thought Marek, *that will slow the devils down*. Undoubtedly, it was the intention of the ferryman who then walked briskly away from the river.

Marek, becoming weaker by each minute, led himself and the carriage in a southwardly direction toward the city of Lublin. They were no more than a quarter of the way there, when they came to the small village of Puławy, which was controlled by the Czartoryski family.

They were directed to the Czartoryski Palace outside the town, where they hoped to find food and rest for the night.

The Czartoryski family had unabashedly supported General Kościuszko's uprising, and Marek hoped to garner both sympathy and shelter there.

As he led the carriage up the path to the gates of the palace, a great fatigue overcame the injured and exhausted Marek. The blood lost from his wounds weakened him severely. His vision became clouded with darkness, and seemed to rock back and forth within him. Thereafter he collapsed, falling from the Cossack's horse onto the gravel below.

44

RETURN TO GALICIA

FALL 1794

After the wounding and capture of Tadeusz Kościuszko at Maciejowice in October of 1794, the uprising came to a swift and bloody conclusion. Warsaw held off the overpowering Russian forces until the next month. Kościuszko was taken to Saint Petersburg, accompanied by a guard escort of two thousand Russian soldiers. Such was the value of his leadership feared by the Russians. Once there, he was imprisoned by Tsarina Catherine, even though his wounds had not healed.

Marek and the two women were cared for at the Czartoryski Palace in Puławy for two days, before they were sent on to the safety of the Galician town of Rzeszów. The Czartoryski were member of the *Familia,* the loose affiliation of noble families that had originally brought King Poniatowski to the throne some thirty years earlier. The Palace was the home of Princess Isabella Czartoryska and her two sons Adam Jerzy and Konstanty Adam. Her daughters had much earlier been moved to safer locations to stay with family. Even as their servants attended to Marek and the two women, Princess Czartoryska and her sons were prepared themselves to abandon the Puławy Palace for the shelter of Vienna, a great distance away from the threat of the Russians advance.

Princess Isabella, even at the age of forty-eight, was renown throughout Poland not only for her still captivating beauty, but also as a patron of the fine arts and culture. She had travelled extensively throughout Europe, and was intent on making the family Palace at Puławy on par with the estates of Paris, Vienna, Prague and London. She had waited for her chance to speak alone with the tortuously wounded Marek before she herself abandoned the Palace.

"What is the fate of General Kościuszko?" she asked Marek, unsure if he could hear her in his stupor.

The gentle, caring nature of the voice called to Marek, who was still deep in the delirium of his suffering. He thought it at first the voice of an angel sent to escort him from this world to another.

"I am told you observed the battle at Maciejowice," said the voice again, this time slightly less cherubically, and bearing a slightly tense edge of concern.

It was then that Marek's eyes cleared somewhat, and he could see hovering over him the long, exquisite face of the Princess Isabella. He could then feel her hands, as smooth as silk, begin to tenderly stroke his face.

Those lovely large eyes that looked down upon him with compassion noticed that a spark of recognition had returned to his own.

"Forgive me, *Pan* Zaczek," the voice said in a third attempt to draw his response, "for interrupting your much needed rest, but before I depart the palace this night for Vienna, I must know what has become of General Kościuszko."

Marek looked upon the elegance of this face without saying a word. The powdered cheeks of this woman were as radiant as the few scattered clouds on a summer's day. The smile, be it ever so tensely drawn, crested her lips like the arc of Cupid's bow. Her beautiful brunette hair hung in curls above him that swayed ever so softly with her every movement, like the willow's leaves on the wisps of a breeze above a lake's mirrored surface. Then he realized the word for the overall effect - it was serenity in its most refined form. Even in the deathly serious approach of the Russians, this face held a tranquility he had not before experienced.

"Who are you?" he asked.

"I am Princess Isabella Czartoryska," she responded, still stroking his face, "you and Maya and her mother are safe here in our palace. Well, at least for tonight. Now, tell me what has come of our valiant General Kościuszko."

Marek had collected his thoughts. He remembered seeking refuge here, before all else went black. He breathed a sigh of relief to hear Maya and her mother were also under the Princess's care.

"I regret to tell you that General Kościuszko was gravely injured and captured by the Russians," said Marek through his pain.

The princess's face drew tighter with concern, but Marek still found solace in gazing upon it.

"But not dead? He did not perish?" asked the princess.

"It is hard to imagine that he will not, given the wounds that I could see even at a distance," he responded.

"He is such a great man, and I feel the heart of Poland itself beats within him," she said. "Some twenty years ago, I met the American Benjamin Franklin in Paris. Even then, that great man queried me about Kazimierz Pułaski. It was not long afterward that same American convinced the young Polish engineer that was Tadeusz Kościuszko to head to America to fight in their revolution."

"You met Benjamin Franklin? I have heard of him, even upon the *folwark* where I was raised..." his voice trailed off.

The Princess feared he was slipping back into a restive state. She quickly added, "Yes, in Paris, he was most highly celebrated, with his 'coon-skin cap'. It was most unlike anything, or he like anyone I had ever met before."

"You are so beautiful," said Marek, his pain at that point rendering him incapable of holding back his thoughts.

"You are so sweet, my valorous young man," she said as she leaned forward to kiss his forehead, which was still hot with fever.

"You know Kościuszko?" asked Marek.

"Yes," she responded, "for after Kościuszko helped the American's secure their liberty, he came back home to fight for Poland's. It was in the War in the Defense of the Constitution that my son Adam Jerzy fought under him. Kościuszko had come back to resist the Russians, not once, but twice for Poland, only to have it end this way..."

"... In ruin," added Marek.

"Perhaps for now, but only for now, for Poland shall rise again," said the princess bravely. "Now you must rest Marek, if you are to fight in the future for our land."

Princess Czartoryska had become concerned that she had unsettled the brave young man far too much. It was to the detriment of his recovery. He seemed flustered and confused, as if he needed to be defending them all, instead of benefitting from the rest he so direly needed.

"Madame," said Marek, "I fear we are barely ahead of the Russians' advance. It would be wise for you to abandon this place at once, and the three of us as well."

Marek looked upon her face and as her lips pursed to silence him, he could not resist the urge to kiss her. However, before he even raised his back from his bed linens, an exhaustive weakness overcame him. Her eyes saw his weakness, and even in the face of her own most grave and personal danger, they were full of sympathy and concern for him.

"Rest," she said in a whisper.

"The Russians! The Russians!" Marek strained to say.

"Yes, well you are leaving with the first light of morning," she said in a soft voice. "I have accommodations awaiting for the three of you in Rzeszów, in Galicia, where you will be safe. As for my sons and I, we leave tonight, beginning a long journey to Vienna. May God keep you in his graces, Marek. I wish that your and Maya's baby is born safe and grows to be a child full of God's blessings."

"You say my and Maya's child?" asked Marek.

"Well, of course," the princess answered with a tender smile, "what other than the fate of your wife's unborn child could have kept you from fighting alongside General Kościuszko. Am I not correct?"

"No, my princess," answered the shamed Marek, "you are exactly correct. Forgive me, for my mind is still clouded from the pain of my wounds."

"Well, it is understandable, of course. After all, you did save your wife, her unborn child and her mother from those two Cossacks. They are more savage than animals, and only the devil knows what they would have done to them. Now rest, my brave Marek Zaczek."

Again, the Princess Czartoryska leaned to kiss him, although this time upon his cheek. The fever raged within it as well. She hoped to herself that he would survive his journey home. Her doctor had assured her that he likely would not.

That night the princess and her two sons left the Czartoryski Palace at Puławy, escaping the forthcoming wrath of the Russians.

The next morning Marek, Maya and *Pani* Polischiuk were placed in a proper carriage, one that was modified to carry the wounded Marek in a litter. Marek's horse was tied by its leads to the carriage, which was pulled by a team of four horses. The Cossack's horse was set free.

Marek and the two women arrived in Rzeszów the next day. This town was halfway between Wieliczka and Lemberg. They were safely once again within Galicia. Word soon followed that the Czartoryski Palace, and the town of Puławy in which it resided, had been plundered and burned by the Russians. This majestic haven was brutally destroyed for the sin of the Czartoryski family having given aide to the rebels of Kościuszko's Uprising.

Once home, in Wieliczka, Marek was allowed to convalesce upon the Count Von Arndt's *folwark. Pani* Polisciuk (formerly the Duchess Sdanowicz) and the pregnant Maya were also taken there. The two women were allowed to share the other great bedroom suite of the guest house. Marek was tended to in the bedroom suite of his mother, who gave him her own bed and she herself slept by his side on a hastily arranged cot. Doctor Olszewski oversaw the wounded soldier's recovery, and it took over a month for him to fully regain his strength.

It was toward the end of November of 1794 when from his

room, Marek could hear a great wailing of the women throughout the house. Doctor Olszewski had just climbed the staircase to attend to his wounds, when Marek asked him what was the nature of the women's grief.

"Warsaw has fallen to the Russians," explained the doctor.

"After Kościuszko was captured," Marek said, "this must have been expected."

"Marek," said the doctor, "the tears are for the fallen innocents of the suburb of Praga. Are you familiar with Warsaw?"

"No, I have never been," he answered.

"Praga is the area on the eastern bank of the Vistula, across the river from the town itself. It held the Russians at the barricades for a long time. We are just hearing that the Russians overcame the defenders and slaughtered them mercilessly."

"Such is war," said Marek solemnly, "it is man's most terrible undertaking."

"They slaughtered the defenders of Praga," answered the doctor, as if he had not heard Marek's comment, "and then they slaughtered every innocent in the community there. Some twenty-thousand souls lost. Men, of course, but women and children also. There are reports of women being defiled in the streets, and then killed immediately afterwards. Of babies, innocent children, being run through with bayonets. It is a wholly avoidable tragedy, even amid the horrors of war. The name of Praga will never be forgotten."

"Those Russian bastards," said Marek, his heart enflamed by the doctor's words, "I can only hope that fate has an especially tragic curse upon their future."

"Marek, there is other news also, I am afraid," said Grzegorz Olszewski, "for your commander was here this morning while you slept. He told your mother that you are being transferred to the West, to fight the French in the Austrian lands just below the Italian Alps. You are to leave the day after tomorrow. She and I pleaded that you are not yet strong enough. However, they said there is nothing that can stop this from occurring."

"I see," said Marek with a great expectation, "*Uhlans* in the Alps? I cannot wait to see those magnificent mountains. To tell the words of the truth, I can't wait to get back upon my horse."

"I am so very sorry to tell you that there will be no horse," said the doctor as gently as he could, "for you are no longer an *Uhlan* cavalryman."

"What?" asked the wounded young man, incredulously.

"For your punishment of abandoning your mission, you are being stripped of your privilege to mount ever again as an Austrian Cavalier, and are to be demoted back to the rank of infantry soldier."

"This is an outrage!" protested Marek. "All I have ever wanted was to ride as a cavalier, whether it be *Uhlan or Hussar*. I have risked my life for Austria's Empire, and this is my reward?"

The doctor continued, "The commander said that you had no authorization to rescue Maya and her mother. In fact, they accused you of never attempting to rescue Kościuszko at all. They said that you must have planned it all along, and evidence of this was offering it as a cover story for your mission. They also said that you even talked them out of sending along additional cavalrymen, because they would have interfered with your true intentions."

A rage built within Marek. His only desire since being a boy was to ride into battle carrying the banner of his country. Now, for the sin of saving Maya - the pregnant, unfaithful Maya - he was to lose that dream forever.

"This is ridiculous. Kościuszko was already captured by the time I reached the battlefield, or nearly so. I had no opportunity to get close to him. Besides, Tolo said the rebels knew all along that I was coming."

Doctor Olszewski was at his bedside, not restraining him as such, but with his hand upon Marek's chest coaxed him into remaining at rest in the bed. Despite this, he went on to rob any real rest from the young soldier.

"Your commander said there were even discussions to hang you as a spy working for Kościuszko. He said that he personally discredited that idea, and they settled upon your return to the troops to fight the French."

"Either is a death sentence," conceded Marek. "What other good news do you have for me, Doctor?"

The doctor looked down at him, wondering whether his perturbed state could take another blow from this onslaught of reality.

"Maya wishes to see you," he said.

"No! No! Absolutely no!" protested Marek vigorously.

"You will leave to rejoin the infantry in Vienna in two days. She wants only to set things right with you," said the doctor.

"Have you seen her? She can never set that right," answered Marek, his voice climbing in pitch, tightening like the tautest string of a musical instrument. "She is a whore! After I waited so long for her, and she has laid with only God knows who?"

"This is wartime, Marek," said Doctor Olszewski, "and many people take advantage of the confusion and breakdown in order to do unfathomable acts. Maya was defiled against her will. She has told me so herself."

"And of course you would believe her. If so, then by whom?" Marek asked. "Who would have taken advantage of such a defenseless woman?"

"She needs to tell you herself," said the doctor. "She is prepared to discuss the entirety of what happened with her, but only with you. She said your anger with her prevented her from doing so until now, but she is ready to talk openly with you."

"Never," Marek said, "I will never speak to her again."

"She thought you would say this," said the doctor, "and asked me to give this to you." He opened his right hand to reveal the amber ring that rested in his palm.

Marek took the ring, and looked closely at it. He resisted the urge to cast it across the cavernous room. Instead, he swatted away the doctor's palm, and began to rise from the bed and dress.

"Marek, you must rest, for these next two days, you must rest," pleaded the doctor with urgency. He was ignored. Marek walked weakly over to the bureau. There, he grasped the gold coins that lay upon it, those he had brought back from the mission, and were due to be returned to his commander.

Marek pulled upon his trousers, and then buttoned his shirt. He continued to then throw on a heavy woolen sweater and boots, and without so much as a jacket, rushed down the steps, past his mother, who cried in horror as she attempted to block the door. Marek cast her forcibly, but not violently, aside and walked through the frigid late November air to the stables. There, he took the first Arabian he could find, and galloped off the *folwark*.

A small crowd of his loved ones had assembled on the forecourt to watch Marek's anger explode on horseback down the crushed gravel path.

Pan Sdanowicz, in his ornate *szlachta* robes, had been walking upon the grounds. His laughter, punctuated only by the terrible hacking coming from his corrupted lungs, was a counterpoint to the solemnity of the assembled crowd. He taunted them, as his sour wit was his last weapon to jab at his enemies.

"Ha! The boy's outbursts still drives all of you out from the comfort of your luxurious mansions," he snarled, as he ran his hand along the crest of his central strip of hair separating the two halves of his shaven head.

"Not now, Father, *proszę*," begged Maya in desperation.

"No one is to follow him," cried out the Count, coming from the manor house only after hearing the great commotion.

"You fear he will not come back, my Austrian usurper?" again taunted Sdanowicz, before choking back a crippling cough.

"*Pan* Cyprian, I know he will not be," said the Count, "for he runs away from his responsibilities, like a child."

The former Duke, having recovered from his hacking interlude, wiped his mouth with a blood and mucous stained rag.

"Yes, he is a child," answered Sdanowicz, "the proud child of a *szlachta* Duke, who runs from nothing, and no one. You only fear that he will be charged with abandoning the army, and it will cast a poor light on yourself."

Maya had heard her father's pronouncement, and realized that he had made a mistake. For Marek was not the son of a *szlachta* Duke, she reasoned, but the grandson, for it was Duchess Magdalena who was the child of a Duke. Of course, she did not understand that her father spoke the truth, as Marek was his son, and her own half-brother.

"As it is," said the Count, "I will not have any one pursue him, should they be mistaken in any way as assisting in his departure. The boy fears the infantry, and so he runs."

And so, Marek was not pursued. When he came upon the bridge over the Vistula, he bribed his way across with one of the coins belonging to the army. Then, at the St. Florian Gate of Kraków, he again bribed his way in with a gold coin. He rode to the tavern near the city's western wall. He flew up the stairs, and without even a knock threw open the door. There sat Reka, alone.

She looked at the young soldier who had once been only a boy before her. Whereas he was once mired in fright and awkwardness, now his eyes burned with a flame of desire. She had recognized this look in men before, and in this case, Reka knew that Marek had come to complete his journey into the fullness of manhood.

He was no longer scared, she thought, *for much time had passed with the regret of his not having had taken Reka when she was offered to him. Now, he is ready to taste the forbidden fruit.*

"I told you, my lovely boy, that she would break your heart and you would return to Reka." The Hungarian then laughed aloud.

Marek moved forward, driven not by his lust, but rather by his rage. He grabbed Reka by the arm and raised her from the chair at the table. He kissed her in a lewd manner, although only for a moment, before thrusting her upon the unmade bed.

"Standing before you is a man, Reka," Marek said boldly, "for the wounds of war have taken my innocence. I come only to offer you what little is left of me."

As he said this, he pulled the sweater from his torso, clearly revealing the wounds upon his chest, arm and hand.

Reka's only response was to smile broadly, for she recognized that all the forces that had been building within Marek for so long were soon to be expended upon her physically.

"Come to Reka, my darling," she said in a voice dripping with expectation. "Reka will release you from what innocence the war did not take. It is what Reka does. And it is what Reka does very well."

Marek stayed with her that night and all the next day and night. His anger was slowly drained from him, taken out upon the fulsome frame of the Hungarian seductress time and time again. He could not satisfy his desires for her, which had long been the temptation against which only the purity of Maya could offer resistance. The latter having been so frivolously squandered, Marek gave in fully to his impure lust, and so, too, what remained of his childhood innocence was soon forever lost.

When he departed early on the morning of the second day that followed, as Reka slept soundly, Marek left the Hungarian his remaining gold coins, stacked upon her table, atop which was a simple ring beset with a small amber stone.

45

THE THIRD PARTITION

1795

After the failure of the Kościuszko Uprising in 1794, the empires of Russia, Prussia and Austria agreed that they could no longer live with an independent state of Poland between them. For even as weakened as it had become, Poland had demonstrated itself time and time again to be a bed of the embers of insurrection. The interval between these revolts was dramatically shrinking. The twenty-one years between the first and second partition was followed immediately by the Kościuszko Uprising. The three empires had decided it was time to alleviate the problem, or so they thought, by eliminating Poland as an independent state altogether.

In 1795, what was left of Poland was once again divided between Russia, Austria and Prussia. The Prussians took the section that contained the capital of Warsaw, while the Russians took even more lands in the east. However, the Austrians gained what may have been the greatest gift, taking not only the city of Kraków, but also adding the lands along the Vistula River all the way up to and beyond, but not including, the capital.

After the implementation of this final dissection of the once glorious Commonwealth, nothing was left of Poland as an independent state. It was wiped clean from the face of Europe. However, the three empires were soon to find that the cultures of these peoples could not be so easily erased. That culture would burn in the hearts and minds of the Polish and Lithuanian families, and as such, would still enkindle the flames of desire for independence. Insurrections would erupt only periodically, but always very violently, over the next century and a quarter.

King Stanisław II August Poniatowski was forced by Catherine to abdicate the throne of the Commonwealth and leave Warsaw in January 1795. He died three years later in Saint Petersburg, where he had been held in a comfortable exile. Catherine, the lover from his youth, had been the instrument of his ascension to the Polish throne, as well as tip of the spear that had dethroned him. Poniatowski was, and is to the day of this writing, the last King of Poland.

General Tadeusz Kościuszko was imprisoned in Saint Petersburg at Catherine's command. He would suffer from his wounds for the rest of his life, but refused to die in Russia, for his role in this story was not yet complete.

General and Prince Józef Poniatowski, the great military commander and nephew of the former Polish King, was in Warsaw after the failed Kościuszko Uprising. Having had his lands confiscated from him, he left Poland for Vienna, where he would stay until the death of his uncle, former King Stanisław Augustus. Prince Józef would go on to have a prominent role in attempting to re-establish Poland over the next twenty years. This would prove to be an undertaking that would eventually claim his life.

In France, the Reign of Terror had come to an end. After the plague of executions that abruptly stopped with the beheading of Maximilien Robespierre, there came a counter-reform known as the Thermidorian Reaction. Soon, the *Girondins*, those twenty-two executions that had taken all of thirty-six minutes only a few years earlier, were publicly honored as Martyrs of the Revolution. France was finally beginning to stabilize internally in 1795. The country began to focus externally on its wars with Prussia and Austria. These wars would soon come to involve Marek Zaczek in a most prominent, if unexpected, role.

Marek had returned after his two night tryst with Reka to the estate. He arrived only hours before he was to be turned over to the Imperial Army. He was then transported to Vienna. After his re-training there, he would later be reassigned to an infantry unit in Lombardy, what today is Northern Italy, in the foothills of the Alps.

The former Duke, *Pan* Cyprian Sdanowicz, had become increasingly more frail as the months advanced. His rendezvous in the graveyard with Marek would remain their last direct contact. However, from a distance, he would watch as the Austrian's took his illegitimate son into custody, removing him from the *folwark*. Sdanowicz would not live to see Marek again, nor the birth of his grandchild from his daughter Maya.

Cyprian Sdanowicz would indeed die from his ailment, which was diagnosed as the Grippe by Doctor Olszewski. Until his last breath, he assumed the unborn child was Marek's, for no one had thought to explain otherwise to him. After all, he had given Marek permission, even if only out of spite, to take his daughter. He knew in his embittered heart that this travesty of nature must surely have occurred.

In January of the year 1795, Doctor Grzegorz Olszewski had been attending *Pan* Sdanowicz's bedside for thirty-six hours straight, expecting the death of the broken, old man. Thinking that his patient had improved slightly, the doctor eventually left him to get a few hours sleep in the comfort of the manor house. It was then that Cyprian Sdanowicz, wrapped in the shroud of his own shadow, released his grip on the tenuous strands of mortality, and died alone. He was found the next day with a wicked, sickly smile painted upon his rigid face.

The former Duke died with only a singular happy thought, although outside his twisted mind it proved to be incorrect. *Pan* Cyprian Sdanowicz passed from this world thinking he had created an abysmal, incestuous situation that would go on to haunt his Magda for the rest of her life. This was a fitting legacy, he thought, for the peasant woman whose vile temptations ultimately stole from him all that he had ever possessed.

Maya and her mother had been living once more upon the *folwark* for a short time before *Pan* Sdanowicz died. After her husband's burial, *Pani* Polisciuk, as she demanded to be addressed, suddenly declared that she was returning to what was left of her brother's farm in Maciejowice, as all the fighting was over. She feared squatters would take over what was left of the farmhouse and lands. *Pani* Polisciuk felt she could wait not even a week longer to return there.

She left behind her daughter, Maya, who was, at that point, too pregnant with child to travel. She suspected, that even had she not been with child, her daughter would have refused to return with her. The farm held only bitter memories for Maya, and her mother fully understood.

Maya had stayed on the *folwark* in the guest house at the invitation of Duchess Magdalena. Magdalena could not look upon the girl and not see herself, so many years earlier, in many ways. Maya would become a mother at twenty-one, only a year or so older than she herself had been. And under nearly identical circumstances, as her innocence also had been taken by one in whose presence she should only have found safety and protection. Magdalena told Maya that she was welcome to live with her in the guest house always, and together they would raise the child.

Maya gave birth to her child during February in that year of 1795. Doctor Olszewski oversaw the birth which resulted in a healthy baby boy, which Maya would name Władysław. She named the child after Magdalena's father, as a show of appreciation for the Countess' kindness to her in her time of need. Maya would even go a step further, as the child's middle name would be Marek. The boy was loved and nurtured by Maya, who would go on to simply call him "*Władek*" .

Only when the child reached the age of six months old, and he could be left under the watchful eyes of his mother and Doctor Olszewski, did Duchess Magdalena set off for a visit to the city of Milan in Lombardy. She could wait no longer than early

September of that year to depart, for even then the threat of the coming winter was once more carried upon the wind. Her intent, worked out in advance with Count Von Arndt, was to travel to Milan, where she would meet once more with her son, Marek, who was encamped nearby with his military unit.

In early November of 1795, the infantryman Marek Zaczek was directed by his commander on a cold winter evening to report to an address in the city of Milan. Doing as he was ordered, Marek was issued a horse to travel to the city. He enjoyed immensely once more being in the saddle, and as he was unaccompanied, thoughts of desertion crept into his mind.

A fine snow began to fall, lightly at first, but then more heavily. The flakes became larger, and soon stung with the chill of a cold, wet Alpine wind. The rolling hills Marek rode through were soon covered with a pristine glaze. He entered the city, and even its usually crowded streets were vacant and disguised in the frock-like coating of white powder.

The beauty of the night aside, Marek arrived at his directed destination: a fine town house not far from the Duomo, the city's elegant Cathedral. It was unusual to be directed to report to a private residence, but as Marek's dealing with Herr Schmidt in Galicia had taught him, the unexpected was always to be expected.

As Marek approached the door, it opened, revealing only a woman dressed all in black on the other side of the threshold. The image so surprised the soldier, that at first he did not respond, until he could be sure he was seeing what he thought might have been a vision. It was when her eyes filled with the salted heaviness of memories, accustomed by a quivering frown that flexed into a tentative smile, that he was sure.

"*Matka*," Marek said in shock, "what brings you so far from Wieliczka? And why are you dressed in mourning clothes? How on earth did you find me?"

She rushed upon him, tears by then streaming down her face as she embraced him. "My Marek, my Marek," she whispered in his ear, "I feared I would never hold you in my arms again."

Marek, who earlier would have rebuffed her embrace, allowed her to wrap herself around him. He had been softened by months of trooping across Lombardy in the spring, summer and fall. The Austrian Army had been attempting to defend these Imperial holdings from the French troops who were seemingly ever threatening to invade them. Both armies were now in winter's quarters, and as such, Marek had been allowed this visit to accommodate the request from his wealthy mother (which had been accompanied by a sizable bribe).

"Come in, my child," his mother said, relieved that her son did not resist her. "This beautiful home belongs to a friend of Count Von Arndt, and was made available to me at his request. The man has many contacts, including those in the military, so it was not difficult to find you, or to arrange for your coming here."

"I should have assumed this night bore the touch of the most generous Count," Marek said satirically, "how could I have not envisioned his hand at play here?"

They entered the parlor, and took seats in front of a marble fireplace which looked magnificent, framing a roaring fire that seemed to celebrate the event of their meeting.

"What brings you so far, my mother?" asked Marek.

"I wanted to personally tell you of the news of the *folwark*," she said, adding, "where you were born."

The last phrase seemed to irk Marek, his mother thought. She wanted so deeply to avoid another argument with him.

"Yes, *moja Matka*," her son replied, "I know where I was born. I only wonder upon which land's soil will I die."

His mother ignored his caustic comment, for it was too painful a thought to consider, let alone acknowledge. "You speak of death, so please know that *Pan* Sdanowicz, the former Duke, has died, my son."

Marek appeared surprised, but not astounded.

"He did not look healthy when I last saw him," said Marek, "and so I am not shocked."

"He died of the Grippe," she said matter-of-factly.

Marek thought of his friend, the trapper Miłosz, and remembered Tolo had mentioned some ailment called the Grippe.

"And this you could not have put in your letters to me?"

"You never answer my letters, Marek," she replied, "how would I ever have known that you had received it?"

"The Duke is dead," he stated, "and while I am sorry to hear this, I do not see why it would cause you to travel so far across Europe in winter."

She wanted desperately to tell him once and for all that the former Duke was his father, but as every single grain of sand passed through the constricted waist of the hourglass, this became more and more of an impossible task.

"I thought you might wish to visit his grave the next time you are upon the *folwark*, my son," Magda said tenderly.

"Is his grave close to my father's?" asked Marek.

"*Pan* Sdanowicz's grave is in the same cemetery behind the manor house, but is away somewhat from that of my Bronisław," his mother answered carefully.

She did not tell him that the Count had refused to have the former Duke's remains within that place of honor until she had interceded on behalf of *Pan* Cyprian Sdanowicz.

"*Dobrze*," snapped Marek, "for when I visit Bronisław's grave, I wish not that even my shadow should be cast upon the soil piled atop the remains of the former Duke."

"You say these things with such venom in your voice, Marek," said his mother. "Do you not consider the pain and suffering of Maya at the loss of her Father? So heavy is her heart?"

"Yes, our Maya," pondered Marek. "Is her heart as heavy as her womb?"

His bitterness toward Maya cut through Magda's own heart. When and how had the compassionate son she had raised become so full of cynicism? It was more than merely his military training. Was it his dissatisfaction with life in general?

"Maya has given birth to a son," Magdalena stately directly. "You certainly know this, even as you have refused my letters. Too many months have passed for her still be heavy in her womb."

The statement immediately stoked a response within Marek. His body stiffened slightly, his face became flush. He had indeed read in a note from Uncle Jacek in Vienna, via regimental couriers, that Maya had given birth to a healthy son. Yet, even after all these months, Marek still held Maya in contempt for not having protected her innocence to share first with him. For not having saved her chastity as a gift honoring his long cherished love for her. Of all the scars he carried upon his body from that day in Maciejowice, it was the sight of her fullness that wounded him most.

"I will always remember the sight of Maya's swollen belly, as it carried only a disloyal seed within her. So, a son, you say? A Polish or a Russian son?" Marek asked, as if to question her virtue.

"Ukrainian, in fact," his mother answered.

"Ukrainian? That is surprising," Marek said, "for though they lived on her Uncle's farm in Poland proper, there were not many Ukrainians that lived nearby. Her mother and uncle were Ukrainian, yes, but they also lived far from that eastern land."

Magdalena could sense that her son did not understand. It did not occur to him that she had not willingly given herself to anyone. An irritation built within her.

"It was her uncle's child," Magdalena blurted, displeasure straining and tightening her voice.

"She gave herself to her own uncle?" Marek asked incredulously.

"He took her virtue by force, my son," said Magdalena, "she did not give it willingly. Her innocence was taken from her by the very man who should have protected it most."

A heaviness came over Marek. It was a mixture of shame, regret and anger.

"My poor Maya," he said, yet he refrained from calling her *Maya Manuska*. "She was set upon by her own uncle?"

"Men will do hideous things when they believe they can get away with it," his mother answered. "Such were this man's thoughts in a time of war."

"Then the boy is illegitimate, a bastard," Marek said coldly.

"Marek," she exclaimed, "never let me hear these words again from you! No child chooses his own father! Each is as legitimate as the next, each is a gift from God. Never question our Lord's ways, my son. Never allow His blessings to be blasphemed by these ugly and hurtful words."

A silence befell them. Marek allowed himself to absorb his mother's rebuke. He became unnerved, then stood and began pacing before the fireplace.

"Of course you are right, *moja Matka*. I was cruel to assume Maya had betrayed me. This is a crime against her. Her uncle will answer for this," said Marek, "for if the French do not kill me, I will visit him and he will pay with his very life."

The Duchess was relieved to see her son work through the situation. If only he could come to know that the situation was nearly an exact reflection of his own birth. Often in life, the consequences of fate imitate the impropriety of heinous acts of the past.

"His last breath is not a currency that he can spend twice, I am afraid," said Magdalena. "The Russians have already taken his life at the Battle of Maciejowice. His head was pulled from a Cossack's pike after the battle."

Marek did not respond. He continued to pace in solitary thought, although his Mother sat still immediately before him. The silence crushed her more with each passing fall of the steps of his boots.

"Poor Maya," he finally said. "You say she gave birth to a son? A healthy son?"

"Yes, very much so. His name is Władysław Marek Sdanowicz," announced Magdalena. "She named him after my own father, but used your name also. She gave young Władek her family name, not the Polisciuk name of her mother and uncle, of course."

"It is surely a cruel world in which we live," her son said to the Duchess Magdalena, as if he was merely thinking aloud.

If only you knew exactly how cruel, his mother thought.

"Marek, you need to forgive Maya," Magdalena said, "for she worries desperately over how you think of her."

"Tell her she has not much longer to worry," he said, "for as soon as the spring thaws the lands, the French are intent to stop me from thinking altogether. Soon enough, they will be upon us."

"My Marek," Magdalena said, knowing her time with him was short, "why do you harbor such anger at her and at me?"

"*Matka*, I harbor no ill will to you," he said, "but as far as Maya is concerned, what you take for anger is only that I have simply come to realize that my love for her was never meant to be."

"Yet, she loves you so much, my son," answered Magdalena. "None of this changes that. Your rejection of her is a cruel disappointment to Maya."

Marek's face became instantly tense as these words were uttered forth from his mother.

"My life is a series of cruel disappointments, my mother," he said, "and I have come to understand and accept this. The hopes of a child die with childhood itself. My childhood hopes were to be forever with Maya, and for my father to watch me ride proudly into battle as the cavalry of my country. Not only could both dreams never exist together, but now I realize each was only the fantasy of a child. For now I am a man, and my father, my country, and the purity of my *Maya Manuska* have all been taken from me."

"Oh, Marek," Magdalena sighed, "you have become such a cynic. How have I failed you as your mother?"

"*Matka*, you have not failed me. I love you, so very much. But I also loved my father, and Bronisław was wrongly taken from us both."

It was then that Magdalena realized that the reason she could not tell her son that Bronisław was not his father was in itself purely selfish. She feared what Marek would think of her. She feared that he would treat her as he had initially treated Maya.

Marek then continued, "I was in love with Maya, and she has been taken from me forever. Whether by injustice or not, she can never be mine."

"Do not cast her aside, just because she has been set upon by her uncle," Magdalena pleaded.

"You would have me marry her and raise a dead man's child?" Marek asked.

"That is exactly what I would be most proud of you to do, my son," his mother answered. Only at that point did it occur to the Duchess that she had pleaded for exactly the opposite of her original intent. She could never allow Maya and Marek to become man and wife. Yet, neither could she allow her son to despise this girl whose innocence had been so forcibly ripped from her.

"Well, that shall not come to pass, *Matka*," he said. "The hour is late, and I must now return to my unit."

"Before you leave me, my son, I have other news," Magdalena said, "that I must share with you."

Her son hesitated, his face telling of the uneasiness of his mind. *What wound will she next inflict upon me?* he thought.

"Count Von Arndt has asked for my hand in marriage, just before the death of the former Duke," she explained.

Marek was shocked.

"I intend to marry him, Marek, after my mourning period comes to an end. If nothing else, to assure I have someone to protect my possessions."

"Why do you even bother to mourn the Duke? He was never your father, never your protector. He cast you into the peasantry..."

"And that rejection lead to my greatest gift from God," Magdalena said, embracing him, "my son, Marek."

Unlike earlier, Marek pushed her away, still arguing with her.

"You mean until the Count gave you all the Duke's possessions. Don't you see that the Count is only offering to marry you to steal those very possessions away from you..."

"He would never do so. He is the reason I have any of what I do possess," said Magdalena. "Why should so wealthy a man as the Count desire what I possess, when he has ten times more?"

"You have answered your own question, *Matka. More. More. More,*" said Marek bitterly. "It is just as well that you marry him. You have been miserable ever since you inherited this great wealth. Once you marry him, and he steals it all again, you will know the happiness of a poor life once more."

Marek's stare cut through her, before he added, "With that being said, do as you will. I take leave of you now to return to my regiment."

Magdalena rushed once more to embrace her son. This time he once more pulled away from her, hurting her deeply. She reached out and took his hands, as a mother would from a defiant child.

"Marek, before you leave me again, know that I love you," she said, "after the war, come home to me."

She then knelt before her son, so that he might know the sincerity of her request.

"That most likely will be in the hands of the French Generals," Marek replied stiffly. "Yet, I promise you tonight, after the war is over, if I am still alive, I will come home to you. The only question to be answered, again should I live, is how long can war possibly last? *Dobronoc, moja Matka*."

Marek then turned away from her and made directly for the door. When it shut behind him, a dense cloud of sorrow had descended upon Magdalena. How could all this misery have come so quickly upon her? How had she become mute once again this night, unable to speak the truth of his father to her son. For she feared the bitterness of his response, but even more, she feared he would cast her from his life forever.

This was something she could not suffer. She had lost her husband. She had lost her country. She knew she could not go on living should she come to lose her son.

46

THE BATTLE OF LODI

MAY 1796

In the spring of 1796, the Austrian Army in Lombardy came under pursuit from the French forces. The French had driven the Austrians from the Kingdom of Piedmont, and captured its capital of Turin. The Austrians and the remaining Italian Piedmontese (Italian troops from the island of Sardinia), were driven eastward. However, instead of engaging the French directly, the Austrian General in charge, Johann Peter Beaulieu, took to a series of retreating actions. He hoped to find a defensive position suitable to his liking, but the French forces proved to be extremely mobile and forced an engagement at the riverside town of Lodi.

The Adda River is sourced in the Alps, and feeds Lake Como, before draining, reforming and flowing southward again to feed into the even more massive Po River. At Lodi, there was but a single bridge that spanned the two hundred yards of the Adda's width.

Here, on the tenth day of May 1796, astride the left, or eastern bank of the River Adda, General Beaulieu ordered the commander of his rear-guard to engage the French. Across the river was the town of Lodi, and the wooden pyle bridge that spanned the river was the only crossing for a great distance.

By crossing the river with his troops, the Austrian General had decided to leave open the road to Milan, the capital of Lombardy, which lied only a short distance to the northwest of the French forces on the western bank. Yet, instead of taking this rich prize, the French forces were intent on engaging the Austrians at Lodi. The French Generals knew that so long as the Adda River crossing was controlled by the Austrians, any movement to Milan would leave their flanks open to attack from the forces across the river.

The French leadership had become uncharacteristically aggressive, and sought to destroy the bulk of the Austrian army. So here, across this very defensible bridge, the Austrian Generals stationed their infantry and decided they would engage the pursuing French army.

In most reviews of this engagement, it is indeed noted as very curious that the Austrians had not destroyed the bridge after they had crossed over it ahead of the French forces. Instead, the Austrians emplaced upon the river's bank a train of thirty cannons, many positioned to fire upon the structure of the span, ensuring that no enemy infantry could survive in attempting to cross it. Near the landing of the bridge, the Austrians also placed many units of infantry, who would be the first to engage any French troops should they possibly survive the Austrian artillery fire.

Marek's unit, consisting mostly of Polish and Czech infantry, were put on the front line at the landing of the bridge. This was typical of the Austrians, keeping the Austrian and Saxon troops in reserve away from the danger of immediate engagement. The Poles and other Slavs were considered expendable, and would make excellent cannon and bayonet fodder.

Marek found himself laying behind a berm of raised soil next to the bridge's landing. He had been in this position for hours, and late in the afternoon he witnessed the arrival of the French troops across the Adda. He had clearly watched the *Republique's Armee d'Italie* readying their artillery in a scattershot fashion across the river's banks, as they came under the withering fire of grapeshot from the Austrian cannons.

As he watched across the river, Marek could see a French

General riding to the front of their forces to personally direct the artillery batteries nearest the opposing bank. The General was young, and moved with the vigor and agility of his youth, although not with the caution and uncertainty that the fire of grapeshot or other lethal projectiles often produces in soldiers.

Even from this distance, Marek could perceive great differences in this French General from those of the Austrian Army he had personally seen. This one was very young, lean and thin, perhaps under thirty years old, whereas the Austrian Generals were most often in their late sixties, or in the case of General Beaulieu, a year beyond seventy. These old, thickened leaders of the Austrian army never came from their rear command positions to the front lines, for they valued their own experience too highly, and feared lest it should be lost in battle. Yet, this youthful French officer rode boldly to the front of the battle line. *Perhaps he too overvalues his own abilities,* thought Marek, *but he does so with such confidence!*

Under a hail of grapeshot, this same General directed the movement of the scattered twenty-four French cannons into tight formations. Personally, he directed the aiming of the guns, as if he was not a General at all, but a Corporal. Indeed, he would later come to most affectionately be called *Le Petit Caporal*, or "The Little Corporal", by his men for his deeds along the river's bank this day.

Once the General was done, the French battery returned a steady stream of cannon fire onto the opposing Austrian artillery positions. Marek consoled himself in knowing that the bowl of dirt within which he had lain for hours was most likely safe only because it was nearest to the landing of the bridge. He knew that the French would not rain artillery fire down directly upon the bridge, for to do so would only make their forthcoming attempts in crossing it all the more difficult.

The one thing that Marek was surest of that day, was that if the French were successful in crossing that river, his life would not be spared. Along with the other Polish and Czech troops, they would be offered as a sacrificial engagement to the French gunfire and bayonets, such that the bulk of General Beaulieu's army could safely withdraw away from the battle.

Marek's eyes had been drawn to the commanding presence of the French General, who demonstrated incredible bravery under fire in directing his troops. This alone would have demanded his attention. Yet, it was the General's magnificent white charger upon which he had ridden forward that had captured Marek's eye. He thought it was perhaps the finest horse he had ever seen.

It was then that the feeling of dread had penetrated throughout him. The sight of the beautiful white charger was a trigger to his mind, reminding him of how he had lived his entire life wishing only to one day bravely command so fine an animal into enemy fire. It had been his earliest dream, since he was a child, gazing upon the Hussar's wings in the manor house. Throughout his years, he had been sure that his ultimate fate was to be a heroic horse soldier.

It had appeared that he was indeed on his way to achieving this goal. In all his short life, Marek had never been as happy as during those days that he had spent in an *Uhlan's* saddle for the Austrian Cavalry. However, his ill-fated quest to rescue his *Maya Manuska* had robbed him of that happiness, of that prestige. Thereafter, he found himself as simply an expendable infantryman, having fallen from yesterday's glamorous heights of the *Uhlan's* saddle, only to land this day in the ignominious Italian dirt in which he felt he was surely soon to be buried.

As the French General across the river had begun to give tactical commands relative to the cannons, a junior officer held the reins of this magnificent beast. Marek found that resting his eyes upon the horse settled his unsteady nerves, and if only for a few seconds, made him forget that in the position he was in at the foot of the span, he would most surely die this day.

Then came the coordinated thunder of the full Austrian artillery, attempting to take out the French cannons in the opening minutes of the battle. No longer did they fire the scattering grapeshot meant to harass and kill the soldiers along the river, but instead they now threw the full weight of individual cannon balls intending to destroy the French guns. The Austrian cannons, firing not far from where Marek lay, shook the very earth. Their vibrations rattled a caustic terror through each man's belly that lay upon that dirt.

If every valiant man is first born the coward that he must overcome, this day there were many who had the opportunity to become heroes. Marek would go on to prove that courageous men come in many forms, and their actions are what define them.

As the cannons roared and the world shook around him, Marek Zaczek instinctively drew himself as close to the ground as he possibly could. However, instead of worrying for his own safety, Marek ill-advisedly raised his head. His worries had become inescapably affixed to the perfection that was that white charger.

Would the horse be killed in this opening salvo? Marek could not think of himself, but instead only of the safety of that wondrous animal of war. It was as if the charger was a piece of himself, perhaps the essence of his dreams. To watch it die, butchered and mutilated by cannon fire, would be like watching himself perish.

Marek looked upon this wondrous horse, when the glare of a shell burst near to it. The junior officer holding the reins was struck and fell to the ground. The beast, unharmed, reared up in panic, and just as a second shell exploded behind it, the General's horse bolted in the only direction open to it: across the open bridge and directly towards the Austrian positions.

"Hold fire," said the forward commander to the Austrian troops, "that is the mount of the commanding General; that animal may quite possibly be carrying valuable battle plans. Someone get up on that bridge and take control of that horse."

"*Ja vol*," answered Marek instantly, as he left his position and ran onto the suicidal span of the wooden bridge. The horse, saddled but riderless, came frantically toward him. The Austrians held fire from their individual weapons as ordered. But, also, did the French, at their General's command. Despite this, the cannon fire continued to arc overhead, including the French barrage in a substantial and deadly response.

Alone on the span, under this umbrella of artillery fire were

Marek and the white charger, racing toward each other. Marek knew that once the horse was captured, whether it carried anything of worth or not, it would most likely be slaughtered by the Austrians just to spite the French General. He looked at the glorious mount as it galloped toward him, and Marek knew he could not allow this animal's demise to come to pass.

Marek stopped on the bridge, near its center span but closer to the Austrian side, raising his arms as high as they would extend. The horse was coming upon him. The confused animal slowed and reared, a look of terror painted in its eyes.

Both shores were erupting in exploding cascades of dirt as the cannon fire landed. Thick plumes of smoke drifted across the bridge, partially obscuring it from each shore. It was a surreal moment, as all that was normal had been turned inside out. Death and disfigurement washed upon each of the river's banks. Yet, upon the center of that wooden span, Marek and the white charger came upon each other in comparative safety.

The horse, still frantically agitated, came at Marek, who did not budge his position in the least. He was still making himself as large as possible with his outstretched arms. At the last possible moment, the horse came to a stop and reared once more in front of him.

Marek moved forward decisively and was able to grab the left rein from its bit with his hand just as the horse came back upon all four legs and just before it turned its head away from him. At as fast a speed as he could achieve in his uniform and boots, he was able to lift his foot firmly into the stirrup and pull himself up atop the beast, throwing his leg over the saddle. It was a maneuver he had performed often on the *folwark* for nothing other than sheer joy. This day it would prove to save his life.

He was on the back of the charger as it began again to rear in the middle of the span. The beast was, however, a conditioned animal of war, and only awaited a rider's instruction. Marek took control and commanded the animal as the two of them began to move as one, first in circles amidst the embattled bridge.

Once atop the white charger, Marek could feel the return of his own self-worth as he settled into the most splendid saddle in which he had ever ridden. The horse responded to his every command immediately, even when Marek's own hesitancy confused the beast. For Marek himself, atop the steed, was unsure for several seconds as what to do next.

He could only think of the alternate fates that awaited him at either end of the long river span. To take the elegant beast to the Austrian side of the Adda River was to condemn it to certain death. The Austrians would kill the fine charger if only to antagonize the French General. Even should he himself survive this battle's engagement, Marek was sure he would be returned to the rank of foot soldier. There would be many more battles ahead of him as an infantryman. And as a Galician Pole, many more opportunities to be offered up to the French guns or bayonets. Death was certain, he thought, although it might be delayed only by luck. So long as he was an expendable foot soldier to the Austrians, death was eventually certain on the battlefield.

As sure as Marek knew he could not return to the infantry, he also knew he could not voluntarily cede the reins of this remarkable beast. Most of all, he could not turn this splendid charger over to be slaughtered. With a kick of his boot heels, and a flick of his wrist, Marek Zaczek consciously commanded the horse to return in the direction of the French forces. It might result in his immediate death, and if not, certainly to be taken as a prisoner of war, but either way, his last actions on the battlefield would be where he always wished to be, in the saddle.

Marek rode upon the wooden planks of the bridge in a full gallop. As he neared the enemy, he yelled in French, "Do not fire! Do not fire! I come to surrender!" It was then that he realized he was already being fired upon by the Austrians behind him, although he was sure he was out of the range of their long guns.

As he continued to ride toward the French artillery on the river's western bank, he felt a stinging burn in his right shoulder. He looked down to see his scarlet blood streaming in rivulets upon the white Austrian uniform. The sight reminded him of the flag of the nation of his birth which existed no longer: the bold and broad red stripe cast low upon the pure white field of the Polish flag.

Marek slumped forward, still screaming in French, "Do not shoot!" The French infantry at the bridge's landing were in a row, bent on knee, their rifles in firing positions. Marek rode directly at them, yet for some reason they held fire. He refused to believe they were adhering to his screams to hold fire. Then he realized that no soldier wanted in any way to risk firing upon their general's beloved horse.

Marek came quickly upon their defensive line at the end of the span, and jumped the horse over them. The charger landed solidly, but the impact of the landing threw Marek from the saddle. He rolled in the dirt, and the horse was quickly reclaimed by another of the General's aides.

Lying shaken on the ground, Marek then heard the forcible command, "Do not shoot, let this man lay where he fell," in another voice, also in French, but with a heavy accent that he would later identify as Corsican. It only then occurred to him this same voice had surely ordered the French forces not to fire upon him as he approached.

Marek was soon surrounded by a multitude of French soldiers. He then heard the voice once more, this time saying, "No further harm is to come to this man! This was the bravest feat of horsemanship under threat of fire that I have ever witnessed. Help him up and attend to his wound."

"*Oui, General Bonaparte!*" a voice answered. Marek whose shoulder was burning, was becoming lightheaded as he was raised to his feet. He was moved to cover and his wound was soon dressed by a field surgeon.

"It is a clean wound. You will be fine, *mon ami,*" the medical officer said to him.

Marek was then propped up after his wound had been cleaned and bandaged. He was told to rest, and from his vantage point he watched as an unending parade of French troops prepared to cross the bridge, and expose themselves to heavy attack by the Austrians.

What Marek saw next amazed him. General Bonaparte, whose horse he had rescued, stood amidst his troops. Marek had been in the Austrian Army for several years and had never seen a General mingling with his own fighting men. Except Bonaparte wasn't only mingling with his troops, instead he was exhorting them on to cross the bridge for the glory of the French Republic.

Finally, the General addressed their sacrifices, their tireless efforts and their famished hunger, before concluding, in as inspirational a voice as Marek had ever heard, *"Frenchmen, here is starvation; there is the enemy, and beyond him - plenty! March!"*

He spoke to the *Carabiniers*, the elite light infantry soldiers named for the carbine long guns they carried. These men would assault the heavily defended bridge. They cheered as they headed out onto the wooden span, into the fire of the combined Austrian and Piedmontese forces.

As the *Carabiniers* enthusiastically fought their way across the bridge they came under blistering fire from the Austrians. The French made it just beyond halfway across the span, before the artillery and the rifle fire of the Austrian long guns overcame them. Soldiers fell one after the other upon the bloody planks of the wooden bridgeway. They began to retreat until the forces were regrouped by the Generals under Bonaparte, who then urged them on in another assault, crying *"Vive la Republique!"* to their troops.

Then, the re-inspired *Carabinier* troops returned to cross the bridge, and once more came under tremendous fire. Yet, this time, they fought through the enemy onslaught. Many French infantry even jumped into the shallows from the bridge on the far bank and waded the last distance to the shore.

At that point, the courageous *Carabiniers* began to emerge from the bridge and the waters that flowed beneath it. What French infantry that had survived the cannon fire upon the bridge, charged the entrenched Austrian infantry units at its landing. The combined Austrians and Piedmontese were driven back from the structure.

Before the Austrian guns could be repositioned, the French Cavalry came charging up the banks. General Bonaparte had sent units both upstream and downstream searching for a place to ford, or cross, the Adda at its shallowest points. The French cavalry successfully forded the river and at this critical moment, attacked the Austrian artillery units, successfully driving the enemy from their cannons.

No longer with the threat of the Austrian cannonade, the French infantry was pouring across the bridge and had overpowered the Austrian rear guard, Marek's former unit included. He could hear the cries of slaughtered men drift across the river's surface, mixed with the thundering hooves of the French cavalry amidst a cacophony of other horrendous sounds. He felt the fright of knowing that had he stayed upon the Adda's eastern bank, he would surely have been maimed and would quite possibly have given up his life as a sacrifice to slow the advancing French forces. All only to assure the cowardly General Beaulieu's main body of troops were allowed to escape the battle. Marek felt compassion for the other Poles and Czechs that were overrun along the river, but he felt no remorse for his actions that removed him from the butchery there.

An all out retreat was occurring as a result of the bravery of the combined French forces. Yet, to Marek, despite the courageous actions of the *Carabinier* infantry, it was the cavaliers who were the heroes of the day. He cursed himself in that he would never drink from their sweet chalice of victory, as these men were surely soon to do.

The retreating Austrian forces did hold off long enough to allow the bulk of Beaulieu's army to escape eastward, away from the river. The battle was deemed a major triumph for France, and for her emerging young General, Napoleon Bonaparte.

After the battle had been won, General Bonaparte instructed his aide-de-camp to take him to Marek. He came to stand directly before the reclining wounded Austrian soldier.

Marek was astounded at the General's youth, only a few years more than Marek's own twenty-four years. In fact, the General was himself only twenty-seven. Marek looked up at the Frenchman, his long hair falling down to his shoulders, framing his strong and confident face. His eyes were riveting to look into, they drew you in, only to then penetrate your seemingly inner-most thoughts. His chest flared with pride, fired with the heart of a lion. His aquiline nose was straighter than the slicing arc of an eagle's beak. Marek found himself captivated by this commanding combination of qualities.

This is a true leader of men, Marek thought, *unlike any man I have ever before met.*

Bonaparte, having heard Marek speak French earlier upon the bridge, spoke directly to his wounded prisoner.

"You have displayed a hero's bravery in rescuing my cherished mount, soldier. Yet, I wonder what drives a man to desert his country to save *only* an enemy's horse, *Monsieur?*"

Marek, weak and weary, but still in awe of the young man standing before him, was unashamed of the French General's intoned charge of desertion. He raised his head high to look the General as directly as was possible in the eye. *The fire in the man's soul shines through,* he thought, before he spoke.

"General, I am a soldier without a country. I am not an Austrian at all, but a Galician Pole forced to serve the Austrians. I saved the horse, because these things of the greatest beauty should not be allowed to be destroyed merely because the rules of war permit it."

"Polonaise?" asked the General.

"Oui, général, je suis polonaise!" responded Marek.

"You are too brave a man to fight for the Austrians," answered Napoleon. "They are fools to waste you in the infantry. You, my valiant *chevalier*, shall fight in the saddle for France."

The French General then turned away from him. However, Marek could not help but overhear the orders dictated by General Bonaparte to his aide. *"Take this soldier to Dąbrowski to join his regiment of lancers."* The General then turned abruptly and walked briskly away from them both.

"Jan Henryk Dąbrowski?" repeated Marek, not realizing he had actually asked this aloud.

"You know of him, your countryman?" asked the aide.

"Yes, of course. He was the hero of the Kościuszko Uprising of '94. He defeated the Prussians with his brilliant cavalry tactics," stated Marek.

"And so he will battle the Prussians once more, but this time for the Republic of France," the French aide replied. "And the General believes that General Dąbrowski can use a horseman of your skills in the brigade of Polish Lancers that he is forming to fight for France. You are receiving a great honor, my friend, from one of the greatest leaders of all the men of the Republic of France, General Napoleon Bonaparte!"

Napoleon Bonaparte soon thereafter rose to prominence for his endeavors in conquering the Northern Italian principalities of Piedmont and Lombardy. Having already conquered Turin, Napoleon only days after the Battle of Lodi, would take control of Milan, having ousted the Austrians from the territory. Venice would in turn fall in the next twelve months, ending over a thousand years of Venetian Doges' rule.

Napoleon himself would later be quoted as stating, *"It was only on the evening of Lodi that I believed myself a superior man, and that the ambition came to me of executing the great things which so far had been occupying my thoughts only as a fantastic dream."*

Five days after the Battle of the Bridge at Lodi, on the fifteenth day of May, General Napoleon Bonaparte entered Milan. The Austrian forces stationed there had rapidly departed. The conquering twenty-seven year old French Commander-in-Chief of the *Republique's Armée d'Italie* was presented the keys to the city. This accomplishment alone would secure his reception in Paris as a conquering hero of the Revolution.

Marek witnessed the tremendous welcome received by the French General. The Milanese welcomed Bonaparte as their liberator from their occupation by the Austrians. They were making the same mistake as would so many other peoples yet to come — mistaking the result of the General's victories with freedom while ignoring his unquenchable ambition.

Marek had been brought to Milan to meet with General Dąbrowski, who was joining General Bonaparte there. Marek met Dąbrowski only a few streets down from the house where he had months earlier met with his visiting mother. Once again, his life had taken a dynamic turn of events. What would his *matka* think of his riding in the services of the Polish General?

It was at this watershed moment in history that Marek witnessed the hero Bonaparte entering though the gates of the fortress that was the Sforza Castle in Milan. That day Marek observed the undeniably sweet essence of victory bestowed upon the General, and became devoted to this great Frenchman. The Bridge at Lodi would enter folklore as the point where an ascending young General of the French Republic would cross over to become a great man of a truly inescapable destiny.

47

EPILOGUE

NOVEMBER 1796

Almost six months to the day after Napoleon's "liberation" of Milan from the Austrians, a series of rapidly occurring events were initiated that would come to cast the entire continent of Europe into deadly conflict. All of Europe's major empires and most of its lesser sovereign states would be engulfed in the most ferocious warfare for nearly the next twenty years.

On the morning of the sixteenth day of November 1796, the servants of the Winter Palace in Saint Petersburg, were relieved to find Tsar Catherine II in improved spirits. She had been in ill-health over the past several weeks. She had told those who cared for her that she felt better that morning than she had for some period of time.

They would return later in the day to find her lying unresponsive upon the floor, breathing shallowly with her face discolored with a bluish hue. Attempts to revive her only resulted in her slipping into a deep coma. What had been diagnosed as a stroke took her life the next evening. Only one year after the final partition of Poland, the third and last of the three conspirators of the initial partition was dead and gone.

Perhaps it is a cruel twist of fate that this Romanov leader today known as Catherine the Great, known then in Russia as Tsarina Yekaterina, had a town on the Asian side of the Ural Mountains that bore her name. Yekaterinburg, actually named after Catherine I, but upon this town Catherine II would bestow many royal honors, would become the location where the Communists 121 years later would murder the family of the last Tsar, Nicholas II.

Those murders took place upon the orders of the Bolshevik leadership in the overnight hours of July 16-17, 1918, forever ending the Romanov dynasty. So, most like a fitting cosmic curse, the last in the line of the Romanov leaders of Russia were gruesomely murdered in the town that bore Catherine's name.

Consider also that the murders in that basement in Yekaterinburg would be so gruesomely executed only eight months after the Bolshevik's Red October Revolution, (which actually began on the night of November 6-7, 1917 on Western calendars). Not many months more would pass before the peoples of Austria-Hungary and Germany would each meet disastrous fates in the ending of The Great War.

After years of fighting between Austria and Germany against Russia on the Eastern Front, the land that had once been Poland was nothing more than a patchwork of horrendous destruction.

The fighting of the Great War ended on the eleventh hour of the eleventh day of the eleventh month of 1918, nearly a year to the day after the rise of the Bolsheviks. The end of World War I brought about the total collapse of the Habsburg's Austro-Hungarian Empire, as well as that of the Prussians, both entities which had joined Russia in the Partitions of Poland. After defeating France in the Franco-Prussian War (1870 - 1871), the Prussian Kingdom had been merged into the unified state of Germany along with the Bavarians, Saxons and other Germanic states. That resultant German nation would survive only to endure an ignominious defeat in The Great War and would be subject to crippling reparations.

World War I's end also re-established Poland's independence after 123 years of being denied the status as a sovereign state. The fate of Poland and Lithuania, as well as the other Baltic States of Estonia and Latvia, would unfortunately be closely tied to the Communist movement in Russia for the next seventy-three years.

Catherine The Great's successor was her only son, Pavel. He had long hated his mother, most likely for the coup she had initiated which brought her to power, and that had claimed the life of Pavel's father, Tsar Peter III. In fact, at the time of her death, Catherine so distrusted her own son that she was in the process of changing the succession rules to preclude Pavel from becoming Tsar, favoring her grandson, Pavel's son, Alexander instead. Her sudden and unexpected demise, however, assured that Pavel would become Russia's next Tsar, Paul I. As it was to pass, Alexander would not have to wait long to reign on his own. Both Tsar Paul I and his son, Tsar Alexander I would play prominent roles in the European response to Revolutionary France, and in particular to the rise of Napoleon Bonaparte.

Almost immediately after Catherine's death, Tsar Paul I started undoing his mother's recent undertakings. He ended Catherine's on-going war with Persia. He reformed the Russian military. Most of all, Tsar Paul detested Catherine's iron-fisted ruling ways, and on becoming Tsar, he ordered the release of all of her Polish political prisoners, including Tadeusz Kościuszko.

Stanisław Poniatowski, the deposed King of Poland, came to Saint Petersburg in the months following Catherine's death. Upon having arrived there, he was denied the right to leave the country. However, he lived in the city, under a pension that had been granted by Catherine before her death, and was honored by the enthroned Tsar Paul. Residing in St. Petersburg's Marble Palace, effectively as a prisoner of the regime, he had nowhere else to go, even had he been allowed. The former King was despised in the lands he once ruled. Poniatowski stayed in Saint Petersburg, until February of 1798, where after only a year and three months, he would die of a stroke, exactly as Catherine had.

Eleven days after the death of Catherine II, Tadeusz Kościuszko was released by Tsar Paul on the twenty-eighth day of November in 1796. Still recovering from his wounds, Kościuszko would by August of the following year arrive in Philadelphia. There, he stayed in a townhome owned by his good friend and, by then, Vice-President of the United States, Thomas Jefferson. Jefferson had once said of Kościuszko that, *"He was as pure a son of Liberty as I have ever known and of that Liberty which is to go to all and not to the few or to the rich alone".*

Tadeusz Kościuszko was convalescing from his wounds in Philadelphia in March of 1798, when he received letters addressed to him from Europe. Upon reading their contents, he was driven from his convalescent bed, and immediately began to dress. He hastily prepared to return to Europe. He would soon depart for France under a passport procured for him by Thomas Jefferson.

The contents of the letters which drove him to return so abruptly to the Continent was the notice that his friend, the Polish General Jan Henryk Dąbrowski, was preparing a Polish cavalry regiment to accompany Napoleon Bonaparte into battle.

Jan Henryk Dąbrowski, the hero of the Kościuszko Uprising, would indeed go on to form the famous Polish Lancers of Napoleon's Army. It would be among these lancers where Marek Zaczek would go on to serve with distinction. Marek would be stationed with Dąbrowski, and became one of his most skilled cavaliers.

Marek, after healing from his wounds at Lodi, would travel alongside General Dąbrowski. The General had instilled in him the discipline that he needed to complement his already well-developed skills as a horseman. Marek would also be trained further in the skills of killing, so that this would become second nature to him. As the cruelty of war against the enemies of the French Republic would unfold before him, Marek would hone these skills to an unspeakable level.

Perhaps one might wonder why a legion of Polish horse-warriors would fight for France? In reality, they responded more to General Bonaparte's decrying the injustice of the Partitions of Poland, and his demands as to how the Austrians, Russians and Prussians must be held accountable for their aggression against the peaceful state. The Polish Lancers under Dąbrowski would fight not for France, but for Napoleon himself, who they hoped would one day restore the independence of their homeland.

Marek found himself in a situation that had turned dramatically since his heroics upon the bridge at Lodi. Before that, he was just an expendable infantryman, a foot-soldier. One that the Austrians demonstrated they were quick to offer up to the cannons of the French. There, on the banks of that river, Marek lay in the dirt, having already given up any hope of reclaiming his dream of a revered life in the saddle of the cavalry. That dream he had already lived as an Austrian *Uhlan.* It was a dream that had been unfairly stolen from him for his well-intended deeds at Maciejowice, in rescuing Maya and her mother.

Marek's life changed dramatically since the Battle of Lodi, where he made the fateful decision to risk his life in rescuing a runaway mount on a contested bridge. His most consequential decision, to surrender himself to the French, he made not for his own well-being, but for the survival of that magnificent white horse.

He was not only allowed to live by the French, but was given a second chance in obtaining his dream. Not alone amongst an army foreign to himself, although he already spoke its language. No, Marek would regain his cavalry mount among an elite unit of horsemen whose ranks were filled of his countrymen. Better still, this French regiment would be led by one of Poland's greatest war heroes in the person of General Dąbrowski.

Marek had transitioned from a position of insignificance and expendability under the Austrians, to a situation of nearly unbridled respect, being held in reverence by the French population. Most of all, Marek valued the camaraderie and fellowship of his fellow Poles.

Marek soon found that the young women of Paris and other towns around France were quick to throw themselves at this uniformed, handsome foreigner of only twenty-five years of age. They would find him romantic, both in his intentions for themselves, but also in his mourning for the great loss of his homeland. They found his tales of rebellion against the Russians and Prussians stimulating and enticing. His longing for the lands and people he had left behind became an aphrodisiac to these women. For in a country that had just undergone a radically violent revolution, beheading its own monarchs, its women were inclined to give themselves more freely. For it was a lesson that they had already learned: it was better to enjoy the small pleasures of life today, than to wait to see what terrors tomorrow may bring.

Marek would go on to drink deeply from the offering that was the sweet flowing fountain of French femininity, of those innocent in their youth as well as others more mature and experienced. Soon, he would all but forget the Hungarian Reka who had been his first conquest, but not his first love.

His memories of his first love, his *Maya Manuska*, would change over this period as well. After his mother had explained the nature of the origin of Maya's pregnancy, Marek went from feeling that she was not worthy of his love, to a remorse of just the opposite. He felt that he had been too rash in his angry return to Reka, so eager was he to take out his frustrations. However, with each new liaison he entered into in France, of which there were many, he felt more and more unworthy of Maya's forgiveness. He saw no way to reconcile his newfound debauchery with her victimhood, and the opportunity would not come for some time, as they found themselves on the opposite sides of a major conflict.

Maya could not care less about the wars of Europe. She stayed with Marek's mother, Duchess Magdalena, who held an affinity towards the young mother. They jointly agreed to raise the child Władek, along with the servant Ewelina, upon the *folwark*.

That is until they were forced to leave the comfort of the guest house. Marek's mother, Duchess Magdalena, had been ready to marry Count Von Arndt, despite her son's protestations. However, that union would not come to pass. Once Marek surrendered himself to Napoleon's forces at the Battle of Lodi, the Count quickly called off the marriage. He could not afford to be married to the mother of a deserter of the Austrian Empire, especially one who was now training to take up arms against Austria.

Soon after, Duchess Magdalena, her informally adopted daughter, Maya, and the infant child Władek, would leave the *folwark* to take up residency in a modest but comfortable townhome within the walls of Kraków. With the Count's generous consent, even the servant Ewelina was allowed to join them.

The former King's nephew, Prince Józef Poniatowski, would go on to fight against the Russian Empire once more, this time under the command of Napoleon Bonaparte, with the hopes of restoring a free and independent Polish State. This engagement would bring him to fight side-by-side along Napoleon's most prominent Polish Lancer, Marek Zaczek, in the years to come. But that is another story in the life of Marek Zaczek, to be told in another writing.

AUTHOR'S NOTES

I have attempted to weave the fictional story of Marek, his mother Magdalena, and his love Maya through the course of historical events as they had chronologically occurred. I had two goals in doing so. First and foremost, to create an enjoyable fiction storyline in which the readers could immerse themselves. All the locations named herein are actual historic sites, and I have travelled to the great majority of them.

Secondly, I aspired for each reader to gain a slightly deeper understanding of the events that transpired over the period of 1772 to 1797. Many of us who delve into periods of world history are often surprised by the concurrency and inter-connectedness of major events. In this case, these included the American Revolution, the French Revolution and the Partitions of Poland. I thought the readers would be interested not only in these events, but also the historical figures that bridged across them including Casimir (Kazimierz) Pułaski, Tadeusz Kościuszko, and to a lesser degree in this story, the Marquis de Lafayette.

As for these men, they paid dearly for their love of independence and liberty. After teaching the Americans how to form and train cavalry regiments near my hometown of Baltimore, Maryland, Casimir Pułaski gave his life to British cannon fire outside Savannah, Georgia. Pułaski's body, long thought to have been buried at sea, was however, discovered in the 1990s within the commemorative marker that stands even today in Savannah's Monterey Square. They were reburied beneath the marker with full military honor in 2006.

Kościuszko lived to return to Europe. When he departed the

United States for the last time, he left behind a personal Will and Testament with instructions to sell his lands and use the funds to free the slaves upon it. This will was never executed. And like his wounds received from the Battle of Maciejowice, Kościuszko never recovered fully from this affront.

Kościuszko would return to France, only to warn against the malevolent ambitions of Bonaparte, who he recognized to be an emerging tyrant. Eventually, after the fall of Napoleon, while living in Switzerland, Kościuszko would die from a stroke, like his nemesis Catherine the Great and countryman King Poniatowski before him. Tadeusz Kościuszko died at the age of 71.

The Marquis de Lafayette, the title of the man named Gilbert du Motier, was in many ways an outlier. He was perhaps the best known foreigner to intervene in the American Revolutionary War. He was one of few aristocrats to survive the French Revolution, being named commander-in-chief of the National Guard. In 1792, when the more radical factions turned against him, he was forced to flee to the Austrian Netherlands. There, he was imprisoned for five years. Napoleon himself would negotiate the freedom of LaFayette during his reign.

After returning to Napoleonic France, LaFayette was once again respected as a man of the people. Even during the second restoration of the monarchy, after Napoleon had been exiled a second time to the remote Atlantic Island of Saint Helena, LaFayette was revered. He would be honored during the July Revolution of 1830 in France, when LaFayette turned down an opportunity to become France's leader himself and instead supported Louis-Philippe to become the next King of France.

LaFayette was also an honorary citizen of the United States. He is credited with naming the town of Havre de Grace, Maryland (after the French town of LeHavre which it resembled), and even presented George Washington with a key to the Bastille, which hangs to this day in Mount Vernon. LaFayette died of pneumonia at the age of 76, and is buried in a Parisian grave under soil shipped across the Atlantic Ocean from Bunker Hill, Massachusetts.

I have intentionally ended this volume with the early rise of Napoleon. It is my intention to continue the saga of Duchess Magdalena, Marek and Maya through the years 1797 to 1815, especially the period that constituted the rise of the Duchy of Warsaw. Of course, I look forward to bringing in the British forces, with their naval heroes (e.g., Lord Admiral Horatio Nelson) and battlefield commanders (e.g., Arthur Wellesley, The Duke of Wellington) into the mix of characters. Expect this second volume to be completed in the next several years, regrettably not any sooner as I have other projects that I have set aside that will consume my attention in the interim.

Allow me a quick explanation about the Polish names and locations. Polish can be a most misunderstood language, but instead of writing it in phonetic style (for example, using "Yan" in lieu of "Jan", or "Yerzy" in lieu of "Jerzy", since that is how they are pronounced), I made a conscious decision to stay true to the Polish spellings, complete with their diacritical markings. Some are foreign to English readers, as Dąbrowski is pronounced "Dom-BROV-skee" and Bronisław is pronounced "Bron-EES-waff". Others look confusing, but are more straightforward, such as Sister Maryja Elizabeta, which is pronounced simply "Ma-REE-ya E-liz-a-BAYT-ta", and the Abbott Dawid is pronounced "DAH-veed". I hope this has been not too much of a cultural reach for my non-Polish readers.

Of course, the Polish speaking readers will recognize a major exception. The love of young Marek is presented as "Maya", and not "Maja" which is the true Polish form. For this I have a personal reason which I will not share, but also I did not wish to have my readers pronouncing that critical name to themselves as "*Ma- Jah*".

Thank you all for taking this somewhat extended journey with me. I hope you found it a great escape, if only for a few hours, from whatever it is that you wished to escape from.

Do widzenia,

David Trawinski

Figure 9: The Beautiful Carvings of the Miners of Wieliczka

*"**... someday, we miners will carve out of the salt a grand cathedral for ourselves down here.**" - prediction of Jerzy the miner.*

The great carvings of the miners of Wieliczka, including the Cathedral of Saint Kinga (above), were skillfully completed about fifty years after the end of this story. Not only are the Cathedral's walls, ceiling and floor carved of natural salt, but so are the individual beads of the chandeliers.

CPSIA information can be obtained
at www.ICGtesting.com
Printed in the USA
LVHW011101020920
664818LV00001BA/64